Off Chance

By
Sawyer Bennett

Published by Big Dog Books

ISBN: 978-0-9894164-9-8

Find Sawyer on the web!
sawyerbennett.com
www.twitter.com/bennettbooks
www.facebook.com/bennettbooks

Contents

Acknowledgments

Two people in particular deserve the largest of shout outs, for they helped me make this book authentic in my research. First, Kizzy Williams, who has been a beta reader of mine from the beginning and my favorite New Yorker and Brooklyn babe! She made sure I was authentic, even if I did have to take a little bit of license with some of the settings. Love you lots girl!

Next, to my hometown Jacksonville buddy, Tim Davis. He is a firefighter for the City of Raleigh and a real life hero. He gave freely of his time to go over my manuscript with me and provided a ton of great material from which I could borrow and help add to the realism of what it takes to serve. I owe you sushi for life, my friend. And I'll never forget, "Two go in, two come out"!

A huge thank you to my cover model, Derrick Vargo. You are just spectacular and I'm so thankful you were involved in this project with me. I hope we can work together again in the future.

Finally, I want to just thank all of my fans, especially those of you I have come to know through Facebook and Twitter. The best part of every day for me is when I can interact with you. You make this job so fulfilling and worthwhile. I am forever grateful.

Now… I'm off to write another book. It won't be the Off Series, and although I said this was my last one, I think it is safe to say you all will see another one in the future. I've heard from too many of you asking me to keep writing them that I just can't ignore.

Love,
Sawyer

PROLOGUE

Flynn

8 years ago

I GLANCE DOWN at my watch.

11:50 PM

In about ten minutes, I'm going to see Marney. In about twenty minutes, I'm going to be buried deep inside of her. My horny, eighteen-year-old body starts to get a boner just thinking about it.

Marney and I have been dating for just over six months but we had sex for the first time very recently.

Five days ago to be exact.

That's one-hundred and twenty long hours or seven-thousand, two hundred excruciating minutes.

We haven't been able to see each other the last few days between school events and work. She's on our high school soccer team and I play baseball. When we're not working our part-time jobs, we have our studies, and although we are just weeks away from graduation, we are both competitive and strive for good grades.

That's a lot of shit we both have going on, which

means our time together has been limited. And that's pretty fucked up in my opinion, because sex with Marney really should be a priority in my life.

Damn… I love my girl!

She is everything a guy could ever want. She's drop-dead gorgeous, smart as shit, and funny as hell. We hadn't been going out barely three weeks and I knew I was in love with her. I was too chicken shit to say anything, but luckily for me, Marney confessed she loved me first, at just the five-week mark in our relationship, and then I was able to reciprocate.

Even though love hit us kind of fast, we took our time with sex. Which is strange, now that I think about it, because neither one of us were virgins. Marney had been dating our high school quarterback, Sam Faber, since the ninth grade, but they had broken it off at the end of our junior year.

Lucky for me!

And while I hate to think about Marney having sex with Sam, I'm grateful I didn't have to worry about deflowering a virgin. I mean, that's a lot of pressure on a dude. I'd been around the block a time or two, so even though I certainly had the ability to eradicate the V-card, I was still glad I didn't have to.

It made that first time together freakin' fantastic. There was no fumbling around or uncertainties between us. We chose our six-month anniversary to have sex for the first time and it was mind blowing. It was exactly how I'd imagined it would be… soft, slow, and shattering. I'd gotten us a hotel room for the night and, armed with a box of condoms, both of us left starry-eyed and sore the next day.

We made plans to sneak out and meet up tonight. Marney lives just two blocks east of me and I'm going to her house to get her. I know just the place to take her. There's a quiet spot in the woods that border Griffith Park and it's perfect because it's an unusually warm spring night. I pilfered a bottle of wine from my parents' liquor cabinet as a surprise and I hope to spend most of the time making love to my girl under the stars. Glancing at my watch again, I note the time.

11:55 PM.

Time to rock and roll.

Bending over, I grab my backpack, which has a blanket and the wine… oh, and condoms. Just as I turn for the bedroom door, the piercing wail of a siren slams into my brain. I walk to the window and pull the curtain back, catching a glimpse of a fire truck as it barrels down the road right in front of our house.

I hope to God the sound doesn't wake my parents up and ruin my escape plan. Just as I start to turn away from the window, an orange glow catches my eye.

Right over the rooftops of the houses across the street… just east of here.

My brain doesn't process what I'm seeing at first, but then I realize the glow is from a fire, and it looks to be pretty big. Now I know where the fire truck is going.

I turn away from the window but then a shiver runs up my spine, warning me that something is wrong. Turning back again slowly, I look back at the fire.

Just east of here.

Oh God!

Marney lives just east of here and my stomach bottoms out as I realize that glow is coming from somewhere in the vicinity of her house.

I pull my cell phone out of my pocket and hit Marney's number. It rings four times before going to voice mail. There's no fucking way she wouldn't answer.

Dropping my backpack, I sprint for my bedroom door, throwing it open so hard it slams against the wall with a resounding crack, knocking my signed photograph of Martin Brodeur to the floor, where it shatters. Adrenaline pumps through me as I take the stairs three at a time. I vaguely hear my dad calling out, "What the hell was that?" but I'm out the front door and tearing down the street.

I would normally go down Pine, then turn east onto Glenford Street until I hit Macon to get to Marney's but fuck that… I don't have time. Angling through Mrs. Capistrano's yard, I scrabble over her chain-link fence, only to take three sprinting strides in her small backyard, and do the same to get over the back part of the enclosure.

Dodging and weaving through the next block of yards, I run out onto Macon Street and come to a dead stop.

Marney's house is just two doors down and my knees almost buckle underneath me when I see it. Flames leap out of the downstairs windows and thick, white smoke pours out from under the eaves. Four large fire trucks are parked outside of her house, two with ladders already extended with water raining down onto the top floor. The rest of the street is filled with police cars and two ambulances. My hesitation lasts only a second before I start running.

Running toward Marney.

I push my way through a sizable crowd, which has filled the streets, knocking people roughly out of my way. I think I even knock a lady over but I could give a shit. Careening around one of the fire trucks, I'm almost knocked backward by the wave of heat that is pouring off her house. With a huge boom, the upstairs windows explode outward, raining glass all around. Huge tongues of flame are now waving from every window but I don't stop. In fact, I kick my speed up a notch.

I'm just steps away from the front porch, holding my arm up to ward off the heat. I can't even fathom how I'm going to get inside with the fire pouring out the front door, but that doesn't slow my progress.

Almost there… three feet from the first porch step and then… I'm tackled from the side.

My body slams into the ground and the air is knocked completely out of me. I try to take in a breath, but my lungs aren't working. Fuck it… I don't need them to get to Marney. I start struggling with the lead weight that is on top of me, vaguely noticing that it appears to be a fireman.

Pushing hard against him, I try to get my legs up so I can kick him off me. I make another attempt to breathe but my lungs still aren't cooperating.

Pulling on the last vestiges of air I have left in me, I rasp, "Get the fuck off."

"All right, kid… calm down," I hear and then the weight is gone.

I suck in a huge lungful of oxygen. Replenished, I spring to my feet and start to make a dash for the porch but arms of fucking steel wrap around my waist, slinging me away from the house. I stumble for a few feet and then right myself.

Spinning around, the fireman is standing between Marney's house and me with his arms held out in front of him. "You can't go in there, kid."

"The fuck I can't," I scream at him. "My girlfriend is in there."

"I'm sorry…" he starts to say but I don't have time

for this shit.

Lunging for the house, I try to juke around the fireman but my skills must be rusty. He easily catches me again, wrapping me in a bear hug that I cannot break free from.

My body strains toward the house, the blazing heat causing rivulets of sweat to pour from my face.

"Marney," I scream. My eyes frantically search the windows, hoping to see her somehow through the angry flames and billowing smoke.

I try to lunge toward the house, time and time again, but the firefighter isn't letting me go. I scream Marney's name, over and over, until my throat feels like it's riddled with glass shards.

"She's gone, kid. No one made it out."

The minute his words penetrate my brain, my body goes still. I can feel his hold start to marginally relax but he doesn't let go just yet.

"Gone?" I whisper.

"Yes. The house was fully involved by the time we got here. There was no way to get anyone out."

The fireman's arms fall away from my body and he takes a small step back. His body is still tense though and he's just waiting for me to spring into action again.

My eyes flick to the inferno and then back to him. "Are you sure?"

The pleading tone in my voice causes him to wince

but he nods his head.

My knees finally give out, and I sag to the ground. Bowing my head, I clutch desperately at the grass in Marney's front yard.

No, no, no, no, no.

This isn't happening.

Marney isn't in there. There's no way she died that way. The thought of Marney's burning body causes bile to rise up in my throat.

I look up to the fireman, who is still standing there. The raging fire behind him causes his body to be nothing more than a dark silhouette… a man without a face.

"Are you okay, kid?"

Shaking my head, I whisper, "I can't bear to think of the pain she was in…"

The faceless man kneels down in front of me and lays a hand on my shoulder. He squeezes it gently. "She was probably long gone from smoke inhalation before the fire reached her. Okay? She probably didn't feel a thing."

I know his words are meant to comfort me but the balmy effect falls flat. My eyes fill with tears and I look back down to the ground.

There's no reason she should have died that way.

The firemen should have tried to push their way in.

They should have sent five trucks instead of four.

They should have gotten here faster.

I should have gotten here faster.

I should have arranged for an earlier time to meet. If I had, Marney would have been out of the house, safe in my arms.

I could have saved her and I didn't.

The hard reality of my failure sets in, and the tears start spilling from my eyes. It's the first time I've cried since I was a little kid. I let them flow, not giving a shit what the fireman thinks, or what anyone thinks for that matter. I watch as my tears fall from my face and hit the green blades of spring grass before me.

"Flynn!"

I turn and see my mom and dad running for me. The fireman stands up and walks away, and then I'm in my parents' arms.

"I'm so sorry, baby," my mom murmurs as she strokes the tears from my face. Fresh ones replace them and I can see through the wavering haze that my mom is crying, too.

My dad's arms engulf both of us and I rest my chin on my mom's head.

I gaze over my dad's shoulder and watch my Marney burn away.

CHAPTER 1

Flynn

"GODDAMN IT, CALDWELL. Get your ass in my office. Now!"

I wince over hearing the Battalion Chief calling from the back of the station house. His voice is booming, echoing from deep inside that barrel chest of his. Studying the cards in my hand… pair of deuces, Ace high… it's best I fold anyway.

Tossing the cards facedown on the table, I stand up. "I'm out."

My buddies, my co-workers, my compatriots… they all keep their eyes pinned to their cards so they don't have to offer me a sympathetic look. They've heard me called into the Chief's office on more than one occasion and I know they feel for me.

But they're also probably a little glad I'm getting ready to get my ass chewed, because my dumbass moves affect them as well.

Walking out of the kitchen, I turn down the back hall, which houses our bunks. The Chief's office is at the very end. As I walk past the open doorway to the sleeping quarters, I hear, "When in the hell are you going to learn, Flynn?"

The room is dark but I don't need to see inside to recognize the voice of my best friend, Tim Davis.

Taking a step back, I lean up against the doorframe and reach my hand inside to flick on the light. Tim is lying on his bed, his hands clasped behind his head. His dark brown eyes look at me with a mixture of affection and annoyance.

I decide to play stupid, just to ramp up his annoyance. "Learn what?"

Tim rises up from the bed, swinging his legs to the side. Resting his elbows on his knees, he clasps his hands and sighs deep before turning his gaze back on me. "You know what, but I'll lay it out for you… when are you going to stop taking stupid risks?"

"Define stupid?" I ask, even though I know the answer. I just don't feel like hearing this shit from Tim, because I'm getting ready to hear an earful from the Chief.

Tim looks back down to his hands and I hear him chuckle, but it's not a sound filled with mirth. Instead, it sounds hard and bitter. When he looks back up at me, there is no smile on his face and his eyes hold just a bit of disgust.

I expect him to lay into me, but his voice is surprisingly soft. It stands at complete odds with his muscular and tattooed frame. "You know what I'm talking about so I won't bother stating the obvious. But the next time you put yourself in unnecessary danger, just remember our motto… *two go in, two come out.* You enter harm's way, you know one of us are coming in behind you. So yeah, I get that you don't care if you get injured or killed in a rescue… but you know you're risking our lives, too. You want that on your conscience if one of us gets killed?"

Guilt flashes like a nuclear explosion through my body. "I wouldn't put you or any of the team in danger—"

Tim cuts me off. "Save it. You already have, and on more than one occasion."

His voice is hard, which is foreign to me. Tim is about as big of a teddy bear as you can find. He has an easygoing nature, which is why we bonded so well.

"I'm sorry," is all I get out before I hear the Chief calling me again.

"Caldwell! Where the fuck are you?"

Taking a deep breath, I stare at Tim a moment longer and then turn my back on him. I can't stand that I've disappointed him. I could give a shit that the Chief is mad, but Tim? He's like a brother to me and I don't like letting him down. He needs to be able to trust me in any given situation, and to know that I've probably breached that trust has sent bitter acid swimming through my stomach.

Steeling my resolve as I head to the Chief's office, I start to calculate the speech which will hopefully get me out of hot water. Unfortunately, nothing good is coming to mind. Fact is, I fucked up and didn't follow protocol. Yesterday when we responded to a structure fire, I didn't wait for the Captain to do a size-up. When I jumped off the truck, I barely had my Nomex hood and helmet on before I was running into the building. Tim was on my heels, cursing at me.

I couldn't help it though. We were told there were occupants in the building—which there were—and I saw a safe entry point. Ultimately, I wasn't even in any danger, but I'm still going to get my ass chewed because I didn't wait the extra two minutes for the Captain to do the size-up.

Just as I reach the Chief's office, but before I can knock, the speakers crackle and roar to life. A series of audible tones chime through, followed by a buzzer. The pager on my hip goes off but I don't bother looking at it because a voice comes over the speaker. "Engine 209, Engine 113, Squad 15, Ladder 102, Ladder 94, Rescue 12, Battalion Chief 1, Air truck 15. Major working fire—532 Pennsylvania Avenue. Residential. Multi-family house, duplex. Be advised Dispatch has received multiple calls."

I turn from the Chief's door and head toward my bunk for my turnout gear. Easily slipping into my boots, I pull my trousers up, looping my arms through the suspenders. I slide my Nomex hood on and shrug into my coat, lacing my thumbs through the wrist gauntlets. After I have my coat zipped and velcroed tight, I push the hood back off my face so it hangs loosely around my neck. Grabbing my black helmet, the color of which signifies I'm a member of an engine company for the FDNY, I head toward the truck.

Engine 209 is on the move.

♦

WE ARE THE first to arrive at the duplex but Ladder 94 pulls in seconds behind us. The Captain gets out to start his size-up, and I quickly don my self-contained breathing apparatus and face piece, pulling my hood over the top. I put my helmet on and pull the chin strap tight, my movements quick and efficient.

I note the housing unit on the right seems to be fully involved and within minutes, our ladder is deployed and spraying water from above. Members of the other engine are entering the front door. I can't see any flames or smoke from the other side at this point, which is a good sign.

As I walk closer, I faintly hear noise coming from the left side of the unit. Since a narrow driveway runs along its side, I walk that way to investigate. The driveway is a luxury here in Brooklyn and I envy the owners for just a second that they don't have to worry about parking.

As I near the windows at the back of the house, I hear the frantic barking of a dog. A big dog by the sound of it and it sounds panicked. I can tell immediately it's coming from inside the house and I easily locate the window where the barking is the loudest. The window ledge sits pretty high, just at my chest as I put my face up against the glass to look in. I can't see shit because the cheap, plastic blinds are partially closed but the dog is definitely in there. I have no clue if a human is inside, so I may only be going in to save a dog, but yup… I'm going in.

And nope… doesn't matter that my Cap hasn't given the okay.

Taking my ax, I break the window and breathe a sigh of relief that no smoke pours out. Making sure that all the shards of glass are clear of the window frame, I reach in and get a good grip on the blinds, pulling hard so they rip from the wall.

"Fuck, Flynn… can't you wait two seconds?"

I knew Tim wouldn't be too far behind but he's not mad at me for entering so quickly. It's pretty clear that this side of the house isn't burning yet. I hear Tim speaking into his radio, letting the Captain know we're making entry. "Cap… we hear a dog and possible subjects inside. Entering window to make a rescue."

I think I hear the Cap curse but then he gives the go ahead. Putting my hands on the ledge, I give myself a mental pat on the back that I'm able to pull myself up and haul myself inside. Working out at the gym five days a week pays off. I make a less-than-graceful fall onto the floor and immediately jump up to take note of my surroundings.

I'm in a bedroom and the door is closed. Smoke is seeping in under the bottom and the air already has a hazy quality to it.

Lying on the bed is a huge dog… probably at least a hundred pounds. Although I only look at him briefly, it's enough to know that he's no ordinary mutt. His coat is jet black, long and glossy. His chest and paws are snowy white with a blaze of the same color down the middle of his face. Russet-colored fur adorns his legs along with two brown stripes right where his eyebrows sit. It makes his face very expressive, and he's looking at me now as if to say, *It's about damn time.*

I say it's a "he" because his head is boxy and his chest is huge, so I'm guessing he's sporting a pair of big, furry balls underneath all that hair. The dog looks at me expectantly and lets out another series of panicked barks, which are still deep and booming.

It's then that I notice the dog seems to be lying on top of something, and based on the size and curves, it's painfully obvious it's a person under a blanket.

Taking a step toward the bed, holding my hand out, palm down, I speak in a calm voice, "Hey boy… you gonna let me help whoever that is you're lying on? Huh? Gonna let me take a peek?"

Not surprisingly, the dog lays his ears back flat and issues a deep growl. My voice just issued through the amp of my mask and I completely sounded like Darth Vader. I know I'm probably going to catch shit for this, but I take my helmet off and toss it near the window. I see Tim standing there, his face peering in. I hold my hand up to him to just wait and I quickly loosen the straps on my face piece to pull it off.

With the mask gone, at least the dog can hear my real voice and hopefully won't be as freaked. I, on the other hand, immediately notice the smoke is thicker and it's hard to breathe. I'm guessing the fire has breached into this unit.

Inching forward carefully, I keep talking to the dog in a soft, reassuring voice. Now that the dog understands that I'm not Darth Vader and I'm here to save, not destroy, his ears perk forward and he just watches my progress with his head cocked to the side.

As I reach the edge of the bed, I take one last look at the dog, which I can now see is lying across the legs of whoever is under the blanket. He just stares back at me… expectantly.

"Do you mind if I pull these covers back?" I ask, feeling ridiculous as I do so.

His gaze at me never wavers, but he cocks his head in the opposite direction as if he's saying, *Well, what the hell are you waiting for?*

Reaching out, I peel the covers back, revealing the face of a woman underneath. Her dark hair is lanky and her eyes are closed, with dark blue circles underneath. She's on her side and it stands out to me that she has several piercings in her exposed ear, traveling all the way around the entire shell. Giving a quick glance at the dog, who still lies across the woman's legs, I peel the blanket back further. When it reaches her shoulders, I realize that she's naked underneath so I halt my progress.

Grabbing onto her shoulder, I shake her slightly. "Ma'am… I need you to wake up now. I need to get you out of here."

She doesn't move or respond in anyway.

Just great… she's probably high as a kite so now I'm rescuing a dog and a bombed-out druggie.

I look at the dog again and he just stares back at me, as if to say, *It's still your job to save her.*

"Yeah, I know… I got it," I answer his silent plea.

I try one more time to rouse her, tapping her on the cheek lightly. "Come on, lady. Wake up."

She still makes no move so, with a sigh of frustration, I reach down to lift her up, sticking my arms under the blanket so it comes with her to keep her covered for modesty.

I give a pointed look to the dog. "Get up, you big lug, so I can lift her."

Much to my surprise, the dog immediately bounds off the bed and walks over to the window, not caring in the slightest that there are glass shards littering the floor. His paws are probably going to get cut but I can't worry about that now.

Bending my knees, I scoop the woman up and lift her from the bed.

Except my momentum is stopped as something pulls against us.

What the fuck?

Lowering her back down to the bed, I flip the blanket back and curse over the sight that greets me.

Her right leg has a manacle cuffed around it and it's chained to the metal bed frame at the bottom.

Now I'm not so sure she has voluntarily taken drugs.

The sight of her chained to the bed makes my blood run cold and now there is a greater sense of urgency to get her out of this structure. Without wasting any precious time, I turn to Tim and call out, "Get the bolt cutters off the Engine. She's chained to the bed."

Tim's face is immediately gone from the window but I don't wait for him to return. I grab my ax and start hitting at the chain. It's thick and stubborn, and under ordinary circumstances, my ax would be useless against the steel links. But when I saw this woman chained to the bed, I had a moment of clarity where I told myself, *This woman will not die the way Marney did. I'm getting her out of here.*

I strike at the chain with all of my might, sparks flying from the metal-on-metal contact. Mentally counting to myself every time I make a blow, it's only on the eighth hit that the chain miraculously breaks apart and the woman is freed.

Tossing my ax near the window, I wrap the blanket more securely around her and easily lift her from the bed. She can't weigh more than a hundred and ten pounds, if that.

When I reach the window, Tim is there with bolt cutters, which he immediately drops when he sees me with the woman. I squat down so her body is level with the window and pass her through head first to Tim's outstretched arms. As Tim takes her upper body, I help to thread her lower half through the window until he's cradling her fully.

"She's unconscious… probably drugged. I can't believe she was fucking chained to the bed."

Tim doesn't respond but he doesn't have to. I know he's as disgusted as I am.

"I'll be right behind you. I'm going to get this dog out."

Tim turns away but yells back, "Don't get bit."

Pulling my head back in the window, I locate and grab my helmet, face piece, and ax, tossing them through the window, hearing them clatter on the concrete driveway below. The Chief will have my ass if he knows I had taken them off, but I know it helped to keep the dog at ease. Turning around, I look at the dog solemnly. "You're not going to bite me if I pick you up, are you?"

The dog gives me a vigorous wag of his tail and I take that as his full acquiescence that he will be good and keep his teeth sheathed.

Squatting down, I wrap my arms around the dog's chest and lift his front paws to the windowsill, resting them there. Squatting again, I reach his back haunches and haul him up, pushing him forward out the window. The damn dog weighs a ton but he doesn't resist me. Once he realizes he's going out the window, he kicks his back legs out against my chest, springing forward and leaping the rest of the way out. I see him land in the driveway with a grace that belies his massive frame.

Throwing my leg through the window, I follow behind him.

As I walk back to the front of the house, I see the fire is mostly contained. This turned out to be a fairly easy fire but I'm thankful that dog was barking, or else we may not have found the girl in time.

Speaking of the dog, I look around but don't see the

shaggy beast anywhere. Shrugging my shoulders, I head over to the ambulance. One EMT is placing an oxygen mask on the woman's face, while the other takes her vitals. She appears to be gaining consciousness and I find myself curious as to why she was chained to the bed.

Reaching up, she tugs at the oxygen mask. The EMT pulls her hand away and tells her to leave it in place. Shaking her head back and forth, she pulls on it again, this time with more force than I would have thought she had, and rips it off.

"Capone," she gasps. "Please, get him out of the house."

The EMT looks at me and says, "Was someone else in the house?"

I nod my head and step up into the ambulance. "Her dog. That's who she's talking about."

Sitting on the bench next to the woman, I lean over and take the mask from her hand. As I start to gently pry her fingers away, I tell her, "I got your dog out. He's fine."

Her fingers immediately go lax and the mask slips from her grip. I start to pull it back up over her mouth and nose, but my hands freeze when I look at her eyes. They are pinned on me and they are the most unique eyes I have ever seen in my life. I can't seem to tear my gaze away.

They are gray—almost utterly devoid of anything

other than that particular shade that is right in between black and white. Except… there's a slight ring of green and gold flecks that hug her pupils and they stand out in stark contrast to the silver. She's staring at me with the most thankful expression I've ever been bestowed.

Reaching out, she locks her fingers around my wrist. "Thank you," she whispers, and then she loses consciousness again.

CHAPTER 2

Flynn

I THROW THE last of my dirty clothes into my duffel bag and zip it up. This last call officially threw me into overtime, having received it just as the end of my three-day shift had expired. Now it's time to go home and relax for the next four days.

Best of all, if I skirt out of here quickly, I can avoid the Chief's wrath altogether. He's been holed up in his office since we pulled back in and has apparently forgotten that he was going to chew me out just a few hours ago.

"You headed out?"

Swinging around, I see Tim standing in the doorway to our sleeping quarters. He's leaning against the doorframe, his beefy arms folded across his chest.

"Yup. How about you?"

"Yeah. Headed over to Sam's school to pick him up. You know… surprise him."

I smile. Tim takes every opportunity he can to spend time with Sam. It's hard being a fireman because you work such odd hours. Ever since Tim got divorced, he takes every available opportunity to spend it with his son. Luckily, Tim's ex is pretty cool and works with him outside of their normal custody arrangement.

"That sounds great. Give the little monster a hug from me."

Tim gives me a grin that flashes sparkly white against his dark skin. "Sure will."

Turning my back, I lift up my duffel and sling it over my shoulder. When I turn around, Tim is still standing there, staring at me.

"Listen," he says, glancing briefly at the ground and then back up at me again, "I'm sorry I said that shit to you earlier. I just don't want you to do something stupid that gets you suspended or fired."

Walking up to Tim, I punch him lightly in the shoulder. It's like hitting concrete. "No worries, man. I get it."

"We're cool, then?"

"We're cool. Are you up for watching the game tomorrow at my place?" Tim and I are die-hard Jets fans.

"Yup. I'll bring the beer."

"And you're bringing Sam, right? I got this killer new Xbox game to show him."

Rolling his eyes at me, Tim just turns around and walks out. "He's coming, too. We'll see you around game time."

Peeking my head around the door and looking down the hall, I see the Chief's office door is still closed so I make a break for it. Just as I'm stepping out onto the sidewalk, I hear, "Caldwell… wait up."

Turning around, I see my teammate, Jim Skellig, trotting toward me. I hope he makes this quick because every second delayed is one that the Chief could be calling for me.

"What's up?" I ask.

"Pete told me you were looking for a roommate."

"Yeah… I'm considering it."

Fact is, I've always had a roommate while living in the city. It was nice to share expenses and it kept the loneliness down to a minimum. My last roommate had been with me for the past three years while he attended NYU-Poly, but graduated this past spring and moved on.

"Cool. I have a friend who has a friend that's going to be moving to the area next month and is looking to share some space. Want me to have him contact you?"

"Sure. Just give him my email if you don't mind."

"Got it."

"All right, man… I'm out of here. Catch you in a few days."

Jim gives me a casual wave and walks back into the station. I turn down Sheffield Avenue and head south. It's the beginning of September and it's finally starting to cool off. I swear I smelled a hint of fall in the air when I woke up this morning.

Luckily, I live close to the firehouse and it's only about a twenty-minute walk for me. I only drive if the weather is really crappy and today I'm enjoying the crisp weather.

As I walk toward my apartment building, my mind drifts back to the woman I pulled out of the house. I can't stop thinking about the fact she was chained to a bed. I mean… what kind of monster does that to someone? And I can't stop thinking that what if she was chained to the bed and the fire was started to kill her? Could she have been a target for murder? It seems unlikely since most of the fire was in the other unit, but that could have been done intentionally to cover motive.

Thank God that dog was barking. He deserves a good chunk of the credit for getting her out safely.

Shit… I really hope the pup is okay.

Now that is weighing heavily on my mind.

Stopping abruptly on the sidewalk, I get a curse from someone behind me that about plows into my backside. I ignore the person and glance at my watch.

Before I can talk myself out of it, I cross the street and head toward the parking deck that has my car.

Yes, I know… I like to save things. I can't stomach the thought of that poor dog out on the streets by himself. He could get hit by a car, starve to death, or hell, someone could shoot the damn beast. My mind runs rampant with all the terrible things that could happen to the dog and my step quickens to reach my car.

Saving the dog, of course, has nothing to do with the fact that I'm curious about his owner. The dog clearly belonged to the woman I pulled from the house, because he was protecting her and barking for help.

Running off to rescue some stranger's dog certainly has nothing to do with the fact that I can't seem to get the image of those gray eyes out of my mind. Nor does it have anything to do with the fact that, based on the hideous circumstances I found her in, some part of my hero-alarm bell is starting to ring.

If my parents, my sister, my cousins, or even Tim, knew I was off to go hunt for this dog and possibly learn more about this woman, they would all be shaking their heads with pity in their eyes.

They would all be thinking, *There goes Flynn… off to save another soul.*

♦

JUST AS I pull out of the parking deck, my phone rings. I don't bother to look at the caller ID, just answer, "Caldwell."

"Hey man… it's Buzz."

"What's up, Copper? Shoot your dick off yet?"

Buzz Matheson is a good friend of mine. He was in my cousin, Nix's, class in high school and we've all remained in touch throughout the years. He's currently working in the Narcotics division for the NYPD.

"Luckily, it's still attached. Burn yours off in a fire yet?"

Chuckling, I tell him, "Nah… all my parts are in working order."

"Listen… I just pulled a case that you're involved in and we need to talk."

"The fire this afternoon?"

"Yeah. I understand you pulled a woman out that was chained to a bed."

Visions of her lying there unconscious swim through my head, causing my stomach to turn. It appears that maybe she was into some deep trouble, just as I'd suspected.

"Yeah. I found her there with a metal cuff around her ankle. She was naked and my best guess is she was drugged."

Buzz curses into the phone. "I'm going to need a formal interview from you. I'm on my way to the hospital now to talk to Miss Page. I've been told she's trying to check herself out against doctor's advice and I need to catch her before she disappears. Think you can meet me over there and I can get your statement after?"

Miss Page? So that's one more part of the mystery unveiled.

"Sure. I'll head that way now. But why do you have

this case? Shouldn't it be with someone that investigates kidnapping or arson or something?"

"It is but I'm coming on to assist. I've been tracking Miss Page's boyfriend, who is a mid-level drug dealer, and she could be my best lead in busting him. If I can get him, then he can flip the larger ring."

So, the drugged and chained Miss Page has a boyfriend? I wonder if he'll be at the hospital to take care of her? Probably not as I imagine he's lying low if he knows he's on the cops' radars.

"I'll head that way now and meet you over there."

"Sounds great," is all I hear before Buzz disconnects.

Unfortunately, the search for the shaggy beast is going to have to wait a bit more. A different kind of duty calls.

♦

AS I WALK down the hall to Miss Page's room, I can hear angry voices that get louder as I approach. Buzz had texted me her room number with a cryptic "could use your help" message after it.

I turn the corner and see her room ahead. The door is open and Buzz is standing just inside, talking to someone else that I can't see. But I can sure as hell hear her, and I can only assume it's Miss Page.

"I don't give a rat's ass what your hospital policy is. I'm leaving and you can't make me stay. And you… I'm not talking to you either. Just leave me the hell alone."

Stepping into the room behind Buzz, I immediately take in the scene. The woman I pulled out of the fire is standing on the other side of her bed, wearing a hospital dressing gown. Her skin is pale and her stringy, dark hair comes down to barely brush the tops of her shoulders. She looks tired and wan, but those gray eyes are spitting fire right now.

It's clear that she's been through an ordeal, and I get the immediate impression she hasn't been allowed to bathe, or even possibly eat, in days. But none of that can hide the fact that she has a delicate beauty about her. Her cheekbones are high, her nose is slender and straight, and her lips are generously full. Even her exhaustion can't cover that up, and I find my interest in her exponentially grows now that I've gotten a good look at her.

There's a nurse standing on the other side of the bed and she looks just as pissed as the lovely Miss Page. Poor Buzz is standing there with his hands in his pockets and his face turned to the ceiling in a look of total frustration.

I knock softly on the doorframe to announce my presence. "What's going on?"

The room erupts all at once and I hear:

"Who the fuck are you?" from Miss Page.

"She can't just walk out of the hospital… we have protocols to follow," from the pissed-off nurse.

"She's refusing to give me a formal statement," from

Buzz.

This situation is about one second away from all hell breaking loose, so I step forward and put on my best Caldwell charm.

"Miss Page? My name is Flynn Caldwell. I'm the fireman that pulled you out of the house. Pulled your dog out, too. Remember?"

She nods her head slightly but I can tell she doesn't really recognize me.

I continue, "I came here to talk about your dog… that is your dog, right?"

She doesn't answer me but starts to chew on her bottom lip in a sure sign of worry. Turning to the nurse and Buzz, I say, "How about you give me a few minutes alone with her, okay?"

The look I give Buzz is one he recognizes… she needs to be calmed down and this is apparently the most calm he's seen her since he's arrived so he's willing to let me have a try.

The nurse and Buzz leave the room, shutting the door behind them.

"Mind if I sit down?" I ask, but I don't wait for an answer. I move over to the only chair in the room and take a seat.

"Where's Capone?"

I point to the bed. "How about you take a seat before you fall over and I'll tell you everything I know. That's one brave dog you have there. So what's your first name?"

She looks like she's going to balk for a second but then she sits on the edge and turns her body to me. I can tell she's still a bit woozy from whatever drugs were in her system and the fight seems to have gone out of her. "It's Rowan. Do you have him? Is he okay?"

"I don't, but I was on my way to go look for him when I got a call from Detective Matheson that he needed to interview me since I'm the one that found you. So I had to come here first."

"Oh God… I can't believe he's out there on his own. I have to go and find him."

She bolts up from the bed and starts for the door. Jumping up from my chair, I gently grab her shoulders and stop her. She's so tiny—I feel like I can snap the bones in her shoulders with just a firm grip.

"Wait just a minute. I'll help you find him, I swear, but you literally cannot waltz out of here in that hospital gown. We need to get you some clothes first, and then we can go."

I can see her calm just a bit.

"You'll help me? Why?" She sounds utterly perplexed that I would even offer her help but before I can respond, she says, "Never mind. I don't need your help. I can find him myself."

She pushes out of my grip with surprising strength

and throws the door open. The nurse and Buzz are standing there.

Looking first at Buzz, she says, "You can just leave… I'm *not* talking to you." She then turns to the nurse. "Get me a pair of surgical scrubs or something I can wear. I'm leaving."

The nurse huffs and turns away. "I have paperwork I have to do to let you out of here and a doctor has to sign off. I'll find something for you to wear but I have to get the paperwork ready."

"Fine," Rowan snaps, "just hurry."

She walks back to the bed and slumps down on it. I can tell she's exhausted and if the dryness of her lips is any indication, I'm thinking she's dehydrated. I pour her a cup of water from the pitcher beside her bed and hand it to her. "Drink this… you need liquids."

She takes the cup and sips at it, staring stonily at her feet.

Buzz has followed us back into the room. "Miss Page… I don't understand why you won't talk to me. I just want to know who did this to you so we can bring him or her to justice."

Very smooth the way Buzz said "him" or "her", especially when I know he already believes it to be a "him". But he wants to make her at ease to talk about her boyfriend, I'm sure.

She doesn't respond but takes another sip of the

water. Buzz apparently takes that as a sign he should continue talking.

"Miss Page… Rowan… I know the house you were in was being rented by your boyfriend." Buzz pulls out his notepad and makes a big deal of flipping through the pages to consult his notes. But I know this is for show… he knows damn well what her boyfriend's name is.

"Yeah… got it right here." He points to the pad. "Like I said, the house you were found in was rented by Mr. Teddy Jones. He goes by "Juice" I believe. That's your boyfriend, right?"

She still doesn't respond but dutifully takes another sip of water. I notice her cheeks get slightly red at the mention of her boyfriend's name.

Buzz goes in for the kill. "Did he chain you to that bed, Rowan? Drug you? Did he rape you? Was he trying to kill you… and that's why he set the fire?"

Rowan's head jerks up at those last words and there is fear in her eyes. I think she's getting ready to spill the beans but the only thing she says is, "He's not my boyfriend, hasn't been for a while."

"Then did he kidnap you? You have to open up to me so we can get you justice."

I think that's a pretty good line, and I'm pretty sure Buzz has said the one thing that will get her to open up.

Wrong!

Rowan's eyes narrow and she actually sneers, her

upper lip curling slightly on the right side. "Justice? You're kidding me, right? When has a cop ever worried about someone like me? You're not fooling me. I smell narcotics all over you. You only want me to help you bust Juice so you can get some fucking meritorious commendation or something. Tell me I'm wrong!"

I have to clamp down hard on my tongue so I don't start laughing. This girl is no dummy. In fact, I'd say she's smart as hell and she neatly put Buzz in his place.

Glancing at Buzz, I can tell he's admitting defeat for today now that she's made him. He pulls his card out of his pocket and hands it to her. "If you change your mind, call me. I can offer you protection against him in exchange for your cooperation."

Turning toward the door, Buzz motions me. "Come on, Flynn. Might as well get your statement now."

I follow him to the door and say in a low voice, "Let's reschedule, man. I'm going to help her find her dog, and maybe she'll open up to me."

Buzz raises his eyebrows at me but doesn't say anything. He just nods and heads down the hall.

Turning, I step back into the room and shut the door. Rowan looks up at me in surprise, the cup of water tilted halfway to her mouth.

"Now, let's spring you out of here and go find that dog of yours."

CHAPTER 3

Rowan

FUCKING COP! I knew he was here only for Juice. No way they'd ever really give a damn about a naked and drugged girl chained to a bed that was almost roasted alive.

The door shuts and I look up to see the fireman standing there. The unbelievably gorgeous fireman.

What a cliché.

"Now, let's spring you out of here and go find that dog of yours."

"I told you, I don't need your help, so you might as well turn around and march out of here, too."

"Well, tough shit… I'm going to help find your dog whether you like it or not. And it will get done a lot faster if we work with each other rather than against each other."

I'm momentarily shocked over his words and I give him another once-over. I'm suspicious of his offer of help, because… well, hey… I'm suspicious of all authority figures. I'd learned that long before I ever got messed up with Juice.

But his gaze tells me the offer is genuine and I take a moment to check him out a bit closer. First of all, he's a pretty big guy… probably a good foot taller than my five-three height. He's also stacked with muscle and I still have enough of my wits about me to notice that he has a face that would make most women fall over in a dead faint if he smiled at them.

It's the eyes.

Definitely the eyes. Lashes so thick you would think they were painted on border the lightest pair of hazel irises I've ever seen. His dark brown hair, which he wears fairly short, only makes his eyes pop that much more. When he smiles, I notice he has a dimple on the left side of his mouth, but not on the right.

"So what do you say?" he asks, bringing me out of my perusal of his hotness.

Shaking my head, because the last thing I need to be thinking about is how gorgeous this guy is, I stand from the bed. "If you think that I'm going to spill my dirty secrets to you so you can run off and tell your cop friend, forget about it."

Flynn holds his hands up in a conciliatory gesture. "I could care less about that. I just want to help you find your dog, and then you can be on your way. Deal?"

My skeptical nature looks hard for the lie, but I can't find it. And I'm a pretty good judge of character. For example, I knew Juice was bad news and trouble from the get-go. But just because I'm a good judge of character doesn't mean I make smart decisions with my knowledge.

Still… he's offering me a way to find Capone and that dog is literally the only thing I have in the world right now. I don't even have any clothes and I have nowhere to live right now, but I figure Capone and I can huddle up together tonight until I figure something out.

"Okay… if you can manage to get me some scrubs to wear and if that beast of a nurse will get my papers ready, we can go."

He shoots me a one-dimpled smile and turns toward the door. "I'm on it. I'll have you out of here in thirty minutes."

♦

FLYNN DRIVES US back to Juice's house and he pulls up to the curb. He had tried to engage me in conversation on the way over but after a few grunted answers, he gave up. Opening the car door, he steps out and I do the same.

"You come get in my car and start driving up and down the streets looking for him. I'll go by foot. We'll be able to cover more ground that way. Let's meet back here in twenty minutes to check in."

I just stare at him for a moment before my tongue

works. "You want me to take your car? I'm a perfect stranger… someone who used to shack up with a known drug dealer. You're really going to trust me with your car?"

Flynn shrugs his shoulders. "Well, it's not like you can walk around looking for him. You don't even have any shoes."

Glancing down at my feet, it hits me harder than ever before that I truly have nothing except for a slightly too large set of blue surgical scrubs. Tears threaten to break free of my eyeballs but I curse them viciously until they retreat.

I look up at Flynn and shoot him a bitter smile. "Sure thing. Your loss if I decide to just up and steal your car."

Walking by him to get in the driver's seat, he reaches out and touches my arm. He doesn't grab it, but just places his fingertips on my forearm. I stop at the silent command.

"You won't steal it. Want to know how I know that?" His voice is low and soft, and I have to admit… it's damn sexy.

Swallowing hard, I reply, "I'll play—how do you know that?"

"Because that damn dog is more important than anything in the world to you, and you're going to do everything in your power to find him. That includes using me to help you find him. No way you're about to take off with my car and leave Capone out here to fend for himself."

He has me pegged. To a tee.

Big whoop. He still doesn't know shit about me. "Great job, Sherlock. You got me. Now let's get to work if you don't mind."

Stepping past him, I climb into the driver's seat and adjust it forward so I can reach the pedals. I don't bother telling him I don't have a license, nor that I've only driven a handful of times. No sense in worrying him.

Putting the car in gear, I drive away, glancing once in the rearview mirror at him. He's already turned his back on me and is trotting across the street, before disappearing into a neighbor's yard.

I methodically drive up and down each street with the windows rolled down. Every few minutes, I yell Capone's name. I also yell out other words he'll recognize like, "treat" or "ball". As soon as I call out for him, I look frantically, left and right, expecting him to come bounding out from behind some bushes.

I'm disappointed time and time again.

As the minutes tick by, I'm starting to get panicked. What if he's been stolen? Or killed? Or what if he's hurt and can't come to me?

I can't lose that dog… not now. Not after everything that he's been through with me. And there's no way I'm ever letting Juice get him back. He only wanted Capone because of his pedigree and because he's a beautiful dog. It was a way for him to show off to his druggie friends that he could afford a two-thousand dollar Bernese Mountain Dog shipped to him all the way from Colorado.

Once the puppy arrived, just over a year ago, Juice promptly named him Capone and then forgot about him. Which was fine by me. I was the one that raised Capone. I potty trained him, taught him how to sit, lie down, and to heel when we walked in the neighborhood. He was smart as a whip and we adored each other. He would sleep in bed with me at night, until Juice would come in and yell at him to get off.

Capone hated Juice and the feeling soon became mutual when Juice realized Capone was completely and utterly attached to me. He wouldn't do a damn thing that Juice asked of him and it would piss Juice off that he would do anything that I asked.

Once, Juice yelled at Capone for a solid fifteen minutes because he refused to sit for him. After he slammed out of the house in anger, I watched in amazement as Capone calmly walked into the bedroom and peed in one of Juice's tennis shoes. Of course, I had to clean it up before Juice got home, because he would have beat Capone if he knew he did that. I tried to chastise the furry monster but I ended up giggling every time I tried to say, “Bad dog” to him. It remained our little secret.

Turning back down the street where Juice lived, I can feel my throat starting to get tight. The burned-out husk of a house is just a block away.

I call for him again.

Nothing.

Pulling back up to the curb, I lower my forehead to the wheel and try to take a deep breath. It comes out in a stuttering gasp and tears pool in my eyes. I hastily blink at them and square my shoulders. There isn’t time to grieve for my dog when I’ve only been searching for twenty minutes. When Flynn meets me back here, I’ll tell him to go on home and then I’ll keep looking.

I’ll look all night and won’t stop until I find him.

Raising my head up from the steering wheel, I look out the front window and my heart almost explodes in joy.

Flynn is standing on the sidewalk in front of Juice’s house, holding Capone by the collar. He’s giving me that one-dimpled smile, but I can’t even return it. My eyes right now are only for my dog.

Throwing the door open, I step out of the car and, as soon as Capone sees me, he bolts out of Flynn’s grip. The move almost topples Flynn over but I see that he regains his footing just as Capone barrels into me. I fall backward onto the two-foot wide patch of grass that constitutes a front yard and he lays his big body right down on top of mine, lowering his huge head to my face and licking me all over.

My hands come up to rub the silky fur just behind his ears and I can feel his fluffy tail furiously thumping against my legs. He even starts to whine a little, he's so happy to see me.

And all of a sudden, I can't hold it in any more. I refused to cry every time Juice tried to hurt me. Not even a drop spilled from my eyes when my escape from him was thwarted and he chained me to the bed. I refused to let the tears come when he stuck a needle in my arm, shooting me up with something that rendered me into a puddle of uselessness. I wouldn't even weep when I gained consciousness in the hospital and learned I'd almost been burned alive.

But now… now that I have my dog back, I feel like it's the most joyous occasion in my entire existence and I cannot stop the tears of happiness that start pouring out. No matter… Capone just licks them up as soon as they spill.

After several minutes of being wrapped up in puppy goodness, a shadow casts over us and I look up to see Flynn standing there. He has a warm smile on his face.

"I'd say the two of you are happy to see each other."

Pushing Capone off to the side of me, I sit up but keep my arm around him, rubbing him constantly.

"Yeah… I really don't know how to thank you. Where did you find him?"

Flynn squats down next to us and points toward the west. "Just a few blocks over. He was meandering in between two houses. He came to me when I called his name."

I focus my gaze on Capone and he looks back at me with his soft, brown eyes. My heart melts even further, and suddenly I could care less that I'm homeless and have just a set of surgical scrubs to my name. I have my best friend with me now, and with that, I can accomplish anything.

Gratitude for Flynn's help overwhelms me and I look up at him. I hope he understands the sincerity in my voice when I say, "Thank you."

"It was nothing."

Reaching out, I grab a hold of his wrist. His gaze flickers down briefly to where we are touching and then back to me. "No… it was everything to me. Capone is the most important part of my life and I don't know what I would have done if you hadn't found him."

To prove he is in puppy heaven, Capone rolls over on his back and bares his belly to me. I start to scratch him there and his eyes roll into the back of his head. Taking a moment, I grab each paw and run my fingers over the pads, checking for cuts. He seems to be good and I sigh in relief he hasn't been hurt.

Flynn rocks backward from his squat and sits down on the grass across from us. Gazing over my shoulder to the burned-out house, he says, "I assume everything you owned was in there?"

"Yeah. Just clothes though. Nothing much."

"What about money? Credit cards? ID?"

"Nope," I say but I don't elaborate further. Juice had taken all of my money except for a small, secret stash I left at a friend's house, I've never had a credit card in my life and I didn't have any ID. When I left home at the age of eighteen, I changed my name but not legally. As far as the real world knew, I was still Anne Marie Cleeden. As far as my world was concerned, I was Rowan Page and had been from the day I stepped foot into New York City.

I've never needed an ID because every job I've worked has always been for cash under the table. Never filed a tax return in my life, but then again, I couldn't… Rowan Page doesn't really exist on paper.

"So where are you going to stay? Can I give you a lift somewhere?"

While I'm gratefully appreciative of the help that Flynn has given me, it's time to part ways. I'm a loner and I hate relying on anyone but myself. So the lie falls easily from my lips. "Sure… I have a few friends I can crash with until I can get back on my feet. You really don't have to hang around here."

Flynn gives me a smile. "Well, at least let me give you and Capone a ride."

I shoot him back an equally nice smile so he doesn't sense my lies. "Oh, no need. I'll just call one of them to pick me up."

Reaching into his pocket, Flynn pulls out his cell phone and hands it to me. "Here… give them a call and I'll wait with you."

When you've lived on your own the way I have, and when you've had to scrape, scrabble, and lie just to survive, I never even hesitate in carrying out my duplicity. Taking the phone, I punch in a fake number and hold it to my ear. I wait a sufficient time for my "friend" to answer and then I carry on a conversation purely for Flynn's benefit.

"Hey Lori! What's up, girl?"

I wait a few moments, pretending to listen to my "friend". I even glance at Flynn and motion with my free hand that she's a chatterbox.

"So listen… I need a place to crash for a few nights. Can you take Capone and me in?" Glancing down at Capone, I give his belly a pat. "That's great. I knew I could count on you. I'm at Juice's house. Okay… see you in about twenty minutes."

I pretend to listen to my "friend" chatter for a few more minutes, rolling my eyes at Flynn. Then I give a fake goodbye and hang up.

Handing the phone back to Flynn, I say, "All taken care of. Lori will come get me. You can go ahead and head home now. No sense in waiting."

Flynn just holds the phone in his hand and watches me for a moment. His perusal makes me a little nervous but then he stands from the ground. "You're sure you don't want me to wait with you?"

Shaking my head and giving him a reassuring smile, I tell him, "No. Honestly, we're good. Capone and I will just hang here and wait for Lauren."

Something flickers in Flynn's hazel eyes and he says, "I thought you said her name was Lori."

Shrugging my shoulders, I don't miss a beat. "It is… Lauren's her full name. I call her Lori sometimes though."

Flynn shoots me a grin that pulls his dimple out in full force. He punches something on his phone and then holds it out to me. I can see from the face of the phone that he's redialed the number I called and then pushed the speakerphone button so I could hear.

The recording comes through loud and clear. *"We're sorry but you have reached a number that has been disconnected or is no longer in service. If you feel you have reached this recording in error, please hang up and try your call again."*

Fuck. Busted.

But I don't even have the grace to be embarrassed. I

shrug my shoulders and smirk at him. "So what? You caught me in a lie. Not the first I've told."

He doesn't even bother to chastise me. "So where will you stay tonight?"

"I'll figure something out. I always do."

Flynn stares down at me, his eyes flicking from me to Capone. When they land back on me, he says, "Come on. You can stay at my apartment tonight and we'll figure out something to do."

"No. No way. I appreciate it but not going to happen."

"Why not?"

"Because I don't like owing people and I don't go home with strange men."

"I'm not a strange man. I just saved your life this morning."

Shrugging my shoulders to tell him I don't care, I say, "I don't need any help."

Flynn gives me a wry laugh. "First, you do need help, and second, you won't owe me a thing. Just consider this something I want to do out of the goodness of my heart."

Anger surges through me for a split second, and my voice is cold. "I'm not a fucking charity case."

I expect Flynn to back away from my wrath, because I can be a mean bitch when I want to, but he just offers me another smirk. "I don't consider you a charity case. I have no doubt you can take care of yourself. But think about this… Capone is probably exhausted and he could use a good meal. If you won't accept my help for you, how about accept it for him?"

I stare at him hard for just a moment, casually noting how the late afternoon sun makes his eyes glow. My resolve is weakening, only because I'm tired, hungry, and I'm finding my own pride may have some limits. Then my eyes go down to Capone. He's sound asleep on his back, my fingers grazing the hair on his belly. I can't help the dopey smile that comes to my face just by looking at the bag of fur lying there, and I'm sure my expression tells Flynn that I've just capitulated.

CHAPTER 4
Flynn

ROWAN PAGE IS one tough nut. If it were just her, sitting in front of her psycho ex-boyfriend's house, wearing nothing but paper-thin scrubs and faced with spending the night in the streets, she would have never accepted my help. But it was a slam-dunk move for me to bring her dog into play. She cares more about that beast than she does about herself and I have no shame in using that against her.

"Well, let's get going. I'm going to need to stop at a store to get some dog food."

I hold my hand out to her to help her from the ground. She ignores it and springs up from the grass on her own. We walk silently to the car and Capone follows. Even as tired as I know she must be—even as beat-down as she must be feeling—I'm amazed that she walks with her shoulders straight and her head held high.

Rowan opens the back door and motions for Capone to jump in. He does and lies down across the seat, apparently exhausted from his all-day adventure outside.

I'm going to be cleaning out dog hair for months, I can tell.

Rowan and I get in the car and we take off toward the nearest Key Food. I briefly contemplate heading to Gateway Center so I can get some clothes for Rowan, but I'm afraid she'll bolt if I leave her alone too long.

To kill some time and try to figure out the enigma that is this woman, I glance over at her and ask, "So... what's your story?"

She looks at me sharply. "Mind your own business. My story's not that interesting anyway."

I'm not deterred, and her standoffish attitude makes me even more determined. "Not interesting? You were chained to a bed and nearly burned alive by your drug-dealing ex-boyfriend, and you're saved at the last minute by your wonder-mutt and a dashingly handsome firefighter. You seriously don't think you're interesting?"

Glancing back at her, I can see the corners of her mouth lift up ever so slightly but they never even come anywhere close to a real smile. I'm relieved to know, however, that this ball-busting girl has a small measure of humor inside. That is completely at odds with her tough persona, and now makes her a gazillion times more interesting.

I literally have no choice but to press on.

"Come on... tell me something to satisfy my curiosity. How old are you?"

She apparently thinks that's safe enough and quickly answers, "Just turned twenty-three."

I let a brief silence stretch on, waiting to see if she'll say anything else. She doesn't, nor does she even appear to have any curiosity about me… the strange man who she is going to be staying the night with.

"I'm twenty-six," I tell her, just to keep the conversation going. "Where are you from originally? I hear a little bit of a southern accent, right?"

She doesn't answer as quickly and her words are softer… more tentative than the brash way she normally talks. "I left Texas when I was eighteen and haven't looked back."

The silence that lays heavy after that statement tells me this is not a subject near and dear to her heart. I can tell that leaving Texas was both a blessing and a curse for her.

I ponder my next question, because while I know this girl and her dog will stay with me tonight, I can't help but worry what will become of her tomorrow. It's none of my business… I *know* that. But she's just demonstrated that she has no one else that will help her, not a single person she could call for help, and there's no way I'm letting her stay out on the streets.

"Listen… I'm not trying to pry into your business and I'm not going to tell the cops anything, but what's the deal with this guy? Was he trying to kill you? You know the cops could protect you."

She snorts at me and when I glance at her, she's giving me a chastising look. "Get real. You saw that cop back at the hospital. They want me to get to Juice. They want Juice to get to his supplier. The safest thing for me would be to just get lost and hope Juice doesn't find me."

She's in a tough place. I get it. I certainly don't know anything about the drug world, but the one thing I do know is that it is big money, and that type of money is always more important than a human life, which does put her at risk.

"I understand," I tell her, and I sincerely mean it. "I'm not so sure I wouldn't do the same thing as you."

She doesn't say anything and I don't ask any further questions. The silence lays heavy between us but it doesn't mean I'm not trying to think of a game plan. Maybe she could stay with me for a while until we could figure out how to get her out of danger. Which sounds fucking ludicrous because I know it's not my problem.

"You really mean that?"

My thoughts are interrupted by her soft voice. "Mean what?"

"That you get why I don't want to deal with the cops."

"Yeah… I do. Sounds dangerous to me, and they have bigger fish to fry. I'm not saying I don't think the cops could be of help at some point, but I do understand you not wanting to trust them. I respect it."

She doesn't respond and I take a quick glance at her. She's just staring at me with bewilderment in her eyes. It's like she's seeing me for the first time and isn't exactly sure what she's looking at.

"So, you gonna share with me anything else about yourself?" I ask her, hoping that I've shown her I have her best interests at heart. She doesn't even have the manners to respond, but just looks out her window, staring at the city rolling by.

"No, huh?" I decide to keep talking, even if she doesn't want to participate. I've always been a chatter-box—my mom's words, not mine—and I want her to see that she can trust me.

"I'm from New Jersey originally… Englewood. Both my parents still live there and I get over to visit as much as possible. My sister, Renner, just moved to Ireland… following her new boyfriend. He plays in a band or some shit like that and he's on tour now."

My heart stutters for a beat… thinking of Renner. I hope she's okay, and I hope she's happy. We text each other nearly every day, and she certainly seems to be both. I'm really happy for her, but damn if I don't miss her like crazy.

The monologue continues. "I don't have any other siblings but I have two cousins that are about as close as brothers to me. My cousin, Nix, lives across the river, near my parents and his dad. He's a metal artist but he also builds custom motorcycles. And his brother, Linc, just moved to Phoenix. He plays—"

"Linc Caldwell? As in the former goalie for the Rangers?"

I turn and grin at her, psyched that I found something to engage her in conversation. "Yup. The one and only. Are you a fan?"

Turning my eyes back to the road, I can't help but take one more quick peek at her. I see a wisp of a smile and her eyes look a bit livelier. "I love hockey and definitely pull for the Rangers. I was sad to see him go."

"Yeah… he was sad to go to. I can get you an autographed picture or something if you want."

Her voice is sharp as a razor. "And just what would I do with it? Frame it and set it on the mantel that hangs over my fireplace?"

Damn, this girl is shrouded in iron.

Just when I thought I had her softened up a bit, she closes back up. Luckily, the conversation is saved from going further as I pull up to the grocer near my apartment. Putting the car in park, I leave the engine running so she and Capone will have the air conditioning.

I point to the backseat where I can see Capone is snoozing hard. "Anything in particular he likes to eat?"

"Just any type of dry dog food. Just get a small bag

though, as he'll only need enough for tonight and for tomorrow morning."

Her statement is clear… she's moving on come sunrise.

"You got it. Be back in a few." I stare at her a moment before exiting the car, but she turns away and continues staring out the passenger window.

♦

THE DOG FOOD has been purchased and the ride to my apartment was done in absolute silence. After parking in my assigned spot, I walk with Rowan and Capone up the three flights of stairs to my humble abode. I've got my duffel bag slung over one shoulder and I'm carrying a thirty-pound bag of dog food over the other. Rowan has her hand lightly on Capone's collar but I don't think she's really afraid he'll bolt off.

When I came out of the store carrying the huge bag of dog food, she didn't say anything, just raised her eyebrows at me. The fact that I bought such a huge bag of food sends a clear message as well… she's welcome to stay a few days longer if she needs to. At least I'm guessing that's what my subconscious is telling her.

When we reach my door, I look down at her. "Can you grab my keys? They're in my front right pocket."

The minute I ask the question, I'm suddenly aware that could be seen as a very lewd and inappropriate request. But Rowan only says a quick, "Yup" and then her hand is disappearing into my pants. She makes quick work of grabbing my keys—which are luckily resting in the part of my pocket that lays against the outer part of my thigh—and holds them up to me.

"It's the silver one on the end. It opens the deadbolt and the door lock."

Rowan makes quick work of the locks and opens the door, stepping back so I can walk in first. Throwing my duffel to the floor, I walk into the kitchen and set the dog food down. I hear the front door close and the locks re-engage, and then Rowan walks in behind me with Capone on her heels.

"Do you mind if I feed him and give him some water?"

"Not at all."

Reaching into a cupboard, I pull out two large, stainless-steel bowls. I hand her one and I take the other to the sink to fill up. I can hear Rowan ripping into the dog food and scooping some into the bowl.

Capone is in doggie heaven when we set both of the bowls down. Poor pup goes immediately for the water, and I'm not surprised with him running around outside all day. After he has his fill, he lifts that big, shaggy head and water spills out from the sides of his mouth all over my floor. Grimacing inside, I resist the urge to get a towel and mop it up. I don't want to do anything that makes Rowan feel uncomfortable to be here, and if I have to learn to live with some dog slobber, then I'll do it.

Capone turns to the food and starts chomping away. We both just watch him silently for a few minutes. He's a clear multitasker because he steadily keeps his face buried in the food, all the while wagging his tail to show his happiness.

When I look at Rowan, she's watching him with a look of worry on her face.

"What's wrong?" I ask.

She doesn't respond at first and then she slowly drags her gaze away from the dog, but by the time her eyes meet mine, the worry is gone. "Nothing. I'm good. Just happy to have him back."

She's lying to me… I know it. She's very smooth at it and makes her transition easily, but I can still see the lie in her eyes.

"Tell you what… let's discuss a game plan for the night. I suggest we order a pizza to be delivered. I'm sure you'd like a nice shower, since you smell like the inside of a fireplace, and I'll give you some of my clothes to wear for the night. Then we'll discuss your next move."

She opens her mouth as if she's going to argue with me about discussing her next move, but then just as quickly shuts it. I'm clever enough to know that she's not capitulating, just putting off having to engage in conversation with me.

"I'll take you up on that," she says. "But I need to walk Capone after he's done eating."

"I'll handle that," I tell her. "Come on back to my room… let me grab you some clothes and you can get in the shower."

She follows me back down the short hall to my bedroom. Opening the door, I sigh inwardly at the mess. I've got dirty clothes strewn all over the floor and old beer bottles on the nightstand. At least I don't keep dirty dishes back here.

Reaching into my dresser drawer, I pull out a t-shirt and a pair of workout shorts that have a drawstring that she can use to keep them up around her tiny waist. She takes them and I point across the hall. "Bathroom is right there. Clean towels are under the sink."

She starts to walk that way but then turns around. "How are you going to walk Capone? You don't have a leash."

I think about it a minute and then I'm struck with an idea. Reaching into my top drawer, I pull out a tie. I don't have many of them but I grab a hideous Donald Duck tie that Renner gave me for Christmas a few years ago.

Holding it up, I show Rowan the tie, hoping I will finally see a smile poke through. It doesn't come but she does give me what could be considered a caustic smirk.

"That's resourceful," she says, her voice only a few degrees warmer than it normally is.

I will not be deterred.

I will not be deterred.

After repeating that silently twice, I give her a huge smile. "I thought so, too. Now, go take a nice, long shower. By the time you get done, I'll have Capone taken care of and the pizza will be here."

Rowan's gray eyes seem to lighten a bit and she opens her mouth as if she's going to say something. Then she just gives a slight shake of her head and turns away to head into the bathroom.

♦

WALKING CAPONE WAS pretty easy. I tied the Donald Duck tie to his collar, knotting it twice in case he tried to pull away from me. But he was well behaved and walked by my side the entire time. The only bad thing was I had to pick up his crap, which was the size of a football, and dump it in the nearest pet receptacle. Thank God Rowan had yelled out to me before I left to take a plastic bag just for that momentous event.

The pizza dude is at my apartment door when I get back with Capone. He keeps a worried eye on the big dog as I dig money out of my wallet and hand it to him.

When we step into the apartment, I see Rowan sitting on my couch, running her fingers through her wet hair. She's swimming in my clothes but she actually looks like she has a little color back in her face. She'll feel even better after she gets some food and has a good night's sleep.

She looks up at me, and I'm again struck by the beauty of her gray eyes, particularly with her dark hair hanging in wet chunks around her face.

"I used your razor to shave my legs."

Her voice is unapologetic about using my razor, but it doesn't matter. My blood boils with sympathy and anger over the fact she was chained like an animal and roughing up my good razor is hardly worth thinking about.

"No worries," I tell her with a smile. "Use anything you like."

She suddenly grins at me wickedly. "In that case, I also used your toothbrush."

Laughing, I walk into the kitchen. Her first real smile and it came with a devilish and cocky attitude. I've not known her long, but I bet I could safely say that is classic Rowan. "Come get some pizza. No telling when you last had a good meal, right?"

Setting the pizza down on my small kitchen table, I turn around and Rowan is right there. She smells like my spicy body wash and, up close, her gray eyes are softer, more liquid. Looking at her now, dressed in my clothes and removed from the horrendous nature of her captivity, she looks different to me.

Beautiful. Angelic. Captivating.

I didn't notice it before, because I was looking at her strictly through the lenses of my fireman's glasses. She was a job… a person to save.

Now that I have her safely tucked away from danger, I'm seeing her through the eyes of a man. And this man likes what he's seeing.

But sadly, I can't go there. I'm doing this to help Rowan out of a bad situation, because that is what I do… I help people. I don't bring home beautiful and tragic women so I can get my rocks off.

Tearing my thoughts away from that direction, I open the box. "I got pepperoni. I figured everyone likes pepperoni."

She leans over the box and inhales deeply. "Oh, my God. I think I could eat that whole pizza. I'm so hungry."

Reaching into the cupboard, I pull out two plates and hand them to her. While she takes them to the table and sits down, I pull two sodas out of the fridge. Popping the tops off, I walk over and sit down across from her, handing her the drink.

She takes a deep swallow and sighs. "Thanks."

I point to the box. "Eat up."

Setting the can down, Rowan reaches in and grabs a slice. She doesn't even lay it on her plate but brings it to her mouth to take a huge bite. The moan that bubbles up from her throat causes my skin to crawl. It's not a sexual moan, but rather the sound of someone that hasn't had food in a while. Anger bolts through me again over what has been done to her.

I just watch her. She gobbles down bite after bite of pizza, polishing the crust off quickly. She reaches for another piece and takes a bite, closing her eyes as she savors the taste. When she opens them back up, she glances my way and stops chewing.

"What?" she asks, her mouth full.

"I'm sorry for what you went through." It's all I can think to say, because it's the only thing I can offer her right now.

Rowan swallows the food in her mouth and sets the remaining slice on her plate. "I don't want to talk about it."

"I'm not asking you to. I just wanted you to know I'm sorry. No one should be treated like that."

She pins me with a hard stare for what seems like forever. I don't waver and I don't look away. I hold her gaze so she knows I'm saying nothing more than I have sympathy for her.

Apparently satisfied I'm not trying to worm information from her, she picks her pizza back up and starts eating again. I use that as my clue to go ahead and start. I pick up a slice and take a bite, wondering what's going to happen to Rowan tomorrow.

CHAPTER 5
Rowan

I SLOWLY COME awake, pushing the covers down to my waist. It's hot… unbearably so, and I'm sure that's what woke me up. Bringing my hand to my face, I wipe at my brow and find it drenched in sweat.

Taking a deep breath through my mouth, I'm confused that the air itself feels hot and dry. My lungs feel compressed and I struggle to take in another breath of air, this time through my nose.

I smell smoke.

It's getting hotter by the second and then flames erupt from the floor, starting to climb the walls on either side of the bed. I try to yell out… to Flynn… to anyone… but smoke is now overwhelming me and I can't even make a sound. A hacking cough sneaks out, and I cover my mouth and nose with my hand, trying to filter the air.

Then I hear laughing.

Peering through the smoke, I see Juice standing by the door. He's leaning against it casually, with his arms crossed over his chest. He just looks at me… and laughs, and laughs, and laughs.

I sit up in bed and reach down to the chain I know is wrapped around my ankle, intent on trying to pull myself free. When I reach down, I'm stunned to find my leg is free and there is no manacle keeping me in this bed.

The smoke is so thick now. I can't see which way to the door, so I drop to the floor where I know the air quality will be better. Frantically crawling in the direction I believe the exit to be, I can only hope the flames haven't spread enough to prevent my escape. I don't even worry about where Juice is. My body is on autopilot and it's working only to get away from the fire.

Suddenly, hands reach down and grab my shoulders. I shudder in relief.

Flynn!

My body is pulled up and I thankfully look into the eyes of my savior.

Except it's not Flynn.

It's Juice.

And he pushes me back down onto the bed and quickly locks a cuff around my ankle, shackling the other end to the bed frame.

Casually tossing the key over his shoulder, he turns around and walks into the smoke, disappearing from my view.

That's when I start screaming.

"Rowan… wake up."

Someone is screaming. A woman, I think.

I struggle to open my eyes and when I do, the shrieking noise stops.

Flynn is sitting on the bed beside me, holding onto my shoulders lightly. He's looking at me with worry lining his face. Capone is lying beside me, his head resting on my lap. His beautiful brown eyebrows are scrunched inward with an equal look of concern.

Sitting up, I rub at my eyes with one hand and absently stroke Capone's head with the other. "Who was screaming? Is everything okay?"

Flynn's hands drop away and his worried look increases. "You were screaming. Scared the shit out of me."

"Me?" I ask, stupefied.

But then, it all comes pouring back to me.

My dream.

Juice laughing at me, a fire raging around me, searching for Flynn to save me and knowing that I was going to die chained to a bed.

"It was just a bad dream. I didn't mean to wake you." My voice is soft, barely above a whisper. My body shudders hard and I feel like I'm going to vomit.

The remnants of the dream still linger with me, so real that I wouldn't be surprised if Juice stepped out of the closet to continue his taunts. I can't help myself when I pull my legs up, just to verify they aren't chained to the bed. Relief floods through me when I realize I'm free from restraints.

In all my life, I know I'll never experience anything as traumatizing as what these last three days have been for me. I hate admitting weakness, but damn if Juice didn't about break me. I had come so close to escaping...Capone and me. So close to having freedom, I could taste it. Just as I can now actually feel Juice's claws sink into my shoulder as he caught me sneaking out the door.

"Think you can handle a shot of whiskey?" Flynn asks.

I nod my head, thinking there's no way I'm getting back to sleep without it.

"I'll be right back," he says as he stands up from the bed.

Flynn had put me in his guest room, which has nothing more than a bed in it, but it was more than comfortable enough for me. I mean... it didn't have chains attached to it.

I should feel comfortable... relaxed... safe. But a sudden surge of fear courses through me and I jump out of the bed. "I'll come with you."

Flynn glances over his shoulder, again with another worried look, but then walks out of the room with me hot on his heels.

I follow him into the kitchen and sit at the table, while he takes out two small glasses and pours healthy shots of whiskey in each. He sits at the table and picks up his glass, waiting for me to do the same.

In the harsh fluorescent light of the kitchen, and away from the darkness of my dreams, I just now notice that Flynn is wearing a pair of sweatpants… and that's all he's wearing.

I knew he was a big guy, but without his shirt on, I can definitely appreciate that this big guy clearly works out. He has a beautifully artistic cut to his muscles… well-defined ripples but not a bulked-up, steroid look.

I'm not interested… but I'm not dead either.

"Here's to a dreamless sleep," he says, and then raises his glass in toast. As his arm reaches out, I notice a tattoo inked onto the inside of his bicep. It says, "Semper" and I wonder what it means but I don't bother asking.

Like I said… I'm not interested.

I clink my glass against his and then toss the whiskey back, reveling in the burn as it slides down my throat, hitting my stomach in a warm puddle. Flynn follows suit and downs his drink.

I don't even wait for him to set his glass back down before I pick up the bottle, finally noticing the brand.

Jameson's. Good choice.

I pour two more healthy shots. There's no toasting this time.

I pick up the glass without waiting for him and shoot it back just as fast.

Flynn doesn't touch his though and just stares at me. "Want to talk about it?"

I run my finger along the edge of the glass and consider pouring another, but I'm really not that big of a drinker. I'm also not that big of a talker, and I can only assume the whiskey has loosened me up because I'm absolutely surprised by myself when I answer him.

"I dreamed I was in a burning room and trying to escape, but then Juice caught me and chained me to the bed. No brainer, right?"

Flynn picks up his glass and takes a healthy swallow. Looking at me over the rim, he says, "It's not unusual after what you've been through."

I can't help myself. I'm always on the defensive. "And you want to know all the sordid details, right?"

Setting his glass down and pushing it away, Flynn looks at me with such seriousness, I want to drop my gaze to the table. "Rowan… I could care less if you tell me the details. If you want to, I'll listen and be a friend to you. If you want to take the story to your grave, I'll respect it. I'm not pushing you for anything."

God, he sounds so sincere. I want to believe him. There's a feeling inside of me that is telling me to trust him. I can only imagine it's because he saved my life.

And he helped me find Capone.

And he gave me a safe place to stay tonight.

But I don't easily trust and I just don't have it in me

to share much more. So instead, I remain quiet and I pour myself one more shot of the amber liquid that beckons from the bottle before me. I'm sure he takes my silence as the subject is closed.

"Let's talk about something that's actually a bit more important," Flynn says.

I look at him in surprise. "What's that?"

"What your future holds. I'm worried about what's going to happen to you."

His words are sweet and they warm me slightly, but I brush them off. Rule number one I learned when I arrived in New York… never depend on anyone else but yourself.

"I appreciate the sentiment, but I can take care of myself. It's not your place to worry about me."

His hazel eyes regard me warmly and a small smile graces the corners of his mouth. He reaches his hand out, grabbing mine, and I want to pull it away but I don't. "Yet, I worry about you all the same. And I even worry about that damned, furry beast of yours, too."

I can't help how suspicious I am. It's ingrained into me. I also cannot help the glare that plasters to my face. The cynicism that is melded to my personality almost makes me hate myself. "Why? We're not your problem."

Flynn releases my hand and leans back in his chair. He links his hands together and rests them on his stomach. As he crosses one long leg over the other, his muscles bunch and then relax against his sweatpants. "I don't consider you a problem, Rowan. But I would like to help you if you'll let me."

"Why?" I persist. He hasn't answered my question, and until he does so sufficiently, I have no more trust in him than I do Juice at this point.

"Why not? You seem like a nice girl, you've been treated like shit, you got a really cute dog, and it's within my power to help you. So, why not?"

I'll admit… that is a good answer. He doesn't pretend to know me, he doesn't seem to want anything in return, and his tone of voice suggests to me that he truly wants to help. I push the third shot of whiskey away from me because I don't want the alcohol clouding my judgment.

Leaning forward, I rest my forearms on the table and lace my fingers through one another. "What did you have in mind?"

"No major plan, really. Just that you can stay here until you get your feet back under you. We can work out the details as we go along, but at least take a few days before you decide what to do, and until you know you have a safe place to stay. We'll get you some clothes, and you and the fleabag can relax for a while, knowing you're safe. I'll help you figure things out, and when we do… you can be on your way, Rowan. I'll help you to get on your way if you'll let me."

The aforementioned fleabag decides to pad into the kitchen. He walks up to me and squeezes his head under my arm, nudging it upward to make room. It's his cue to me that he wants attention and he expects me to give it to him. I don't hesitate and my hand immediately drops to start rubbing his neck.

Damn spoiled dog.

I lean down and run my nose along the top of his head. "What do you think, Capone? Want to stay here for a few days?"

He doesn't answer me, of course, but I didn't expect him to. I only asked the question out loud so I could ponder it further.

I quickly run down the pros and cons of accepting Flynn's offer.

Pros include having a safe place for Capone and me to stay, food in our stomachs, and precious time to figure out my life. I don't think I'll need long to do so, but at least there won't be a ticking clock.

Cons include loss of independence and pride. I'll probably kick myself repeatedly for my weakness.

Lifting my head, I look at Flynn. "Are you sure we aren't imposing?"

"I'm positive. Stay… relax. It's not a big deal."

I don't like being beholden to anyone and accepting help is foreign to me. But again, something is telling me to trust Flynn. "I actually have a little bit of money stashed away that I can pay you with, especially if you can front me a little for clothes. I can get a few things at Goodwill or something."

He regards me for a moment and then nods his head. I know he wants to refuse my offer to pay, but I think he knows me well enough to know I won't accept charity.

"I'll also handle cleaning your apartment and cooking while I'm here but I'll immediately start looking for a job."

"Did you work before…?" His words trail off steeply and his eyes look sad for me.

"Before you found me chained to a bed?"

He nods and I give a very small smile. Not a huge one, but a tiny, tiny one, and it feels weird. "Yeah… I had a job at a bar before Juice put the shackles on me. I bet I could still work there but that's not really an option. That will be one of the first places Juice will look for me."

Again, he nods and doesn't push me for any further details past what I've given. "Sounds like we have a deal."

Reaching my hand across the table, I say, "So… want to shake on it? Temporary roommates?"

His hand engulfs mine and my skin actually tingles from the contact. His hand is dry and I can feel calluses rubbing against my skin. He holds my hand for just a bit and we stare at each other. I don't know what I'm seeing reflected in his eyes, but whatever it is, it doesn't make me feel bad. It makes me feel warm… safe… secure. The feeling is alien to me but it's nice.

Flynn releases my hand and grabs his whiskey. He looks at mine, indicating I should pick it up. I do and he holds his glass out. "To being roommates."

"To being roommates," I murmur.

We knock our glasses together and shoot the amber liquid back.

CHAPTER 6

Flynn

THE NEXT MORNING, I'm up just as dawn is breaking because there's a lot of shit to take care of to get my new roomie settled in. The first thing I do is shoot a text off to Tim and tell him I can't hang today to watch the game. I don't tell him why, only that something important came up and I'd fill him in later.

Peeking in on Rowan, I see she's still sound asleep with Capone lying over her legs at the bottom of the bed. I'm betting she'll be out for another few hours, which should give me plenty of time to run my errands and get back.

I hate to admit, but part of me is afraid she'll bolt once I'm gone. She clearly has a hard time trusting, and an even harder time accepting help. I also have no clue why it's so fucking important to me to help her out. She's a stranger to me, and the only bond we share is that of savior and victim. In my line of work, that does not make for a lasting bond. I save someone, I go home, and I forget about them.

But there's no forgetting Rowan Page.

What I'll go ahead and admit is that I'm lying to myself just a bit when I act ignorant of my reasons for getting involved. Ever since Marney died, I'm obsessed with saving people. Clearly, it's the reason I became a firefighter and it's the reason I take some unnecessary risks that have landed me in hot water with my Chief and crew. But it extends beyond just pulling people from the flames. I also get involved where it's probably not my business, and try to make situations better.

Case in point... Rowan Page.

Clearly none of my business, and yet I want to make things better for her.

I think about this vexing woman the entire trip over to Nix's house. She's an enigma and I'm probably a bit obsessed with finding out more about her. How does someone that is clearly intelligent with a good dose of street smarts get involved with a drug dealer? Is she involved in the drug trade? I also wonder why she left her boyfriend, and I wonder if he's coming back for her to finish the job.

All of these thoughts have me on edge, and I know I can't solve all of her problems today. But I am intent on helping her solve them if she'll let me.

I pull into Nix's driveway and jog up to his front porch, knocking on the door rapidly. It opens up and Nix eyes me up and down.

"What's up, loser?"

"Not much, bonehead. Is Emily around?"

Nix's eyebrows rise in surprise but he nods, stepping aside to let me in.

"Are you having an illicit affair with my fiancée?" he asks with a grin.

I chuckle but then deadpan, "Yes, we are *illicitly* having an affair… right here… in front of you. In fact, I made sure you were here before I came knocking on the door."

Nix responds with a boisterous laugh and it warms my heart. My cousin didn't have a lot to laugh about in the not-to-distant past. Struggling to overcome physical and emotional injuries from his time spent in the Afghanistan war, he became a recluse and the once close bond I shared with him growing up had eroded to almost nothing.

That was until he met Emily Burnham. That's when my boy became a new man.

Right on cue, Emily comes skipping down the stairs. "Flynn," she says in surprised delight. "What brings you out here?"

Emily throws her arms around me in a hug and I grin over her shoulder at Nix, waggling my eyebrows. "See… we're very illicit."

Pulling back, Emily looks between Nix and me. "What's illicit?"

I shrug my shoulders. "The affair you and I are having under Nix's nose."

Emily just gives me an accommodating smile and starts walking back to the kitchen. "I see. We're very stealthy, aren't we? Well, come on back and let's have some coffee. We can make future illicit plans. I was just getting ready to make some breakfast."

Nix and I follow Emily into the kitchen. I hadn't called before coming over and just took a gamble that Emily would be here. Even though she has an apartment in the city that she shares with her college roommate, Fil, she stays over at Nix's house most nights.

Glancing over, I see Nix's dog, Harley, lies in front of the kitchen windows, basking in the early morning sun. He raises his head, gives me a lazy look, and then goes back to sleep.

"So seriously, what brings you over here?" Emily asks as she pours a cup of coffee and slides it across the counter toward me. She knows I take it black so doesn't offer anything else.

"I need to borrow some of your clothes."

Emily just stares at me blankly, and Nix rolls his eyes. "First, you're having an affair with my fiancée and now you want to dress up in her clothes?"

"Yeah, it's not as kinky as it sounds. Short version of a very long and whacked story is that I have a temporary, female roommate who I rescued from a fire yesterday.

She has nothing to her name except a pair of surgical scrubs they released her from the hospital with. I was hoping to borrow a set of Emily's clothes, particularly shoes, so I can take her shopping for some stuff today."

After I finish my story, I watch to gauge their reaction. Both Emily and Nix just continue to stare at me, not saying a word.

I wait, particularly for Emily to pipe up that she'd be glad to help.

I'm met with silence.

Sighing deeply, I say, "What's the silent treatment for?"

Emily and Nix exchange a quick look, but it's filled with a little bit of worry, and a whole lot of frustration.

"Okay… go ahead and spill it out. Let's get this over with." I pull a kitchen chair out from the table, turn it backward, and straddle it, resting my arms across the back.

Nix leans back against the counter and crosses his arms. "Isn't it a little out of the norm for a firefighter to bring one of his rescues home?"

It's a legitimate question coming from anyone, but I know where Nix is headed. "You already know the answer to that, Nix. Why don't you just say what you really want to say?"

My voice is hard and unforgiving. I've heard these concerns before from practically every family member and close friend.

Before Nix can say anything else, Emily steps forward, laying a restraining hand on Nix's arm so he doesn't say anything further. Nix isn't known for his tact. "Flynn… you know we're just worried about you. You tend to take on every hopeless and lost cause there is, often to your detriment, many times causing you pain."

"And it often comes in the form of a woman," Nix adds.

I shoot him a glare and then look back to Emily. "Don't you think you're exaggerating?"

"Flynn, it's just that—" Emily starts to say but she gets cut off by Nix.

"You tend to date broken women and then you try to fix them. And when you find out you can't fix them, or that they don't want to be fixed, you're left behind holding a broken heart and usually their debt."

"Nix," Emily says in a chastising tone.

"It's true, Em. I know you haven't known Flynn long, but ever since Marney died, he thinks every woman needs saved from some dark catastrophe."

Emily opens her mouth to say something but I beat her to the punch. "Leave Marney out of this, Nix." My voice is laced with so much venom, I can see Emily actually take a step backward.

There was a time in his life that Nix would have just

as soon punched my lights out for talking to him that way, but he only drags his hand through his long hair in frustration.

"I'm sorry," he says. "That was out of line. I just don't want to see you hurt. You're like a brother to me and I protect what's mine."

The anger deflates out of me and the tension leaves my shoulders. Standing from the chair, I clap a hand on his shoulder. "I know, man, and I love you for it. But this is a little different situation."

"How so?" Emily asks.

"First… I'm not dating her and have no intentions of doing so. It was just a really interesting situation, and it's a very temporary sort of help."

Picking my coffee cup back up, I take another sip and then proceed to tell them the entire story of how I met Rowan Page. I speak in impersonal tones, so they don't even catch a whiff of the fact that my interest in Rowan isn't completely professional. Those gray eyes don't just haunt me anymore, they've piqued an interest in me that has me looking at her as a woman, and not as a victim.

But I'm not about to let them know that. I lay out the scenario, and assure them that I just want to help get her on her feet. I don't hold back about the fact that she could be in danger so they understand that Rowan is truly in a bad situation and needs help.

By the time I'm finished, there's no doubt in my mind Emily would have taken her in had I not. She rushes upstairs to pull together a few outfits that Rowan can borrow until I can buy her some new clothes.

Once she's gone, Nix turns to me. "I'm really sorry for bringing Marney up."

"It's okay. I've been told I have a hero complex on more than one occasion."

"With good reason, buddy. But just remember… you don't have to fix everything. It's not your responsibility to save the world."

Fuck if I don't know the truth of that statement, but it doesn't stop me from trying my damnedest anyway.

♦

I RETURN BACK to my apartment with a very satisfied feeling that I'm making progress toward helping Rowan get back on her feet. I unlock the door and step in to silence. My first thought? It's too quiet, and I'm immediately thinking that she's left.

When I shut the door, she immediately calls out, "Flynn… is that you?"

"Yeah," I answer and walk back toward her voice.

When I get to the bathroom, I look in and find her bent over the tub, scrubbing it out. And, yeah… because I'm a man, the first thing I notice is how slammin' her ass looks all perked up into the air. It's not something I had noticed before because my clothes are so damn big on her, and there was never any opportunity to notice her shape.

And what a shape it is, with my gym shorts pulled tight against her.

"Whatcha doing?" I ask.

She looks over her shoulder at me, her bangs hanging over her eyes. Blowing a puff of breath up to get them out of the way, she gives me a stern look. "What does it look like I'm doing? I'm cleaning the scum out of your tub that clearly hasn't been cleaned in years."

Grinning at her, I shrug my shoulders. "It's a known fact… single men are slobs."

"You can say that again," she says, and then turns around to continue scrubbing.

"You really don't have to do that though… you're my guest."

She doesn't even bother looking back at me. "Don't even go there. We have an agreement. If I stay here, I need to earn my keep."

Keeping my eyes pinned on her ass, I tell her, "Fine. I won't say another word."

She doesn't respond and I lean up against the bathroom door, shamelessly ogling while I can.

"Are you looking at my ass?" Her tone is still hard, a Rowan Page trait, but if I'm not mistaken, there is a miniscule amount of teasing in it. It catches me off guard for just a second. So far, Rowan has been closed off, moody, and distrustful. I would never have thought she'd have the ability to tease. It actually lightens my mood even more.

"Yup. Busted me."

I can hear her snicker and then she says, "Well, do something more useful and go put away those weeks' worth of dishes I washed for you in the kitchen."

"Sure thing. But when you're done, I've got some clothes for you to wear and I thought we'd go out shopping for some more."

Her scrubbing motion stops and I can see tension stiffen her shoulders. "Fine, but we need to make a stop first so I can get my money."

"You got it." I give one last wistful look at her ass, and head toward the kitchen.

I'm just putting up the last dish when Rowan walks in. When I look at her, I'm surprised by how lovely she looks. Now that her hair is clean and dry, it lends a new level of attractiveness to her. She has it cut so the ends just drag the tops of her shoulders but lays in shaggy lengths with long bangs that angle over one side of her face. The look is carefree and wistful. Coupled with her delicately boned face, she looks like a fairy pixie having stepped straight out of a fantasy movie. It's very at odds with the hard life that I believe she's had.

Pointing to the plastic bag on the table, I tell her,

"There are a few outfits and some shoes in there."

She opens the bag and pulls out a blouse laying on top. It's dove gray and looks to be made of silk. It matches her eyes perfectly, which is an odd coincidence that Emily would choose it.

Rowan holds it up against her body and looks down at it. When she looks back up at me, her nose wrinkles in distaste. "It's a little fancy, don't you think?"

"Beggars can't be choosers," I tell her. The minute the words are out, I know they were a mistake.

Her eyes turn dark… the color of dirty steel, and she actually bares her teeth at me before she snarls, "I'm not a fucking beggar and I told you I don't need your help."

She throws the silk shirt back in the bag and storms down the hallway to the spare bedroom.

I'm stunned stupid for just a minute and then I take off after her. Rounding the corner of the bedroom door, I skid to a halt, mesmerized by the sight before me.

Rowan is jerking my t-shirt over her head and she throws it angrily to the floor. Her back is to me but I can see the curve of her breast from the side, and while I want to be captivated by the half-naked sight of a beautiful woman, I'm immediately dismayed when she reaches over and picks up the surgical scrub top that she had neatly folded and laid beside the bed.

"What are you doing?"

She doesn't answer me immediately and apparently

has no shame, because she turns to me and I have a momentary flash of two perfect breasts before she's yanking the scrub top over her head. "I'm leaving—what does it look like?"

Her hands start working at the drawstring tie around my shorts she's wearing and I leap forward, taking hold of her hands to stop her action. "Wait… please, just wait."

Her hands still and she looks up at me. Her eyes are still dark and filled with fury. She doesn't say anything.

"I'm sorry, Rowan. I didn't mean anything at all by that statement. It was just a cliché that popped out, but I don't think of you as a beggar."

She regards me for a moment and while I'm happy to see her eyes lighten up a shade, her tone is frosty. "I don't take handouts, Flynn. Not from you… not from anyone. I stand on my own."

"I got it," I hastily assure her. "Seriously… I didn't mean anything by it."

Her eyes pin me and we wage a silent staring war. This woman standing before me… I wonder what has happened in her life to make her so averse to getting help from others. It makes me a little leery over the fact that I just really want to help her. I will have to be careful so that she doesn't see me giving her a handout, but rather a hand up. Even then, she's going to insist on repaying me in some way for that hand up.

I take a deep breath and continue on. "Rowan, I know you're perfectly able to take care of yourself. I haven't known you long, but gaging by your resilience and determination… well, I just know it about you. But just this once… let me give you a little help. You can pay me back, with interest if you want, but take this little bit that's being offered."

I hold my breath, waiting for her reaction. It comes in the form of her hands dropping away from the drawstring. "Fine," she says after issuing a long-suffering sigh. But then she grudgingly adds, "And I'm sorry I'm so sensitive. It's just something I take seriously."

I take a step back. "I won't forget that, trust me."

She regards me for a moment. "See… that's just it. I don't trust you. I don't trust anyone. But I'll take your help, and yeah, I'll pay you back. Make no mistake about that."

Yes, there is no doubt in my mind that Rowan is broken.

And it's equally as clear that I want to try to fix her.

CHAPTER 7
Rowan

I'M SITTING IN Flynn's car and I'm feeling guilty, which is not a feeling I'm used to. I was fuming mad at him over his "beggars" comment; a reaction that I now see was probably just a bit over reactive.

I'm touchy—I get it.

But because I've lived my entire adult life learning to only trust myself, learning to only depend on myself, I get a little heated when my ability to do so is called into question. When I left home—and my father told me that I would be nothing but a failure—I was determined to prove him wrong. When he told me I'd never be able to provide for myself, it only made my spine stiffen with resolve.

I may not have amounted to much in his eyes, but I've kept myself alive and surviving all on my own, and I'm damned proud of it. Besides… I'm still young, and if I can ever distance myself from this Juice fiasco, I'm going to buckle down and really try to make something of myself.

I pick subconsciously at my new "slightly used" plaid, pleated mini-skirt, which was one of the many great things I found at a local thrift store Flynn took me to. I paired it with a black tank top and a really, really worn-out, black leather jacket I picked up for just ten bucks. My biggest score was a pair of broken-in, leather combat boots I found in the freebie pile. They were slightly too large for me so I just doubled up on the socks.

After I made my purchases, I asked Flynn to wait a second while I went into the dressing room and took off the expensive clothes that he had brought me. He had told me his cousin's fiancée had loaned them, and they probably cost more that I made in a month at Zeke's Bar. I hated wearing them because they reminded me of my old life, but I folded them with care to show my gratefulness over their use.

When I came out of the dressing room, Flynn roamed his gaze over me with lazy interest, but I swear he spent extra time looking at the way my legs were showcased in the mini-skirt. Spending the last five years working in bars, I knew how to dress to get maximum tips and, frankly, it was the only way I knew how to dress now.

When we had left his apartment, I gave Flynn the address to my friend Amy's apartment. I wanted to go there first to get my money, but Flynn insisted we go shopping for clothes first and that I could pay him back. I didn't like that but I eventually gave in, not needing to win every battle with him just yet. I just hoped that Amy hadn't spent my money and that I could, indeed, pay him back.

I call Amy a friend but she's more like a casual acquaintance, a former co-worker type of friend. She used to work at Zeke's with me but quit saying she got a better job. My instinct says she's hooking, but I never asked her outright. The only thing I asked was if I could start storing some extra cash at her place. I had hoped that this emergency fund would help me disappear if my break up with Juice didn't go so well.

"We're here," Flynn says.

I look up in surprise, my fingers smoothing out the edges of the skirt I had been fiddling with. I was so lost in my thoughts that I hadn't even realized where we were.

Turning my head, I look at Flynn and he's wearing that casual, friendly smile that I'm getting used to seeing on his face. I don't know many people that wear friendly smiles all the time.

It's weird… but nice.

Which also ramps my guilt up further over the way I reacted this morning.

"I'm sorry," I blurt out.

Those are two words that don't come easily to me

because I rarely apologize for my actions. It's not that I don't ever think that I'm wrong, but in my world, you have to react on instinct most of the time, and you have to be confident about it. Apologizing for foolish actions could get you in trouble down the road and ruin your street cred.

"Sorry for what?" he asks as he turns the car off.

"For being a bitch this morning. I know you didn't mean anything by that "beggar" comment. I was just being too defensive and you didn't deserve it. Not when you've been so nice to me and all."

His casual smile turns into a full-blown grin, that deep dimple showing brightly. "Let's not forget I saved your life, too."

I giggle just a bit and then immediately bite down on my tongue to stop the foreign sound from coming out of my mouth. I can't manage to turn down the corners of my mouth that unwillingly lift up. "Of course not… I could never forget that."

My gaze falters a bit from the open acceptance of my apology on his face, and I stare back down at my skirt. I've never met anyone like Flynn Caldwell and his generosity unsettles me.

Because generosity is something I've never encountered in my entire adult life.

Not once.

Before I can act even more a fool over the way he ties

me up, I grab the door and open it. Giving him a quick look, I tell him, "I'll be back in just a minute, okay?"

He nods. "Sure. Take your time."

Just before I shut the door, I tell him one more thing. "Do you mind if we make another stop before we head back to your place?"

His smile is warm and accommodating. "Sure… what do you need?"

"I need a cell phone and underwear," I tell him. "It's a bit drafty under this skirt without it."

For some reason, I cannot fathom why, I get a surge of satisfaction as I see Flynn's eyes flicker with heat and his gaze travel to the edge of my mini-skirt. I can practically see inside his head, as understanding dawns on him that I'm going commando.

"You're not wearing underwear?" His voice is rough and for some reason, it causes me to have a reactive shiver.

Our eyes hold each other, and while I started out telling him this as a way to show him I didn't have to be so serious all the time, it's now turned into something a little sensual.

I shake my head. "I guess I better be careful… this skirt *is* awful short." His gaze flicks back down to the hemline, which rests against my upper thighs, and back up again.

While his eyes seem to grow warmer as they look at

me, his lips curl up when he says, "Don't bend over and you'll be fine."

My face involuntarily reacts and I shoot him a grin as I shut the door. As I turn away to walk into the apartment building, I know his eyes are on my ass the entire time and it doesn't bother me in the slightest.

♦

AMY OPENS THE door after I pound on it for about five minutes. I've clearly woken her up, even though it's almost noon.

Her eyes are foggy as they try to focus on me but when recognition hits, she grabs my arm and pulls me in, slamming the door shut quickly.

"My God, Rowan… What are you doing here?"

"I came to get my money you were holding."

She looks twitchy but says, "Sure… no problem. But then you have to leave."

Her statement makes the hair on my neck stand up. "Has Juice been here?"

She nods as she reaches over to the counter for a pack of cigarettes. Pulling one out, she lights it, inhaling deeply and then letting a huge plume of smoke out. "Last night. He told me about the fire and that he's been looking for you. He thought you were here and that I was hiding you."

I can only imagine the intimidation tactics Juice

would use and I feel terrible I put her in this situation, just by the mere fact we know each other. "Are you okay?"

She turns her back on me and walks into the kitchen. Reaching into a cupboard, she pulls out an old coffee can and pops the lid. "I'm fine. He scared the shit out of me though. Threatened me if I didn't cough you up. He searched every inch of this rat-trap and when he didn't find you, he left."

Reaching into the can, she pulls out a roll of green and hands it to me. "It's all there if you want to count it."

Shaking my head, I stuff the wad into the pocket of my leather jacket. "Nah… I trust you."

I really don't trust her but I don't want to stick around. The mere thought that Juice could be watching her place is giving me the willies.

"Thanks, Amy. I'm sorry he came here."

I turn and head toward the door. As I reach for the knob, Amy touches my shoulder and I turn to look at her.

"Juice may not be looking too hard for you right now, so you might be okay."

"What do you mean?"

"He was really bent out of shape about the fire. Said he knows who did it and they were going to pay. I'm thinking his energy is going to be focused on finding that person."

"I doubt that. I'm pretty sure he set the fire himself."

Amy looks at me in surprise. "No way!"

I grab the door handle and give her a hard look. "That shit kept me chained to the bed for three days. I don't think he's above taking me out. He's fucking crazy, Amy."

"I don't know, Rowan," she says, while shaking her head. She's completely unfazed by my statement that Juice kept me chained up. "He was really pissed about the fire."

Is it possible that Juice didn't set the fire? I had just assumed that he was tired of keeping me chained to the bed, particularly because I was fighting him every step of the way. There wasn't a time he came into that room that I didn't curse at him for what he was doing to me. He had to have known, for sure, that I would never stay with him voluntarily.

"Give me some paper and a pen," I tell Amy.

When she hands over the implements, I jot my cell number down and hand it to her. "Do me a favor… call me if Juice comes back or if you hear anything, okay? I should have a replacement phone this afternoon."

"Sure. Take care of yourself," she tells me, but I'm not sure she'd actually call me if she knew something. She'd be smart to stay far away from this, and that's what I expect her to do.

Giving her a look of thanks, I leave Amy behind and head out to Flynn's car. When I hit the sidewalk, I look left and right, expecting Juice to jump out at me. I half run to the car and throw myself in. When the door slams shut, I tell him, "We need to go… now."

Flynn gives me just a cursory glance, then he starts the engine and swiftly pulls away from the curb. Turning in the seat, I watch to see if anyone pulls out behind us. After a few minutes, I feel like we're in the clear and turn back around, latching my seatbelt on.

"Want to tell me what that was about?" Flynn asks.

I really don't, but I feel like I owe him a heads up. Juice is out there looking for me and he's pretty fucking resourceful.

"Juice was looking for me at Amy's last night. I was afraid he might be around… watching her place."

I watch as his jaw muscles clench and he looks in the rearview mirror. Pulling his gaze briefly away, he looks at me. "I'm not telling you to do this, but shouldn't you consider going to the cops now?"

His words aren't even entirely out before I'm shaking my head in the negative. "No way. I don't trust them."

"Rowan… he tried to kill you. You should take this a bit more seriously."

Chewing on my lip, I consider what Amy said. "I'm not so sure he set the fire."

"Why's that?"

"It's just something Amy said. She said Juice was really freaked out by the fire and that he knew who set it."

Flynn is quiet for a while and I stare blankly out the window while he drives. Finally, he says, "What do you believe?"

"I don't know. Juice isn't a nice guy… He'd probably kill someone in a heartbeat. But… I don't think he wanted me dead. He just wanted me back."

"He kidnapped you and chained you up," he reminds me.

"I know… I mean… I don't know. I have no clue what the hell is going on. I really just need to disappear and start over again." I hate that my words have a whiny sound to them but I'm starting to feel the pressure of my situation.

Just this morning, I was thinking it would be cool to hang at Flynn's for a few days, absolutely positive I'd figure a way out of this mess. Now I don't know what to do. And now I have Flynn involved, and while I've known him for less than twenty-four hours, he's done so much for me that I don't want him to be at risk.

"It's probably best if I move on, Flynn."

I'm startled when Flynn moves one hand off the steering wheel and grabs ahold of mine. The warmth of his skin against mine immediately sets my pulse fluttering. "Absolutely not. I told you I'd help you out, and I will."

Sighing, I squeeze his hand so I have his attention and his eyes flick to mine briefly. "No cops, though."

He squeezes my hand back. "No cops. I promise."

CHAPTER 8

Flynn

"I BETTER GO put some underwear on."

Those words practically make me groan as I watch Rowan walk down the hall to the guest bedroom, her shopping bag filled with what I can only imagine is black lace.

When we got to Gateway Center, she reached into her jacket and pulled out a roll of cash. She peeled off a few bills to pay me back for her thrift store purchases, and then hopped out of the car, promising she'd be back soon.

While she was inside shopping, I tried to keep my mind off the fact that she was bare under that tiny mini-skirt and I tried not to imagine what she was buying. Instead, I tried to focus on the bigger issue… and that was what to do with Rowan. I'm bothered by the fact that she has a deranged ex-boyfriend searching for her, who may or may not have tried to murder her, but certainly was deviant enough to chain her to a bed so that he could keep her. That's about as fucked up as you can get.

Rowan's talk about disappearing has me slightly freaked and I have no clue why. It would certainly make my life easier if she left, and I have no allegiance to her, nor do I owe her anything. Except, for some demented reason, I feel utterly compelled to see this through.

And while this started out, no doubt, as nothing more than a manifestation of my old hero complex running amok, it's turning into something different. Now, there is not only a connection to Rowan forged out of the bizarre circumstances of her rescue, but I'm feeling a personal attraction to her as well. And not just an attraction to her beauty, although there is plenty of reasons to have me fantasizing about what lies underneath that mini-skirt, but I'm attracted to her entire character.

Her stubborn pride has me intrigued, and her bravery in the face of some scary fucking danger makes me respect her. She's tough as nails and as beautiful as an ocean sunrise. I find that combination to border on the addictive side.

Yes… it's too fucking late for me. I'm fully invested in seeing this through with her.

My mind briefly goes to Marney. I don't think of her every day, but I do think of her often. I wonder if she's looking down on me now, shaking her head and thinking, "Poor bastard." While not many thoughts of

Marney have me smiling, this one does.

"What's so funny?"

I look up and Rowan is walking back into the living room, followed by Capone. She's changed into another thrift store outfit—a pair of worn jeans and a tight, vintage t-shirt that says "Mountain Dew" on the front. The material is thin, because the t-shirt is probably older than dirt, and hugs her breasts like a glove. I'd be dead and buried not to notice her nipples are popping hard against the soft cotton and while she may have put on panties, she certainly didn't put on a bra. She's fucking sexy as hell but I really can't be thinking like that. We have more serious things to worry about.

"When you're done staring at my boobs, want to tell me what's so funny?"

My eyes slowly lift to hers. "You're not wearing a bra."

Rowan smirks at me. "And you find that funny?"

"There's never anything funny about a beautiful, bra-less woman. That's something I take very seriously," I tell her with a slight grin of my own. "But apparently, I got sidetracked from what I thought was funny."

I'm actually startled when Rowan breaks out into a soft laugh. It's rich, warm, and filled with amusement. Completely at odds with the general taciturn nature I've seen so far.

"Well, you better get used to it, roomie. I hate wearing bras. Too confining."

Holding my hands up in mock surrender, I tell her, "Hey… no complaints here. In fact, I'm betting there isn't a man on this planet that would complain about it."

She snorts as she walks by me and grabs the Donald Duck tie that I had looped over the front doorknob. "I'm going to take Capone for a quick walk."

"And we'll talk when you get back?"

She regards me for a moment and I can see barriers starting to form. But then, she takes a deep breath and lets it out slowly. "You've done a lot for me, Flynn. I owe my life to you. We'll talk some when I get back."

I watch as she bends over to knot the tie around Capone's collar. She regards me as a hero, a thought that both pleases me and scares me at the same time.

I hope I won't be a failure to her.

♦

WHILE ROWAN IS out walking Capone, I decide to give Tim a call. He answers on the second ring. "Man, you're missing a helluva game."

"Damn," I respond and walk into the living room to turn the TV on. I quickly find the Jets game and mute the volume.

"So what was so important today that you ditched me and the Sam-meister?"

I sit down on the couch and let out a pent-up sigh.

"Dude… it's a strange and fucked-up story."

"No worries… it's almost half-time. I can lend an ear to you for a bit."

How do I start my story with Tim? He's going to give me the same shit that Nix and Emily did, except he'll try to be more subtle about it. Outside of my family, Tim is the only one that knows what happened to Marney. He's one of the few that understand what drives me at times.

"So, that girl that was chained to the bed yesterday?"

"Yeah."

"Well, she's sort of staying at my apartment for a few days."

Tim makes sort of a low whistling sound through his teeth, which is his version of saying, *What the fuck?*

Pressing on, I tell him, "I had to take her out today and get some clothes. She lost everything in the fire. That's why I had to ditch."

"Doesn't she have any place else to go?"

See, I knew Tim would be subtle. I read that question to mean, *What the fuck are you doing bringing a strange woman to live in your apartment?*

"Nah, man. And she left the hospital with only a set of surgical scrubs to her name. She was going to sleep out on the streets with that dog of hers. I had no choice. It was the right thing to do."

Tim is silent for just a minute, and I can tell he's

choosing his next words carefully. "Flynn… buddy… she has some serious shit going on. She was chained to a bed and I don't even really want to know how that came about. Are you sure this is the wisest thing for you to do?"

If he weren't a firefighter, Tim would make a great politician. What he's really saying is, *Not only is that not the right thing to do, it was the craziest fucking move you could make.*

It's a good question and the answer is, *It's probably not the wisest thing.* But there is no backing away now. Like I said… I'm fully invested in helping Rowan.

Before I can even tell Tim that, he pushes on. "Flynn… just listen to me for a second. This woman… she was chained to a bed. I can only assume that she was there against her will, and that is some serious felony shit going on. She almost dies in a house fire, so I'm thinking there may be attempted murder involved. I don't even want to think about the emotional baggage she's bringing into your life. I mean, for all you know… she could be scamming you. This is a mistake, man. I know you don't want to hear that, but I need to say it anyway."

I take a deep breath and let it out slowly. It gets tiring… having my motives questioned all the time.

Still, it is with patience that I say, "Tim… you're my best friend, and I respect the shit out of you. But this is the right thing. She needs help and I had to fight her hard to get her to take it. But more than that… she's a good woman, Tim. She deserves to have someone on her side right now. I don't know what her background is, or what led her to this situation, and frankly, I don't give a shit. I just know that… in my heart… it's the right thing to help her."

I can hear Tim sigh but then he proves to me why he's my best friend. "I still think it's a fucked-up situation but I trust your judgment. If you need any help, you just let me know, okay?"

"I will. Thanks, man."

I disconnect the call and throw my cell phone down on the couch beside me. Laying my head back, I stare at the ceiling and hope that Tim's faith in my judgment is strong enough for the both of us.

"Hey," I hear from behind me.

Sitting up, I look over my shoulder and see Rowan standing there with Capone. She had come in so quietly, I hadn't even heard the door open or close.

"That was a quick walk."

"Yeah, well, my boy here got down to business pretty fast." She unknots the tie from his collar and he pads into the kitchen for some water. After she lays the tie back over the doorknob, she walks to the couch and sits on the opposite side of me.

After staring at the muted TV for a few seconds, she turns my way. "I caught part of your conversation… I didn't mean to eavesdrop."

I shrug my shoulders. I wondered if she had heard any of it, but I didn't say anything to Tim that I wouldn't say to her face.

Clasping her hands in her lap, she looks down at them, seemingly lost in thought. She promised me she'd talk to me about what was going on, and I assume she's trying to collect herself. I wait patiently.

And I wait.

And then I wait some more.

I actually start watching some of the game on TV, letting my mind take a break from all the craziness that has been my life the last twenty-four hours.

Without any warning, Rowan stands from the couch and says, "I'm hungry. How about I make us some lunch?"

She's stalling and I know it. But I'm hungry as well so I stand up and say, "Sure. We can talk while we're eating."

Rowan actually grimaces over that statement but then turns and heads to the kitchen. I follow her in and lean against the counter while she pulls out all the stuff to make us some sandwiches.

Her back is to me and she silently works on making us lunch. I don't press her for information, taking my time enjoying the view of her backside. It's just as lovely as the front.

"How do you know?" she asks as she turns to me.

I manage to sling my gaze up from her ass to her eyes and I don't think she caught me checking her out. "How do I know what?"

"That I'm a good woman. You said that to whoever you were talking to. I mean… you've known me for a day. How do you know I'm a good woman?"

For a split second, I feel like I'm caught in the glare of a spotlight, and I've just been asked the million-dollar question. My mind blanks, and outside of knowing for certain that her tits are exquisite and her ass is slammin', nothing is coming to mind.

But then I focus on those gray eyes of her, watching me carefully, and it all comes to me in a rush. "I know for lots of reasons. You're brave enough to try to leave a guy that's so demented he kidnapped you. You have pride… a little bit stubborn, but respectable all the same. You don't like handouts and you have a hard work ethic. You like to earn your keep. You're distrustful, for sure, but I'm thinking that's just to protect your heart, which I'm guessing has been bruised. But that means you have a heart. I know you're a good woman because of that damned dog in there. He saved your life as much as I did and that means you inspired love and loyalty in him. That means you have a soft touch and the heart you have is warm and caring. You don't like to see people get hurt. You were worried for me today at Amy's. You wanted to move on after you realized Juice was looking for you, and that was so that I wouldn't get caught up in this. There are so many reasons, but more than anything, Rowan… I just know. It's an instinct, and I'm going to trust it."

She just stares at me, those gray irises wide and unblinking. Then I see her lower lip start to tremble ever so slightly and a veil of tears forms in her eyes. Her voice quavers but she smiles when she says, "Boy… you sure do see a lot."

"I see you," I tell her simply.

Taking a deep breath, she blinks her eyes rapidly and the tears disappear. She turns her back on me and goes back to making the sandwiches. Maybe it's because we aren't making eye contact, but she feels brave enough to share with me, "Thank you, Flynn. No one has ever said nice things like that about me."

Picking up the plates from the counter, she walks to the kitchen table and I follow her. As we sit down, I tease her, "I find it hard to believe no one has ever said nice things to you. Not a hottie like yourself."

It cracks me up that Rowan actually blushes over that remark. I never would have pegged her for someone that would get embarrassed.

She picks her sandwich up and takes a bite. After she swallows, she says, "Sure… I mean, guys are always saying nice things… I mean, it's what you do when you want in a girl's pants, right?"

I snicker, because that is exactly what we do.

"But not you, Flynn… you meant those things you said. I heard the truth in your voice. And you said it, expecting nothing in return from me. You think I'm a good woman, and I'm not so sure about that. But I know you're a good man. Like you… I just know."

I'm stunned for a moment, because her words touch me, and that doesn't happen often. She stares at me, and I return it, both of us silent… both of us thinking over the things we just said to each other. It's a definitive turning point in our relationship and by the look on Rowan's face, I'm not sure she's ever opened up to anyone like that before. She looks slightly stunned and a little fearful for allowing herself a moment of vulnerability.

I decide to lighten the mood, so she won't have the opportunity to close herself away from me. "Yeah, well, who says I don't want in your pants?"

I try to keep a serious face and she blinks at me, trying to comprehend what I just said. Then I break out into a huge grin and shoot her a wink.

A smile slowly comes to her own face and then a devilish gleam sparkles in her eyes. "Who says I won't let you get in there?"

CHAPTER 9

Rowan

MY LIFE IS whacked.

When my family turned their back on me five years ago, I created a new life. I was scared shitless, but I did it anyway. I moved to a new city, and became a new person.

I don't always like the new me. I've had to sacrifice some qualities along the way. You'll never get sweetness from me. I won't cater to your feelings. I call things the way I see them and there's no rosy tint on my glasses. My laughs don't come easy, and when they do, there is always an underlying hint of skepticism in my humor.

With all of that being said, something has happened in just three days that has made my life even wackier. I think I've met someone that doesn't have a single ulterior motive for being in my life. Up until now, everyone wanted something from me, and I never got anything without first giving up a piece of myself.

Until Flynn.

Life as Flynn's roommate has been great, even

though I know this is only temporary. He has made Capone and me feel completely at home, and the more time I spend with him, the more I find myself loosening up. He is funny, gracious, and self-deprecating. He doesn't have a mean bone in his body that I've been able to see, and he's done nothing but treat me with kindness and respect. I even came in the door the other day after running down to the grocery, and found Capone curled up on the couch with Flynn. This, despite the fact he calls Capone "the flea-bag" all the time.

I've gone five years without a real friend. In just three short days, I can no longer claim that accomplishment on my resume. I've met a man so multi-dimensional, that he makes my head spin trying to keep up with all of his great qualities.

When Flynn told me why he thought I was a good woman, it's like he was bathed in an almost holy light. I not only saw it in his eyes, but I heard it in his voice. He was being genuine with me, and that is something that has been sorely lacking from my life. You would think someone that had never experienced genuineness before would not understand it when faced with the same. But just the opposite occurred. The first time I saw it… a true, genuine soul… I recognized it immediately because it made the rest of the world around me seem dull and lifeless.

So why am I not jumping up and down with joy over

my newfound friend?

Well, because while Flynn has all of these wonderful qualities that put him squarely in the category of "friend", he has additional qualities that, unfortunately, make me look at him in a different light.

Yes, I'm talking about the fact that the guy has some serious sex appeal. There is no hiding the fact he's stunningly gorgeous—a fact I've only thought about every time I'm in the same room with him. He also has flirting with me down to a science, and every time he makes a cheeky comment that is laced with innuendo, my heart starts a mad thumping. If I catch a glimpse of his bare skin, like yesterday when he walked out of the bathroom after his shower with nothing but a towel slung around his narrow hips, I start thinking the dirtiest of thoughts. A vivid fantasy of him slamming me up against the wall and capturing my lips in a scorching kiss flashed through my brain and made me blush like a little school girl.

Sadly enough, but completely true, Flynn Caldwell's mere presence has the ability to make me feel like a horny teenager. Sometimes he'll look at me, those hazel eyes will get warm, he'll quirk those sexy-as-hell lips, and it makes me want to just climb on top and rub myself against him. It's unsettling, the powerful pull I'm feeling, and we've never even done anything more than just some casual flirting.

Last night, I went to sleep thinking of Flynn and all the kind things he has done for Capone and me. Sometime in the early morning hours, I had a dream about him. I don't remember the full details, but I know he had my naked body pressed down into the mattress of my bed and he was worshiping me with just his lips. There were no other details in the dream. Just Flynn, the mattress, and me… and soon the mattress faded away from my thoughts. Then it was just Flynn and what he was doing to me.

In my dream, he never touched my breasts or between my legs. But he paid exquisite care to every other part of my body. The longer he touched me, the more skin that his lips grazed, the more I felt the pressure building inside of me.

And with just a light kiss behind my knee, I had an orgasm so powerful that I came out of my sleep, sitting straight up in bed while spasms rocketed through my body. When I came fully awake and understood what happened, my body was drenched in sweat and my chest was heaving. Poor Capone was standing at the foot of my bed, watching me with curiosity. My covers were kicked to the floor and I can only imagine what I must have been doing in my sleep. I could only hope that I had not been making any sounds that Flynn could hear.

I sat there in my bed until my heart rate returned to normal and my breathing became steady. Knowing there was no going back to sleep after that dream, I decided to jump in the shower before Flynn got up.

I step out of the shower and wrap a towel around me. After wiping the steam from the mirror, I lean in close and take a good look at my face. The dark circles that seemed to have been ingrained into the skin beneath my eyes have finally disappeared. That's merely a testament to the good food and sleep I've had the past three nights that I've been here.

All thanks to my new friend, Flynn Caldwell.

Perhaps, my first true friend.

You know… the one that gives me orgasms in my dreams.

Some who know me would say, *And why is this really a problem, Rowan? Geez… jump on that shit!*

I'll tell you why it's a problem.

I don't want to lose Flynn Caldwell as my friend.

Because no matter how unbelievably sexy Flynn is… no matter how great I know he would be in bed… everything will change between us if sex is involved.

I just know it.

Up until this point in my life, sex has been a tool for me. It's been a stress reliever, and sometimes I've used it to get what I want. It was always so easy to manipulate Juice early on in our relationship with sex. I could diffuse his anger toward me with just a look, and even now, I'm a little ashamed I would resort to such tactics.

But with Flynn?

Sex with him will be something entirely different. It will open up a new level of intimacy that I don't think my cynicism will be able to handle. He has the ability to undo the entire basis of my existence for the past five years, and I don't think I'm ready to let go of the safety net that my walls provide me.

I search my own eyes in the bathroom mirror. They look back at me and tell me I'm a fool for thinking such things. They taunt me with the knowledge that a friendship with Flynn will never be as ultimately satisfying as a love affair with him.

I close my eyes and tell myself to shut the fuck up.

I say a tiny prayer of thanks that Flynn Caldwell is my friend and that he was brought into my life.

I need to be content with friendship and leave it at that.

♦

WALKING INTO THE kitchen, I try to mentally prepare myself for how to deal with Flynn today. I tell myself I will not engage in flirting and that I will find a way to strengthen the new friendship that we have.

Now that I have a taste of what it feels like, I want to cultivate it further.

Without annoying, sexy thoughts getting in my way.

Flynn is leaning back against the counter, drinking a

glass of water. He's dressed in a pair of shorts, a gray t-shirt that is soaked with sweat, and running shoes. His face glistens with moisture and his hair is sticking up in a thousand different directions.

I try not to notice the way his bicep bulges when his arm curls upward to bring the glass to his lips.

Or the way his lips rest softly against the glass.

Or the way his throat moves as he swallows.

I have to restrain myself from walking to the refrigerator and slamming my forehead into it so these thoughts will go away. Instead, I walk to the coffee pot and pour myself a cup.

"You're up early," he observes.

I pull the milk out and add a splash to my cup. "So are you. Already went for a run?"

"Yeah. I had strange dreams last night and just couldn't get into a good sleep."

"You and me both," I mutter.

"Mine were crazy… I was at a party with Eminem and Prince Charles and they were arguing over how to make the chicken potpie that we were eating. That was the one that woke me up." He flashes me a dimpled smile. "What were yours about?"

I almost choke on the coffee I'm drinking but I'm able to force the hot liquid down the right pipe. "I don't remember. I'm sure nothing important."

Finishing off his water, he lays the glass in the sink.

"I'll take Capone out for you before I hop into the shower."

Oh, God. Thoughts of him in the shower cause my mind to burst with color for just a moment, but then I shake myself back to reality. "No need. I took him out and fed him before I had my shower."

His eyebrows rise. "Wow. You were up really early. Must have been some dream."

If only he knew.

"So, what are your plans on your last day before heading back to work? I'll finish up your laundry for you."

"Rowan," Flynn says, his tone only slightly chiding. "You don't have to do my laundry."

The old Rowan… the one who, just three days ago, would have torn into Flynn for that, doesn't make an appearance. The new Rowan… the one that wants to build this friendship with Flynn, handles it just a bit differently.

"Yes, I do." I smile at him but my tone is firm. "You promised you'd let me earn my keep until I could get a job."

Holding his hands up in surrender, he says, "Fine. Have at it. Just don't starch my underwear."

I snicker. That would be a good prank to play on him, and that makes me snicker even more, because the old Rowan didn't pull pranks or joke around.

"What's so funny?"

Shaking my head and trying to wipe the smile from my face, I take another sip of coffee. "Nothing. But no starch in the underwear, I promise."

Flynn shrugs his shoulders and pushes away from the counter. He walks up to me and stands very close… just staring down. My breath hitches and I fight hard to hold his gaze. He does nothing more than raise a hand to tuck my hair behind my ear, and the light touch of his fingertips on my skin almost causes me to convulse.

I take a quick step back, enough to put room between me and his overwhelming closeness. His hand drops and he also takes a step back, looking embarrassed. I'm equally hot in the face, because that wasn't casual flirting. That was a moment of tenderness that scares the crap out of me and makes me yearn at the same time.

Clearing his throat, he says, "Actually… I was thinking about going to the movies today. Are you interested?"

I mentally calculate the money I have left. After buying clothes, a cell phone, some toiletries and groceries that Flynn chewed me out for buying, I have $283.00 left to my name. I put in applications to a few of the businesses around Flynn's apartment, but no one has invited me to an interview yet. I need to take care of the few bucks I have left and I need to find a way to earn money so I can pay my own way.

"I don't think so. But thanks."

Flynn studies me for a second. "If it's about the money, I'll pay."

I shoot him an exasperated look and walk into the living room. Capone is curled up on the couch, snoozing hard. "Don't go there, Flynn. You've done too much for me already."

"Come on, Rowan. It's just a movie… and maybe some popcorn."

"No, thanks," I say firmly. "Besides… I do have to run an errand today."

I head down the hallway, walking into Flynn's room. The second day here, I cleaned his room from top to bottom, and he has amazingly kept it clean since then. I open his closet and grab his clothes hamper.

When I turn, Flynn is right there and grabs the hamper from me. "Need a ride for your errand?"

He walks out of his room and heads back to the kitchen, setting the basket down in front of the stacked washer/dryer unit that takes up the majority of his pantry.

"Thanks," I mumble in appreciation for carrying the hamper for me. Although, it sort of defeats the purpose of me earning my keep. "But I don't need a ride. I can take the train."

"Okay," he says, but I can tell he's disappointed. "Where are you going?"

I hesitate, because I know Flynn won't like where I'm

going. The old Rowan would have come up with a lie. It would have flown from my lips without a second thought and without a trace of guilt. But I can tell my friendship with Flynn is important because I don't want to lie to him.

I start sorting through his laundry, throwing the whites in the washer. "I'm actually going to get some money that's owed to me… at the bar where I used to work. They owe me a paycheck."

One of the things I like best about Flynn is that he doesn't get mad, or angry, or loud… especially when he has reason to. He merely raises his eyebrows at me and says, "Are you sure that's a good idea? Juice could be waiting for you."

His calm reasoning helps. It's something I've thought about a lot and it's what has put me off from heading to Zeke's before now. But Zeke owes me about three hundred bucks and that could go a long way toward paying some expenses to Flynn.

"I know," I answer. "But I need that money. I figure if I go early in the day, chances of Juice being there are slim. He's like a vampire…loves the night too much."

"Well, I'll come with you—just in case."

"Absolutely not," I tell him emphatically.

Flynn turns away and heads back toward the bathroom, no doubt to take a shower. "Try to stop me," he says over his shoulder. "And if you try to leave out of here while I'm in the shower, you won't like it once I catch up to you." His tone is firm, slightly menacing, and the alpha nature is a little hot.

Okay… a lot hot!

I open my mouth to yell out a retort but I hear the bathroom door shut and realize it would be useless.

Flynn will be in the bathroom for only about ten minutes. He always showers fast and doesn't shave on his days off.

Weird… the things I'm coming to know about him.

I glance at the clock that hangs on the kitchen wall, calculating if I can get down to the train station before Flynn catches up to me.

Probably not.

CHAPTER 10

Flynn

I THINK MY head may seriously be fucked up.

Otherwise... why would I be sitting on this train, seriously contemplating grabbing Rowan and plunging my hands into her hair? Why do I have this almost insane urge to pull her to me for a kiss? Why is this woman plaguing all of my thoughts?

Watching her now, she's completely oblivious to how I feel. I've tried to be very careful with my feelings, which have morphed from concerned bystander, to over-protective friend, to someone who now wants nothing more than to immerse myself in her body.

No, that's not exactly right. I mean—I do want her. Badly. I jerked off in the shower thinking about her this morning, imagining her going down on me with the hot water pouring all around us.

But it's more than that. So much more.

I thought Rowan was brought into my life because she was broken and needed fixed. I know that is exactly why I offered her help, why I opened my home to her. I was trying to make up for all the ways in which I failed Marney. There is no way I can ever completely atone for that, but my warped sense of justice makes me try to add up all the checks in the "Flynn Does Some Good" column, and hope they can get me close to being even.

That's what I thought about Rowan—at first. But over the past three days, I'm starting to realize something.

She's not broken. Not in the slightest.

Oh, she's dinged up a bit. And she's clearly been through things that have damaged her. But whatever has happened in her past, it has created a person that is strong and independent. She's not broken—she's just a bit hard.

And now I'm obsessed with softening her up.

The past three days, we have settled into an easy friendship. She's actually lightened up, and our relationship just feels natural. Unfortunately, this has made it easy for me to look past the circumstances that brought Rowan into my life, and look toward circumstances that may keep her there.

She intrigues me and I want to know more about her.

I *have* to know more about her.

"Why are you staring at me like that?"

Forcing myself to focus, Rowan comes into sharp relief and her gray eyes are pinning me with a quizzical look. Luckily, I'm saved from answering as we come to our stop and the train rocks to a standstill.

We stand up and exit the train, stepping out onto the crowded platform. Since I'm not overly familiar with Prospect Heights, the neighborhood where Rowan worked, I follow her up and out of one of the many subway stations that come out on Flatbush Avenue. She turns left down Bergen Street and walks swiftly.

"Zeke's is just a few blocks this way," she says.

"Let's make this quick, okay? I don't like the thought of you being in places that he could find you."

"No need to tell me that. I want my money and then Zeke's will be a fading memory for me."

"How long did you work there?"

Rowan shrugs her shoulders. "Maybe nine months? It's just one bar on a list of many I've worked at. It's all I've ever done really. I guess it's all I'm good at."

"That's bullshit," I tell her.

She looks over at me in surprise and gives me a patronizing smile. "You don't know me well enough to know what I'm good at, Flynn."

"What about dogs? You're awesome with Capone. Look how well trained and behaved he is. You're like a dog whisperer or something."

Her head swings back toward me, and she searches my eyes. It's a look that I've come to recognize from Rowan. She wants to know if I'm telling the truth, and she believes the eyes are the gateway to the soul or something.

No matter, I am telling the truth. She's fucking amazing with the fleabag.

Whatever she sees reflected back to her causes her cheeks to turn red. She turns quickly away from me, but not before I see a satisfied expression on her face.

It makes me feel invincible that I put it there.

She rounds the corner of a building and we stop in front of Zeke's Bar. It's an unassuming place, nestled in between a small supermarket and a locksmith. The worn sign over the door has seen better days, and the windows are a tad grimy. The neon "Open" sign beckons us in, and Rowan doesn't hesitate.

As we step inside, my eyes take a second to adjust to the gloomy atmosphere. The place is completely empty and had the door not been unlocked, I would think it was closed.

"George?" Rowan calls out.

"Who's George?"

"He owns the place."

"Then who's Zeke?"

Rowan shrugs her shoulders. "Never bothered to ask. Wasn't important."

I smile inside. That's the Rowan I've come to know. She doesn't sweat the small stuff and is very much a big picture kind of person.

A door from the back opens and a small, wiry man comes out from behind it. He's probably close to sixty if the gray hair he wears in a military buzz cut is any indication, but his forearms are laced with ropy muscles, indicating this guy is in shape.

He looks at me, then at Rowan, and a grin splits his face wide open. "Damn, Rowan. It's good to see you, honey. I was worried sick."

I'm assuming this is George and he walks up to Rowan, giving her a hug. I notice it's short because Rowan steps away first. She has a warm look on her face, but I'm guessing physical displays of affection bother her. It's probably why she stepped away from me so quickly this morning when I tucked her hair behind her ear.

"Hey, George. I was wondering if I could get my pay from the last week I worked?"

"Sure thing, darling. But sit down for a second. You have to tell me what's happened to you. When you didn't show up for work, well, I just feared for the worse."

Interesting. This guy was worried for Rowan and I'm guessing it has everything to do with her ex.

Rowan looks around, and I can tell she's on edge. "We really don't have time, George. If you don't mind, I'd really like to just get my money and go."

George's eyes flick to me, lingering just a second in an attempt to figure out who I am. Then they slide back to Rowan. "Are you hiding from Juice?"

Rowan grabs her lower lip in between her teeth and gives him a short nod. She looks vulnerable, which is not a good look on a woman as tough as her, and it makes me just want to sweep her into my arms and hug all of her problems away.

George sees it too, and his gaze hardens. "All right. Sit tight and let me get it."

When George disappears back through the door, I reach my hand out and softly lace my fingers through hers. She doesn't even turn to look at me, but just stares down at our hands. I give her a short squeeze, telling her it will be all right. She squeezes back and then releases me from the grip.

True to his word, George is back almost immediately with the money. He counts out three-hundred and fifty dollars into Rowan's hand.

"This is too much, George. I should only be getting three hundred." She tries to hand the money back to him but he lays a gnarled hand over her, pushing it back to her.

"Take it," he says. "Take it and just be safe, okay?"

"But—"

George grabs her by the shoulders and turns her my way. Giving her a gentle push, he says, "Get out of here, kid. It's not safe for you to be around this area."

Rowan gives George one last look, and I can see the

affection written all over her face. It says, *I want to hug you, old man, but I don't know how.*

Instead, she gives him a nod and walks past me toward the door.

I look at George one last time and his look says, *Take care of her.* I also give him a nod and follow her out.

When I step out on the sidewalk, Rowan is tucking the money into her back pocket. She looks up at me. "I can't believe that old goat did that. I'll have to figure out some way to pay him back."

I mentally roll my eyes at Rowan's need to shy away from generosity and take her by the elbow. "That's fine, but let's get out of here, okay?"

I start leading her away from Zeke's—back west down Bergen Street, toward the train station. But we don't make it twenty feet before doors are opening on a dark sedan parked by the curb, and two burly men step out into our path.

Rowan immediate freezes and I can feel recognition pouring off her. The guys are dressed in jeans and t-shirts, completely innocuous, but the menace pouring off them tells me there's going to be trouble.

The back door of the car opens, and a guy steps out. He's dressed in jeans too, but they look designer and he's wearing a black silk shirt. His dark blond hair is slicked back from his face and he's pinning Rowan with a look that makes my blood instantly flame.

"There's my girl," I hear him say, and there's no doubt I'm looking at the infamous Juice—kidnapper and potential murderer.

Rowan takes an involuntary step backward, stepping right into my body. I immediately take my arm and push her behind me, never taking my eyes off the three men standing before me.

Juice's gaze narrows on me as he watches my protective move. His lips peel back and he sneers, "Ah... my girl is stepping out on me. Interesting."

"Not your girl anymore," I tell him, keeping my arms loose beside me.

He doesn't take kindly to my proclamation and his face darkens in fury. He never even hesitates before he says, "Get this piece of shit out of my way. Rowan and I have places to go."

I tense because I know the attack is coming, and it's quicker than I can even prepare for. Both guys lunge at me, grabbing me by the shoulders and driving me down toward the sidewalk. I manage to tear one arm free, swinging my elbow at the nearest face. I hear a resounding crack when my elbow meets his mouth and blood sprays everywhere.

I don't even have time to enjoy the victory of that blow, because the other guy lands a solid punch to my right kidney while the other dude's knuckles drive into my left temple. My knees buckle and the sidewalk rises up to meet me, but not before a knee rises up and catches me under the chin. My teeth slam together with my bottom lip caught in between and blood fills my mouth.

Fuck, that hurt!

Rowan lets out a piercing scream, the word "Stop" reverberating through my bones. I'm dizzy and struggling to hold onto consciousness as both guys really start landing some blows. They have me at such a disadvantage with their coordinated attack, I'm only able to block a few of the punches and kicks they're aiming at me.

To my surprise, Rowan screams again and tries to jump on the back of one of the guys that's hammering on me. Then I see Juice come up behind her, grabbing her around the waist to pull her back. She screams again in outrage and my stomach flips over when I see Juice actually nuzzle her neck.

The sensual move practically shuts Rowan down and I can see the light exit her eyes, her body going limp. I'm enraged this fucker has the power to do this to my girl… yes, *my* girl… and I push my way to my feet, throwing one of the guys backward. I don't hesitate, ramming my shoulder into the other guy, driving him back onto the hood of the car.

But again, it's another short-lived victory and, within a matter of seconds, both guys have me back down on the ground again. While one holds my shoulders, the other aims a well-placed kick into my ribs, which causes stars to burst in my head from the pain.

My mind is frantically still working though—trying to figure out how to get me out of this mess and get Rowan out of that fucktard's arms—when I hear the unmistakable sound of a shotgun cocking.

"You tell your goons to get off that boy or I'm going to splatter your brains all over the sidewalk in front of my bar."

Everyone goes still—one of the guys who is whaling on me has his arm cocked back, ready to throw another punch. But I don't have time to worry about that… my gaze goes to Rowan.

She's staring back at me with a look that is so intense with worry, I can feel it down into the marrow of my bones. Juice, on the other hand, is gritting his teeth together, a vein in his temple throbbing in anger.

"Now, let Rowan go."

Juice doesn't comply at first and George takes the shotgun that he has pressed up against the back of Juice's skull and nudges him hard. Juice slowly unwinds his arms from around Rowan's waist and she shoots out of his grip, running to my side.

The two goons immediately back away, their arms out slightly to the sides. I watch warily as Rowan crouches beside me, her face awash with fear. Her hand comes up and she grazes her thumb softly against my jaw, possibly the only place I had not been hit.

"Rowan… you and your fella get over here behind me," George says.

Rowan stands up and tries to pull me to my feet. My ribs scream in agony as I stand but it doesn't stop me from putting my arm around Rowan's waist and leading her to George.

Giving another hard shove with his shotgun, George pushes Juice toward his cronies. He turns to look at George and murder is reflected in his eyes.

"You just fucked up, old man," Juice sneers. "Nobody crosses me."

George only laughs at Juice. "You think a two-bit punk who walks around with thugs because he's too scared to take on someone himself bothers me? You're pathetic and I suggest you get out of here because my trigger finger is getting a little twitchy."

Juice doesn't make a move to leave and neither do his goons. I suspect they have guns on them and they're figuring out how to get the drop on George. I instinctively push Rowan behind me, anticipating an unloading of bullets in the near future.

George calmly keeps the shotgun trained on Juice and reaches into his pocket with his other hand. Pulling out his cell phone, he hands it to Rowan.

"Call the cops, honey. Tell them we have some trash

to pick up."

Rowan grabs the phone and I can see the look in her eyes is conflicted. She's afraid of this situation but she's afraid of the cops as well. However, before she can make the choice whether to dial or not, Juice lowers his hands down and turns toward his car. He never says a word, but shoots a last, lingering look to Rowan before he gets in, his cronies following.

We all three watch in silence, tense and ready for something to happen, until the car pulls away from the curb and it disappears from sight.

Satisfied that I'm safe for the moment because George is still holding his shotgun, I hobble over to the steps in front of his bar and sit down with a grunt. Holding my hand against my ribs, I find that helps the pain diminish from a ten to a nine.

"Call the cops, Rowan," George says.

"No." She hands the phone back to him. "They're gone. And we need to get going."

Her face is panicked and, given her aversion to cops, I'm not surprised she wants to get gone. I force myself to stand, grunting with the exertion. Holding my other hand out to her, I say, "Let's go."

"Call the goddamn cops, Rowan!" George yells.

Both of us startle and turn toward George. He is pissed and thankfully, his gun is pointed to the ground.

"Excuse me?" Rowan says. She's shocked that George

yelled at her, and so am I.

"You heard me." His voice is just as hard and is brooking no nonsense.

I can feel Rowan stiffen beside me. Even though she is scared, she's feeling backed into a corner and is going into protective mode. "Yeah, I did hear you, but I'm not doing it. I don't like cops and I'm not calling them."

George stares at her for a few moments and then he sneers, "You ungrateful little snot. I just saved your ass—
"

"Now hold on a minute," I growl, stepping toward George, shotgun be damned. "Watch how you talk to her."

Rowan lays a hand on my arm to stop me. "No, I want to hear what he has to say. So say it, George."

My heart actually lurches, because I can tell by the tone of Rowan's voice, that George is getting ready to say something that's going to hurt her. It lurches because Rowan doesn't have to stick around and listen to it. I'm more than willing to leave with her right now. But for some reason, she's going to take her lumps and listen to what the old man has to say.

George takes a deep breath and lets it out. His voice is extremely gentle when he says, "Rowan… I know how you feel about cops, but we have to involve them. I know you don't like it, but think about others for a change. By defending you, I probably just signed my own death warrant. You don't think Juice isn't going to come back and demand a little vengeance for my interference? And what about your fella there? You saw the way Juice looked at him. He's as good as dead, too. You may not need the cops help, but I do. And you two are my witnesses to what just went down here."

Oh, man, I never even thought of it that way, and I'm sure Rowan didn't either, judging by the stricken look on her face. I have a feeling George is completely right about this but I'm not going to make Rowan do something she doesn't want to do. I promised her early on we wouldn't involve the police if she didn't want and I'm not about to go back on that promise.

"It's okay, Rowan. I can handle myself, and I'm sure George can, too." I grab her hand and start pulling her down the street, while George looks after us sadly. She moves along with me passively for a few steps, then she digs her heels in and stops.

"No, wait."

I look down at Rowan and she's scared… I can tell. I reach up, running a thumb down her cheek, and her eyes close from my soft touch.

"We don't have to do this," I assure her.

She shakes her head and opens her eyes, pinning me with resolve. "Yes, I do. It's the right thing and until Juice is in custody, none of us are safe. If it were just me, I wouldn't do it. But I'm not going to put you and

George at risk."

Releasing my hand, she walks back toward George while she pulls her own phone out. To my surprise, she also pulls out the card that Buzz had given her a few days ago. Giving me a small smile, she turns her phone on and dials.

CHAPTER 11

Rowan

I PACE BACK and forth down the hallway, pausing every few seconds to listen at the bathroom door.

I'm waiting for Flynn to get out of the shower, waiting for him to fully understand the fucked-up craziness that is my life and boot me out of his apartment. I wouldn't blame him if he did. I'd completely understand.

When we got to his apartment, he didn't say anything other than a curt, "I'm going to take a shower," and then he disappeared into the bathroom. That was ten minutes ago and he should be out soon.

I can't believe I almost got him killed. And George for that matter. I'm like a poison to those around me, and had it not been for George pointing out the danger I put him in, I would have never relented to calling the cops. But now that it's done, I'm glad.

Detective Matheson arrived fairly quickly, along with another detective whose name I didn't catch. He interviewed George first, and then Flynn.

He took Flynn's statement, not only about what happened in front of Zeke's, but also about my rescue from the fire. I sat there and listened to him as he recounted everything in an extremely organized and linear fashion. As I watched him talk, I literally watched as a bruise appeared on his temple. Once, he raised his right arm to rake his hand through his hair, and I saw his elbow was bloody. My chest actually cramped over the thought that Flynn got battered in an effort to defend me.

When it was my turn, he asked if I wanted to do the interview in private. I shook my head *no*, not quite having the courage to say out loud that I wanted Flynn there. It was a comfort that he sat beside me—not even touching—but just his presence was palpable.

Detective Matheson's questions were straight and to the point. He only had to interrupt me twice for clarification, but otherwise let me tell the story I wanted.

Yes, I said. *I had been dating Teddy "Juice" Jones for over a year. I moved in with him about eleven months ago.*

Yes, I said. *I had wanted out of the relationship and tried to leave the house with Capone. I hadn't made it down the front porch steps before his hand grabbed me, pulling me back in. He chained me to the bed and when I wouldn't stop screaming for him to let me go, he injected me with some type of drug to keep me quiet. I believed he kept me there for three days, naked and chained, only allowing me to go to the bathroom a few times a day. He never touched me sexually during that time and was hardly ever around.*

No, I admitted. *I wasn't sure that Juice was the one that started the fire. Without giving away names, I heard through the grapevine that Juice had been upset about the fire and said he knew who did it and would make them pay.*

No, I concluded. *I had nothing else to add.*

My words seem to be enough for Detective Matheson because he didn't push me further, although he said he might be back in touch with more questions. To my relief, he told me that he felt there was enough based on my statement for probable cause to arrest him—at least for the kidnapping charges.

The only other thing he did was encourage Flynn to get some medical attention, but Flynn declined. He said he was fine, but I know he wasn't. We walked back to the train in silence. He rested with his head against the window and his eyes closed for the entire ride back to his neighborhood.

And other than his short announcement that he was going to take a shower, there hasn't been any other conversation. I feel nauseated over it because I'm seeing my first real opportunity at a friendship starting to circle the drain. Why would someone like Flynn even want to have a freak of a friend like me? I'm sure none of his other friends have psycho kidnapping, drug-dealing ex-boyfriends stalking them.

So lost in my thoughts, I'm unprepared when the door opens and a waft of spicy, scented steam billows out of the bathroom. Flynn steps out and my tongue practically sticks to the top of my mouth. He wears only a blue towel wrapped around his waist, with another smaller one hanging around his neck. I can't help it when my eyes flick across his chest, taking in the beads of water still clinging there before I meet his eyes.

"You shaved," I say with surprise.

For the past three days, Flynn has let his beard grow in, claiming I ruined his blade when I shaved my legs. It was only after I was headed out the door to buy him a new razor that he laughingly told me he was joking, and that he's just too lazy to shave on his days off.

Flynn rubs his fingertips over his chin. "Yeah. I figured I'd go ahead and knock it out since I have to be at work early tomorrow."

"You're going in to work?" I'm surprised, given the fact he looks like he's been through a meat grinder.

"Sure, why not?"

I look down at his ribs pointedly. "Maybe because of that."

His gaze follows mine down to where a dark purple bruise, just about the size of a boot, covers his right ribcage. A slight grimace passes over his face and then he looks at me, shrugging his shoulder, "No biggie. I've had worse."

He moves to the left to walk by me, obviously heading to his room. My hand snakes out and wraps around his forearm. His warm, moist skin is almost electric against mine but I hold on. He stops and looks at me in question.

"Are you mad at me?" I don't know why I blurt that out but if he's going to end this short-lived friendship, I'd rather get it out on the table.

Flynn looks genuinely surprised. "Why would you think that?"

My hand falls away from his arm and I jam both of my hands in my pockets. My gaze lowers and I stare at the tips of my combat boots, shrugging my shoulders like a shy child.

Gah… since when is Rowan Page at a loss for words? Or since when does Rowan Page lower her gaze in embarrassment to anyone?

Flynn sticks his forefinger under my chin and pushes up. My head follows and the last thing I raise is my eyes to his. When I do, he's looking at me with understanding, warmth, and amusement.

Amusement?

Yes, there it is.

I amuse the man and that fact immediately causes the constrictive feeling in my chest to ease up.

"You find me funny?"

"I find it adorable that you would think I was mad."

His words send a course of pleasure through me, not only because he has reiterated our friendship is intact, but because he thinks I'm adorable.

Suddenly, I'm no longer focused on my own insecurity but I become painfully aware of his closeness and near-naked state. I can smell his soap and feel the warmth radiating off his skin as he stands near me. We just stare at each other, both of our eyes locked.

When he starts to lean in toward me, his eyes lower to my lips and I know he's going to kiss me. I am both elated and scared all at once. I want him to kiss me but I don't want to hurt our friendship.

Panicking, I take a quick step back and blurt, "Did you disinfect your cuts?"

The heat stays in his eyes for just a few seconds and then simmers down. His lips curl upward in a smirk, but he shakes his head no.

Moving past him into the bathroom, I reach under his sink, where I had seen a bottle of rubbing alcohol. I grab a few cotton balls, a box of Band-Aids, and turn to him.

"Sit down on the toilet and I'll patch you up."

He turns his back on me and walks to his bedroom. "Come patch me up in here. It's too damn hot in the bathroom."

My eyes close briefly at the thought of sitting in his

bedroom with him while he wears nothing but a towel to cover himself. I utter a small prayer for the strength not to drool over him and head that way.

When I enter his bedroom, I find him sitting with his butt perched on the very edge of his bed, his legs slightly apart. The position causes the towel to gape open over his right thigh, exposing several inches of powerful muscle. Just a few more inches of movement, and I'll be seeing what is in between his thighs. I hope he holds absolutely still for the sake of my sanity.

I walk to stand beside him and lay my supplies on the bed near his hip. Pulling his left arm out, I look at the elbow I had noticed was bleeding. I briefly flick my eyes over the tattoo on the inside of his bicep. It's in the same size and font as the "Semper" tattoo on his other bicep, except this one says "Fidelis". I start to ask him what the words mean when my gaze captures the gash on his elbow. It's oozing blood from the ragged wound.

"You got a really nasty cut back here," I tell him as I reach for the cotton balls and alcohol.

He turns his shoulder inward, causing his arm to rotate so he can see his elbow. "Good. I thought I caught that motherfucker in his mouth. I hope he lost some teeth."

I try to keep a stern look on my face but I smile inside. Opening the alcohol, I warn him, "This may sting."

Glancing at him, I see his eyes are leveled at me and I wonder what he's thinking at this moment. I break the connection and look down to his elbow. Holding a few cotton balls underneath the cut, I tip the bottle and pour some alcohol over it. I expect him to wince, or hiss, or even try to pull his arm away. I sneak a peek at him and he's still just staring at me. He hasn't even flinched. I quickly avert my eyes down and watch as the alcohol mixes with this blood and runs away from his wound in a pink river.

Sopping the mess up with another cotton ball, I open up one of the larger Band-Aids and stick it firmly on his elbow.

Clearing my throat, I stand straight. "All right…any other open wounds?"

Those serious eyes continue to just stare at me, but he says, "I'm not sure. You better give me a once over."

I know he means nothing by it. I just know it. But damn if his words don't sound like sin, and my skin tightens in anticipation of looking over his body.

"Okay," I say, internally wincing at the fact that my voice sounds breathless.

Flynn doesn't move and I assume he expects me to inspect him from where he's sitting. I do a quick lean across the bed to take a look at his back. I didn't expect to see anything there, but it didn't stop me from enjoying the smooth skin and hard muscles that greet me.

As I straighten up, I look over the side of his face that is nearest to me, since I know he took a few blows up there. I see nothing but a purple bruise near his temple and my fingers reach out to touch him. Gently prodding the skin, I assure myself there is no cut and let my fingers drift away.

Sneaking a quick glance at Flynn, he's still looking at me with the same somberness as earlier, but now his eyes look a little more heated. If I'm not mistaken, my touch has done that and that thought alone causes my stomach to flip end over end with awareness.

Walking around to his other side, I check out that part of his face, relieved to see it looks fine. I look over his other arm and it is also unmarked. Outside of the large bruise to his ribs, I can't see any other injuries that need tending on this side, and part of me is a little disappointed.

I reach over for the bottle cap and say, "I think that's it."

"You missed one."

Straightening up with the bottle still in hand, I look at him. "Where?"

"My lip. One of those guys caught me under the chin with his knee and my lip got caught in between my teeth slamming together."

I can't see an obvious wound so I walk around to his

front and lean in, peering at his lips. They are full and look soft, and in my dream, they felt like satin. "I don't see anything."

"It's there. You might have to look a little closer." As he says this, his legs shift apart just a tad more, making room for me to walk closer.

Whether the move is made innocently or not, my blood chooses to surge through my veins the minute my brain considers stepping in between those powerful legs. I pull my eyes up from his lips and when they meet his, my lungs contract painfully. His brows are furrowed in slightly and his eyelids are at half-mast. He's looking at me with a lazy, sensual appraisal and in that moment, there is no doubt that Flynn Caldwell is sexually attracted to me. It causes my lower stomach to tighten and my panties immediately get wet. The sudden rush of sexual awareness is so intense on my part, I actually have to squeeze my legs together to alleviate the pleasurable pulse I'm feeling there.

Before I can even think what to say, Flynn's hands come up to my hips and he pulls me closer. My hands reach out to grip his shoulders, not because I'm in danger of falling, but because I want to touch him the way he's touching me.

We are so close now; our faces are only inches apart. There's just as much room separating the tops of my thighs from the dark mystery that lays beyond the blue towel, which I'm sure has parted even further, although I don't look for fear of perishing from pleasure.

Our eyes are locked on each other, neither one of us moving, neither one of us saying a thing. I move my right hand from his shoulder and bring it up to lay lightly against his cheek. Then I drag my fingers across his face, over to his chin. I lightly run my thumb across his bottom lip and his mouth parts for me.

Just on the inside of his lower lip, I see two cuts, presumably made by his two front teeth. They aren't bleeding but they are red and angry looking.

"Oh my God… you do have cuts here!" I pull his lip down further so I can take a better look.

Flynn starts chuckling. "I told you so. Why did you think I asked you to look closer?"

His words slam into my like an icy glacier and I try to pull back, but his hands hold my hips tight. I start fumbling around for words. "I thought… I mean, you said you had a cut, but then I couldn't see one… and then you pulled me closer… so I thought…"

I feel Flynn's fingertips dig into my flesh and he pulls me in a fraction closer. My hands go back to his shoulders and his muscles jump when our skin makes contact.

"How about you just kiss it and see if you can make it better?"

My confused brain is trying to catch up. I thought he

was attracted to me, and then I thought he wasn't… now it appears he is. I'm not even sure I know which way is up right now.

"You want me to kiss you?"

"Well… how else will I know how bad the cut is until I try to use my lips?" His voice is so serious, his eyes reflecting the same, but the slight curve to his mouth tells me he's enjoying this banter.

With Flynn sitting on the bed, my face is at the same level as his. Our bodies are perfectly aligned for me to kiss him soundly. I could just lean forward, ever so slightly, and my lips would touch his. I can tell that is exactly what he expects me to do.

I take one step in further until the outside of my thighs graze the inside of his and our chests touch. The closeness demands I wrap my arms fully around his neck and I do so. I hold my head back just a touch, so our lips are the last thing that will touch.

We stare at each other, silently. Our faces are so close, my eyes glaze over a bit trying to look into his.

"I'm going to kiss you now," I whisper.

His arms wrap around me, squeezing me closer.

"Okay," he whispers back.

I don't waste any time before I press my mouth against his. We mutually open up to each other and I tilt my head sideways. Our mouths move against each other, tasting… testing boundaries.

One of Flynn's hands moves from around my back to hold the back of my head, pushing me in tighter to him. His tongue slips into my mouth at the same time and at the first contact with mine, both of us groan loudly.

The kiss turns more fevered and I'm riddled with the need to touch more of him. As if sensing the urge within me, Flynn's hands drop and grip under my ass. In one smooth move, he scoots his butt further back on the bed and hauls me onto his lap. As my legs part to straddle him, my gaze travels down and I see the towel has opened completely. A moan of appreciation slips out when I see how hard he is.

"Fuck," he hisses. "If you keep looking at me like that, I won't be responsible for the way you walk tomorrow."

His sinful words shoot lust through my body as I imagine Flynn fucking me so hard I can't walk and my eyes slam back into his. The gaze only lasts a second before his mouth is back on mine and his hands are tangled in my hair.

I'm completely overwhelmed by the intimacy that swirls around us. Flynn's mouth is almost inducing catatonia in me while his hands are causing mini-volcanic eruptions everywhere they touch.

Falling, falling, falling… fast.

I struggle to clear my head, and remember that we

are friends.

Just friends.

I should pull back and stop this before we both do something stupid and ruin our friendship.

Yes…pull back. That's what I should do.

I will.

In just a moment.

After we kiss for just a bit more.

CHAPTER 12

Flynn

I'M INTO THE second day of my three-day shift and I stare at the loudspeaker on the wall, willing it to crackle and spit to life with a call. I'm jonesing for a call… even if it's to get a fucking cat out of a tree.

Something.

Anything to get my mind off Rowan.

We had made out like two sex-starved teenagers the other day, both of us too hesitant to move past second base. I'm not sure why we didn't go further, because there was nothing more that I wanted to do than strip Rowan naked, lay her out on the bed, and make her come hard. I wanted her to reach down between my legs, take my aching dick in her hands, and give me the same pleasure.

But none of those things happened. We kissed… deep, long, hot kissing. There was plenty of moaning, lots of tongue, but our hands still remained on good behavior and didn't venture too far. I kept mine mostly on Rowan's head, sometimes stroking down her back and, yes, once… I gripped her ass and reveled at the groan she rewarded me with.

Rowan ran her hands over my shoulders, down my arms… digging her fingers into my biceps. She touched my chest, laying her warm hands flat against my pecs, and lightly stroked my skin. It drove me crazy and I silently begged her to touch my nipples.

I have no clue how long we made out. It could have gone on another five hours and I would have been deliriously happy, despite the fact I would probably be sporting the biggest set of blue balls in the history of mankind. But at some point, Rowan pulled back, her hands resting on my cheeks. She looked at me… the deepest, softest look she had ever bestowed my way… and she said, "We should slow down."

I groaned. I couldn't help it. Guys are conditioned to involuntarily groan when a woman puts a screeching halt on our sex-capades. I flexed my fingers open and closed with frustration, wanting to just pull her back in and start kissing the fuck out of her.

But then, I realized it was Rowan sitting on my lap… a girl that I was apparently willing to lay my life down for on two occasions so far, and I knew that she was right. We should slow it down. Starting an intense relationship under the already bizarre circumstances that threw us together was probably not a good idea.

So I kissed her lightly, one more time, and I gently

pushed her off my lap. Her face was flushed, her lips were swollen, and her chest was heaving. I still get a rush of satisfaction over that image. She merely gave me a small nod of her head—after sneaking a glance down at my erection—and walked out of my room. I got up, headed for the shower, and jumped back in so I could jerk off… *again*… to thoughts of Rowan.

After that, the rest of our night was uneventful. We ate dinner and played cards. I wanted to kiss her again but she put up a wall and maintained a slight level of aloofness that told me it wasn't going to happen. She went to bed early and was still sleeping when I left for work the next morning.

My phone buzzes in my pocket, startling me from my thoughts. I pull it out and my heart leaps a bit when I see it's from Rowan.

Met Food called. I didn't get job. Back to the drawing board.

My heart now hurts for Rowan. She was so excited yesterday about having an interview at a grocery store just a few blocks from my apartment. She had texted me right after, telling me that she thought it went well and was hoping she got it.

This girl is amazing. Yeah, it's a simple job as a checkout clerk, but her enthusiasm and pride over getting any job humbles me just a bit. I've never met anyone that is so intent on doing things the hard way, just to show that she can do it.

No worries. You'll get something soon. Faith in you.

And I do… have faith in her. There is no person I know in this world that wouldn't land on their feet with as much grace as I know Rowan will.

Thx. At least your apartment is sparkling. Bored so cleaning.

That's my girl. Keeping busy… earning her keep. I grin inside thinking of her bent over my bathtub, and immediately start getting a boner. I need to dial it back a bit!

I start to text her back but my phone rings. It's Buzz Matheson calling.

I connect the call. "What's up, Buzz?"

"Got some good news. I tried to call Rowan but got her voice mail."

"Yeah, she's more of a texter than a talker. Tell me you got the bastard."

Buzz chuckles. "Yeah, we got him. Picked him up this morning. He was holed up with some woman over in Long Island."

Well, it didn't take long for him to start fucking around. For the life of me, I can't figure out why he wants Rowan so bad if he can just go shack up with another woman so quickly.

"How'd you find him?"

"We got a tip from an informant who actually gave us a bit more than just his whereabouts. They pulled a body out of the Hudson yesterday… apparently, a rival drug dealer of Juice's. Rumor has it that Juice whacked him."

I'm silent for a moment, digesting that piece of news. It makes my hair stand on end, knowing that this guy is probably a murderer. "You think that was the guy that set the house on fire?"

"Who knows? Could be. Doesn't much matter to me since I have enough evidence on the kidnapping charges to hold him and he won't make bail. Hopefully, homicide can build a case for the murder, too."

"Hope so, man."

"Yeah, well, listen… tell Rowan thanks again for talking to me but prepare her… if this goes to trial… she's going to have to testify."

Yeah, good luck with that, I thought. "What do you think the chances of that are?"

"I'm hoping he'll cut a deal in exchange for giving up his supplier. It would be best for him if he did. I'll keep you posted, okay?"

"Sure. Thanks, Buzz."

After I disconnect, I dial Rowan's cell. She probably won't answer if Buzz just tried to call her but I take a chance.

She picks up on the second ring.

"Hey," she says, and just the sound of her voice washes over me like a drug.

"Buzz just called."

"Yeah, he tried to call me but I didn't answer. What did he want?"

"They got Juice in custody."

I wait for her to respond but I'm met with silence. Then I hear it… faintly. A long exhale of relief.

"You okay?" I ask gently.

Her voice warbles just a bit when she answers. "Yeah. Just happy is all."

"Me too. You're safe now."

The minute I say those words, I think to myself, *She's going to leave now that Juice is off the streets.*

"Don't leave," I blurt out.

"What?" Her voice is startled, which gives me a small measure of relief that she wasn't thinking the same exact thing I was at that same exact moment.

"Just because Juice is in custody… I don't want you to leave. In fact, I want to open up the position of roommate to you permanently. I was looking for one anyway before I met you. And once you get a job, you can split expenses with me fifty-fifty. So… don't leave, okay? At least not until I get home."

Man, that was a mouthful and my face heats up a bit that I just sort of bared my soul to her. She has to know I'm not asking her to stay because I want rent, right? She has to know I want her to stay because I want her to stay.

I'm met with a soft laugh of amusement. "I'll stay, Flynn. Don't worry. I'll see you day after tomorrow."

My breath rushes out in relief. "Good. I'll see you day after tomorrow."

I go to disconnect the call but I clearly hear her say, "Stay safe, Flynn."

She cares… I know she does.

The loudspeaker hisses and issues a long crackle, then I'm jumping up from my rack as the call comes in.

♦

AFTER WE RETURN to the Station, I take a quick shower and hang out on my bunk for a while.

"Hey, Caldwell." I look up and one of my crewmates, Gigi Scaletti, stands in the doorway. "You have a visitor out front."

"Oh, yeah?"

"Yeah… tall, long hair… broody looking." She flashes me a grin.

"Must be my cousin, Nix."

"Is he single? Because if so, I'm willing to be all over that if you know what I mean."

Yes, I do know what she means and I just shake my head with a smirk. Gigi tries hard to be one of the guys, when she really doesn't have to. She's proven her worth as a teammate a million times over, so I let her down gently.

"Sadly, he's very taken. Engaged in fact."

"Damn," she says but she really doesn't look heartbroken in the slightest. "Guess I'll keep looking."

When I get to the front bay, sure enough, Nix is leaning up against the truck talking to Tim. As I approach, I hear Tim say, "See ya, Nix." They fist bump and Tim heads toward the kitchen.

"Hey, man. What brings you over to this corner of the world?"

He jerks his thumb over his shoulder. "I was just delivering a piece of art to an accounting firm here in Brooklyn and thought I'd stop by. See how things are going."

"You mean, see how it's going with the victim I moved into my apartment that I'm trying to fix?"

Nix at least has the grace to look slightly embarrassed. "Yeah, something like that."

Leaning back against the truck, I cross my arms over my chest and look out the bay door at the traffic driving by. I want to be mad at Nix for being judgmental with me the other day, but I can't find it within me. He's my cousin—one of my best friends in the world—and all of his words are born of love. I get it.

"All's good. In fact, it looks like Rowan's problems are over. Buzz caught her ex-boyfriend and he's in custody, so she's safe."

"So, she'll be moving on?" His eyes are so serious, and I know… again… this stems from love.

"Actually, I've gone ahead and asked her to officially

be my roommate. She's trying to get a job now."

Nix looks to the concrete floor and scuffs a boot over it, presumably thinking over his next words. "Flynn, are you sure she's not trying to scam you… or abusing your hospitality?"

Chuckling, I slap Nix on the shoulder. "Man… trust me, this girl doesn't know how to take advantage of someone. If you met her, you'd know it in about five minutes. I guarantee once she finds a job, she'll probably insist on paying me back-rent with interest. That's just the way she is."

Nix looks at me and holds my gaze. I make sure mine is unwavering so he understands that I believe the truth of what I'm telling him and that I'm not romanticizing her involvement in my life.

"Really? You trust her motives?"

"I do," I say emphatically. "I'm not wrong about this. She's a good person. More importantly… she doesn't need fixed. She'd be fine with or without my help."

Nix pushes away from the truck and comes to stand in front of me. "So, what type of job is she looking for?"

I shrug my shoulders. "She's not picky. Just something where she can earn a decent wage. She's worked in bars before but she's applied to some local businesses around the apartment. Retail stuff."

Nix rubs the scruff along his jaw, contemplating. "She know how to work a computer?"

"I don't know. I guess so. I mean—doesn't everyone in this day and age know how?"

"You'd think, right? Hold on just a sec… I'll be right back."

I watch as Nix steps out of the open bay doors and out onto the sidewalk. He pulls his phone out and dials. He paces back and forth while talking to someone on the other end, and I'm assuming he might know about a potential job for Rowan. The thought that he would do that touches me and I'm reminded how very lucky I am to have the family that I do.

Nix isn't on the phone long before he disconnects and walks back toward me. "That was Emily. She agrees with me… if your roommate is familiar with computers, and can work some basic software I have… I'll offer her a job as my secretary. We'll do a trial for thirty days and I'll start her at thirteen dollars an hour. If at the end of thirty days, she's doing a great job, we'll talk something more permanent."

"What?" I ask, completely startled.

"Emily's trying to buckle down this last year of school and she just hasn't been able to stay on top of my stuff that she had been helping me with. We've been talking about me hiring someone to take over for her. Now seems as good a time as any, I guess."

I cock an eyebrow at him. "Wait a minute… just five minutes ago you were questioning Rowan's integrity.

You've never met her, you don't even know if she can do the job. Why are you offering this?"

Nix gives me a smile and shakes his head with amusement. "Because I know you, dude. And if you tell me she's solid, then she's solid."

I push away from the truck and take a step toward Nix, holding my hand out. He grasps it in a hard shake and then pulls me into a quick half-hug, clapping me on the back.

"Thanks, Nix. That really means a lot. I'll call Rowan tonight and tell her. Although, she'll probably bitch about this being a handout. The girl has maybe a bit too much pride."

"That means she'll work hard. I like it."

"That she will. When do you want her to start?"

"When does your shift end?"

"Tomorrow is my last day."

"Probably the day after that. Give me a call when you get home and we'll iron out the details."

After Nix leaves, I head into the kitchen to get something to eat. I think how I'm going to approach this with Rowan, because she won't like that I had a hand in getting her a job. I just hope she's not too stubborn to accept this help.

CHAPTER 13

Rowan

I STARE OUT the passenger window at the tree-lined street. It's weird… because I haven't stepped foot out of the city in five years. I'm used to the concrete jungle, not this fall oasis where the leaves are just starting to get a touch of color and the air is refreshingly crisp in the morning.

Flynn is driving me to his cousin's house in Englewood, New Jersey. I'm apparently starting a new job today, brought about by the generosity of Nix and Flynn Caldwell. I'm torn, because on the one hand, I want to be elated that I'll have a way to make money. But on the other hand, I'm feeling like a failure that this job was sort of handed to me.

Flynn's line—beggars can't be choosers—flits through my mind and I sigh inwardly. I suppose I need to swallow a bit of my pride and go ahead and look at the bright side of things. So I'm telling the new Rowan to suck it up and be nothing but appreciative of this job.

The old Rowan still exists though, because Flynn and

I had a knock-down, drag-out fight last night about him driving me here. I insisted I could take public transit. I even showed him on the computer a nice little route that, between the bus and subway, I could make it in just a little over an hour and a half. Flynn then promptly pulled up driving directions on Google Maps and showed me how he could have me there in about forty-five minutes by his car. Then we got into a major pissing contest about it, but he eventually won by telling me he wanted to visit his parents while Nix showed me the ropes.

"Are you still pissed at me?" Flynn asks with a good-natured attitude.

"Yup. Leave me alone." I try to sound harsh but truth be told, I'm really not pissed at him anymore. I find it very difficult to hold strong against his wit and charm.

Flynn reaches over and tugs on the end of my hair. "You're cute when you're mad."

I lean my head to the right, dislodging his hand from my hair. Not because I'm mad, but because his touch affects me too much.

"Am not mad."

"Are, too. Admit it. You don't like the fact I won our argument."

I turn my head toward him and he takes his eyes off the road for a second to return my gaze. I shoot him my best fuck-off glare but he only laughs at me. His dimple pops out, his eyes crinkle up at the corners, and I think he may be the most gorgeous man alive.

Seriously.

I turn my head to look back out the passenger window, not because I'm mad, but because of the smile that is involuntarily creeping onto my face.

Damn that Flynn Caldwell and his devious charm.

♦

NIX'S FIANCÉE GREETS us at the door, telling us that Nix is doing some welding in his shop and that she'll be teaching me the ropes. Emily Burnham is a pretty cool chick. She clearly comes from money, and I make that snap judgment based on the designer clothes she's wearing and the expensive salon cut of her hair. I had those same things once upon a time, and I can honestly say I don't miss it. The price that came with having those luxuries just wasn't worth it to me.

Still, the one thing Emily Burnham is not, is snobbish. She immediately hugs me when Flynn introduces us, then coos over me like a mother hen for the ordeal I'd been through recently. Once that is out of the way, she eagerly takes me out back to show me Nix's shop, and I throw a casual wave to Flynn as he gets back in his car to go visit his mom and dad.

I follow Emily to a workshop in the backyard. We

enter and I immediately take in the surroundings. It's lit with bright, overhead, fluorescent bulbs and it's neatly organized. The walls sport shelving stacked with various tools and implements that I have no idea what they do. In the corner, there is a tattered recliner and a mini-fridge. In another corner, there is a desk with a laptop, and I'm guessing it's Emily's workspace because it's adorned with framed photos of her and Nix, as well as a vase of flowers. She girled the space up a bit.

"So, this is where you'll work," she says as she walks to the desk. "Flynn said you're pretty computer savvy."

I nod. "Yeah. I don't own one but I use the one at the public library a lot."

"Well, it's mostly bookkeeping and tracking supply orders. Pretty basic software like QuickBooks and Excel. I'll be able to teach you everything today, so consider this just an orientation."

Emily boots the laptop up and drags a short stool from the large workbench that takes up the middle of the room. "Sit here and just watch. I'll go through everything and then let you try some invoices. The password to log on is *badthings*."

"Bad things?" I ask.

Emily gives a very un-lady-like snicker. "Yeah… I was singing the song *Bad Things* by *Jace Everett* when Nix and I had our first kiss. It seemed appropriate."

I take the seat and peer over her shoulder as she explains how to keep Nix organized and his business running smoothly. It only takes her about an hour to show me the basics and, admittedly, it doesn't look too hard. I'm pretty good with numbers and I expect after I do a few invoices myself, I'll be working with no problems.

A door that sits on the far side of the room opens, and I get my first look at who I assume is Nix Caldwell. He gives me a quick glance and takes off his work gloves, throwing them on a nearby shelf. Without a word of greeting, he heads to the sink and washes his hands. Emily is engrossed on the computer and doesn't seem to notice he's entered.

Had I not known that Flynn and Nix were cousins, I would have pegged them as brothers. They have the same dark brown hair and hazel eyes, although his have a bit more green in them, but they also have the same nose and lips. Nix's attitude seems a bit surly from the start, so I'll have to wonder if he has dimples when he smiles.

If he smiles.

"Hey, babe… remind me what account I put this invoice under from Shogran Motors."

Apparently, Emily did notice he walked into the room because she never even pulls her nose away from the computer to ask that question.

Nix turns away from the sink and he now has a smile on his face that is so warm and tender, I actually swallow a tiny lump in my throat. The smile isn't for me though… it's directed straight at Emily and he walks toward her without ever taking his eyes from her back.

I watch as Nix walks up behind Emily, bends over, and wraps his arms around her shoulders, crossing them over her chest. He leans his chin on top of her head and looks at the computer screen. "Put it under the account labeled 'Kit Vendor'."

Emily taps a few strokes on the keyboard and I follow her progress on the screen, making a mental note to myself to do the same the next time I get that invoice to enter.

"Thanks," Emily says as she tilts her head back so she can see Nix. "You are an amazing man."

Nix leans over and gives her a swift kiss on her lips. "I know. You lucked out with me."

I'm almost embarrassed that I'm watching this interplay between them. I've never been an openly affectionate person and this display makes me a little uncomfortable, and just a little bit envious. I try to imagine Flynn wrapping his arms around me like that… leaning his body into mine… giving me a tender kiss. Just the thought causes a longing to rise up in me, but I quickly push it back down. I've struggled with my feelings for Flynn and it helped having him gone the last three days. The alone time helped me to refocus and I kept repeating the mantra, "Flynn and I are better off as friends" as much as possible. I hoped that by repeating it, it would sink in and I would accept it.

Emily stands up from the chair, dislodging herself from Nix's embrace. "Nix… meet Rowan. Rowan… meet Nix."

Nix straightens and leans a hip on the edge of the desk. He doesn't reach out to shake my hand and he certainly doesn't offer me a hug the way Emily did, which is just fine by me. Her hug weirded me out just a bit. Rather, Nix crosses his arms over his chest and gives me a quick once-over. I see distrust in his eyes and I have to wonder what I've done this early on in our relationship to earn that look.

"So… what's your story, Rowan?"

His words seem pleasant enough but his body language doesn't compute. Shrugging my shoulders, I tell him, "Not much of a story. Just an out-of-work girl looking for a job."

My answer is evasive and Nix knows it is. The look of distrust in his eyes magnifies more. "Where are you from?"

"Brooklyn," I tell him.

"And before that?"

"Texas… Lewisville to be exact."

"Why did you come to New York?"

"Just wanted to see the world… got sidetracked by the glitz of The Big Apple."

"Family still there?"

"To my knowledge," I answer, starting to get irritated by his questions.

"To your knowledge? You don't know?"

Okay… I've had it with his nosiness. "Is this a job interview because I was under the impression I already had the job?"

Glancing at Emily, I can see she's worried by the way I snapped at Nix. By all appearances, he was making casual conversation, but I know he's rooting around because he's skeptical of me.

Nix just casually shrugs his shoulders, completely at ease with my bitchy attitude. "You have the job. I was just curious, is all. You start tomorrow… eight to five with an hour for lunch. You're more than welcome to eat with me in the house if I'm here. If I'm gone, you're on your own but there's sodas in that fridge. And don't be late."

I'm not sure I like Nix very much… or at all. But he is now my employer, and he's my new bud and roommate's cousin, so I try to play nice. "Got it. Anything else you need to show me, Emily? Because if not, I think I got it."

Emily pulls her puzzled gaze from Nix and looks at me. "That's it. I'll show you Nix's stockroom and then we can go in the house and have a drink while we wait for Flynn to come back."

Nix doesn't say another word, just turns around and heads back through the door from which he had just exited a few moments ago.

"I'm sorry," Emily says. "Nix wasn't being nosy; he was just trying to get to know you."

Yeah, those are one in the same, I think to myself.

"No problem," I assure her. And it isn't a problem. I'm pretty sure I put Nix in his place and he'll be avoiding share time with me from now on.

♦

FLYNN TAKES ME out to dinner, to celebrate, he says, for getting a job. He's in good spirits the entire time and it eventually rubs off on me. It's so hard for me to maintain my surly distance when he's constantly smiling and joking around with me. He's like a drug that makes me happy, and once again, I offer up a small prayer of thanks for bringing him into my life.

After taking a sip of his drink, Flynn looks at me. "So, I wanted to ask…what was the deal with you and Juice? How did you end up with someone like him?"

I shrug my shoulders. "I don't know. I knew he was bad news but I was drawn to him. It was part of the rebel that still existed inside of me, I guess. And knowing I wouldn't ever be good enough for someone better than a guy like him, I sort of just settled."

"Now, that's just not true. You could have anyone

you wanted," Flynn says with admonishment. "But he definitely wasn't good enough for *you*."

"It took me a while to figure that out. Plus, he just became so possessive. When I tried to leave, I didn't even have any grand plan. I just quietly packed a bag, hooked Capone's leash on, and tried to sneak out of the house. He wasn't as sound asleep as I thought he was."

"And that's when he chained you up?"

"Yeah… but after I told him that I would just leave again the next opportunity I got. Dumb move on my part, I suppose, but I never thought he'd keep me prisoner."

"Was he on drugs or something?"

"Actually, no," I tell him. "I tried to stay pretty removed from his drug deals, but from what I did see… at that level, you don't really use the stuff yourself. He treated it very much like a business and I guess you got to have a sharp mind to be successful at it."

"And stay one step ahead of the cops."

"That is definitely a good reason not to let your mind get clouded with that shit."

Flynn gives me a knowing look. "You've overcome a lot, Rowan. I'm proud of you."

My insides warm from his words… the first time anyone has said that to me. They are said with such sincerity, I have no doubt he truly means it.

When we get back to the apartment, Flynn offers to

take Capone for his evening walk and I acquiesce, wanting nothing more than a long, hot shower and to get to bed so I can be fresh for my first day of work tomorrow. I let the hot water soak into me as I reflect over the day.

Nix is certainly a piece of work but I really like Emily. I think in my old world, she and I probably would have been friends. In my new world, I've only just accepted Flynn as a friend and that's enough for me right now.

When I finish the shower, I dress in the t-shirt and shorts that Flynn had given me my first night here. I've commandeered them as my pajamas but he hasn't asked for them back so I'm not going to worry about it. Besides… I like wearing Flynn's clothes to bed. It's a way to be close to him without really being physically close to him. It's a way to touch him without ruining our friendship.

I step out of the bathroom, running my fingers through my wet hair. In the kitchen, I grab a bottle of water and twist the cap off, taking a long swallow. Glancing over, I see Flynn left his breakfast dishes in the sink so I put the bottle down and start to wash them.

"You don't have to do it." Flynn's voice washes over me, warm, comforting, and even exhilarating. I hate that my body reacts to him this way.

I turn around and give him a casual shrug. He's

standing in the doorway with Capone beside him. "No biggie. But tomorrow, once I start working, we're sharing in the cleaning duties, fifty-fifty, right?"

"Right," he assures me. "But will you still clean the toilet? That gives me the heebie-jeebies."

Rinsing the last plate and wiping it down, I turn around to him. "Seriously? You get freaked out over a toilet? You're a freakin' firefighter. Aren't you supposed to be all macho or something?"

Flynn puts on his most hurt look and places a closed fist on his chest. "You wound me, Rowan. You seriously wound me."

I lean my hip against the kitchen sink, rolling my eyes at him. "I seriously doubt that wounded you."

"It did," he proclaims as he walks to the kitchen sink. Pulling a glass out of the cupboard, he fills it with water and takes a sip. "And when people make fun of me, I tend to retaliate, so I'd be careful if I were you."

His tone is light and teasing and I instantly smile at him. I fucking just can't help myself. With a laugh, I playfully punch him on the arm. "Oooohh… I'm so scared. What could you possibly say to me that would wound me?"

Swallowing the last of his water, he sets the glass in the sink and turns the water on. He picks up the sprayer and starts rinsing the glass out. "Well, on occasion… well, really only once before, when someone dared to question my masculinity… I did a little something like this…"

Without warning, Flynn turns the sprayer my way and sprays me right in the face. I'm so stunned, I can't even react, and he takes the opportunity to wave the sprayer up and down, soaking my entire shirt in the process. Capone sees the water flying and scurries out of the war zone with his tail tucked between his legs.

I finally snap out of it and my first thought is payback. I lunge for him and wrap my hands around his, trying to wrestle the sprayer from his grip. He starts laughing and raises his hands higher, now spraying water down on the top of my head.

"I'm a firefighter. Look at me!" he exclaims as water rains all around me.

I shriek in mock outrage, and decide I'll never be strong enough to rip it away from him, so I go in for a secondary attack. I drop my arms to his waist and, taking a big gamble, I start to tickle him. I have no clue if he's ticklish or not, but if he is, the sprayer… and thus victory, will be mine.

The minute my fingertips dig into skin, he jerks almost convulsively. The sprayer drops but I can't make a grab for it because Flynn now has my hands in his and he's trying to push me away. He's now laughing hysterically while I try to tickle him and we are now engaged in a battle to keep my fingertips away from his stomach. As we push and pull against each other, both of us out of breath from laughing, our feet start slipping and sliding on the wet linoleum.

My eyes lock with his, just for a brief moment, and I see pure happiness and joy radiating from his face. Then our feet fly out from under us and we start a free-fall to the kitchen floor. I'm not sure if it's his firefighting skills, or he's just a damn good rescuer, but Flynn's arms wrap around my waist and he manages to turn both of our bodies so he's underneath me as we go down. We land with a jarring thud, with Flynn taking the impact from the floor and my body on top of his. He winces and exhales loudly.

"Oh, shit," I say. "Your ribs."

I sit up immediately and straddle his thighs, my knees coming to rest against the wet floor on either side of him. I carefully lift his shirt up from the hem, revealing his torso. The purple bruise on his ribs is fading and is now a lovely yellow-green. I skim my fingers lightly over it. "Does it hurt?"

His voice comes out gruff. "Not in the slightest."

I move my eyes to his and they are filled with such intensity and longing, my heart stops cold in my chest. When it resumes its life beat, it starts hammering so hard I think I can hear it.

"Flynn," I say, but then I trail off, words failing me.

"Kiss me, Rowan." His hands come up and rest

warmly on my thighs. His gaze travels down briefly to my chest and I glance down to see what has caught his attention. My shirt is soaked through and my nipples are pushing hard against the material. When I look back at Flynn, he runs his tongue over his bottom lip while he stares at my breasts.

When he looks back to my eyes, he merely says, "Please" and it's all over for me. I lean forward, bringing my hands to cradle his face. When my lips meet his, his mouth is already open and waiting and my tongue dives straight in. The kiss is instantly molten and desire rockets through my body.

Proving that Flynn's workouts clearly focus on strong abs, he sits straight up, bringing my weight up with him. Without breaking the kiss, he wraps my legs around his waist and pushes me down onto his lap. I'm met with the thick bulge that is pressing against his fly and I can't stop myself when my hips move to run myself against his hardness.

Flynn answers my move by gripping my waist and pushing me down even harder against him, all the while ravaging my mouth. My head is spinning, lost in the sensation of this kiss, the way our hips moving against each other causes moisture to flood between my legs.

Tearing his lips off mine, Flynn pushes his nose into my neck and whispers his lips against me, "Fuck, Rowan… I want you so bad. Tell me you want me, too."

Somewhere—deep down in my brain—something is yelling at me to stop. I push it away from me, refusing to listen. My body is taking over and my brain has no business butting in.

"I do," is all I say and then he's kissing me again.

Flynn's hands grab the bottom of my shirt and he peels it upward. Our faces break apart so he can get the offending material up and over my head. He throws it carelessly aside but rather than kissing me again, he merely leans back and looks at my breasts. Bringing his hand up, he lightly runs his knuckles over the swells and valley. "Christ… you're perfect. Absolutely perfect."

His voice is so reverent I have to close my eyes so I can just revel in it for a moment. No man has ever looked at me with such worship.

My eyes snap open when I realize Flynn has leaned forward and flicked his tongue over my nipple. I gasp in surprise and pleasure. He peeks up at me with a mischievous smile, his hazel eyes barely showing through his lashes, and places his lips back against my breast.

"You're so responsive," he says, while his lips graze my skin. It causes a ripple of pleasure to shoot through me. I've never been this reactive with a man before, but with the barest of touches or a few sensual words, my body almost explodes in pleasure.

I remember the dream I had about Flynn—the orgasm that fired through me with him just kissing behind my knee, and I realize that I'm responsive to Flynn because there is a deeper connection there than any I've ever felt before.

It is born of a relationship that was forged under very unique circumstances, and then cemented due to the fact that Flynn is a genuine soul. He's been about the most perfect friend I could ever wish for.

And that thought douses me with cold water. Because it all comes flooding back to me. Flynn is my friend, and that is all I want him to be.

Right?

Yes, right. That is all he can be. If we make this sexual, then friendship is excluded. I think that is the way things work, at least to my limited knowledge.

Even though Flynn's mouth is working at my nipple and I want nothing more than him to fuck me into oblivion, the voice in my head is now screaming so loud, I can't ignore it.

Grabbing Flynn's head, I gently push him away.

"I'm sorry," I say, as I scrabble up from his lap. Grabbing my t-shirt, I hold it in front of me. I look down into Flynn's confused expression. "I can't do this."

Then I turn and run for my bedroom.

CHAPTER 14
Flynn

I'M SITTING IN the driveway outside of my parents' house. We're having an impromptu family dinner to which I invited Rowan, but she declined. It's been a tiny bit awkward between us for the last few weeks, and I'm awash in frustration.

Closing my eyes, I lean back against the headrest and think of the kiss we shared in the kitchen. It was filled with as much passion as the first kiss but with added sexual intensity. There is no doubt in my mind that we were headed for a full-blown fuck-a-thon when Rowan pulled away from me.

When I think about the look she had on her face, my stomach twists into a painful knot. It was filled with longing and sadness but even worse, there was fear.

I followed her back to her bedroom to find her sitting on her bed, hands by her side, head hanging down. She had put the wet t-shirt back on and didn't look up when I walked in.

"Rowan… what's wrong?" I had asked.

She shook her head, refusing to meet my eyes. Not to be deterred, I stepped right up to her and knelt at her feet. Placing my hands on her knees, I asked again, "Please tell me what's wrong. Did I do something to upset you?"

I held my breath while I waited for her answer, because honestly, the only thing I could think of—the most terrible thought that was running through my head—was that Rowan had suffered from some type of sexual trauma.

Her eyes met mine and they were still sad, but there was no longer fear there. I'm assuming because there wasn't an ounce of sexual tension between us right at the time. "No, you didn't do anything wrong."

"Did I misread your signals?" I asked, wanting to know fully why she pulled away.

Again, she shook her head. "I wanted you as much as you wanted me."

"Then what's wrong?"

Rowan brought her hands up and placed them over mine. She looked at me with such sincerity I knew that whatever she was getting ready to lay on me would be a belief so rooted into her very fiber, that there would be no swaying her from it.

"Flynn," she said, her voice filled with resolve. "I can't risk my friendship with you. Turning this into something sexual would do that. It would ruin our friendship and frankly, you're the first real friend I've ever had. I don't want to lose that."

"But it wouldn't—" I started to insist but she cut me off.

"It would. Things always change when sex is involved."

They get better, I wanted to shout at her. *It would be fucking fantastic if we could build this relationship higher.*

But Rowan wasn't having any of it. She just leaned forward and laid a very chaste kiss on my cheek, and murmured, "I'm sorry. But I can't."

Rowan woke up the following morning, and greeted me with exuberance. She chattered away about being excited to start working for Nix, and that we were out of laundry detergent but that she'd pick some up on the way home, and that she appreciated me looking out for Capone during the day while she was gone. It's like nothing had ever transpired between us and the kiss was forgotten.

The only small measure of satisfaction I got was from throwing the friend card out and slapping her in the face with it. We had a small argument the next morning when she got ready to leave. I grabbed my keys off the counter and tossed them at her.

"Take my car," I had said.

She caught them deftly and then tossed them right back. "No way. I'm taking public transit."

"Rowan," I warned, tossing the keys back to her, "as your *friend*, I am offering you my car and saving you forty-five minutes on your commute. Don't be an ass—be a friend. Just take the damn car."

She caught the keys and opened her mouth to argue, but then she snapped it shut. "Fine. But I'm filling your car up with gas each week."

"Fine," I muttered and turned away to go take a shower.

Opening my eyes, I look out the windshield to my parents' house. I'm looking forward to seeing everyone so I need to shake off my morose thoughts. I need to accept things the way they are between Rowan and me.

She's absolutely right. We have a great friendship, and while I've known the joys of close friends throughout my life, I'm honored that I'm her one true friend.

The only problem is, I want to be more than friends, and I know she does too… she's just too scared to take the risk.

♦

"HOW'S IT GOING with your new roommate, Flynn?"

I swallow the last bite of apple pie before I answer my mom. "Going great. We get along well."

And I want to get her naked and worship her body for hours on end, but I don't voice those thoughts out loud.

"Next time we get together, you have to bring her."

I smile as I relish the faint Irish lilt my mom still bears, even though she's lived in the States for the last twenty-seven years. Nora Caldwell, with her fiery red hair and vivid green eyes, is forever gracious and has always opened up our family home to my friends.

"I will, Mom," I assure her, hoping she drops the subject.

"Nix told us all about how you met her." This from Nick Caldwell, my dad.

I glare over at Nix, who is staring hard at his empty plate. Emily is sitting next to him and tries to suppress a grin.

"He did, did he?"

"It's kind of romantic, don't you think?" my mom asks.

Still glaring at Nix, I answer, "We're just friends, Mom. Nothing more."

"Oh," my mom says, clearly disappointed I haven't found the love of my life yet. Although who knows if that's Rowan. She won't give me the time of day to see if we can have more than a friendship.

Nix raises his head up and catches my glare, which is still aimed his way. He does nothing more than give me a smirk before he says, "Well… Emily and I have some news."

Everyone goes silent and turns to stare at them. They had gotten engaged a few months ago while visiting Linc and Ever in Phoenix. I assume we're getting ready to hear about their wedding plans, and I'm not disappointed.

"We've decided against a big, formal wedding. In fact, we only want our immediate family attending. And we want to do it on December 25th because Linc only has a small break in his season where he can come."

Everyone breaks into talk around the table, excited that the date has been set and it's a little less than three months away. Nix holds his hands up to get everyone's attention. "There's one more detail I need to mention. We're going to have it in the U.S. Virgin Islands… St. John to be exact."

"Oh, a destination wedding," my mom says as she clasps her hands to her chest, her eyes getting misty.

"Don't cry, Aunt Nora," Nix says as he steps from his chair and gives her a hug.

I smile at Nix's uncharacteristic display of affection. It comes so easy to him nowadays and it's a damn sight better than the grumpy-ass attitude he wore after returning from the war.

Once Nix rose up from his chair, it was like open season. We all stand up, pushing our chairs back, and hugs and kisses are passed around in congratulations.

I step up to Nix and we clasp hands, pulling each other in for a manly hug/back-slap combo.

"I'm happy for you, man."

Nix looks over at Emily, who is standing there with

her arm wrapped around Uncle Hank's waist. "I'm a lucky guy."

The tenderness in his eyes pangs my heart, and I feel envious. I want to look at someone like that.

Emily glances over at Nix and gives him a smile. It is full of love and devotion.

"Emily is a lucky girl," I tell him.

"She's my everything," he says, and my green-eyed monster starts roaring. I'm still able to pull out a happy smile for Nix as I head over to Nix's dad and Emily to give my congratulations.

Emily steps into a hug. After giving her a squeeze, I turn to Uncle Hank and clap him on the back. "You're losing your babies," I tell him.

Uncle Hank chuckles but then looks over at Emily. "Nope. I'm gaining a daughter and a damn fine one at that."

It tickles me but Emily blushes a pretty pink over the compliment. She gives him another hug. "And I'm gaining another dad."

"Okay, you two," I say. "You're making me sick. Stop it already."

Uncle Hank chuckles. "You'll understand it one day, Flynn. When you find that someone. Everything changes."

God, I hope so. I really do.

"So, Emily… have you already talked to Linc and

Ever?"

"Yeah, we had to find out when Linc could make it before we finalized the date. He has a game against the Sabres on the 23rd and he'll fly out that night to St. John. Then he has to be back in Phoenix on the 28th."

I nod in understanding. Linc's schedule is crazy during the NHL season. "What about Renner? Have you talked to her?"

Emily shakes her head. "We were going to call her in the morning. It's past midnight there."

My sister, Renner, lives in Dublin with her rock star boyfriend, Cillian. "You don't give my sis enough credit," I admonish Emily. "She's living the rock-star life. She'll be up."

Pulling my phone out of my pocket, I hold it up to Emily and ask, "Do you mind?"

She smiles and shakes her head. "Go for it. She can yell at you for waking her up."

I hit Renner's name from my Favorite list where she resides at the top because my sister is my most favorite person in the world. I talk to her a few times a week in addition to almost daily texts because, hey, I'm her brother and I worry about her. I don't know this Cillian dude very well and although he seems to make her happy, it's my duty as an older and over-protective brother to make sure she stays that way.

The phone rings four times before Renner answers.

Her voice is heavy with sleep. "This better be good, Flynn, or I'm going to fly back to Jersey and murder you."

"What the hell are you doing sleeping? Shouldn't you be out partying with Cillian and his band or something?"

Renner lets out a big yawn. "Contrary to popular belief, our life isn't all about sex, drugs, and rock-n-roll. It's just about the sex, and I'm exhausted after the fun Cillian had with me tonight."

"Ewwww, Renner. TMI. I don't need to know that shit."

"Well, then quit calling me at ungodly hours. I'm cranky," she snaps back.

We're silent a moment and then we both start laughing, her giggles ringing through like a charming melody.

"So, why did you call, O brother o'mine?"

"We just got done having a family dinner and Nix and Emily announced their wedding plans. I wanted to make sure that you and Cillian could come. It's going to be on December 25th in St. John."

Renner lets out a high-pitched squeal and I hear Cillian yelling, "What the fuck's wrong?" I have a clear mental image of him sitting straight up in bed, looking around in a panic.

Renner whispers a, "Sorry babe. Go back to sleep. I'll tell you all about it in the morning."

After a moment, she whispers into the phone, "Yes…

we can definitely come. Over The Edge is taking a break from their tour over the holidays."

"Awesome! I can't wait to see you, Ren."

"Same here. So how are things going with the roommate situation?"

I look around the room. Everyone is engaged in conversation, but I don't want anyone to hear what I'm about to say.

"Hold on," I tell her as I walk through the living room and step out onto the front porch. The early October weather is chilly and I'm glad I wore a long-sleeved shirt tonight.

I had told Renner about Rowan. About how I had rescued her, how she came to live at my apartment, and I told her all about Juice. She knows Rowan is living with me on a permanent basis now, but she doesn't know much more than that. I'm thinking I can use some girlie advice right now.

"I could use some guidance… about Rowan."

"Shoot," she says, matter of factly.

"Well… we've become really good friends over the last several weeks. I don't know much about Rowan's background but she says I'm really the first true friend she's ever had."

"Awww. That's so sweet."

"Yeah… my teeth hurt it's so sweet. Quit interrupting."

"Sorry… grump-ass."

"Anyway… we've kissed twice, and it was… well, it was explosive. I mean… we both have an intense attraction to one another."

"But?" she prompts.

"But, last time, we were getting pretty hot and heavy and she pulled away. She stopped it and she said she couldn't go there with me because she didn't want to risk our friendship. She said sex would change everything and she didn't want to lose me as a friend. And it's driving me fucking nuts because I know she wants me the way I want her. And I'm all messed up about it and don't know what to do."

Renner is silent for a moment and I wait for a pearl of wisdom to come through the phone and save my sanity. Instead, she only says, "I'm sorry, Flynn. That sucks."

"That's it? That's all you got for me? Sorry… and it sucks?"

"Well, I get where she's coming from. Sex does change everything. It opens up a whole new level of intimacy, which will naturally bring you closer."

"But that's a good thing, right?"

"Yes, but the consequences if it doesn't work out would be disastrous. You can't go backward to friendship. If you take it to the next level, and it doesn't work out… then it's over. If she cherishes this friendship the way you say she does, then this would be a very scary proposition for her."

"Bullshit," I tell her. "We could still be friends. Besides… why wouldn't it work out? We have a lot in common, and I really like her, Ren. A lot."

"I hear you, Flynn. I'm just saying I get where she's coming from. I think as women, we tend to worry about that stuff more than men do. I mean, let's face it, you probably just want to get in her pants."

That's true… I do want to get into her pants. But fuck, I want so much more. I want someone to be my everything. I've wanted it so bad since Marney died that I can taste it on my lips… and it tastes like ambrosia.

I know Rowan will taste like ambrosia.

"So what should I do?"

"Be her friend, Flynn. That's all you can do, and hope that one day, she'll want you enough to step off the ledge with you."

This just blows. I was hoping my sister would have the magic-ball answer to worm my way into Rowan's heart. And all I get from her is to do nothing but cultivate the friendship.

Well, piss on that, I think to myself. I'm not about to sit back and watch this woman slip further away from me. Friendship isn't good enough, and I intend to get her to the next level.

I'll just make sure I'm subtle about it.

CHAPTER 15

Rowan

"DAMN IT, ROWAN. What the hell did you do to my stockroom?"

I look up from the computer and rub my eyes. I was in invoice hell, and now I'm in Nix hell. Reaching down, I rub Harley's head as he snoozes by my feet. I have a fleeting moment of satisfaction that Nix's dog likes to lay near me. I think it drives Nix nuts that his dog became attached to me so quickly.

Looking over my shoulder, I try to answer with as much calm as I can. "What do you mean?"

"You re-arranged the whole fucking room and I can't find anything. Why did you do that?"

"I put all your supplies in alphabetical order. You didn't have any structure to it and it was driving *me* nuts."

"I did too have structure," he explodes. "I knew exactly where everything was."

"But I didn't," I snap back at him. "And since you expect me to keep your storeroom well stocked, I needed it better organized so I could see when you were getting low on supplies."

"But I can't find anything," he says like a whiny, snot-nosed brat.

"It's not rocket science, Nix. It's alphabetical. You see… there's this concept that's called 'A to Z'," I say slowly. "If you're looking for bolts, just start with the A's and proceed forward. You'll then get to the B's and lo and behold, you'll find the bolts. Geez."

Nix glares at me for a moment and then turns his back, growling in displeasure. I do a happy dance in my head.

Oh, you'd think that Nix and I hate each other based on that display, but quite the opposite. We get along fantastically. We just fight like squabbling siblings. I think, personally, that I provide an outlet to Nix that allows him to be surly and grumpy, an attitude I understand he used to exhibit quite frequently. Emily told me about Nix's time in the Marines and his injuries from the war. I didn't know much about PTSD but Emily explained it all to me, and it made me look at Nix in a different light. It's why I have such extreme patience with him, and why I let him snarl and snap at me most days. It's the least I can do for the sacrifices he made for our country.

"Hey, Nix," I say, opting for a complete change in subject. "What does your shirt mean?"

I had noticed it earlier and had been meaning to ask. It was red with gold lettering that said, *Semper Fi.* I thought it might be the same thing as the tattoos that Flynn had on his biceps.

"It's short for *Semper Fidelis*, which is Latin. It's the Marine Corps slogan. Means, *Always Faithful.*"

"Why does Flynn have them tattooed on his biceps? He wasn't in the Marine Corps, was he?"

Nix shakes his head and walks over to his fridge. He pulls out a beer and holds it up to me, silently asking if I want one. I shake my head and watch as he flops down in his ratty, old recliner, twisting the cap off. After he takes a long swallow, he answers me, "He did it shortly after I came home from Bethesda, where I was recovering from my injuries. He did it to honor me."

I digest that information, and take note of how my heart swells and then pangs for what Flynn did. Honoring his cousin for his sacrifices. And the words clearly have meaning. Flynn is one of those guys that is *always faithful.* It's why he stuck by me, and why he is so well loved by his family and friends. The thought comes unbidden to my mind that he will make a great husband one day, and I'm immediately hit with a flood of jealousy that it won't be me.

I'm jealous because I won't have that chance with him, because I'm too chicken shit to risk my friendship with him. And I'm also jealous of the woman who will one day wear his wedding ring, because I'm all of a sudden fretting that he won't look at me the same way, and won't be my friend anymore. In fact, I've convinced myself that the bitch he marries won't let him have any female friends, and I want to kill this unknown woman that he will marry one day.

"Geez, Page… What in the hell is going through your head? You look like you could murder someone right now."

I shake out of my thoughts. "Nothing. I wasn't thinking about anything."

"Yeah, right. Come on, Page. Lay it on me. I'm done for the day and I feel like gossiping."

"Stop calling me Page," I testily say. "And I don't do gossip sessions. That's for you and your other dork friends that like to sit around and paint each other's toenails a pretty shade of pink."

Nix gives a shout of laughter and lifts his beer to me in salute. "Good one."

I turn around to the computer and start entering invoices again. But Nix isn't through with me.

"So how are things going with you and Flynn?"

My shoulders stiffen involuntarily and I take a deep breath. "Everything's great. Peachy keen."

"You know he's in love with you, right?"

I swivel around in my chair so fast I almost throw myself out of it. "What? What do you mean?"

"You seriously can't be that dense. When you two were over here for dinner last weekend, he could barely keep his eyes off you. But he walks around like a kicked puppy so I assume you don't reciprocate those feelings."

Holy shit. Nix saw all that at dinner? I mean, I saw it… I see it every day and every night I'm around Flynn. I know what his eyes are telling me. They are saying, *I want you but I respect your boundaries.*

I decide to play stupid. "I don't know what you mean."

Nix quirks an eyebrow at me. "Page, you seriously are not that stupid. Give it up. Now. Talk to me, girl."

I shake my head. This chatty Nix is freaking me out. He's never delved into my personal business before but I'll have to admit, over the last few weeks, I've become very comfortable around him.

I have no clue what makes me answer, but I say, "He's not in love. He's in lust."

"Semantics. Love and lust are so closely woven together, they're practically the same for all intents and purposes… at least from the male point of view," Nix says, as he shrugs his shoulders. "It may not be love yet, but he has it bad for you is the point. Don't you feel anything for him?"

Nix's question is honest and sincere, but I never forget for a moment that he is related to Flynn and he is also protecting him. I remember all too clearly how suspicious he was of me when I first started working for him. He even admitted to me that he thought I might be scamming Flynn and that was why he was rude to me when I started.

I take a deep breath, and decide to go all in, because I've kept these feelings bottled up inside of me and maybe this will prevent an explosion. "Of course I feel for him. I feel for him a lot."

"Then act on it."

"I can't," I say lamely. Then I bolster my voice with confidence. "I won't."

Nix takes another sip of beer and looks at me with genuine curiosity. "Why not?"

"Because… I love my friendship with Flynn. It's the best thing that's ever happened to me—in my entire life. I've never met anyone like him, and never will again. I don't want to lose that."

"Why would you think you'd lose it?"

"Because," I tell him, giving him my best, you're-a-doofus look, "everything gets messed up when sex is involved. The friendship will die. He'll only care about me for sex. I've had that… and it's never worked out for me. The friendship is more important than getting my rocks off."

And oh, God… how I know Flynn would get my rocks off. I'm betting he'd launch me so high, I'd orbit the moon. It's a feeling I yearn for badly, but refuse to give in to.

"Rowan," Nix chides me and I know he's serious because he's using my first name. "That's not the way of it. Not all men are like that."

"How would you know?" I snap, because I don't want him to give me any more reason to hope for something I can never have.

"Because I've been there… done that. I was the guy that only wanted to get in the girl's pants, and then I wanted to kick her out the door as soon as possible. I wanted that with Emily when we first hooked up."

"Really?" I ask, suspicious he's feeding me a line.

"Cross my heart. You can ask her. In fact, we agreed on a sex-only, no-emotional-involvement relationship. But it didn't work out that way. Being with Emily… intimately… it opened up my heart to a whole new level of relationship. It strengthened my friendship with her. It made me want to help her, protect her, and love her even more. Sex doesn't always kill things. It can strengthen… with the right person."

"But how do I know Flynn is the right person? I mean, maybe he's only destined to be a good friend to me."

"Maybe he's destined to be so much more," Nix counters.

Yes… maybe.

I look Nix squarely in the eye. "But it's not a risk I'm

willing to take. Maybe isn't good enough me."

♦

WHEN I GET back to the apartment, I take Capone on a long walk. Flynn had to go back into work today for another three-day shift and he left a note telling me he did all the laundry for both of us. My heart swells up in gratitude over his simple kindness. For someone that hasn't been able to rely or count on anyone but herself for the past five years, I find a simple act such as that to be overwhelmingly endearing. I wish he were here so I could hug him, and I smile at the new Rowan.

Old Rowan was most definitely not a hugger.

I feed Capone and change into Flynn's t-shirt. I have the apartment all to myself so I don't bother with his gym shorts.

I'm restless, I don't feel like watching TV, and I'm not much of a reader. So I boot up Flynn's laptop. He told me I could use it any time, and I rarely take him up on the offer unless I'm scanning the news headlines.

Pulling up Google, I type into the search field "John Cleeden". Too many results pop up, along with a bazillion ads for Ancestry.com. I clear the search and type in "John Cleeden Lewisville, Texas". I'm immediately rewarded for what I was looking for.

And I settle in to torture myself.

The first article is entitled "Esteemed Judge Rules In

Landmark Trade Dispute". I don't bother reading the details because I've read it before and have no desire to read it again. Trade disputes just aren't my thing.

The next result reads "Charity Auction Yields Highest Result With Judge's Donation". It's an older article but I click on the link and stare at the picture before me. It's of a tall, distinguished man who I know to be currently seventy-one years of age. His hair is dark with silver at the temples, but that is about the only thing that belies his true age. He is fit and looks to be in excellent shape. His arm is around the waist of a petite woman, also with dark hair. I know her to be forty-five.

Hello, Mom and Dad.

The article goes on to extol the virtues of The Honorable John Cleeden, District Court Judge, and how his donation of $50,000 put the Kid Strong Foundation over their million-dollar goal for the year.

My dad is looking serious in the picture, and I believe it's because he truly doesn't know how to smile. My mom, however, is showing her pearly whites, eager to be in front of the camera, I'm sure.

I search their faces, trying to see if there is anything lurking there that would indicate how they feel about me. They don't look like two people that have a missing daughter. While my dad doesn't look overly thrilled to have his picture taken, they certainly don't look forlorn or look to be in despair.

It's as I thought. They don't think of me at all, and even though I torture myself with this game every now and then, it never diminishes the hurt I feel.

Going back to the Google search field, I type in Anne Marie Cleeden. It returns 178,000,000 hits. I narrow it down… Anne Marie Cleeden, Texas. Three hundred and forty-eight results appear. I scan the first page, searching for the words I long to read.

Parents Search For Missing Daughter

Hope Still Alive For Texas Couple Searching For Daughter

Esteemed Judge Hopeful Daughter Is Alive.

Page after page I search but it yields me nothing. My parents aren't looking for me. They could care less whether I'm alive or dead.

It's what I should expect.

When I left home at the tender age of eighteen, withering under my parents' lack of interest in me, my dad told me. He warned me well.

He said if I left, I would never be welcomed back. He said I'd be as good as dead to them, and apparently, I was.

CHAPTER 16

Flynn

"OKAY… NOW REACH in and start pulling out the guts."

Rowan looks at me with only a small level of disgust on her face. "It smells horrible."

"Stop being a baby and start gutting. Pretend those are Juice's innards," I tell her, throwing a grin over my clever idea.

She looks beautiful tonight with her hair pulled up in a ponytail and her face scrubbed of all makeup. She's wearing an old Steely Dan t-shirt and faded jeans with holes in the knees. Casual and sexy at the same time.

Rowan grins back at me and dives in with both hands. Pulling out a huge glop of pumpkin guts, she throws it on the newspaper covering the table and says, "Take that you, bastard!"

I laugh out loud. "You tell him!"

She reaches back in and pulls out another handful. It hits the table hard and splatters on me a bit. "That's for kidnapping me."

Rowan pulls a third handful out. "That's for chaining me to the bed," she yells with a silly smile on her face.

Splat! The guts hit the table again and a few pumpkin seeds fall to the floor. Capone walks over and sniffs them with interest.

"Rock on, girl," I encourage her.

She plunges back in, pulling out a huge pile and slams it on the newspaper. "And that's for having your thugs attack my bestie, Flynn."

I chuckle over her antics, happy to see that she can find something to laugh about. "That was probably the best therapy you could ever do to move past Juice."

We both share a secret smile over that, continuing to work on our pumpkins. Then our chuckles die down and we work in silence for a while.

Rowan had brought these stupid pumpkins home and said she wanted to carve them for Halloween, which is less than a week away. I didn't particularly care to do it, because I think it's a useless holiday, but her enthusiasm was infectious and here we now stand, shoulder to shoulder, mutilating these poor cucurbits.

Stepping back to survey our now empty pumpkin shells, I ask, "What do we do with all the innards?"

"Well, I read online that we can roast them."

We stare at the huge pile of pulp and seeds on the table, then look at each other. At the same time, we both shake our head, and say, "Nah."

"I'm too lazy to do it," Rowan says.

"Me too."

I gather all the corners of the newspapers, rounding the entire pumpkiny mess up, and toss it in the garbage. Rowan lays fresh newspaper under our shells and we both give our hands a scrubbing in the sink.

"So… now what?"

She hands me back my knife, holding the blade and presenting me with the handle. "Now we carve."

I'm not much of an artist and I don't have the patience to skillfully chip away at the pumpkin, so I opt for the classic triangle eyes and nose. Glancing over at Rowan, I see she's trying something a bit more exotic. Her pumpkin's eyes have a cat-like slant to them with delicately arched eyebrows.

I'm impressed.

"Nix told me what your tattoos mean."

The statement comes out of left field and for a second, I have no clue what she's talking about. Then I understand.

"Always faithful," I confirm.

"He told me you did it to honor him."

I nod, jabbing my pumpkin in the left eye. "In hindsight, it's kind of silly. I mean, how do you ever really honor someone like Nix for what he did, right?"

"Oh, I don't think it's silly at all. I think having

those words inked on you is beautiful. I think the words also fit you perfectly."

Surprised, my eyes fly upward to meet hers. They are gray pools of warm mercury, swirling with tenderness and affection, and the look hits me hard. I've been spending weeks with Rowan, vacillating between wanting to fuck her and wanting to cultivate this friendship that she puts such stock in.

But this look she's giving me now? It makes me want it all… badly. It makes me ache with desire to just hold her, not in a friendly fashion, but not in a sexual fashion. I want to hold her intimately, and have her pour out all of her pain to me. I want to take care of her, covet her, and make everything in her life better. Not because I think she's broken, but because she makes me a better person and I want to honor that.

"So what else did you and Nix talk about?" I ask, averting my eyes so hopefully this overwhelming need to sink into her goes away.

She's silent for a moment but then she says, "He said you were in love with me?"

My eyes fly up to hers again, and there is the sadness and the fear I saw before. "And what did you think about that?"

"I told him you were just in lust with me," she says with a bitter smile on her face.

"Hmmm," I muse. "Is there a difference?"

Rowan shrugs her shoulders. "Nix doesn't seem to think so. He says it's a man-thing."

I watch as Rowan continues to push her knife into the pumpkin, twisting it slightly to chip small pieces out. She looks strong and vulnerable all at the same time and I have no control over what I do next.

Reaching a hand out, I smooth it along her face and cup her behind her head. She's surprised by the touch, and instinctively turns to look at me, allowing me to grip her neck. "I want to kiss you, Rowan."

I pull her closer and she doesn't fight me… at first.

But as soon as my mouth is just inches from hers, her hands sneak up to push against my chest. "Stop, Flynn."

My chest constricts painfully over her denial but I don't release her. She doesn't push me farther away either.

I look at her… deeply… intently. "Rowan… why? There's a connection here. You feel it, right?"

She quickly nods her head to assure me. "Yes… I feel it like the sun… it's warm and encompassing. But I'm too afraid. I just can't."

I release her suddenly, needing the physical distance. Taking a few steps back, I lean against the counter, placing my hands on the edge by my hips. "Then explain it to me… again. Let's talk about it. Let's see if we can figure something out."

I think she's going to balk for just a second, because

Rowan isn't exactly known for her openness. However, she pulls the kitchen chair out from the table and sits down with a sigh, laying her carving knife down in front of her.

"My dad is a judge—very well known, highly respected. My mom is a socialite, also well known, probably not as respected since she was a trophy wife for him. He's twenty-six years her senior."

I don't say anything but walk up and pull the other chair out, sitting down across from her. She continues.

"My dad was, I think, like around forty-eight when they had me, and frankly, I don't think he was interested in having kids. He was well on his way to a successful career on the bench and his career was everything. But my mom was young and wanted them, so he gave in."

"So you probably grew up in a pretty posh lifestyle, right?"

"Yup, although judges don't make as much as you think they do. My mom is the one that had family money. Her family are ranchers… cattle mostly, but they are very successful at it. At any rate, growing up was okay. My dad paid no attention to me, and while my mom did at first, over the years even that faded away. She was never able to get pregnant again, and she filled her time by playing tennis and having lunch with her lady friends at the country club."

Rowan pauses and gives me a sly grin. "Do you know

what happens to a teen girl who gets no attention from her parents?"

"You rebel," I answer, because that's an obvious answer.

"That's right. And boy, did I rebel. I was drinking and doing drugs by the time I was fifteen. I lost my virginity at that same age. I came home shit-faced that night, and bragged about it to my parents. Told them how Sam Cantor popped my cherry in the back seat of his daddy's Lexus. I used that exact wording."

"What did they do?" I ask, slightly horrified. I couldn't ever imagine doing something like that and bragging about it to my parents. But then again, my parents doted on Renner and me. We never lacked for their attention.

"My dad just looked at me… but it was like he was looking right through me, you know? And he said, 'I'm sorely disappointed, young lady'. Then he turned to my mom and said, 'You need to handle this outburst, Susan. I can't have this shit marring my public image'. He walked away and never mentioned the incident to me again."

"What did your mom do?"

Rowan gives out a little laugh, filled with bitter humor. "She at least took a little time with me. She asked me to please behave so I didn't disappoint my father, and also wanted to make sure I was practicing safe sex."

"That was it? You didn't get in any trouble?" I'm astounded her parents would ignore that. If it were my daughter, she would have been grounded until she was twenty-five at least.

"That was it."

"I take it that didn't satisfy your need to have your parents pay attention to you?" My words come out hard, because I'm angry as shit at them for driving their daughter to do those things, and not having enough interest to make her take responsibility.

"No. It didn't satisfy it. I became even worse, trying to get them to notice me. I started dressing Goth… died my hair black, wore black lipstick, got an eyebrow ring. Nothing. They didn't say a word, although my dad wouldn't take me with them to any functions where cameras were involved. So I became even more removed from them. Then I started really acting out. I would come to the dining table drunk or high. I'd say outrageous things to try to provoke a reaction."

"Like what?" I'm genuinely curious how far she would go—how bad she was hurting for their love.

Rowan actually gives a girlish giggle and I'm glad that her past trauma hasn't caused her complete bitterness and hate. "Once, while we were eating breakfast, I was pissed because my dad just sat there with the newspaper in front of his face. So I announced to my mom that I was thinking about getting my clit pierced."

"Holy fuck. You did not?"

"I did too," she says with a huge grin.

"Holy fuck," I say again in amazement. "What did your dad do?"

He didn't even drop the newspaper. He just said, 'Susan, please get your daughter under control.' He didn't even sound mad. Just annoyed."

"His choice of words is interesting… 'your daughter'."

Rowan nods. "That didn't slip past me. In fact, I actually wondered if maybe my mom had gotten pregnant by someone else, but that's not something I ever figured out."

"So, what caused you to leave? You said you left about five years ago, right?"

"I finally got my parents' attention." Her words come out as a mere whisper and she lowers her gaze to the floor. The hair stands up on the back of my neck.

I can't help myself. I lean forward and reach over to grab one of her hands. I hold it gently in between mine, noticing that her skin feels like ice. While my palm tries to warm the outside of her hand, my thumb slowly strokes over the inside, trying to offer her a measure of security.

She looks up at me, and there are no tears in her eyes. Just pain. Pure, unfiltered pain and I feel like I want to vomit.

"You can tell me anything, Rowan. Anything."

She nods. "A few weeks after I graduated high school, I was out with friends. We were drunk, high… We were out of our minds. And the funny thing was, I really don't think that night I was even thinking about trying to get my parents' attention. I just was having fun. At any rate, we decided to break into a house in my neighborhood. I knew the people were out of town because they were friends with my parents. We trashed the house good… I'm talking spray painted the walls, cut up the mattresses, gouged up all the furniture…"

She trails off and there is a smile on her face as she's lost in the memory. It's not a smile that says she's happy in the memory. It's actually a shameful smile, one she's forcing herself to wear.

"And you got caught?" I guessed.

"Oh yeah," she says. "We got caught big time. Neighbors heard the racket and called the cops. We all got arrested. That finally got my dad's attention. I mean… a judge's kid getting caught doing that shit?"

"What did he do?"

"After he bailed me out? Well, he took me home and sat me down in his study. And for the first time I can ever remember, he lectured me. He talked for probably an hour on what a rotten child I was. How I was an embarrassment—an abomination. That he regretted the day my mom got pregnant with me, because I had been nothing but a thorn in his side. He told me that this behavior was stopping now, or he would disown me… cut me off without a penny. He was finally putting his foot down with me. And at first, I was just happy. Happy that he was paying attention. But then I really started listening to his words, and I started getting angry."

"Because they weren't the words you needed," I observe. She needed her parents to tell her they loved her and that they were interested in her.

"No… they weren't the words I needed. I was so furious. I told him that I didn't need his money and I didn't need him, or my mom for that matter. I walked out of his study, went to my room, and packed a bag. I had some money saved up that basically bought me a bus ticket to New York. I walked out and didn't look back."

"Did he try to stop you? Did your mom?"

Rowan shakes her head. "No. He held the front door open for me. My mom stood there behind him, worrying at the pearls around her throat. I think she wanted to say something, but she never did. Just as I walked out the door, he told me I'd never make it on my own and that I wouldn't be welcome back. I heard the snick of the lock after he closed the door behind me." She pauses a second and a ghostly smile appears. "Funny… how loud the sound of the lock turning was… I can still hear it in my head so clearly."

I just stare at Rowan, completely heartsick for her. I want to pull her onto my lap and hug the sadness out of her. But she won't accept it… I can tell. Instead, I pull her hand to my mouth and lay a short kiss on her palm before I release it.

"But look at you now," I tell her. "Look how you survived… look how strong you are."

She stares at me, almost blankly. "You think?"

"I don't think… I *know*. You're amazing, Rowan. You proved your dad wrong and you have turned into a hell of a woman. And you did it despite what they did to you."

Rowan shakes her head, her beautiful hair glinting as it swings back and forth. "No, Flynn. Don't you see? I'm not worthy of love. History has proven it. It's why I can only do a friendship with you. Anything more is going to turn to shit… I just know it."

"That's bullshit, Rowan. You're smarter than that, and you're stronger than that. I can't believe you're afraid of the risk."

She tilts her head to the side and looks at me with curiosity. "Why do you have such faith in me?"

"Because I know a little something about heartache and how events that happen to us can shape and define us. I know what it's like to be a little warped by the past, but I also know what it takes to try to overcome it."

"Tell me," she whispers, and I have no choice but to

bare my soul to her, the way she just did to me.

I take a deep breath and let it out slowly.

Then I tell her about Marney. I don't leave out any detail, including the fact that Marney's death led me to my career as a firefighter. I'm as honest as I can be, and I even tell her that my hero complex can get in the way sometimes, that is drives me to fix broken things. I admit to her that my hero complex kicked into overdrive and that is why I sought to help her out originally.

When I finish, she's looking at me with a look of profound sadness. "Don't you see, Flynn? You just proved my point. You think I'm broken… that's the only reason you want to be close to me. You want to fix me, and I'm here to tell you… I can't be fixed."

"No," I deny. "Maybe at first, but not now. You're the most capable woman I know. There's not a thing about you I'd fix… except maybe your fear of taking risks. I'm hoping we can work on that though… together."

Rowan stands from the table and scoots the chair back in. "I'm sorry, Flynn. I can't do it. I know the pain of rejection and I know what it is like to want someone to love you desperately. So desperately, you slice yourself up in the process of trying to achieve that love. I don't have it in me to be hurt like that again, and if there's one thing I know… it's that you, Flynn… you have the power to destroy me if I had your love and then lost it.

I'm just not brave enough to want it the way you do."

I watch as Rowan walks out of the kitchen but I don't make a move to stop her. It's for the best because after what she just said, words are failing me.

CHAPTER 17

Rowan

IT'S THE FIRST week of November and we are having unseasonably cold weather for this time of the year. I'm waiting for Flynn to finish getting dressed because we're taking Capone out to the park. I've got on a heavy wool coat I just bought last week on sale, along with a pretty, red knit scarf to wrap around my neck. It was a splurge for me, but I wanted to buy something for myself with my recent earnings and a coat seemed practical. Especially since winter was approaching and I didn't have anything except that beat-up, old leather jacket.

"I'm ready," Flynn says and I turn around to see him walking toward me.

It never ceases to amaze me the way my pulse thumps like a Texas jackrabbit's leg when I see him. He looks like he just stepped out of a fashion spread for Ralph Lauren with his dark brown cords, cream, cable-knit sweater, and a caramel-colored, wool coat that he slips on and turns the collar up to ward against the cold. His hair looks like he just got out of bed, but, strangely, it works for him. As he approaches, I catch a whiff of cologne. It's subtle but I smell sandalwood and citrus, and it suits Flynn to perfection.

"Don't you have a scarf or something?" I ask.

He gives me a look of horror and scoffs. "Real men don't wear scarfs."

"Fine," I tell him. "But don't complain when your neck gets cold."

"Real men never complain," he counters as he winks at me.

I snicker as I reach over to attach the leash to the New York Jets collar that Flynn had bought for Capone last month.

Figures.

We head over to a small park that is about seven blocks away and we aren't thirty feet from the apartment when I realize I forgot my gloves.

I hand the leash over to Flynn. "Here… you walk Capone. My hands are freezing."

He takes the leash from me and I jam my hands in my coat pockets.

"Do you want my gloves?" he asks.

"Nah. Real women don't wear gloves."

Flynn bumps his shoulder to mine with a laugh. "There is no doubt—you are a real woman, Miss Page."

I bump him back and shoot him a playful smile. "Why, thank you, kind sir."

I find myself loving this new level of companionship that Flynn and I have settled into since our serious talk last month. We both opened ourselves up and let it all hang out.

And while there was plenty of stuff that was probably left unsaid, the important things that needed to be said were voiced. Flynn now understands the root of my fears, and he now understands why I just can't pursue anything more than a friendship with him. He hasn't pushed or pressured me in the slightest since our talk, but has managed to be nothing more than a true friend to me.

The friendship has been amazing and we actually hang out together all the time. Since telling Flynn about my parents, a secret I haven't shared with anyone, I find myself able to tell him just about anything. I can do so without fear of judgment and the most important thing that is happening is that we are building trust with each other.

For example, just the other day, I started my period and asked Flynn to run to the store to grab me some tampons. I had to bite down on my tongue not to giggle over the look on his face. But then he manned up and said he'd be happy to. When he returned from the corner market, he handed them to me and said, "Next time I get myself in a situation, and need condoms… you're going down to the store to get them for me."

I laughed and said, "Sure thing", but there's no way

in hell I'm ever buying him condoms. I must be the world's most terrible person because while I won't let Flynn get into my pants, I don't want him to get in any other woman's pants either.

I'm twisted, for sure.

"Want some coffee or something?" Flynn asks as we walk toward a street vendor.

"Hot chocolate would be good. My treat."

"Cool. Make it two."

See, that is proof right there that the friendship thing is working. Before our talk, Flynn would have insisted on paying, which would have felt more like a date to me and moving squarely out of the friendship scenario. But Flynn letting me buy him something, that right there proves this friendship is working just fine.

We get our drinks and head toward the park. I choose to wait before drinking mine after I watch Flynn burn the shit out of his tongue when he takes a sip.

"So my mom called today and wanted me to officially invite you to the Caldwell Thanksgiving Day Extravaganza."

"Oooohhh," I exclaim. "It sounds magnificent. What all is involved in a Caldwell Extravaganza?"

"Well, let's see. There's food… then football… then naps. I think that's about it."

I laugh, particularly at the mental image of Flynn, Nix, and their dads passed out in the living room with the football game blaring.

"I don't want to impose."

"Rowan," Flynn says in warning. "Friends don't let friends eat a microwave turkey dinner on Thanksgiving. Besides… Tim will be there. You know my parents open the door to everyone."

It's true. I've been over to their house twice with Flynn, and Nick and Nora Caldwell are two of the most gracious and welcoming people I have ever met. They're the type of people that expect you to come into their house and plop your feet up on the coffee table, or they expect you to feel comfortable enough to get whatever you want from the fridge if you're hungry or thirsty. They have no walls built around them, and their hearts are filled with generosity.

I can only imagine what Thanksgiving would be like with the Caldwells. There will be plenty of good food, lots of laughter, and probably some naps when it's all said and done.

"And Capone can come, too," Flynn throws in to entice me further, but I'd already decided to accept.

"Okay. We're in. Can you ask your mom what I can bring?"

"I'll ask but I know she'll say 'don't bring a thing but yourself'."

I laugh over Flynn's impersonation of his mom's Irish accent. "In that case, don't bother asking and I'll just bring something. Maybe a pie."

"You can cook?" Flynn asks with astonishment.

"Of course I can cook," I tell him with indignation.

"Then how come all we ever have is pizza or bologna sandwiches when it's your turn to cook?"

"Just because I can cook, doesn't mean I want to. This is the twenty-first century pal… get with the times. Women have shed the chains of slavery and we no longer serve you menfolk."

Flynn throws his head back and starts howling with laughter, then he pitches forward, holding the hand with Capone's leash to his stomach while he laughs, with the other holding onto his hot cocoa. It's infectious and I start laughing along with him.

He looks at me and our eyes meet.

Then it happens… there is almost a crackle in the air, like electricity is flowing between us. Flynn's laughter immediately dies away and the smile slides from my face. The same happens to me and nothing is left in our expressions except a focused intensity on each other. It's almost as if I can feel heat swirling all around us, and the backdrop of the world fades to black.

Until nothing is left but just Flynn and me.

I call it "The Happening" and it represents those few times when the resolve to just be friends seems to melt away into oblivion. It occurs at the weirdest of times and I have no control over it. When I'm in that moment with

Flynn, I want nothing more than for him to grab me and kiss me like I was the oxygen his lungs crave. I want to strip him bare and use just my fingertips to trace every inch of skin on his body. I want to get lost… *deeply* lost, in Flynn.

"The Happening" hits Flynn just as hard as it hits me. I see the desire light him up from within. I feel the sexual tension pouring off him with visceral awareness, and I swear I can feel his heart moaning for me.

When "The Happening" occurs, I am powerless to fight it. In fact, if Flynn ever made a move to touch me during the event, I would completely submit to him body and soul. But thankfully, Flynn is a stronger person than I am, and he is clearly the more responsible of the two of us. He'll usually snap out of it first, and bring me crashing back to reality.

Like he does right at this moment.

Reaching out with his hand, he tweaks my nose. "You're adorable when you start spouting your feminist viewpoints."

I blink my eyes hard, still a little under his spell, and offer him a smile. He gives me one back that is sad and understanding all at once. To lighten the mood, he takes my hand, tucks it into the crook of his arm, and starts walking again. My feet have no choice but to move and keep up with him. He starts chattering about his Fantasy Football League… something innocuous that will make my mind… my heart… my body, forget about "The Happening".

He is always looking out for me.

My heart swells up, huge and pulsing, with Technicolor love for him.

Yes… I love Flynn. He is my dearest friend in all the world.

And I will have to be satisfied with that.

♦

"WHATCHA DOING?" FLYNN asks as he plops down on the couch beside me. I have his laptop open and he leans in to look at the screen. It never even occurs to me to hide what I'm doing so I turn it a little so he can see it better.

"I'm doing a torture session."

He just looks at me with one eyebrow raised.

Turning the laptop back toward me so I can type, I enter in new search terms, and when the results are displayed, I turn the screen toward him. I watch as he skims his eyes down the screen, and I notice how long and thick his lashes are from this angle. Why I never noticed it before is beyond me.

"Who's John Cleeden?"

I click on the article about the charity donation and when the picture appears, I point at it. "Meet my mom and dad."

Flynn's head snaps toward me and his eyes are soft as he holds my gaze. I give him a quick smile and point back toward the screen.

He reads the entire article and then looks back to me. "John and Susan Cleeden? Where does Page come from?"

"Rowan Page isn't my real name. It's Anne Marie Cleeden."

"You're kidding?"

"Nope."

He surveys me closely and even runs his eyes down my body. I can't help the tingle of awareness that his gaze brings upon me, even though his look isn't sexual at all. "You don't look like an Anne Marie," he muses.

"And I'm not. My name is Rowan Page now."

"When did you change it?"

"The minute I stepped on the bus that brought me to New York."

"But when did you change it legally?"

"I haven't… never needed to."

"Seriously?"

"Yup."

"How do you get anything done? You don't have a social security number. How do you pay taxes? Or rent an apartment? Have a bank account? How do you even get a driver's license for that matter?"

I'm so enjoying this. The look on Flynn's face is a

mixture of comedic horror and respect. "Well… I've never paid taxes as I'm always paid in cash, including by your dear cousin, Nix. I've never had to sign an apartment lease because the lease has never been in my name and I've never needed a bank account because I've always paid my roommates just my share of expenses. Oh, and I don't have a driver's license."

"You don't have a driver's license?" he asks in disbelief.

"I don't have a driver's license… at least not in Rowan Page's name," I confirm.

"But… you drive my car." He cracks me up because he actually sounds a little affronted.

"Lighten up, serious sally. I haven't been caught, have I? Besides… I technically have a valid Texas license. I just think I may have been required to get a New York license after I moved here."

I shrug my shoulders. Oh, well.

"Criminal!" he accuses me with a pointing finger. "I'm living with a criminal."

I start laughing and assure him with concession, "I know… I really do need to get it done legally at some point. I even got my birth certificate last year just for that reason. I just never got around to doing it."

Flynn is shaking his head in disbelief and wonder. "You are unbelievable, do you know that?"

I close the laptop and lay it on the coffee table. Curling my feet up underneath of me, I turn to face him. "Is that a good unbelievable or a bad unbelievable?"

"It's a good unbelievable. A crazy, wonderful unbelievable. You're not exactly the most law-abiding citizen, but you are amazingly inconceivable and I love that about you."

The blood in my veins sings out with happiness over Flynn's compliment. My heart does a mad dance that he used the "L" word. Peace settles in my heart that I don't have to fight for his attention. That he finds true interest in me, and he likes what he sees.

I know I'm not perfect, and I know I've done things that aren't admirable in the past, but I try to do good. I try to live my life without intentionally hurting others. It would be natural to expect some people to look at me with some measure of disgust because I haven't paid taxes, or because I drive without a license.

But not Flynn. He doesn't admire that behavior but he does admire and like the way I have survived. I'm finally getting validation from someone that I am more than what my father ever believed I would amount to.

Flynn is staring at me with genuine affection twinkling in his eyes. I want to reach my hand out and ruffle his hair with my fingers, trail them down his temple and feel the scruff of his beard along my nerve endings.

I'm in danger of falling prey to "The Happening", and if I do, I am in danger of falling hard for Flynn. I want it… *badly*. But I'm as equally afraid of it. It pulls me left and right, turns me upside down, and ties my stomach in knots. My heart tells me to let go and enjoy the free-fall. But then my brain pulses images of my dad's face as I walked out the door five years ago. I can hear the click of the lock as clear as a bell and my chest seems to cave inward upon itself.

I need space and I start to stand up. Flynn's hand jets out and grabs a hold of my fingertips. "Hey, there was something I wanted to talk to you about."

His face is so serious that my stomach flips. Oh, God… is he kicking me out? Did I do something wrong?

I lower my butt slowly to the couch, afraid of the words that will come out of his mouth once I get settled in. It reminds me of the time that I was trying to teach Capone how to sit. He was so stubborn and didn't want to do it at first. He would lower his butt to the floor at the speed of molasses, staring at me intently. It's like he was waiting to see if I would change my mind before ass met linoleum.

I feel that way now. Maybe Flynn will release my hand and change his mind before my butt hits the cushion.

But no such luck. I sink down and Flynn gives my hand a quick squeeze before he lets go. He angles his body more toward me and flips his arm over the back of the couch.

"So…" he says slow and drawn out, which tells me that he's nervous. "You know Nix and Em are getting married over Christmas in St. John, right?"

"Duh… it's all she talks about when I'm around her. Which reminds me… I better start looking for a gift for them."

"Well… you know it's just for family, but since I'm the only single person attending, Nix and Em said I could invite someone. I was kind of hoping you'd come with me to the wedding."

I know I heard Flynn wrong because I just stare at him, my mouth hanging open. This is wrong on so many levels, but mainly because the minute he invited me, a freakin' fantasy image of him and me kissing on a sandy beach flashed through my mind.

Before I can answer, Flynn says, "And I'm only talking about as friends. I actually thought about asking Tim if he wanted to go… you know, get away for a quick vacation, but then I remembered he'd never leave Sam on Christmas. So I thought about you… because next to Tim… you're my closest friend."

Flynn's words hit the mark and cause me pain at the same time. I'm happy to know he was only asking as a friend, but I can't help that it hurts my feelings just a tad that he considered Tim first.

And being the woman that has repetitively held up a barrier to Flynn's feelings for me, I am one seriously twisted chick to even be offended by that.

Still, it's not possible for me to go. "It sounds great, Flynn. Truly. But I don't have that type of money to spend and before you even open your mouth to offer to pay for my expenses, I just want you to know I'll punch you in the face if you do."

Flynn's mouth was halfway open to argue with me about the expenses but my threat to punch him has it snapping shut.

I stand up from the couch, giving in to the urge I had a few minutes ago… to ruffle Flynn's hair. I reach down and do just that, his eyes burning into me with frustration and affection. "Now, I'm going to go get some sleep. See you in the morning."

I turn away before the brief touch of my hand against Flynn's head induces "The Happening" to occur and content myself to allow my dreams to give me what I really want.

CHAPTER 18

Flynn

TONIGHT IS GOING to be interesting. Emily has talked a group of us into going out to a new nightclub, called Grind. She cooked this up with her roommate, Fil, because both of them love to dance. She wanted Nix to go, who would rather have his right nut cut off, so I got roped into going with him so he would have someone to talk to while Emily and Fil tear the dance floor up.

Of course, I wasn't going to leave Rowan at home by herself. When I told her about it, I expected her to balk because she doesn't seem like the type to go clubbing, but she jumped all over that, even exclaiming, "I love to dance."

That obviously sent my brain into overload with vivid scenes playing out before me of her dancing. I imagine it would be provocative and sexy, and yeah, my dick perks up in interest just thinking about it.

The past several weeks have been amazing in a unique way, just not exactly in the way I want. I've developed a very strong bond with Rowan. She's the first close friend that I've had that was a girl, and Renner doesn't count because she's my sister and a pain in the ass more than fifty percent of the time.

Rowan is never a pain in the ass though. She is always there to listen to me, and even though she is only twenty-three years old, her life experience has made her wise with sharply honed common sense. She's given me advice that has been sound, well thought out, and fair on more than one occasion. She is patient and thoughtful, and my day brightens when I'm in her presence.

Best of all, I have watched Rowan morph into an amazingly confident and self-possessed woman. It's not that she wasn't confident before, because she was. But it was a confidence that was bordered with sharp angles and deep edges. It was built from a tough life and by being rejected by her parents. Rather than breaking her down, her dad's final rejection of her emboldened her to become everything he said she would not be.

And she survived.

But Rowan's new confidence is something to behold. It's softer, and it's bright. It comes from deep inside a woman who has decided to let go of her misery and forge a new path. I truly believe that has come about after Rowan opened up and told me about her parents and their lack of affection or interest.

Now, while the past several weeks have been spectacular as I build a solid friendship with Rowan, I feel absolutely empty at times because I want so much more. I want to take this friendship we have, and I want to build on it. I want to take it to the next level, and yes, that means I want to make love to her.

I believe she wants it too, and I truly believe she will come around. I only have to wait until that day when she can trust fully that it's okay to take the risk.

So I am patient.

Now, when Rowan steps out of her bedroom and I see how she's dressed to go clubbing, I don't know that I am so patient. In fact, all the resolve that I have been manifesting in respecting her friendship barrier seems to be disappearing at this very moment.

She's got on a black and white dress that fits her body like a glove, and it's the first time that I've actually ever seen her body outlined in such sharp relief. The top portion of the dress has thick, black stripes across her breasts, which only serves to draw my eye to the deep cleavage she's showing. Thin, black straps hold the dress onto her shoulders, and she's got it all topped off with some killer black heels that have little straps that wrap around her ankles.

I try to stop myself but I cannot help the way my eyes travel slowly up and down her body. If my dad were here right now, he'd knock me up against the back of my head for the way my gaze is molesting her. When I reach her eyes, she's looking at me with amusement, which shakes me out of my lust just a tiny bit.

"Like what you see?" she teases.

"I'd be dead not to," I quip. "You look amazing."

Rowan is so brashly confident, I would expect her to maybe spin around and show off all her assets. But my compliment actually has her eyes lowering to the floor and her cheeks heating up with a blush. That actually strikes a chord of hope inside of me, because that means she was affected by my perusal of her.

Sometimes… I think there are moments when Rowan wants to give in to her feelings. I can't describe it but it's a look we share. I feel we are on the verge of connecting but then her words come back to haunt me.

I'm not brave enough to want it the way you do.

When the memory of those words penetrate my brain, I push myself away and try to shield my heart. I make myself be brave for Rowan, because she is the one that has suffered in the past, and like I said, I'm willing to wait for her to come around.

♦

THIS CLUB IS packed and it's like one seething, waving mass of bodies on the dance floor. Luckily, Emily, Fil, and Rowan are dancing near the edge so Nix and I can keep an eye on them. In fact, Nix all but demanded to Emily she stay within his line of sight, to which she just snorted at him and walked away without a backward glance.

However, I notice she did what he asked and I'm sure it's because Emily had been attacked by a guy that couldn't take no for an answer at a nightclub before Nix came to her rescue. Thus, she's being respectful of his worry and gives him what he wants. I imagine relationships are supposed to be like that, right? It's about trying to give the other person what they want without sacrificing too much of yourself. In return, the other person does the same for you.

I think in today's day and age, we call that compromise.

The throng of people actually pulses as a whole, looking like a massive, beating heart under the disco lights. But then I focus on Rowan, and everything else ceases to exist. My girl loves to dance, and yes, I'm aware I just referred to her as *my* girl again. And she's fucking good at it. Her body moves with a natural rhythm and she undulates her hips in a way that is like a walking orgasm. The only problem is, that show isn't just for me and every horny male within eyesight of Rowan dances their way toward her.

I curl my fingers into my palms and dig in, trying to force my attention away from her, and one particularly looking sleaze bag who is staring at her ass while he pumps his hips back and forth behind her. I swear… if he touches her, I'll go ballistic and knock his teeth down the back of his throat.

Just as the douche is getting ready to touch her, I start to stand up from the table. But then I watch in amazement as Fil intercepts the guy and gets right up in his face. I obviously cannot hear what she's saying but she is laying into him. He looks pissed at first but the longer she yells at him, the more his shoulders sag and I swear he looks like he might cry. He finally turns around and slinks off.

Fil merely turns around and starts dancing again, as if nothing happened.

Leaning over, I yell at Nix. "Looks like you weren't needed tonight, buddy. Fil apparently can keep Em and Rowan safe."

Nix smirks at me. "Yeah. I'll deny it if you say anything but I'm a little afraid of her."

We both turn back to the dance floor, watching the women work it, and I have a hard time keeping my eyes off Rowan.

After several songs, they return to the table—which apparently it's the men's job to protect—and order more drinks. We've been here a few hours and all of us are sporting a nice buzz. It won't be too long before it's time to leave.

The music is so loud there is no way to have a discussion amongst the group because you have to yell at the person sitting next to you just to be heard. Rowan is sitting to my right but she's turned her back to me, talking to Fil.

That's fine by me because I'm being treated to a lovely view of her upper back, since her hair only comes down to the top of her shoulders. Her skin looks smooth and creamy, and with the flashing lights bouncing off, it's practically hypnotizing.

Nix leans back over to me and yells loud enough that thankfully only I can hear. "Rowan and Fil seem to be getting along great."

I nod. This was the first time they had met but they seemed to become fast friends. It makes me wonder if Rowan would have been so open with her just a few short months ago, and I tend to think not. But that could be my ego talking, because I think part of her ability to be open with people stems from her finally giving me some of her trust.

"Maybe they're interested in each other," Nix yells into my ear, leaning just a little bit closer so for sure no one can hear.

I'm startled by his comment and I turn my head to look at Rowan and Fil.

No way! I mean, Fil is admittedly one-hundred-percent, out-of-the-closet gay, but there is no way Rowan is.

And I tell Nix that with certainty. "You're wrong,

man."

Nix just shrugs and then says, "I bet you ten bucks that Fil will ask her to dance when the music turns slow."

"You're fucking high, Nix. You're so misreading that."

Nix just smirks at me and leans back in his chair, watching the two women talk. I see what he sees now… intimate smiles, Fil laying her hand on Rowan's arm when she says something funny.

What the fuck? Is Fil hitting on Rowan?

I can't believe I'm getting jealous over the prospect. I glance back at Nix. He's grinning at me and I can't figure out if he's pulling my leg or not.

I'm vaguely aware that the music idles to a snail's pace crawl and I see Fil start to stand from her chair in slow motion.

She's actually going to ask Rowan to dance.

Before I can even fathom what I'm doing, I stand quickly, knocking my chair back into the next table over and reach down for Rowan's hand. Pulling her from the table, I say, "Let's dance."

Fil smiles at us and yells over the music, "You kids are so cute. I'm heading to the bathroom because I'm about to burst. Anyone want anything while I'm up?"

We both shake our heads and watch her go. Then Rowan takes the lead and heads toward the dance floor. I shoot a quick glance back at Nix and he has his hand over his mouth, hiding the fact he's laughing at me.

Fucker!

Oh, well… at least I'm going to dance with Rowan.

When we hit the dance floor, I don't waste time letting her lead us too far in. I pull back on her arm and she turns, stepping easily into me. She lays her hands briefly on my chest, and then runs them up over my shoulders until she links them behind my neck. Mine naturally circle around her waist and I pull her in as close as I can without mashing our bodies together.

I have the swirl of good liquor in me, soft music playing, and a beautiful girl that my heart pines for in my arms. This is a recipe for disaster… or triumph, depending on how you look at it.

"What are you thinking?" Rowan asks.

"You don't want to know," I tell her with a mischievous smile.

Rowan leans her forehead into my chest and her shoulders shake with laughter. When she looks back up at me, her eyes are bright. Her tongue darts out and licks her lower lip, and its wetness reflects the flashing lights around us. It is taking all of my willpower not to lean in and grab her lip my teeth.

"Want to know what I'm thinking?" she asks with a flirty giggle. She punctuates the question with a tiny hiccup, which starts her laughing again.

"Are you drunk, young lady?" I ask, pretending to be

indignant.

Her eyes are silver pools of light as she smiles at me. "Maybe a little. So, want to know what I'm thinking?"

I do… God, I do, so I nod at her. I want to know—especially if it's dirty and she'll let me sneak in just one kiss before we need to be all responsible and respect the friendship.

Rowan tugs on my neck and my head lowers. She stands on her tiptoes and places her mouth near my ear, which also fortuitously pushes her breasts into my chest. "I'm thinking I want you to kiss me, Flynn. And I want it to be hard, and hot, and wet. That's what I'm thinking." She ends the statement by flicking her tongue out so it just catches me on the tip of my ear.

That small but simple touch nearly makes my knees buckle and I pull back to look at her. She's smiling at me with carefree abandon but there is a world of sensual heat in her eyes. I know this is fueled by alcohol and I know she's probably going to regret it in the morning, and I'm the biggest schmuck for doing this, but I'm going to kiss her.

And it's going to be hard, and hot, and wet.

♦

I UNLOCK THE door to our apartment and my hands are practically shaking from what may be about to happen. I glance in and see Capone raise his shaggy head from where he is lying on the couch and then he lays it back down, completely bored with our arrival. He'll need to go out soon, but he can wait. There are more important things at stake right now.

When Rowan asked me to kiss her at the club, I obliged. And I thought it would be everything she asked for, but it was actually so much more. I didn't go in hard like she asked, but rather feathered my lips softly against her. I let my hands spread out over her back and I rubbed her through the thin material of her dress. I softly slipped my tongue in her mouth and it flirted with hers.

The entire kiss was so amazingly delicate compared to the ways we had kissed before, and it was the exact thing that would probably guarantee I would have not one ounce of resolve left in me when it comes to staying away from Rowan.

When we broke apart, I glanced over at Nix and he was pointing to his watch, indicating it was time to go. We made our goodbyes, with Fil and Rowan hugging and promising to text each other. It appears she had a new BFF.

The entire train ride back to the apartment was surreal. We sat side by side and I casually draped my arm across her shoulders. I was hyper aware of the way her leg pressed into mine, and the way her hair skimmed over the back of my hand while I stroked her shoulder with my thumb.

We didn't say a word but I could feel the sexual tension vibrating between us.

Unfortunately, the short, but frigid, walk from the station to the apartment did nothing to cool my desire; it only served to sober me up slightly so I might be thinking a bit clearer.

I push the door open and step aside for Rowan to enter in front of me, my hand on the small of her back, guiding her in. I have no clue what my next move should be, or even if there should be a next move. All I know is that I want her back in my arms and I want to try out her idea of that hot, hard, and wet kiss.

As soon as I step through the door and close it, Rowan spins around and launches herself at me. Her arms curve around my neck and with a quick jump, her legs wrap around my waist, causing my hands to involuntarily reach down and grab her under her ass to hold her in place.

That may not have been such a good idea because her dress is now hiked up to her hips and she's apparently only wearing a thong because I am now holding on to sinful, naked ass.

Her mouth latches onto mine and we are now fully engaged in hard, hot, and wet. I spin her around and push her back into the door, and as I grind my dick against her, I can only think to myself, *Yes, this is what I've been waiting for.*

Rowan gasps into my mouth, "I shouldn't have done that. We should stop."

I respond by moving my tongue hard against hers, and then I pull away, nipping at her lower lip. "I'll stop if you want."

"Yes," she says, and my heart bottoms out. Then she says, "No… don't stop," and she kisses me harder, knocking our teeth against one another.

The minute she gives me the go ahead, I shift one hand. As I'm still gripping her bottom, it brings my middle finger in proximity to her thong. She feels the change in my position and moans. I shift again, and hook my finger in the bottom of her underwear, pulling it aside.

For a second, Rowan goes still and I think she has snapped out of her lust-induced haze, but she moans low in her throat and rasps, "Not good, Flynn. Not good."

Then Rowan pushes her hips downward and twists them to the side, bringing her slick core in direct contact with my finger. The heat is searing and I only stroke against her one time… because that's all I have in me, before I push my finger deep inside of her. Her hips buck hard, lodging me even deeper, and a strangled gasp comes out of her mouth while her nails flex into my scalp. I silence it down with another kiss and push her harder into the wall.

My world is fracturing and every semblance of normalcy is flying out the window. I give one last, lingering thought to stopping this… because Rowan's inhibitions are lowered because of the alcohol and I should protect her from this. I'm betting in the harsh light of day and completely sober, she wouldn't want this.

I consider it… just briefly, and then I tell myself to piss off. I want her too much and I'll worry about the consequences later. I'm inflamed with lust, and love, and it's all tied up into one painful knot, but it's going to unravel tonight.

I pull my finger out and add a second before plunging back in. She cries against my lips and it sounds sweet to me.

Pulling my face back, I look at her and her eyes are partially closed. When she realizes my lips aren't against hers anymore, she opens her eyes. My fingers are pumping in and out of her slowly and her hips tilt against my hand with every thrust. We stay like that, for just a few moments, just watching each other as she rides my hand.

"Rowan," I whisper, and her eyes focus more sharply on me, even as a little gasp of breath hitches out past her lips. "I want to make you come, and then I want to make you mine. Say you want it, too. Tell me you want this."

I'm pleading for her to say the words that will ease my own guilt, because if she tells me point blank she wants me, I don't have to worry so much that I may be taking advantage of the situation.

"I..." she starts to say, but a particularly deep push of my fingers cuts her words off. She grasps her lower lip in between her teeth and her eyes close as she moves against my hand.

"Say it," I urge her, desperate for the words. "Say you want more than just a friendship with me."

When I look back and analyze how things went to shit so quickly, I'll pinpoint the word "friendship" as the pivotal moment that stalled my impending apocalyptic orgasm. The minute the words are out of my mouth, Rowan's hips go absolutely still and the heat dies out of her eyes. Her eyebrows furrow inward and she slowly closes her eyes, lowering her forehead to my shoulder.

"We need to stop, Flynn," she says softly.

I'm not willing to give in just yet so I move my fingers against her inner walls, curling them to hit that spot that I've seen splinter women apart before. She moans into my shoulder but then pushes back against me.

"Stop," she says with more force, and I immediately stop, pulling my fingers out of her and holding her in place under her thighs for just a moment before I lower her to the floor.

It is only then that I notice my chest is heaving with exertion and Rowan has a fine sheen of sweat on her forehead as she pulls her skirt back down. I hadn't realized how hot and heavy we were going until just now… how far things had gotten out of control and how fast.

My hands may not be on her anymore and my head is cleared a bit, but I'm not ready to give up. "Rowan… don't pull away. Let it happen. You were right there with me. I know it."

She looks up at me and there is a thin veil of tears in her eyes. My heart is breaking for her. "I was… right there with you. But I can't. I know you're tired of hearing that and I'm so sorry I led you on. I had too much to drink and was terribly wrong to do that. But I can't risk our friendship."

"You can, Rowan. You're braver than this. If you just give it a chance, I know we will work. I can feel it. I want you to—"

"NO!" Rowan yells at me and I take a small step back from the venom in her voice. Her eyes flash hot and pissed for a second, but then it dies just as quickly. Her voice is softer when she says again. "No. Don't ask me again, Flynn."

My heart slices open at those words and I bleed pain all over. I know Rowan enough to know when she's drawing a firm line in the sand and this is it. Still, I'm going to try one more time.

"Rowan… wait…" but she cuts me off by holding up her hand to me.

"Flynn… hear me out. It's not going to happen. I'm

not going to let it and I need you to let it go. In fact, you have got to move on from me. Find yourself someone deserving and make a new start. I'm here… as your friend. But *only* as your friend."

She gives me one last look and heads to her bedroom, Capone padding after her.

CHAPTER 19

Rowan

DIPPING MY SPOON into the pot, I pull out a small bit of sauce and taste it. My stomach grumbles because I'm starving but I'm going to wait and boil the pasta when Flynn gets home from work. I haven't seen him much because he's picked up some overtime the last few weeks, so I'm excited for him to walk in that door.

I've missed him a lot.

Walking into the living room, I glance at the clock. He should be here any moment. I turn on the TV and after less than thirty seconds of flipping channels, I know that won't keep my mind occupied. I pick up a magazine from the coffee table but as soon as I open it, I throw it back down in frustration.

My mind is whirring with excitement over seeing Flynn, but I'm stressed as well because I have no clue where I stand with him. Every day, I feel crushing guilt over pushing him away. I'm mortified that my body reacted to him… almost viscerally, and my mind took over and stopped what I'm sure would have been a night of mind-blowing passion. I'm weighed down by the knowledge that I led Flynn on, my face turning red when I think about the way I pushed myself up and down on his fingers. I egged him on every bit of the way, and then I shut him down, officially making myself the world's biggest prick tease.

When I closed myself in my room that night, I cried my eyes out because I knew I had hurt him. But I kept telling myself over and over again, it would be okay. We'd wake up the next day and things would be just the way they were. We could take Capone for a walk and stop at a bakery for breakfast. We could laugh at silly things and compare our knowledge of famous movie lines. We would be the Rowan and Flynn of old… the best of buddies.

Except, that isn't what happened. While Flynn hasn't been anything but his usual nice and charming self when he's around me, he offers me nothing more than that. It's like he's making himself keep a respectful distance from me, because… yes, that's what I told him to do.

And yes… it hurts, and I have no right to be hurt, and yet I hurt all the same. My head is so fucked up over this, and when push comes to shove, I'm not sure I made the right decision. What if I missed out on the opportunity of a lifetime? Sure, that's a possibility, right? Because, otherwise, why am I constantly yearning for all things Flynn Caldwell?

For example, not two weeks ago, I was content with our friendship. Every little thing we learned about each other was an amazing discovery. Every time I opened myself up a little bit more to Flynn, I discovered another part of my heart that wasn't irrevocably damaged.

It was all enough for me.

Until I pushed him away and shut the door on him for good.

And now, I'm just miserable over the fact that this could have been a very bad decision. Our friendship has taken a hit, I'm sure. We don't have the same level of ease that we once did. I was so worried all the time about the friendship ending that I never realized that it could possibly be hurt by not moving forward. At this point, we're just stagnating.

I guess that's why I'm so anxious for Flynn to get home. I want to look in his eyes and see if there is a spark of attraction left or have I killed all of it. That explains why I took a shower late this afternoon, blew out my hair until it was soft and silky, and took great care with my makeup. It's why I put on my most flattering jeans and a blouse rather than a t-shirt. I've sunk so low that I even put on some lip gloss, because I heard that a woman's lips can capture a man's attention faster than anything.

This is a sick game I'm playing with Flynn. I've repeatedly kept him at bay, only to now want to pull him back in. I absolutely hate myself that I could be hurting him further, and yet I can't stop the compulsion that is making me reach out to him. I miss what we had, and I really want more.

I think.

I'm still not quite sure about anything.

I hate myself.

When I hear the keys rattling in the locks, my heart skips a beat and then I jump from the couch and sprint into the bathroom. I turn on the light and give myself a quick once-over, rubbing my fingertip at the corner of my lips to remove stray gloss.

When I head back into the living room, Flynn is dropping his duffel bag to the floor and greeting Capone. He bends over and puts his hands on both sides of his face, vigorously rubbing behind his ears. Capone actually lets out a groan of satisfaction and Flynn chuckles. His dimple pops out and my heart sighs in response.

"Hey," I say, grabbing his attention.

He looks up and smiles. It's friendly, charming, and affectionate. "Hey, yourself." He then looks at me a bit harder and I hold my breath. "You look really nice. What's the occasion?"

He noticed and I want to break out into a jig over the fact. Instead, I put on a friendly smile and say, "No occasion. Just wearing some different clothes is all."

"Very nice," he confirms. "I'm going to go grab a shower, okay?"

"Sure," I tell him. "I'll take your duffel and start a load of clothes."

"Awesome," he says and flashes me a grin. "You make a great housewife."

"You're funny, Caldwell. But you stink… go shower."

He gives me a mock salute and heads down the hallway.

I quickly grab Flynn's bag and start a load of laundry. Then I put the pot of water on the stove and anxiously watch it. It takes forever to boil but at least it gives me time to open a bottle of red wine I picked up today. I had discovered just last week that Flynn likes this particular brand and I thought it would be nice to get it for him.

I hear the bathroom door open and then Flynn's bedroom door close. He's getting dressed so that gives me time to start the garlic bread and I dump the pasta in the pot. I just have the table set when Flynn walks into the kitchen, and oh, my God, he looks divine.

He's put some effort into his appearance as well. He's freshly shaven—although I do prefer the scruffy look—and he's wearing a pair of dark jeans that are perfectly formed to his ass and a dark gray dress shirt that fits his chest like it was custom designed. His hair is even styled with his short locks brushed forward and then tufted upward at his forehead.

"Wow," I say, my voice slightly rough. "You clean up nice."

He gives me an embarrassed smile and points to the stove. "What's all this?"

I shrug my shoulders nonchalantly, like it's not a big deal that I made dinner for the two of us, but it is so a big deal. I don't cook, a fact that Flynn has bemoaned on more than one occasion, and I have been jonesing for two weeks for some quality time with him. I'm hoping that we will naturally glide into a serious conversation about our feelings because I need to confront them before they drive me insane.

"Oh, nothing much," I say, waving at the pot of sauce bubbling merrily. "Just a little something I whipped up. Thought you'd be hungry when you got home."

Flynn sort of glances around the kitchen, taking in the pasta, the uncorked bottle of wine, and the plates that I had set out. I even put a little vase with flowers on the table. He looks down at the floor and sort of shuffles his feet back and forth, like he's nervous.

I think it's adorable, and I even notice his cheeks are a little red.

"What's the matter?" I tease. "Is the setup not to your liking?"

He looks up at me and his eyes are filled with apology. "No… not at all. It looks great. It's just… I have plans tonight for dinner and I can't stay."

I feel like I just got sucker punched in the chest and for one terrifying moment, I think my breath may be gone for good, but then I recover. My head is buzzing, though when I manage to ask, "Oh… heading out with the guys tonight?"

Flynn looks back down to the ground and tucks his hands into his pockets. When he looks back up at me, the apology is gone and his eyes are a bit aloof. "I have a date."

"A date?" I ask, completely aware of the disbelief in my voice. It rings through loud and clear, and I actually see Flynn's eyes turn cold that I would be surprised that he has a date.

"Yes, a date. Remember… you told me… two weeks ago, to move on from you. That's what you told me to do, so I went and did it."

I inhale sharply because his words are like razor blades soaked in stinging alcohol against my heart. He's actually moved on… past me. And here I am putting on an incredibly stupid display of a romantic gesture with this dinner, and the entire time he's getting ready to go on a date.

Karma is such a bitch!

And he has every right to do this yet that does nothing to ease the burn of rejection. It's as I had imagined it would be… sharp and cold. It ravages deep inside of my chest and grabs my heart in an icy grip.

I turn my back on Flynn, because I have no clue what expression my face is wearing right now. I hope he didn't see the hurt and mortification. Where I possess the strength, I have no clue, but I manage to say in a semi-steady voice, "That's great. No worries on the food. You can have leftovers for lunch tomorrow."

Even I'm impressed with how even my tone is and I think I managed to sound happy for him at the end. So I play it all the way up and turn toward him, pinning him with a dazzling smile. "I'm happy for you, Flynn. I hope you have an amazing time tonight."

He looks back at me, his eyes still hard. But then they soften and he rewards me with the very softest of smiles. "Thanks. I appreciate that."

Flynn reaches over and grabs his keys and wallet from the counter, stuffing them in his pockets. "I probably won't be in until late, so I'll see you in the morning."

"Sure," I say, with that fake smile plastered on my face and a touch of hysteria in my voice. I'm on the verge of losing it and I just want him to get the hell out before I meltdown in front of him.

He gives me one last look, and his eyes seem to be searching hard for something. I can feel my cheeks trembling from the effort to smile. He finally turns away and heads toward the door. "See you later."

When the door shuts, I walk up to it and engage the locks. Turning around, I lean back against it, my palms flat on the wood. Then I slide downward, the first teardrops spilling from my eyes as my butt meets the floor.

I stare straight ahead, numb from the shock that Flynn has indeed moved on. Now, nothing is left for me to have except that stupid fucking friendship that I was so keen to hold on to.

Capone walks up to me and I loop my arms around his massive shoulders, pressing my face into his fur. It will help to mop up the buckets of tears that are leaking out. I cry with abandon, knowing that the only one to share my pain at this moment is my dog.

CHAPTER 20

Flynn

I JUST CAME off an extra two-day shift I picked up at the Station and this early morning run I just finished is exactly what I need before I'm able to collapse into my bed and get caught up on some sleep. We were insanely busy and I'm lucky if I've had a total of eight hours of shuteye in the last two days.

Opening the door to the apartment, I quietly enter so I don't wake Rowan up. All was silent half an hour ago when I opened the door to just drop my duffel bag in the foyer before heading out to run. I gently close the door and turn the locks.

"Is that you, Flynn?" I hear Rowan call out from the kitchen.

Walking in, I see her sitting at the kitchen table, nursing a cup of coffee. She looks up at me and smiles a greeting, but it doesn't actually reach her eyes. "Guess I wasn't as quiet as I thought I was."

The smile slips and she says, "I heard the locks clicking."

I cringe from that statement, a brutal reminder that Rowan still has issues that she is dealing with and thus keeps me firm in my resolve to move on.

But it's fucking killing me.

The minute I walked into the kitchen and saw her, with the morning sunlight pouring down on top of her from the small, high window that sits above the fridge, I thought she looked like an angel.

A sad angel.

There is something different about Rowan and it clearly changed the night I went on my first date with Jennifer. She has become a little more withdrawn from me, and I can't figure out if it's because she's angry or if she's sad. Hell, it may be that our friendship has run its course and what was once new and exciting has now become old hat for both of us.

I know one thing though… I do miss the camaraderie we had shared before, and while I still find myself pining for what may have been with Rowan, I am trying my damnedest to leave the thought of an intimate relationship with her behind.

I'm done being mad at her though.

And I was mad. I mean, *really* pissed after she spurned me that night. I was mad that she couldn't see past her fears to something that could have been miraculously wonderful for both of us. I was furious that this brave, strong, independent woman didn't have the chops to venture even further. Red was the color I saw when I looked at her because I was hurting so bad.

But then I decided I had to move past it. I had to move on, just like she told me. And while I hadn't really been looking for a relationship before I met Rowan, I got to thinking that maybe it was time for me to find one. A woman that would want to venture forth with me rather than standing timidly in the shadows. A woman that I could look at… the way Nix looks at Emily and says, *She's my everything.*

That's what I wanted and if I couldn't have it with Rowan, I'm sure I could have it with someone else.

I let one of my co-workers hook me up with his cousin, Jennifer. She's two years older than me and an investment banker. She's polished, educated, and outgoing, and I even emailed my mom the morning after that first date to tell her all about it because I knew she would be thrilled at the prospect.

So, there you have it. I'm officially dating. Jennifer has a slammin' body from what I've been able to see through her tailored clothes and designer heels. I also know this because she told me… exhaustively… about her workout routines. It seems Jennifer is a bit of a health nut, and while I'm all for working out and taking care of the body, I'll never be one of those "drink nothing but spinach and kale shakes" type of people.

Like Jennifer.

On our first date, I almost laughed because not only did she order just a side salad for her entire dinner, but she asked for it with no dressing.

That's right… no fucking dressing.

She didn't even ask for it to be brought on the side… she had cold, plain lettuce for her meal. It would have been the cheapest date ever but she did order an expensive sparkling water to go with it, which was fine by me. I didn't want to have to hear her stomach grumbling through the movie.

Still… I've had a good time the few times we've been out. We've never been at a loss for things to talk about, and while she tends to show more interest in herself that she does anything else, it's not a bad way to spend my free time.

The best thing though, is that we are taking it slow and so far there have been no expectations to move this to anything deeper than some casual dates at this point. And that's fine by me because while I'm doing exactly what Rowan suggested I do, I'm not exactly throwing one-hundred percent of my effort into it.

It's kind of hard to do when you're still stuck on someone else.

Walking over to the refrigerator, I open it and pull out a bottle of water, twisting the cap and drinking it down. I watch Rowan as I chug, and she's staring a bit vacantly at her cup. She looks sad and lonely… which makes me sad, and I have to wonder if it is because I haven't been around a lot lately? I have been picking up some overtime and I've had a few dates with Jennifer, so we definitely don't hang as much as we used to. There's also been a bit of an emotional distance between us since "that night" but because she clearly believes the friendship is the most important thing we have, I've been all for continuing that like we always have. It's just I haven't had much time lately.

"So anything new in your life?" I ask her.

She shakes her head and takes another sip of coffee. "No, not unless you count the fact that your cousin was even more of an asshole this week, and Capone threw up on my bed the other night, but other than that… it's been pretty status quo." She shoots me an impish grin and relief shoots through me like a lightning bolt. There's a bit of the Rowan that I was looking for.

"Yeah, Nix has his mood swings. Just ignore him."

"Hell no, I'm not ignoring him. I give it back to him tenfold." She now gives me a smile that lights up the room and my heart swells. It's an involuntary reaction I have to her.

I chuckle at the thought, and I know Rowan can take care of herself. "How's Capone? Is he sick?"

Standing up from the table, she walks to the sink and dumps the remainder of her coffee. As she rinses the cup, she says, "Nah. I think he just ate too fast or something."

The brief moment of humor that Rowan showed me just seconds ago is now gone, and her face looks blank again. She turns to walk out of the kitchen without another word, and something just doesn't feel right to me. I'm exhausted and I know I should hit the sack for some sleep because I have another date with Jennifer tonight, but I can't let Rowan walk away from me knowing that she's very sad about something.

"Hey, Rowan," I call out, and she stops to face me. "Want to go do something today? Maybe hit a museum or go do some touristy stuff?"

"Really?" she asks and her eyes spark. "Aren't you exhausted?"

"No way," I assure her, although I feel like I could drop into a deep slumber right on the kitchen floor. "Besides, it's been too long since we've hung out together."

And it has been way too long. I step up to her and put an arm around her shoulder, giving her a quick squeeze. She actually leans into me and even after I release her, she doesn't move back right away.

"Okay," she says as she finally steps back and I'm overjoyed to see her eyes are sparkling with light now.

Just like that… Rowan is back, and I know for a fact that she has been missing me. I fight to keep the feeling of elation I'm feeling down, because surely that doesn't mean that she wants me for more than a friendship, right? Surely, it can only mean that we've both been busy and haven't spent any time together.

We are missing our friendship. That's what it must mean.

Still… I wonder.

♦

AFTER SOME DEBATING over what to do with our day, we decide to head over to Museum Mile and hit the Met. Rowan has never been before and I figure on this chilly November day that it's warm and fairly quiet, and we can just hang out.

We take our time as we travel through the various galleries. Neither one of us are the type to seriously study a painting, but we do at least move past each one and give it more than a cursory glance. We could spend months in the Met if we wanted to study everything but I wanted to give her a taste of it all.

We make idle chitchat when we can, but for the most part, we are silently enjoying the art.

As we walk among some Spanish Renaissance pieces, Rowan stops before a painting and studies it a bit longer. I hold up and wait for her but she doesn't move, so I walk the few steps back to stand beside her.

She's gazing at *El Greco's View of Toledo*. I've never seen it before, or if I have, I've forgotten it, but it's quite beautiful with its dark storm clouds shadowing the lush, green hills, and the medieval city of Toledo, Spain in the distance. The more I look at it, the more I can see why Rowan is taken with it. It's both peaceful and edgy, which is a good way to describe Rowan.

"It's old," she says quietly.

Peering at the placard beside it, I see it was painted over four hundred years ago. But so were many of the paintings we've seen so I don't understand the significance of her statement.

"I can't imagine what it takes to preserve something this… special."

There's something about the tone of her voice that is haunting and I turn my eyes to her. Her profile is so fucking beautiful. Her lashes are long and lay like whispers on her cheeks, and her nose has just the slightest tilt upward that gives her that pixie look.

"I imagine a lot of techniques have been learned over the years," I muse, turning my gaze back to the painting.

"I imagine it takes a lot of hard work. I bet there's painstaking focus on the details."

I nod. "If it wasn't hard, then it wouldn't be so treasured."

She turns her head and I meet her gaze. She looks at me thoughtfully for a moment before she says, "Exactly."

Rowan turns and walks on to the next painting, and I'm not quite sure if we were just talking about art or something else.

♦

WE DECIDE TO eat a late lunch in the cafeteria at the Met, which has a surprising array of food. I choose a pastrami sandwich and Rowan tries their sushi, which I'm a bit dubious about eating from a cafeteria. She swears it's good after she takes the first bite and offers me some, but I decline. I'm not about to get food poisoning.

Her mood does seem to be lighter though, and after I decline her offer of sushi, she demands I give her a bite of my sandwich. I laugh and willingly hand it over to her, watching as she takes a huge bite.

She only chews twice and then she closes her eyes in rapture and lets out a moan. She clearly thinks the sandwich is amazing but damn if the sound she makes doesn't cause a surge of lust to drive through me. I thought I had made it past these feelings, but apparently not. I watch as she finishes the bite, giving a final swipe of her lips with her tongue, and I realize I am no further removed from my feelings for Rowan than I was right at the moment I first sunk my finger into her while she was pressed up against my door.

The image of that night flashes hot in my brain and I take a deep breath to move past it.

"Is something wrong?" Rowan asks.

I drag my gaze to hers and shake my head. "No. I'm good."

I'm anything but.

I still fucking want a woman that doesn't want me the same way. I decide a change of subject is in order.

"So, what are your plans for the rest of the weekend?" I ask her. I have four glorious days off and I have no clue what I'm going to do for all of it.

Rowan shrugs her shoulders. "No major plans, but I'm up for hanging out if you want to."

"Sure," I tell her, although I'm sure I'm setting myself up for some serious frustration. "And before I forget, we need to leave for my mom's house around noon on Thursday. I think she wants to eat around 2:00 PM, if that's okay with you?"

I hadn't mentioned Thanksgiving to Rowan lately, and I assume she's still on board with going, but since our friendship had been a little rocky the past few weeks, I'm greatly relieved to see her smiling.

"Sounds great. I'm going to make the pie early that morning but that's plenty of time."

"We won't stay over there too late because I have to be back to work the following morning."

"Not me. Nix gave me that Friday off."

"I thought he was an asshole," I tease.

She smirks. "He is, but he does have some nice moments."

Rowan reaches across the table and sneaks one of my fries. "So you want to rent some movies tonight? Order a pizza?"

Swallowing a bite of my sandwich, I take a quick drink of my soda before replying. "Um… I actually have a date tonight."

This is a bit awkward but no sense in hiding it.

Rowan glances down at her plate for a moment but when she looks back at me, there is a warm smile on her face. "So, when are you going to tell me all about your mad dating life? I mean… aren't friends supposed to share that stuff?"

Her smile looks genuine but I think she may be putting on an act because her voice sounds a little shaky. Could it be that Rowan is having second thoughts? Because if she is… she needs to fucking tell me so we can get on with it.

"Hmmm… let's see. Her name is Jennifer and she lives here in Brooklyn. She's a few years older than I am and works in a bank. She's like this really hardcore fitness nut though… I mean, really intense."

Rowan snorts. "Don't tell me she only drinks spinach shakes?"

I about spew the soda I'm taking a sip of because she's pegged Jennifer. "Sort of. It's actually a bit annoying when we go out to eat and she only nibbles on raw vegetables."

"Oh, God… I was just joking. She really does that?"

I laugh and nod. "But she's really nice and she's gorgeous, and…" I search for other words to nicely describe Jennifer but nothing is coming to mind. "And she's really successful... she's a banker." I throw that last part out because I don't know what else to say and I feel slightly guilty for even telling Rowan something about Jennifer that annoys me.

Rowan's smile slides off her face, and I have no clue what I've just said to make that happen, but she clues me in. "Wow... banker. You really landed yourself someone great."

She's trying to say it to give me a compliment on my new girlfriend, but she's saying it as a backhanded slap to herself, because she isn't an investment banker, which in turn doesn't make her good enough.

I reach across the table to grab her hand and she instantly tries to pull it away. I hold on tight.

When she looks at me, there is moisture in her eyes and my fucking heart cracks. "I didn't mean anything by that, Rowan. I was just struggling with what to say about her to you and that is the only thing that came to mind."

Blinking her eyes rapidly, I watch as the tears dissipate and she gives me a smile. "It's good. I know I'll never be successful like that. I had my shot at that type of life and I fucked it up."

"No," I tell her harshly. "Don't ever talk like that. You didn't miss your shot."

She's quietly staring at me so I continue on. "And who's to say what success is anyway? I look at you and your ability to take care of yourself in a very mean city, and you did it all on your own. How many people do you really think could do that without succumbing to things like crime or homelessness?"

Rowan blinks and then nods her head slightly. "You're right. I hear you."

"I'm serious about this, Rowan," I tell her. "You are amazing."

She smiles at me, and this time it has more light to it. "Thanks. You always know what to say to make me feel good about myself."

The thought that my words make Rowan smile causes happiness to bubble and well inside of me. It makes me realize that I used to feel this way a lot around her, but that I haven't felt this way in a while.

I squeeze her hand and take a deep breath. "I feel like our friendship's taken a bit of a hit lately."

She sighs and squeezes back. The look on her face is one of deep affection and her smile is as warm as a desert breeze. "Yeah… I feel that way, too."

"Let's rectify that, okay?"

"Absolutely," she says, her smile flashing with joy.

CHAPTER 21
Rowan

WE'VE COMPLETED PHASE One of The Caldwell Thanksgiving Day Extravaganza. The food has been eaten and the top buttons on our pants have been undone. Flynn and Nora are in the kitchen, cleaning or miraculously eating another piece of pie, but everyone else has been shooed out to the living room.

Nix and Emily are on one end of the loveseat, with her on his lap, both of them sound asleep. Nix's dad, Hank, is on the other end with his head tilted back. It took that group only three seconds to fall asleep. Nick is stretched out in his recliner and, every time I glance at him, he's struggling to keep his eyes open.

Tim ate with us as his ex-wife has Sam for this holiday, and he's passed out on the floor with Capone snoring softly beside him.

That leaves just Fil and me. We are sitting on the couch and she's trying to teach me about football.

I absolutely adore Fil. Since meeting her earlier this month when we went clubbing, she and I have developed a good friendship. We've gone out together a few times, which ironically seem to coincide with the nights that Flynn has gone out on his dates, and we text each other all the time. She has a hilariously filthy mind and loves to text me shocking photos, usually of naked men. She tells me I'm in a dating slump and wants me to get out there and steam up the sheets with someone, and she figures the photos will get me in the mood.

The other day, my phone buzzed with a text and I saw it was from Fil. It had an attachment that said, *Hawt guy in kilt with huge pole!*

I immediately scrambled to open the picture, because she has sent me some really hot men before. When the jpeg opened up on my screen, I started laughing. It was a man… in a kilt, and yes, he was hot. But the pole? Yeah… not what I was expecting. He was literally carrying a huge, wooden telephone pole in his beefy arms. It looked like one of those Highland games or something.

"Okay, now pay attention, Rowan, because I'm going to give you a complete run down of all the rules today as we watch this game."

Fil leans forward on the couch and gazes seriously at the TV. The Raiders and the Cowboys are playing and although I've heard of the Dallas Cowboys—I mean, who hasn't—I have no clue who the Raiders are. Sorry, but hockey is my game.

Fil gives me a rundown of the National Football League and how it's broken into two conferences with four divisions in each. I look longingly over at Nick Caldwell, who has succumbed to a nap.

"Now, this is important," Fil says with flourish. "Our team… the Giants… are in the NFC east, same as Dallas. Which means we hate Dallas and so we're pulling for the Raiders today."

"Wait… why am I a Giants fan?"

"Because you're a New Yorker, that's who you root for."

"But maybe I'm a Jets fan. That's who Flynn roots for and besides, he got Capone a Jets collar."

Capone raises his head after hearing his name and looks around with bleary eyes. When no one says anything further to him, he gives a deep sigh and lays his head on Tim's stomach.

"Fine… whatever… be a pansy-assed Jets fan, but don't come crying to me at the end of your pitiful season."

I'm pretty sure I won't be doing that because past watching the games today, I have no intention of following football.

After silently watching for a few minutes, I ask, "Okay, here's a question for you… what's that yellow line on the field?"

Fil doesn't answer me so I poke her in the ribs.

"Teach me, Yoda."

She looks at me with frustration and then looks back at the TV. "That splits the field in half."

"Liar," I hear from the doorway and I turn to see Flynn there with a plate of pie in his hand.

Fil turns around and looks guilty for just a second, then her face splits into a grin. "Busted."

"Wait… that line doesn't split the field in half?" I ask, because that made damn good sense to me.

Chuckling, Flynn walks in and comes over to the couch. "Scoot down," he says.

I try to move to the left, but Fil is ignoring me in favor of the football game. I jab her in the ribs again, she moves over a quarter of an inch, and I move along with her. It gives enough room for Flynn to jam his body in between the end of the couch and me, and the heat of his leg against mine sends my pulse dancing.

He takes the last bite of pie and sets the plate down on the coffee table. After he swallows, he says, "Okay… the yellow line represents the first down marker. You do understand the concept of downs, right?"

"Sort of," I tell him. "Not really. And what's the blue line?"

"That's the line of scrimmage," Flynn says and, before he can explain further, Fil lets out a curse. "I can't believe he got sacked. The offensive line sucks."

"What's a sack?" I ask.

Flynn chuckles. "Slow down there, Speedy. One question at a time."

He takes my hand and turns it palm up. "Here's the easiest way to understand it. See these two lines running parallel on your palm?"

I glance down and his fingertip traces two of my lifelines, which do indeed run exactly parallel across my hand. The feel of his skin against mine causes me to shiver slightly and I'm mesmerized by the movement.

"Yeah," I say and it feels like it comes out in a croak.

"So, this line right here is the line of scrimmage. It's where the offensive line starts and the quarterback will be roughly in the middle of the line." Flynn traces the line of scrimmage on my palm and then taps the area where the quarterback would stand.

"And this here," he says, as he runs his finger across the other line. "This is the first down line. This is the distance, which is ten yards, that the offensive line has to get the ball to be able to advance further. They have four tries to get there… and those are called downs."

I want to know more, not because I give a shit about football but because I want Flynn to keep holding my hand and tracing patterns on my skin. Which is decidedly not within the purview of a regular friendship.

"And a sack?" I remind him.

He pushes his index finger into my palm and holds it there. "When the quarterback starts the play at the line of scrimmage, he will most times step backward to get some distance from the defensive players that are coming toward him. If at any time they get him behind this line," and here he pauses to drag his finger across my palm, "that is called a sack. Understand?"

"Yes," I say but really, no. I don't remember a damn thing he just told me and could care less. I am, though, trying to think of other questions to ask so he can teach me more palm football.

Sadly though, Flynn releases my hand and props his feet up on the table. He leans back into the cushions with a sigh. I'm sitting almost ramrod straight, trying to follow the game, while Fil sits beside me, alternating between cheers and curses that, funny enough, don't wake up any of the nappers.

After just a few minutes, Flynn touches my shoulder. "I can't see the TV, Rowan, with you sitting forward like that."

Before I can respond, he grips my shoulder and pulls me back into him. As I sink back into the couch, he raises his arm and drapes it over my shoulder. I'm stiff and unsure, but then Flynn leans over and whispers in my ear, "Relax" and I let myself melt into him.

Pressed up against his side, his scent and warmth calming me, I tentatively lay my head on his chest. He responds by giving me a slight squeeze and then his thumb starts rubbing the edge of my shoulder. It is heaven and I close my eyes so I can concentrate on the feel.

♦

WHEN I WAKE up, I'm completely disoriented. I first take in the fact that the same football game is on so I must not have been asleep long. Next, I immediately realize that I am lying down with my head in Flynn's lap, and his arm is holding me around my waist.

Carefully, I ease my shoulders up and sneak a peek. His head is tilted back against the couch and he is sleeping soundly. I pick up his hand and move it off my waist, gently rolling off the couch so as not to wake him up. Glancing at Fil, I see she is curled up on the other end of the couch fast asleep, and everyone else is still down for the count.

I step gingerly over Flynn's legs and head into the kitchen to find Nora sitting at the counter, drinking a cup of coffee and reading a magazine.

"Hey," she says when she sees me. "I just peeked in a few minutes ago and you were sound asleep."

My cheeks burn slightly that she found me sprawled on her son. "Yeah… all of a sudden, I was out."

"Turkey does that to you," she says warmly.

Walking to the fridge, I open it up and pull out a bottle of water. "Then how come you aren't sleeping?" I ask.

She shrugs her shoulders. “I guess I just like taking advantage of the quiet when I can. I have plenty of time to sleep later when I’ve gone from this earth.”

My father used to say that very thing when my mom would try to urge him to come to bed late at night when he would still be working. The unbidden memory actually makes me smile and I realize that this is the first time in five years that I’ve had a memory of my parents that didn’t cause me pain.

“Now that’s a lovely smile on your face,” Nora says, her Irish lilt ringing like music.

“I just thought of a nice memory, is all. My dad used to say that very thing… that he would have plenty of time to sleep when he was dead.”

Nora smiles and rests her chin on her hand. “You miss your parents, huh?”

I meet Nora’s gaze and keep the same smile on my face, but I’m honest with her. “Actually… I don’t.”

“I’m sorry, honey,” she says. “I didn’t mean to open up a can of rotten worms.”

“No, it’s okay. It’s kind of funny… but I used to miss them. Even as toxic as our relationship was, I would miss them a lot during holidays. But for some reason… right now, I don’t.”

Nora cocks her head to the side, curious, but she doesn’t ask. I go ahead and volunteer. “Thank you for inviting me into your home, Nora, and for such a great time today. You created a new memory for me that I'll have to cherish."

Understanding sweeps across her face and she reaches across the counter to grab my hand. Giving me a squeeze, she says, "You are welcome here anytime. You're practically like family to us."

"You treat me like family. It's… comforting," I say in a rare moment of vulnerability. This is only my third time in her house but she and Nick have made me feel utterly comfortable in their home.

"Flynn told me you're not coming to St. John with us for the wedding. I wish you'd change your mind."

"I'd love to, Nora, but it's just not something I can afford right now. Besides, it should just be family."

"You know Nix and Em aren't doing it this way to be excluding of others. It's just happening so quick that they know most people won't be able to come or won't want to attend a destination wedding. They're going to have a huge wedding party sometime in the Spring."

"I know," I assure her. "It's not that… it truly is about the money. It's just not within my budget."

"But Flynn said—"

Holding my hand up, I say, "No, Nora. I'm not accepting money from Flynn. Now, I'm going to eat another piece of pie. Do you want one?"

Nora shakes her head and takes a sip of her coffee, thankfully dropping the subject. I grab a plate and cut a piece of pumpkin pie, foregoing the whipped topping.

As I go to take my first bite, Nora surprises the shit out of me. "You know… Flynn never brings that girl he's dating over. I've been on him to do it but he always has one excuse after another."

My fork is poised halfway to my mouth, which is halfway open as well. I can't think of a damn thing to say.

"Do you have any idea why he wouldn't want me to meet her?" Nora whispers, sneaking a glance at the doorway so we won't be overheard. "Is she like an ogre or something?"

I lower my fork back down, completely uninterested in pie right now. "I'm not sure. I mean… I haven't met her either."

Flynn has always liked to make fun of the fact his mom is dying for him to meet someone special, so I sort of expect her face to fall over my proclamation and inability to provide her with insider information.

Instead, she smiles at me conspiratorially. "I bet I know why neither one of us has met her. I bet he secretly likes someone else and he's just waiting for that woman to notice him."

Thank God I had not taken a bite of pie or I would have choked on it. Is Nora making a wild-ass guess or does she know something that I don't? Has Flynn said something to her, or is she seeing things that I am not seeing clearly?

These thoughts flood through my mind and I mentally try to remember every conversation I've had with Flynn in the last few weeks. Does he still feel something for me? Do I still have a chance?

I'm careful when I say, "I don't know. He seems pretty focused on dating Jennifer."

Nora just looks at me thoughtfully and I wait for her to tell me I'm wrong.

Please tell me I'm wrong.

"What are you two doing?"

I spin around with guilty color flooding my face to find Flynn leaning up against the doorway, his arms crossed casually over his chest. How much of our conversation had he heard?

"Nothing," I say hastily, sounding like I had just robbed Fort Knox or something.

"Actually, I was just asking Rowan why I haven't met your girlfriend yet. I surmised that maybe you had secret feelings for someone else but Rowan seems to think you're pretty into this girl."

Oh. My. God.

Does Nora not have a filter on her mouth? I can't believe she just outed us on that personal, and somewhat inappropriate, speculation we were doing about Flynn.

I raise my eyes to Flynn and he's looking at me intently. "Is that right?"

"Yes," Nora continues, even though Flynn's eyes keep me pinned in place. "So what's the deal, Flynn? Why don't you bring her over to meet me?"

After a painfully long moment, Flynn turns his eyes from me over to his mother. "Tell you what… how about I bring Jennifer over for dinner next weekend when I'm off?"

Just hearing those words causes my throat to close up and my stomach to bottom out. I thought for a moment there Flynn was going to confirm his mother's suspicions and confess he still had feelings for me. But he apparently has feelings for Jennifer and it must be getting serious if he's going to bring her to meet Nora.

"You're kidding?" Nora asks, and I notice she has her eyes narrowed at Flynn.

"Why would I kid?" Flynn asks with a smirk, although he's not looking at his mom… he's staring back at me. "You just asked me to bring her over, and I said I would. That's what you want, right?"

Nora starts stuttering. "Well… yes, but… I mean… I just thought…"

Flynn turns away from me and looks at Nora again. "Look, Mom… Rowan and I need to head back. I have to get up really early tomorrow." He steps in and gives her a kiss on the top of her head.

Nora looks as confused as I feel.

CHAPTER 22

Flynn

WHAT A FUCKING day!

I sit here in the emergency room waiting for the doctor, and I'm unbelievably annoyed that I'm even here. But the Chief wasn't brooking any nonsense today, and I didn't have it in me to take an ass chewing, so here I am.

At least I'm not the only one suffering under a medical microscope. There were three of us caught in the apartment when the flashover occurred, and three of us were sent scrambling backward to avoid the 1100-degree heat. In addition to the steam burns at the top of my chest, which aren't very bad in my estimation, I also wrenched my left shoulder against a doorjamb as we were making our escape.

Stupid fuck!

But I'm not telling the doc that. A shoulder injury will get me sent home on medical leave for a good month at least, and no way am I having that. I'd die of boredom.

I will have to admit, the burns are starting to hurt like a motherfucker, and when the nurse comes in and offers me something for the pain, I go ahead and take her up on it. I might be a tough son of a bitch most times, but burns tend to be in a different realm of pain level.

A shot of Morphine five minutes later and I'm feeling pretty good. The doctor comes in and examines me, telling me what I already know. I have two second-degree steam burns—each about the size of a quarter—from the flashover. They'll require dressing changes and an antibiotic ointment. I'm put out of work for one week and told to return for a re-evaluation, but that they could take three to four weeks to heal.

Well, shit! I probably should have told him about my shoulder then, but the Morphine sort of chased that pain away, so whatever.

His last words to me were that I'd need to get a responsible adult to take me home because of the narcotic medications they had given me. Just great! I don't feel like waiting for my parents or Nix to come get me, and Tim is back on duty at the Station, so that's a no-go.

Which leaves me to dial the one person who I really want to pick me up and who would be my first choice anyway, but I put her at the bottom because… well, because damn it, I'm trying to maintain a respectful distance from her.

Rowan picks up on the second ring. "Hey, Flynnster. What's shakin'?"

Her voice is so cheerful and happy, it makes me internally sigh. I imagine the way she looks and I feel like I could drift away with her beautiful face in my mind. It would be easy because my eyes feel so heavy.

"Flynn? Are you there?"

What? Oh, right… I need a ride.

"Hey, beautiful. I need you to pick me up." Damn, but my tongue feels thick and I'm not quite sure I even understood what I just said.

"Oh my God," Rowan says with a groan. "You got drunk on duty?"

"What?" I ask in confusion. "I'm not drunk. High, probably, but not drunk."

"Flynn, what the hell is going on? I'm freaking out here."

I snicker, because this seems pretty funny. "I'm at the hospital. They gave me a shot of something but I can't leave unless someone can take me home."

"The hospital?" She practically screeches and I have to hold the phone away from my ear. When I put it back, she's in the middle of a sentence and I struggle to catch up. "…but I'm going to have to take your car so you better not be pissed. Now where are you?"

Now I'm confused. "What about my car? What's wrong with it?"

"Nothing's wrong with it. I'm going to have to drive

it there. Just tell me where you are."

"I'm at Brookdale."

I think.

"Are you okay? What happened?"

"I'm fine," I assure her, and it's true. Not feeling any pain right now. "Just come get me and I'll tell you all about it when you get here."

"Okay… I'm leaving now."

"Thanks… and Rowan?"

"Yeah?"

"You know I still think you're the one for me, right?"

There's no sound from her end, and I think she may have hung up, so I let my eyes start to close. Just as I feel myself drifting off, I think I hear her say, "I hope so."

♦

THROBBING PAIN WAKES me up and my eyelids feel like they're glued shut. With a solid effort, I open them and stare around, confused. I expect to see the Station sleeping quarters, but I'm in my bed… in my apartment… and I have no clue how I got here.

Then the memories come rushing back and I remember the fire and my trip to the hospital. I have vague memories of Rowan coming to get me, and maybe I'm delusional, but I think she may have been crying when she showed up.

The rest of the night flashes in bits and pieces. Her

buckling me into my car, helping me take my shirt off, sitting beside my bed and holding my hand.

I gingerly poke at the bandages on my chest and suck in my breath when the pain ratchets up. Rolling off the bed, I stand up and look down to see I'm naked. A very distinct memory assaults me and I'm quite positive I insisted to Rowan that I sleep naked, demanding that she help me out of all of my clothes.

Oh, God. What in the hell did they give me at the hospital?

I pull on a pair of sweatpants and head toward the bathroom so I can take the monster of all pisses. My bladder feels like it's going to explode.

Just as I step into the hallway, Rowan's bedroom door flies open. "What's wrong? Are you okay?"

I smile because she's standing before me in just my t-shirt. The one I'd given her to wear months ago when she first came to stay with me. Normally she wears some shorts with it, but this morning, I'm treated to miles of gloriously bare legs with the hem just teasing me short of her panties.

"I'm good. Just going to the bathroom."

"Are you in pain?"

"Actually, yeah. I'd love some Ibuprofen if you don't mind."

Rowan turns to head into the kitchen. "They actually gave you some stronger stuff."

"No," I call to her. "I don't want that shit. Just Ibuprofen."

She looks back at me in astonishment. "Are you sure?"

I grin at her. "Yup. Seems it makes me do strange things… like demanding that you strip me naked."

Rowan actually blushes scarlet. "Remember that, do you?"

"Bits and pieces."

She gives me a smile. "Well, come into the kitchen when you're done and let me check the wounds. The doctor told me what to look for when changing the bandages."

After I finish my business, I head into the kitchen, scratching my stomach and trying to stifle a yawn. I feel so groggy and need caffeine immediately.

I find Rowan bent over Capone's water bowl to pick it up, and I'm treated with a boner-inducing view of her ass barely hanging into a pair of white, lace panties. Fuck, I'm going to pitch a tent right here in the kitchen so I quickly avert my eyes and head to the coffee pot. I concentrate on the burns on my chest, and I let the throb of pain invade my senses, which completely works to help me avoid embarrassing myself.

Rowan steps up to the sink and fills Capone's bowl. "Why don't you sit at the table and let me look at the burns?"

I see a cup of coffee already poured with two Ibuprofen laying beside it. I pick them up, toss them in the back of my throat, and chase it with the hot coffee, which burns like hell going down.

Taking a seat at the table, I sip at my coffee a bit more carefully while Rowan feeds Capone. When she's done, she washes her hands in the sink and quickly dries them with some paper towels. She steps up to me and moves right in between my legs with no hesitation. Memories of that first time we kissed, with her standing between my legs, floods over me. I try like hell to avert my eyes so I'm not staring straight at her breasts as they sway softly under the cotton shirt when she moves.

Focus on the pain, Flynn. Avert the hard on.

"Lean back," she says softly. "I'm going to take the bandages off and put some ointment on."

"Maybe I should take a shower first."

Rowan shakes her head. "No, let's be careful today with it. Bath is all you get so we can keep the bandages dry."

I grumble because I hate taking baths. Our tub is large enough to barely bathe a child, much less my overgrown frame. But I comply with her request and lean back in the chair, tilting my head back slightly so she can get a good look.

Carefully peeling the bandages back, I silently will the Ibuprofen to work faster, and bring the throb down from a roar to a dull ache. When the first bandage comes off, the cool air at first feels good, then the pain starts to intensify. I grit my teeth and stare at the ceiling, hoping I don't cry like a little baby in front of her.

The second bandage comes off and Rowan bends over to look at the wounds. "They actually look pretty good." Her finger comes out and lightly touches the good skin around the burn, but even that hurts and I suck air in between my teeth.

"Quit being a baby," she says.

I don't say anything but let Nurse Ratchet continue her ministrations.

"One of them is blistering pretty badly, but right now there are no open wounds," she comments. "The doctor told me what to look for, so I think you're good right now."

"How big are they?" I ask, because I can't get a good look at them since they sit right below my collarbone in the middle of my chest.

She holds her hand up and touches her forefinger to her thumb, making a circle. "Not too big… probably like this."

I nod and watch with dubious eyes as she now advances on me with a tube of cream. "What's that?"

"An antibiotic ointment I have to put on, and then I'll put on clean bandages."

Rowan squeezes a dab of cream onto her forefinger

and leans forward. She touches the burn softly and starts to smear it in a circle. The pain spikes even though her touch is gentle and I jerk, issuing a curse from my mouth. "Fuck, that hurts."

She stands back and looks at me with affection and amusement. "God, I can't believe what a sissy you are."

"Well, damn Rowan… you have a touch that is about as soft as a concrete cinderblock."

Rowan leans back down with another dab of cream to torture my other wound. "Quit complaining or you can just get Jennifer to come over and take care of your sorry ass."

She's teasing, of course, because I can hear the laughter in her voice. But I also hear a twinge of jealousy and that works faster than the Ibuprofen to ease my pain. It must be the rush of pleasure endorphins.

"Yeah, well… that will be kind of hard, seeing as how I broke things off with her two days ago."

Rowan's head snaps up so fast, she almost catches me under the chin. Her eyes bore hard into mine, and her brows furrow inward. She looks pissed at first, but then I see she is just shocked over the pronouncement and has no clue what to do with the feelings they invoke.

And they definitely invoke feelings. I can see them swirling in her eyes. She stares for just another moment and then goes back to her task, rubbing the ointment in.

"So you broke up, huh?"

"Yeah… we just weren't destined, I guess."

"Did she take it hard?"

"Not really," I tell her, and it's true… she didn't. She actually shook my hand when we parted ways outside the restaurant where I had met her to break the bad news.

Rowan opens a bandage and with much more care, gently lays it over a burn and presses it into place. "Well… I'm sorry. No matter, it always sucks to go through a break up."

"Are you?" I ask, watching her intently.

She looks up at me, another bandage in her hand. "Am I what?"

"Sorry we broke up."

She doesn't answer right away and leans forward to put the other bandage on. But then she softly says, "No… I'm not sorry. Not really."

I can't help myself so I put my hand under her chin and force her eyes up to mine. "My mom is a wise woman, don't you think?"

Her eyes flare wide with surprise, because I'm quite sure she wasn't expecting me to bring my mom into the conversation.

She nods her head slightly. "Very wise."

"Well, I overheard her conversation with you on Thanksgiving. I just… think she's very wise."

I can actually see the wheels spinning in Rowan's head as she drifts back to that conversation and tries to remember everything Nora Caldwell said to her. I smile softly and decide to put her out of her misery.

"She said that she suspected I was into someone else… and that's why I didn't bring Jennifer over to see her."

Rowan stands straight but doesn't back up from between my legs. I love her closeness to me and inhale her sweet scent. "Is that right?"

"Pretty much."

"You said something like that on the phone last night… when you called me."

"Hey," I say and hold my hands up to deny culpability. "I deny anything I say while under the influence of drugs."

Her face drops and her gaze lowers to the floor. She says, "Oh" and starts to turn away from me but I grab her wrist. When she turns to look back at me, her eyes are stormy gray and filled with confusion.

"But," I tell her. "I'd say the same thing here in the bright light of day."

Rowan's eyes go from dark to light in just a matter of a few seconds. She just looks at me and I return her stare.

Then slowly, she reaches her hand out and places her fingertips at the edge of my forehead where my hairline starts. She pushes her fingers in slowly until she's three-knuckles deep into my hair and she combs her fingers through. She repeats this a few times, just lazily running her hand through my hair.

With a smile that is laced with trepidation, she says, “I’m still scared, Flynn.”

I reach up and grab her hand, pulling it to my mouth. Holding her fingertips to my lips for a moment, I slowly release them. I stand up from the chair and Rowan has to back up to give me room.

Looking down at her, I give her an encouraging smile. “I know you’re scared. But I won’t push you for anything you don’t want to freely give.”

I lean down and give her a soft kiss on top of her head while I gently cup the back to hold her there. I let my lips linger for a moment and then I release her.

She smiles at me and I turn away… intent on cramming my body into that tiny bathtub so I can get cleaned up.

CHAPTER 23
Rowan

FLYNN AND I walk through the apartment door, loaded with bags upon bags of stuff. Capone rushes up to meet us, dipping his big head in the bags as we lay them on the floor to unburden our arms.

"It's your turn to take Capone out," I tell him. "I'll start putting everything away."

"That's a fair deal. We'll be right back."

I smile as I watch Capone prance in place when he sees Flynn grab the leash. It's amazing how fast they've bonded, especially since I didn't think Capone would ever take to a man because of the way Juice treated him.

Flynn leaves tomorrow for Nix and Emily's wedding in St. John. I really wish I could go but it just isn't feasible. So, we decided that we would celebrate Christmas early, just the two of us. We spent the majority of the day shopping for gifts, although I had bought mine for Flynn a few weeks ago, but it needed some work and I just finished it last night. We picked up some decorations, too, although we decided not to put up a tree.

Neither one of us wanted to bother cooking so we agreed on Chinese. I pick up the phone and place an order for us…Shrimp Fried Rice for me and General Tso's for Flynn, along with two egg rolls. I carry our Christmas gifts back to put them in our respective rooms. I don't have that many as I really only bought a few things. I got a beautiful sterling silver frame for Nix and Emily, so they could put a wedding photo in it, and a crystal wine chiller for Nick and Nora. Finally, I bought a box of cigars for George and some perfume for Fil. The Caldwell's gifts will have to wait until they get back from St. John but I plan on sending Fil and George's over to them in the next few days.

Opening my closet, I pull out Flynn's gift. I wrapped it the other day and I'm so nervous about giving it to him. I wanted something that would let him know how much he means to me, but without it being too intimate. Because at this point, I really want Flynn but I'm still too chicken to take the dive.

When he was dating Jennifer, I sort of came to a realization. There will eventually be a woman in Flynn's life. He is too good of a man for there not to be. Now, my big fear of involving myself with Flynn is that I will get crushed if it doesn't work out and I will probably lose my friendship with him.

However, I saw while he was dating, that if another

woman is in his life, I'm going to lose him anyway to a certain extent. He is not going to be able to spend the time with me that he does, and the even bigger risk is that his new love probably would not want him having a close female friend. So, it seems I'm probably damned either way.

Now I find myself debating the best way to have Flynn Caldwell in my life, with the least amount of risk to myself. But most importantly, I also have to figure out how to do this without hurting Flynn. Because even though I'm afraid of getting hurt myself, it's becoming more important to me that he remain unscathed.

"We're back," Flynn yells and I bring his gift out with me.

"I ordered the Chinese. It should be here in about half an hour."

Flynn looks pointedly at the present in my hand. "What's that?"

"It's your gift," I tell him, setting it on the coffee table. Capone nudges it and gives it a sniff. "Don't even think about it, Capone," I give him a warning. He doesn't even look abashed and nudges it again, but then he loses interest.

"Can I open it now?" Flynn asks, his eyes lit up like a five-year-old.

"No. We have to decorate first, then eat, and then presents."

"Why does it have to be in that order?" he sulks.

"Because… I just decided to make that rule. Besides… the anticipation is what makes it great, right?"

Flynn's childish and goofy grin melts away and a smirk replaces it. "Anticipation can kill you, too."

I snort over that comment, because I know exactly what he's talking about.

We're able to decorate the apartment by the time the food arrives. It wasn't like it was a massive undertaking though. We basically bought some cheerful, colored lights and hung them around the living room windows. He strung tinsel across the mantle of the fireplace, which has been broken the entire time Flynn has lived here. And we lit some Cinnamon-Apple candles, turning the lights down low so the room just glowed from the lights and wavering flames.

Flynn and I ate our Chinese food on the floor, both using the chopsticks. "This reminds me of *A Christmas Story*," he says.

I start laughing and point my sticks at him. "It does! Where at the end they eat Christmas dinner at a Chinese restaurant."

"Yup. That's a great movie. We should see if it's on TV and watch it tonight."

"That would be fun," I agree, taking my last scoop of rice. I'm stuffed and can't hold anymore, even though I only ate about half of it.

Pushing my container away, I watch Flynn polish his food all the way off, even grabbing my container and eating some of mine. When he's finished, he lies back on the floor and groans. "I'm dying. That was way too much food."

"It's not like someone forced you to eat all that."

"I know, I know. I got carried away."

With Flynn lying on his back, the hem of his shirt inches up and I see a small strip of skin above his jeans. It glows golden in the flickering lights and I have a hard time pulling my eyes away from the thin patch of dark hair that is disappearing under the waistband. My eyes do finally move and travel upward. He's wearing a V-neck, black sweater and I can still see the two burn marks peeking out. They've healed well, with only a slight reddening of the skin remaining, and he swears they don't hurt anymore. Flynn was only out of work for a week, although he had to spend another week on light duty. Just about the time he got released to full duty, his vacation started, so I think he's getting a little restless. Flynn is definitely not the type that likes to sit around and do nothing.

"Do you want to open presents?" I ask.

Flynn raises his head from the floor and cracks one eye open at me. "Does Chinese food make you want to barf if you eat too much?"

"I don't know, does it?"

Sitting up with a groan, Flynn says, “Hell yeah, it does, but I’ll get over it. So let’s get this party going.”

Standing up, I walk into the kitchen. “I got a surprise. Stay there.”

When I return, I’m holding a chilled bottle of champagne and two flutes. Flynn looks at me with interest.

“What you got there?”

Holding my implements up, I say, “I figured we could celebrate Christmas and also do a toast to Nix and Emily.”

Flynn hops up from the ground and takes the bottle from me. He deftly removes the foil and wire cage from the cork and, holding it to the side and angled away from me, he easily pops it open. I hold the flutes out and he pours us each a glass before setting the bottle on the coffee table.

Holding my glass up, I say, “Merry Christmas, Flynn. I can never thank you for all you’ve done for me. And here’s wishing Nix and Emily a beautiful Christmas wedding.”

Flynn taps his flute against mine and we both raise our glasses, staring at each other while we sip. Even after our glasses lower, I still can’t tear my eyes from his and I love how the hazel color gleams under the Christmas lights, causing sparkles to appear.

Flynn finally breaks away and sets his glass down. He smacks his palms together and then briskly rubs them back and forth. "I want presents. Now. Now. Now."

Laughing, I set my glass down and then pick up my present from the coffee table. We both sit down on the couch, side by side, with only an inch of space between us. I hand the gift over with a qualification. "It's not much. I hope you don't think it's too lame."

Flynn shakes the small box near his ear, trying to harbor a guess as to what it holds. He then sets it in his lap and tears into the paper, revealing a brown box underneath that is taped shut. He picks at the edges of the tape, and rips it back. Peeling the flaps away, he reaches inside and pulls his gift out. It's wrapped in tissue paper, which he easily removes, and then he holds it up before him.

It's a brown leather journal and has embossed on the front, "The Story of Me". Flynn reaches over to his right and flips on the table lamp so he can see it better. He shoots a curious glance at me but I don't say anything.

I watch as he opens the cover and reads the words out loud I had written just this morning.

Flynn,

You saved my life and you are my hero. You offered me friendship with no judgment, and kindness when I needed it most. You've shown me that it is okay to trust, and I want to always continue to develop our bond.

For a while, I divided my life into pre- and

post-Flynn, because my life seemed so much better after meeting you. But then I realized, my entire life is what makes me… well, me, and thus I need to celebrate it all.

I want to share all of it with you.

So, I've written furiously the last two weeks, and I'm giving you The Story of Me, so that you can know me better than anyone on this earth.

Love,
Rowan

With a smile on his face, Flynn takes his fingertip and strokes it gently over my name.

I lean in closer to him and turn to the first page of the book. It reads, *What is your favorite childhood memory?*

"See… it's a journal that asks probing questions about your life. You just fill in the answers. I tried to answer everything as honestly as I could, even though some of them were lame."

Flynn is quiet as he reads my answer. It wasn't the coolest of memories, but it was actually when my mom let me play dress up with her. I must have been about five or so, and she let me wear her heels, she styled my hair, and she let me put on makeup. It was a great memory, because it wasn't too long after that she started to lose interest in me.

When Flynn finishes reading, he doesn't say a word

but flips through a few pages until he finds one that catches his eye. I peer closer and it asks, *Describe your high school years.*

Flynn starts reading, lost in my words. I just watch him… silently, as he reads about all of the terrible things I did to get my parents' attention. I told him some of it before, but I didn't hold back now on all the ways in which I was an awful child.

When he finishes reading, he turns the book face down on his lap to save his place and turns to look at me. "This is, without a doubt, the best present anyone has ever given me." He picks up my hand and brings it to his mouth, placing a tender kiss on my knuckles. My heart melts into a soft puddle and I actually sigh.

Flynn starts to pick up the book to read again, but I grab it from him. "Uh-uh, buddy. I get a present, too."

He looks at me and cocks an eyebrow, giving me a devilish grin. "You do?"

"Damn tootin' I do. Now get it. Pronto." I stand up from the couch and grab his hand, pulling him along. "Shoo. Go get my present."

Chuckling, Flynn walks down the hall to his bedroom. Within just a minute, he's back, carrying a huge box. He must have had it hidden in his closet. He sits it down on the living room floor with a thud. It's big enough that the top of it comes to the middle of my thigh. I stare at it, wondering what in the hell he got me.

He sweeps his hand toward the box and says, "Dig in."

I look at him for just a split second and then I dive for the box. I rip the paper in a frenzy and make short work of the tape holding it closed. When I open it, I'm met with thousands of Styrofoam peanuts completely hiding its treasure.

I thrust my hands into the billowy mess and start rooting around. Peanuts go flying everywhere, and Capone immediate starts eating them.

"Flynn… get him away from those."

I keep digging in the box while Flynn is repetitively saying, "No, Capone. No!"

When I get near the bottom, my entire upper body is practically hanging in the box. My fingers brush against something hard and I latch on, hauling it out.

I stare in astonishment at the… cinder block I'm holding in my hand.

My gaze moves to Flynn, and I must have the most confused look on my face because he takes the brick from me with a laugh. "That was just to weigh it down. Keep digging."

Giving a frustrated grunt, I dive back in and start throwing out armfuls of peanuts. "You're cleaning this mess up, Flynn… just so you know."

He chuckles and I hear him say, "Gladly. It's so worth it to be able to stare at your ass while you're bent over that box."

"Perv," I mutter but I smile.

After a few more moments, my fingers brush against something and I pull on it. Standing up, I'm holding an envelope. Just a plain, white envelope with nothing on it. I sneak a brief look at Flynn and he's watching me intently. I slip my finger under the edge of the flap and tear it open. I pull out a piece of folded paper and open it carefully.

It appears to have several handwritten messages on the inside and one message that appears to be taped to the paper.

I look at Flynn one more time. He actually sits down on the couch and props an ankle on his knee, draping his arm across the back. He watches me like a hawk and I have a feeling he's trying to gauge my reaction.

I start reading. The first note says…

Rowan,

Awaiting for you tomorrow at JFK is a round-trip ticket in the name of Anne Marie Cleeden to St. John. You only need your driver's license and your birth certificate to fly to the US Virgin Islands, both of which you have. The ticket has already been paid for and it cannot be refunded. If you choose not to use it to come to the wedding, you can use it to fly anywhere else for up to one year, so it is yours to do with what you wish. You also have a room booked for you in St. John that is paid for. And before you get mad at me, please know that I did not buy this for you myself. I had a little help. Read on.

Love,
Flynn

My heart starts beating madly and I'm pissed, but I'm also incredibly humbled by this gesture. I read the messages and they are from all the people who chipped in to buy the ticket and pay for my room.

Nix writes that if I don't come, he will be forced to fire me so he had no choice but to chip in. That actually makes me laugh out loud. Emily writes that she would be devastated not to have me there, which I think is a little over the top, but then she presses her point and tells me the wedding photos will be ruined as there will be too many male guests in the photos. I can't help but snort because that is brilliantly manipulative.

Nora writes the most, telling me how much she wants me to be there, not only for Nix and Em, but also for Flynn, so he won't be odd-man out. She tells me how much she adores me and she knows that I won't let her down. And oh, shit, does that put the pressure on. Nick just wrote a brief, "Please come. We'd love to have you."

And at the bottom, I even notice there is a printout of a text message from Renner that has been taped there. It says, "We haven't met but I'm dying to do so, and what better way than to hook up in the tropics. Please come and I'll tell you lots of juicy secrets about Flynn". That one also makes me laugh.

I fold the letter back up and return it to the envelope. Walking up to Flynn, I look down at him. "I'm mad at you."

"Why me? I didn't pay for it by myself."

"Yeah, but you orchestrated it."

He gives me a sly grin. "Got me. Please say you'll come."

Holding my hand out to him, he takes it and I tug so he'll stand up. I stand on my tiptoes and wrap my arms around his neck. Putting my nose into his chest, I breathe in, and then I squeeze him in a tight hug.

Flynn squeezes me back and rests his chin on my head.

"Yes, I'll come with you… you big bully."

Pulling back, Flynn brings his hand up and caresses my cheek. "Thank you."

Before I can say anything, Flynn leans down and gives me a soft kiss on my lips. My mouth willingly opens and I press back, sliding my tongue in briefly. I can feel Flynn jerk with surprise and he pulls back, his eyes searching mine.

"I'm ready, Flynn. I want more."

His eyes flash hot and his lips turn up sensually. He takes a deep breath and says, "I can't believe I'm getting ready to say this, but maybe we shouldn't. Maybe we should take our time."

Yeah, that's not going to work for me. I've waffled on this issue for far too long, and caused Flynn untold grief and frustration over my indecision. He's not going to wait a minute more, and neither am I.

Reaching my hand out, I press my palm to the front of his jeans, feeling him grow amazingly hard beneath me. I squeeze him gently and he sucks his breath in harshly, growing harder yet beneath my hand.

"We're not waiting," I tell him.

CHAPTER 24

Flynn

SHE DOESN'T WANT to wait and I release my breath in a rush.

Her touch is everything I thought it would be.

And so much more.

It's soft but confident, and I bet she could make me come just stroking me through my jeans. But I'm not about to let that happen.

I reach down and grab her hand, pushing it behind her back and pinning it there. With just a tug, I pull her forward so her body is pressed into me. Both of our free hands hang loose by our sides and we just stare at each other. I take in her gray eyes, which are bathed in the soft glow of colored lights and looking at me with that openness that I've come to appreciate about Rowan. I let my eyes travel, taking in her cheekbones… the slope of her nose… how her bottom lip is just slightly fuller than her top. I roam my eyes all over her face, memorizing it so when I close my eyes to sleep, I can appreciate the details.

Leaning down, I brush my lips lightly back and forth against hers. She sighs into me… a sound that is so peaceful… so content, that I'm all of a sudden nervous over the power I may hold.

I hold Rowan's body in my hands, but more importantly, I hold her heart. She's guarded it fiercely and now she's opened the door to it and invited me in. The responsibility is huge and while I have no clue what the future holds for us, I know I'll never intentionally hurt her. Not the way her parents did.

I push these thoughts aside because I don't want to talk myself out of sinking into Rowan tonight. I know that may be selfish of me, but Rowan gave me the go ahead and I'm not stopping unless she tells me to.

Moving my lips, I feather them over her temple, down her cheek. I softly graze over her ear, and then move down her neck. Soft, light, warm kisses. Mostly just my lips, sometimes a little lick of tongue. Her skin is so soft, I could run my lips across it for hours and never tire.

With every touch she shivers, or squirms, or flexes her hips into mine.

She's growing restless from my lazy touches and brings her hand up to wrap around my neck. She tries to urge me on, but I'm not having any of it. She's made me wait, for what seems like an eternity, and for all I know she could spook and run tomorrow. But for tonight…

she's mine and this will be done on my timetable.

When I whisper my lips back over her mouth, I gently run my tongue along her bottom lip before moving toward her jaw. Rowan grips me by the hair and demands, "Kiss me, Flynn."

"I am," I tell her as I nibble along her skin.

"No," she says with a moan laced in frustration. "Not like that."

"Oh… you mean like this?" I move back to her neck, and just slide my lips along its silky slope. She shivers but shakes her head.

"Then how?" I ask.

"My mouth… hard… please."

Releasing Rowan's wrist, I move my hands up to hold her face. Her eyes are wide… luminescent. They are pleading with me to make her mine, in every carnal way I know how. It tests my resolve to take this slow because the way she's looking at me now, I could have this over and done within a matter of minutes.

Instead, I reward her with what she asks. I lean down and seize her mouth, taking it in a brutal storm of lust. My tongue plunges… masters, and I feel like a fucking caveman that brought home the biggest rump of dinosaur roast when I feel Rowan tremble and practically sag against me.

Wrapping a hand around her waist, I pull her tighter into me, pushing my thickness into her belly. My other hand snakes under her shirt and I trail my fingers up her ribs and over the bottom slope of her breast. It is one of the times I'm grateful my girl doesn't wear a bra and her skin feels like fire when my entire palm covers her, causing Rowan to moan out and push herself harder into my hand.

I keep molesting her mouth while I gently squeeze her breast, teasing her every so often with a flick of my thumb over her nipple. Each time I do it, her breath catches and her hips move, and it gives me a heady feeling of power that I can control her body this way.

It makes me wonder what else I can do.

After a slight pinch of my fingers on her nipple, I pull my hand out of her shirt. She gives a cry of distress into my mouth and I pull back just enough to say, "Shhh."

My hand immediately goes to her pants. I easily pop her top button and slide the zipper down. Rowan gives a groan of approval, although she holds her breath when my hand starts its descent down. I efficiently burrow into her panties, and just like I remembered from that night several weeks ago, she is liquid heat. I move my finger back and forth through her slickness, then rub her in tight circles.

I want her to come for me, right here and right now. I pull my mouth from hers and say, "Look at me, Rowan."

Her eyes open and she focuses on me, although her hips buck every time I hit her just right.

"Watch me, baby. I want to see those beautiful eyes." I work my finger against her, every so often plunging inside, but immediately retreating to caress against her. The pressure I'm using is causing her to shake and I know she's not long for this plane of existence.

Her eyes start to roll backward and her lids flutter as she gets close.

"Uh-uh," I chide. "Eyes on me."

She refocuses and I smile at her. "That's my girl. This feels good, doesn't it?"

She nods and I rub the pad of my finger against her faster.

Our eyes are locked, our breath coming in choppy spurts. "You don't know how much I've dreamed of this, Rowan. Of doing this to you." I plunge and caress a little harder and I can feel her body start to stiffen. "I want to do so many things to you… really, *really* dirty things. Will you do anything I ask?"

Rowan gasps as I push two fingers in and then pull them both out to spread her moisture around. "Yes," she gasps. "Anything."

"Will you come for me? Right now?" I push against her as I say those words and holy fuck, she fractures apart in front of me. A scream comes out of her mouth and I swoop down with my lips to swallow it up, all the while keeping my hand firmly wedged between her legs as the orgasms rends her body.

When I feel her start to sag, I pull my hand out of her pants and scoop her up in my arms. She's as limp as a rag doll as I walk swiftly down the hall to my bedroom. Capone is on our heels and he tries to follow us in, but I close the door in his face. "Sorry buddy. I'm not doing this with an audience."

Rowan giggles and I look down at her. Her head is resting against my chest and she's looking at me with playfulness.

"What's so funny?" I ask.

She gives another tinkling laugh. "It's just a dog, Flynn. It's not like it's a person watching us."

I capture her mouth for a quick kiss, pulling back and biting on her lip. "Baby… what I have planned for you will have that dog blushing, trust me."

Her entire body shivers in pleasure and there's that caveman feeling again. I set her down on the floor and she immediately starts working at my pants. "I need to touch you," she says.

I pull her hands away and push her back gently. "And you will… in time. But I have other things planned first."

Rowan's eyes widen and her tongue darts out to wet her lips. "Like what?"

"Like making you come again. With my mouth."

Her lips part as she sucks in a wisp of air for fortification. "I want to do the same."

"And you can… later. I want to play first."

I expect Rowan to balk but instead her mouth curves upward in a sensual smile and her eyes flicker with heat. Her voice comes out all soft and breathy when she says, "Okay. Tell me what to do."

I cross over and sit on the bed, resting my hands by my hips. "Take off your clothes for me."

She grins. "Want me to do a sexy dance?"

I laugh and shake my head. "I've seen the way you dance. If you do that while taking your clothes off, you'll kill me. Dead."

Chuckling, she pulls her shirt up over her head and tosses it to the side. My eyes go to her breasts and they are perfect. They are soft, round, and sit high with pink nipples that are hard against her satin skin.

She pushes her jeans down, sliding them over her bare feet and kicking them to the side. She's left in nothing but a pair of pale pink panties that are mostly lace. I can see the dark triangle of hair shadowed between her legs. She hooks her thumbs at the waist and starts to push them down.

"Wait," I say abruptly and she stops, eyeing me with curiosity. "Come here."

Rowan walks over to me, stepping in between my legs. I hadn't intended on touching her again quite this soon, but I can't help when I lean forward and suck one of her nipples into my mouth. Her hands wrap around my head and she holds me to her tightly.

I lave at her breast for just a few seconds, and then I pull back. "Crawl on the bed and lie on your back."

She immediately complies, completely trusting me in my requests. I stand up and step back a few feet to watch her. "Touch yourself for me, Rowan. Show me how you want me to touch you."

I expect her to blush and maybe hesitate but she does nothing more than take a second to flash me a knowing look, and then her hand dives down her underwear. And oh holy hell, I didn't expect her to go for the main prize so soon. I sort of expected her to run her hands over her body, caress all of her skin, maybe pluck at her nipples a bit. But she's not wasting time and I think this is a devious plan on her part to get me to hurry up.

I go ahead and remove my clothes while I'm watching her. I really can't see exactly what she's doing because those damn panties are blocking me, but I can see her hand moving between her legs and her teeth are gripping her bottom lip. She keeps her eyes open though and watches me as I strip.

I'm fucking hard as a rock and after I get my pants off, I grab my dick and stroke it a few times, trying hard not to groan over the contact. Releasing myself, I stride over to the bed and grab Rowan's ankles. I pull her to the edge and she gives a tiny yelp but her hand never comes out from between her legs.

I lay my hand over hers and hold her still for a moment. "Are you close?"

She shakes her head and tries to move her hand but I won't let her.

"Want me to take you the rest of the way?" I ask.

"God, yes," she says and I gently pull her hand away from her body. I peel her underwear off and toss them over my shoulder. Kneeling at the edge of the bed, I pull her closer and drape her legs over my shoulders. I bring my hands over her stomach and look at her.

"Rowan… sit up on your elbows and watch me."

She immediately props herself up, which thrusts those magnificent breasts outward. My hands unlink and glide up her stomach, taking a perfect mound in each hand to squeeze before grabbing each nipple between my forefinger and thumb to pinch. She rewards me with a long moan and her hips buck up, hitting me in my chin, which reminds me of what my ultimate intention was. I release her breasts and move my hands south, taking a hold and spreading her wide. I stare at her femininity laid bare before me, almost disbelieving it is mine to do with what I want.

And I know what I want to do.

I glance up and she's watching me keenly. "You're so beautiful, Rowan. You make everything else around me seem barren."

She doesn't respond but takes in a slow breath that I can see is stuttering out and her eyes are swimming with more emotion than I've ever seen. She's feeling right now… with her heart. She's all in, completely with me.

I lower my mouth and plunge into her with my tongue, and I hear her flop back down on the bed with a cry. Her hands come up and grip my head, pushing me harder into her… which is fine by me. I want her to feel every bit of me down there while I lick and suck her off. I want to see how fast I can make her come and, apparently, it's pretty fast. When I feel her starting to tremble hard, when her fingers flex into my scalp with a stinging bite, I know it won't take much to push her over. I work at her with my lips, feathering my tongue quickly, and then I suck on her hard.

Rowan screams so loud that I hope to fuck the neighbors don't call the cops and her whole body stiffens while she tries to push my face harder into her. I don't let up and continue to lick at her, while her legs squeeze me in a vice.

"Fuck, Flynn," she says and finally pushes my head away.

I stand up and wipe my hand across my mouth. "If you insist," I tell her, reaching into my bedside drawer and pulling out a handful of condoms. I toss them all on the bed beside her and she gives me a salacious smile, while she reaches over and grabs one. She sits up on the bed and kneels before me.

Her fingers are sure and while she covers my boy up, she leans in and runs her tongue over one of my nipples. And while it feels oh so fucking good, I need something different.

I put my hand on her chest and gently push her back. Following right over on top of her, I crawl in between her spread legs. Looking at her lying there, her neck and chest flushed red from her orgasms, her bottom lip swollen from where she was chewing on it while I was eating her out, I don't ever remember being this horny in my life.

I want to slam my way home and once I get there, I want to slam into her repeatedly, almost like I'm branding my place inside of her body. But there's time for that later. I want to go slow tonight and I want to drag this out. I want this first time to be so memorable, that we'll strive for the rest of our lives to try to outdo it.

I put my hands behind her knees and lift her legs, bending them back until she's spread wide open. My dick is sticking out at the perfect angle and with just a downward tilt of my hips, I'm able to bring the head right to her opening. I keep ahold of her legs the entire time, not even needing my hand or hers to guide me in.

I give a slight push and although I know she's soaking wet for me, I also know she'll be tight because I didn't spend enough time with my fingers inside of her… getting her ready for me. So I go slowly, pushing in with the greatest of care, feeling her body sigh in welcome.

When my pelvis is resting hard against hers, I take her legs and wrap them around my waist, then I lean over her more closely, resting my weight on my arms. My face hovers over hers and she watches me with wonder. We just lie there together, with me sunk deep inside of her, and we do nothing but stare. Her hand comes up and touches my face softly, her fingers skimming down. My eyes flutter closed for a moment and then open back up. I pull my hips back slowly, and then sink inside her again.

"That feels good," she murmurs.

"Feels so good," I agree, and I do it again.

Then again.

And again.

I establish a very slow rhythm but I make sure that she feels every inch of me as I pull back, and every inch going in. She grips me tight and hot, and I swear… it's the best fucking feeling ever.

Everything builds slowly. My movements, our breaths, even my orgasm starts as a minor rumble in the base of my spine and stays on idle, waiting for me to push us both into blinding pleasure.

But I'm not ready… not right yet. I want to watch

Rowan some more.

Because I love the way she tries to keep her eyes on me, but she can't help it when the pleasure causes them to close. She starts chewing her lip again, and once I even move my hand up and grab it from between her teeth, leaning down to lick at it. Redness creeps up her neck, flushing her pale skin with the blood that is racing through her veins. Her heels dig into the backs of my thighs, urging me on.

"Flynn… I want to come again."

"You will," I promise her as I make lazy pushes in and out. A bead of sweat travels down my temple, slides along my jaw, and drops onto her cheek. I lean down and nuzzle it away.

"No… I want to come now. I'm close."

Her words spur me on and I pick up the pace. She rewards me with a gasp and a barely audible, *Yes*, which excites me even more.

I push up from my elbows to my hands so I can get better leverage and I give in to my compulsion to slam my way home. When I hit her deep inside, she cries out and immediately says, "Do it again."

I retreat and thrust, faster and faster, and now I hook one of my elbows under her leg, and let this new angle suck me in even deeper.

My world starts spinning as the pleasure builds and everything starts to fade.

Everything but Rowan.

Faster and faster, harder and deeper… flesh smacking wickedly against each other.

Rowan's eyes close tight and her upper back arches off the bed.

"I'm coming," she gasps.

She doesn't need to tell me because I can feel it contracting all around my cock and the knowledge sends me into overdrive. I unleash a firestorm of thrusts on her body, wrapping my arms underneath of her and pulling her to me tight… letting my hips do all the work. I can feel a tingling ball at the bottom of my spine and then it rockets upward, blasting off through every nerve ending in my body.

"Fuck!" I shout as I start coming… and coming… and coming. It seems to go on forever and I don't want it to ever stop, because it's the best fucking nut I've ever blown in my life.

Rowan's arms are wrapped tightly around me and our chests are mashed together. My nose is stuck into the crook of her neck and my hips continue to shallowly thrust against her, even as I feel tiny pulses of spasms gripping me from below.

My breath is coming out so harshly, I can feel how it blows away and then pulls her brown locks against my mouth. My bones feel like rubber and I'm doubting I'll ever be able to walk again.

I'm shattered… destroyed… probably wrecked beyond repair.

And I could give a fuck because that was probably the best thing that's ever happened to me in my life.

CHAPTER 25

Rowan

WE ARRIVE AT the resort on St. John mid-afternoon, after a forty-five minute boat ride from St. Thomas. It's a balmy eighty-two degrees and I'm in awe of the lush, tropical scenery. I've never seen anything like it in my life and I'm not sure I ever will again. We were on the same flight with Nix, Emily, Hank, Nick, and Nora. Everyone else will be arriving soon and we've made plans to meet in one of the outdoor bars for drinks before dinner.

Flynn steps up to the desk to register us and Emily nudges my shoulder. She leans in and whispers, "So… you and Flynn… finally hooked up?"

I try not to grin because she makes it sound so seedy, and what Flynn and I did last night is anything but. It was beyond explosive, and there's not a part of my body that Flynn doesn't know intimately right now, but it's definitely not seedy.

It's everything that I said I wouldn't give in to, but things were just getting so blended in my mind that I had a hard time figuring out where my friendship with Flynn stopped, and the sexual intimacy began. I mean, even before we had sex, I had engaged in a level of intimacy with Flynn that surpassed any other relationship I'd had before. I thought friendship and intimacy would not go together, but the truth is, they are so closely related, I stepped into a relationship that was already a blended mix. When Flynn kissed me last night… ever so soft and tentative, I felt my entire being give in to my desires and I decided to stop worrying about what may or may not be.

It's not to say I'm not still worrying about it, because when I woke up this morning before the alarm went off, and just luxuriated in the feeling of being wrapped in Flynn's arms, my first thought was perhaps I made a mistake. I know that if Flynn and I don't work out, the hurt is going to be unimaginable.

Emily nudges me again and I realize I've ignored her in favor of daydreaming about Flynn. "I guess," I say lamely. "I mean… yeah, we took it to the next level."

She throws her arms around me and squeals. "That's so wonderful. The last of the Caldwell men have fallen. But then again, I knew this was going to happen."

"You did?" Because I sure didn't. Even though I had yearned painfully for Flynn on a sexual level, I was still pretty unsure whether this would happen just a little over twenty-four hours ago.

"Yup," she says smugly. "You two are perfect for each other."

Looking around, I see Flynn still at the desk, and the rest of the group is standing nearby. I grab Emily's hand and lead her further away from everyone so they don't overhear. "How do you know, Emily? I mean… what if this is just sex, and then when it fizzles, our friendship is what gets lost?"

There… I've managed to succinctly voice my greatest fear.

Emily lays a reassuring hand on my shoulder. "Here's the thing, Rowan… I really don't know for sure. No one can. All you can do is go into it with your eyes wide open and work hard to build the relationship. And it *is* work. Trust me on that."

I don't say anything at first, mentally digesting this tidbit. Of course, it was a little too late to worry about it now. The dam had been broken and there was no undoing what we did last night. I'll have those memories to keep me hot and bothered for the rest of my life.

And I know every minute that I spend with Flynn… every touch he gives me, I'll fall in deeper.

♦

FLYNN AND I are walking to our rooms. The resort is huge, encompassing almost two-hundred acres of rolling hills covered with tropical trees and plants. A narrow cement path crosses and winds along the hills, sometimes bringing you out in a clearing that overlooks one of the seven private beaches. Every time I see the crystal blue waters and bleached white sand, I'm a bit dumbstruck because it's beyond anything I've ever imagined.

We reach our building, which houses just eight rooms that sits ten yards from a small beach tucked into a cove. We were told this tiny bay houses a sea turtle population that we can snorkel among, and I want to do that while we're here but I first need to find out about the likelihood of sharks. I'm terrified of them.

Flynn leads me up a staircase to the second floor. There's no elevator because this resort frowns upon modern conveniences. The rooms have electricity but past that, not much else. There is no air conditioning except lazy fans that twirl overhead, no TVs, no Wi-Fi, and no telephones. It's truly designed to get away from it all.

When we reach Room 210, Flynn inserts the antique metal key into the door and opens it. He motions me inside and follows.

"They'll be bringing our bags up in about half an hour," he says as he steps up behind me, laying his hands on my shoulders.

I lean back into him. "Is my room next door?"

"Nope. I canceled your room. We're bunking together, roomie." He punctuates the statement by laying a warm kiss at the base of my neck, right where it meets my shoulder.

I let out a soft whimper at his touch and curl my arm backward to wrap around his head. "Is that so?"

"Yeah… and I figure we have half an hour to fool around before the bags get here." His hand snakes down to the hem of the dress I decided to wear for the trip and pulls it up. His knuckles trail along my outer thigh as the dress moves higher.

I push backward into him and I'm not surprised by how hard he is already. The idea that just the thought of having sex with me turns him on, completely turns me on. Which as jumbled as those thoughts are, actually makes complete sense to me.

"Tell me you have a condom concealed on you somewhere," I say, reaching behind me and feeling him through his shorts.

Nuzzling under my jaw, Flynn chuckles and pushes into my hand. "I've got it covered."

I giggle. "No pun intended, right?"

Flynn slips his hand into the front of my underwear, smoothly dragging a finger between my legs. My hips have no will and push back against him.

"Let's make this fast," he says. "I'm betting we can go twice before the bags get here."

The thought causes me to tremble, and I know I certainly have the ability to get two quick orgasms in because Flynn proved that to me last night. I wonder if he can do the same.

"Let's do this," I say, my breathing starting to become shallow the more he moves his fingers against me. My body feels wired tight with the anticipation of him fucking me fast.

Flynn's hand comes out of my panties and he pushes me toward the bed. His words are hurried… urgent. "Get your underwear off and get on all fours while I suit up. Oh, and keep touching yourself. I'm not going to last long and I want you with me, okay?"

His words are simple orders but damn if they don't have me groaning at the way he has things mapped out. I don't waste any time and shimmy out of my panties. I hike my dress up around my waist and jump on the bed, presenting my ass to him. As he commanded, my hand goes between my legs and I start working at myself. When I glance back over my shoulder, Flynn has his shorts unbuttoned and he's rolling the condom over his massive length. My mouth goes dry at the thought of him pushing into me and my hand moves faster.

He glances up and looks at me, eyes then traveling over my ass, my pelvis thrusting gently against my hand. I even let out a moan so he knows how turned on I am. Flynn holds himself in his hand and he closes his eyes for just a moment, taking a deep breath. He looks like he's trying to get himself under control but that's the last thing I want.

"Flynn," I say softly.

His eyes snap open and lock onto me.

"I'm waiting," I tell him.

Groaning, he steps to the edge of the bed and climbs on behind me. His hands come up to my hips and he holds me gently, flexing his pelvis forward and rubbing his dick between my legs, brushing up against my own fingers, which are still rubbing hard. Flynn smoothes one of his hands across my ass, and drags his finger down between my cheeks. The move is decidedly erotic and I gasp and flinch forward when his finger skims across my anus.

"You're sensitive," he teases. "I like that."

His finger ventures forth and he slips it inside of me. "God Rowan… you're all ready for me."

"Always," I breathe as he adds another finger, stretching me for him.

While Flynn said he wanted to go fast, he seems content to play with my body, pumping his fingers in and out… rubbing and pushing… causing me to groan from the contact.

Finally, I have to remind him, "I thought we were going to do this fast."

He removes his hand from between my legs, pushing himself to my opening. He is on target and he enters me with one smooth stroke, pulling a groan from each of us.

"Fuck, Rowan," he says between clenched teeth. "Fuck, fuck, fuck that feels good."

I answer by pulling myself off him and pushing back, and his moan in response has me smiling.

Then it's on.

Flynn sets a hard, fast pace while he grips tight to my hips. Sweat drips from his chest onto my back, soaking through my dress, and his thighs slap against mine. He's hitting me deep… so very deep, and I can feel an orgasm building fast. I try to hold it off, so I can wait for him, but I don't know if I have that much willpower. I want to succumb too greatly.

"Rowan," Flynn says in almost a pained voice. "I'm not going to last… I can't hold it. If you're not with me, baby, I swear I'll take care of you after."

I suppress my giggle that Flynn is so turned on, he has no control, and my heart melts that he's still thinking of me… always thinking of me. Those words alone cause my body to start spasming. "Too late, Flynn… I'm coming."

Flynn gives one super hard thrust, practically knocking me onto my stomach, and then he groans, "I'm coming, too."

His fingers dig into my ass, and I'm sure I'll have ten little bruises showing for all the world to see when I wear my bathing suit.

Oh, well. So worth it.

Flynn makes a few more pumps into me and then collapses onto my back, pushing me into the mattress. I turn my head to the side at the last second to prevent getting smothered by the pillows, but then Flynn immediately rolls off me.

We are both gasping for breath. I turn my head to look at him. He's lying on his back, staring at the ceiling with a silly smile in full bloom. He reaches a hand out and glides it over my naked butt.

Turning his head to face me he says, "You wreck me."

"You wreck me, too," I whisper.

♦

THE CALDWELL AND Burnham clans make quite the entrance to Parrot's, the outdoor beach bar that sits just off the main building. Steel drum music beats low and the sun is dipped halfway into the water, throwing orange and pink sparkles everywhere.

Flynn holds my hand the entire time, and introduces me to everyone. Sometimes he moves his hand to my back, lightly rubbing through the cotton material of my dress. My mind keeps flitting back to the carnality we just enjoyed in our room, and I want nothing more than to abandon these people and figure out what other dirty things Flynn can do to me.

But we must socialize first.

First up is Emily's brother, Ryan, and his wife, Danny, along with their six-month-old daughter, Amelia. They're both gracious, saying they had heard all about me from Emily. I'm not sure what to make of that, but I'll have to assume she said good things.

Danny is interesting. She's one of those people that you just have an instant connection with. While both Ryan and Danny give me a warm hug upon introduction, when Danny wraps her arms around me, I feel an instant trust with her. It's freakin' weird and I'm really looking forward to getting to know her to find out why that is. About the only other person I've ever felt that with before was Flynn, and even then, I was distrustful. I suppose maybe opening myself up to Flynn, and seeing that not everyone is out to hurt me, is opening me up to other people.

I'm completely intimidated by meeting Emily and Ryan's parents. Flynn has filled me in on them, and apparently, I'm meeting an honest to God U.S. Congressman and his wife. To make matters worse, apparently Congressman Burnham… who insists I call him Alex—yeah right—is thinking about running for President, and that thought alone has my hands breaking out into a slimy sweat. Which is completely awkward when he holds his hand out to me to shake. Still, they seems nice enough and then I watch as Celia Burnham practically wrestles her grand-daughter away from

Danny, who laughs as she gives her up, only to step into her husband's embrace and lay her head on his massive chest.

Yup… Ryan Burnham is a hottie.

Next up is Flynn's cousin, Linc, and his girlfriend, Ever. Again, no doubt that Linc and Flynn are related, and they could easily pass as brothers… which puts him in the smokin' hot category. Ever is ethereally beautiful with the loveliest and widest blue eyes I've ever seen on a human. It's like she knows everything about you.

Linc and Flynn are the closest in age of the Caldwell clan and are very close. Flynn talks to Linc by phone or text almost as much as Renner, and he has the NHL package at the apartment so he watches as many of Linc's games as he can. He also watches the Rangers and Ryan, but he pulls for the Coyotes now that Linc is playing there. I'm still a die-hard Rangers fan though and that's not going to change.

As we're talking to Linc and Ever, we hear a scream from behind us and Flynn whips around, his entire face lighting up in a smile. A red-haired woman across the bar has her eyes locked with Flynn's, and then she's running to him. She jumps up and he catches her soundly as she wraps her arms and legs around him. He hugs her tight and it only took the flame hair for me to know this was Renner.

Walking up behind her with a smirk is a holy mother

of God hottie that I can only guess is Cillian. He's the only one thumbing his nose at the tropics as he wears a pair of black jeans, a black t-shirt with his band's logo, and a chain hanging from his back pocket, extended over to clip to a front belt loop. He has two shiny, silver hoops stuck in his bottom lip and yeah… he's a panty dropper.

So this is the lead singer of Over The Edge? Flynn introduced me to their music not long after I moved in, and we play it quite frequently around the apartment, although I doubt Flynn would ever admit that to Cillian. It seems they didn't get off to the greatest of starts.

Flynn releases Renner and I watch as Cillian extends his hand to Flynn, who doesn't hesitate and shakes it. But they quickly release and then Flynn pulls Renner in for another hug. While he does so, Cillian turns to me.

"You must be Rowan. I'm Cillian." He holds his hand out and I shake it.

"Nice to meet you," I say quietly, again a bit overwhelmed with the amount of famousness I've been meeting today. Hmmmm… let's see… a Congressman, two NHL players, and an Irish rock star. Yeah, nothing unusual about this day.

Flynn releases Renner again and pulls me to his side. "Ren… this is Rowan."

Renner grabs me and pulls me into a hug so swiftly, I almost get whiplash. She babbles in my ear. "I'm so glad to meet you. Flynn talks about you all the time. I almost made Cillian bring me to the States last month so I could get a gander at the girl that has my big bro all worked up."

I blush over those words but I'm secretly pleased as well. It's one thing to know that Flynn has feelings for me, because I see it in his eyes… the way he talks to me, and now the way he touches me so intimately. But it's a completely different thing for me to know that Flynn shares his feelings about me with others. It humbles me, and yeah… scares me just a little because I'm starting to understand that Flynn may have already gone off the deep end where I'm concerned.

Me? I feel like I've stepped over the edge, but lashed out and grabbed ahold of a rocky ledge, with my toes just dangling in the water… afraid to let go and take the plunge. I wonder if I'll ever really trust and just do it… just let go?

Pulling back, I smile at Renner. Before I can even respond, she's grabbing me and pulling me to the bar. "Come on, girlfriend. Let's drink something coconutty and bond."

I glance back at Flynn and he's laughing at me, his eyes warm and full of something so powerful, it makes me swallow hard. It exhilarates and frightens me, and I have to wonder which emotion I'll ultimately let overtake me.

CHAPTER 26
Flynn

"WANNA GO SWIMMING again?" I ask Rowan, glancing over at her as she lies beside me on the warm beach.

She's stretched out on her stomach, her cheek resting on her hands, with her eyes closed. She looks so peaceful and it's a look that I'm so glad can lay naturally on her face.

We've been out here all morning, soaking up the sun and just chillin' with each other. Nix and Emily had to go into St. Thomas to get their marriage license, and Renner and Cillian decided to tag along. I have no clue where all the parents are, but for now, I'm enjoying some alone time with Rowan.

After renting some snorkeling gear, we swam out in the small lagoon and tried to find some sea turtles. No such luck but we did swim over some really pretty reefs, teaming with colorful fish. I tried to talk Rowan into some scuba diving but she was having none of it. She muttered something about "shark bait" and "not enough money in the world". I didn't have the heart to tell her sharks could swim into this lagoon since I'd never get her back out in the water if I did that.

Rowan sits up and I can't help but notice the way her breasts sway underneath her tiny bikini top. She didn't own a bathing suit so yesterday afternoon, she bought one in the resort's gift shop. I tried to talk her into a sedate one-piece because, frankly, I don't like the idea of her assets hanging out for everyone to see. Those are for my eyes only. She merely threw it back at me and grabbed the tiny pile of dental floss that she's now wearing. I have to admit, though, the turquoise blue material looks beautiful against her skin and it makes me want to peel her out of it.

In fact, I'm thinking maybe we should take a beach break and hit the room for a while. I'm now obsessed with getting that bikini off her. I lean over and rub my nose along her neck. She sighs and brings her fingers up to glide through my hair. She tilts her head and brings her lips against mine. I press the advantage and slip my tongue in, deepening the kiss.

"Hey you two, get a room."

Cursing, I pull back from Rowan, who wipes at her lips with the tips of her fingers and smiles. Glancing over my shoulder, I see Linc headed our way. He's wearing a pair of board shorts and a New York Rangers t-shirt.

"Isn't it sacrilege or something for you to wear that

shirt?"

Linc looks down at his chest, no doubt not even conscious of what clothes he threw on. Shrugging his shoulders, he says, "Hope I don't get struck by lightning."

He takes the towel in his hand and unfurls it, laying it in the sand next to mine. He plops his butt down with a sigh.

Glancing over his shoulder back toward the building where our rooms are housed, he looks back to me. "Okay… I need your advice before Ever gets down here." Linc glances at Rowan. "You're a woman! I could use your advice too."

"Thanks for noticing," Rowan says dryly.

Linc's mouth turns upward and he wiggles his eyebrows at her. "Oh, I noticed all right."

A low growl emits from my throat. "Hey… eyes back on me, buddy, or I'll introduce your face to my fist."

Linc lets out a chuckle and I smile at him, but I'm dead serious. If he looked at Rowan's perfect body a second longer, we'd have gone at it. "So, what's up?"

He glances one more time over his shoulder and then leans in toward us conspiratorially. "Okay… so I'm going to pop the big question to Ever the night after the wedding. I talked to the resort manager, and he's going to arrange for us to have a private dinner on the beach. He's going to set up a small table, candles… they even have this canopy that is like nothing but some bamboo poles stuck in the sand with some filmy material or some shit like that that goes over the top. So Rowan… do you think that sounds romantic?"

I glance at Rowan, because I am curious as to what she considers romantic. She gives him a wry smile and holds her hand to her chest, "My heart just went pitter-patter when you said 'some shit like that', Linc. Very romantic."

A bark of laughter escapes my mouth and Linc punches me in the shoulder. "Dude, not funny. Seriously, what do you two think? Because I really wanted to do something huge and over the top. Let her know how much I love her… you know, sort of like what Ryan did for Danny."

Rowan looks puzzled so I take a minute and explain how Ryan proposed to Danny on the big Jumbotron at Madison Square Garden before a Rangers game. She's dutifully impressed and a fleeting thought goes through my mind… I wonder what type of proposal it would take to get Rowan to agree to marriage. I have no clue what her views are, but I know her ideas of parenthood are skewed based on her family experience.

Turning to Linc, I tell him, "Look man… I don't really know Ever all that well, so I can't say for sure what she'd like. But I do know you. And you're the low-key, subtly romantic type of dude. You're not an over-the-top, in-your-face, shout-to-the-world-my-feelings kind of guy. So I think this beach dinner sounds perfect. What I do know about Ever is that she loves you… just the way you are. So she'd much rather have something that reflects the real you."

"But what if it's not enough? I'm so nervous, I'm practically sick to my stomach. What if she says 'no'? I don't think I'll be able to handle it."

"She'll say yes, man. Trust me," I assure him.

"Really?" Linc asks and he sounds so pathetically miserable over this whole proposal not working, I start to feel really bad for him.

"Absolutely," Rowan chimes in. "No woman could resist that."

I stow that piece of information away for future reference. I also add, "Quit stressing, Linc. I swear she'll say yes."

Linc lets out a huge sigh and flops back on his towel, eyes raised to the sky. "God, I hope so. I'll be miserable if she says no. I've never been so stressed in my life."

"Stressed over what?" Ever asks as she walks toward us. She's wearing a red bikini top that looks perfect against her pale skin and dark hair, with tiny, white shorts. Yeah… she's beautiful, but she's got nothing on Rowan.

Linc sits up ramrod straight and his mouth hangs open like a dead fish. I can see panic on his face, having no clue what to say. Before I can even swoop in to save him, Rowan says, "Linc was worried about his toast at the wedding dinner. Says he's a bit of a pansy-ass when it comes to public speaking."

I snicker and Linc turns a stunned face toward Rowan. Ever drops down in Linc's lap and his arms wrap around her waist while he rests his chin on her shoulder. He looks at Rowan and mouths the words, *Thank You* to her, relief swimming in his eyes.

"That's true. Linc hates being the center of attention like that. But you'll do great, baby." Ever leans her head back to look at Linc and he kisses her temple. When she straightens back up, she looks at us. "What do you two have planned today?"

"Just relaxing… but we're actually going to go swimming right now. You want to join us?"

"Nah," Ever says. "I think I just want to lie out here for a while."

Linc chimes in, "What she said."

Standing up from the towel, I hold my hand out to Rowan. She takes it and I tug her up from the towel. When she's standing, I bend over and catch her legs with my shoulder, tossing her over me as I stand up. She squeals as I start walking toward the water.

"This is what is known as a fireman's carry," I tell her.

She squirms as she laughs and I pop her on the butt.

"Don't do that. I might drop you."

"As if," she giggles.

I walk straight into the warm water and when I get waist deep, I let her slide down the front of my body. The contact of legs gliding over my crotch starts my dick twitching.

Rowan wraps her arms around my neck and her legs around my waist, and I walk out until the water is just lapping over my shoulders. She has to hold on to me now, because she can't touch the soft sand from where we are.

I lean my face in and give her a soft kiss. "Are you having a good time?"

"The best," she says and she kisses me back.

When she pulls away, she dips her head back into the water to wet her hair. The move pushes her breasts up, and I stare down at the creamy swells just inches from my mouth. My dick raises its head up with genuine interest.

When she pulls back up, water runs down her face, making her skin glisten like dew drops on spring flower petals. The sun reflecting off the water lightens her eyes to a shimmering silver and I'm stunned for a moment by how gorgeous she is.

"Do you have any idea how beautiful you are?"

Her cheeks actually get pink and she smiles at me shyly. "I don't know. I don't think anyone's said that to me before."

"You steal my breath sometimes," I tell her.

Laying her head on my shoulder, she says softly, "You're too good to me, Flynn. I don't deserve it."

I reach my hand up and grab her hair, pulling back so her head rises up. I look at her somberly. "You deserve the world, Rowan. The entire fucking world should belong to you."

Her mouth opens like she's going to say something, and then it snaps shut. Whatever was going to come out is locked away, but she speaks to me in another way. She lays her lips against mine, opening her mouth, and I slip in. Our tongues touch each other with confidence, and I let myself get immersed in the feelings of desire and affection I have for her.

She pulls her tongue back, just enough so she can speak, but never letting her lips leave mine. "Touch me, Flynn."

My face jerks back in surprise and the thought of all the things I could do to her in this water gives me an immediate and full-blown, raging hard on.

"Right now?" I ask, disbelieving.

She stares at me, her eyes hooded and unblinking. "Right here," she whispers.

I shoot a hasty glance at the beach and Linc and Ever are both on their backs, faces tilted up to the sky. They're not watching us. I look down the beach to a young couple that have been out there all morning, and they're actually making out pretty hot and heavy. I'm assuming honeymooners.

Scanning the area, I notice that the family of four that I had seen earlier are gone, maybe to get an early lunch?

Who gives a fuck?

It appears right now, I could probably have my way with Rowan and none would be the wiser.

Keeping my eyes locked on her, I remove one of my hands that were wrapped around her waist, dragging my fingers over her hip and down between her legs. I brush my fingers lightly over the material separating me from my goal and the contact causes Rowan to jerk almost violently as she throws her head back.

I pull my fingers back slightly and grin at her. "Uh-uh. Can't have that. You need to hold still, okay? Can't give away our secrets to anyone on that beach."

Bottom lip firmly gripped between her teeth, just so her front two teeth peep out, she nods at me.

"Okay," I tell her. "Let's try this again. And you need to behave. Just keep talking to me like we're just casually hanging out in the water."

"Okay," she pants. "But I hope I don't scream."

I chuckle over the thought and dip my hand back down again. I test her out, grazing my fingers over her lightly and, to my respect, she keeps absolutely still, although her eyes flutter close.

"Good girl," I tell her before pulling her bottoms to

the side.

I tease between her legs for a few minutes, taking my time and making sure she can handle what I'm doing to her. She remains perfectly still, although her breathing is getting faster.

When I dip one long finger inside of her, her breath rushes out in a wave of peppermint breath and she gasps, "Oh, Flynn, that feels good."

"Going to feel better," I promise her.

I lean in and grab her lips in a kiss, just as I plunge another finger inside. She lets out a tiny cry into my mouth and I start moving in and out of her in a consistent rhythm.

"I can't take it," she whimpers.

"Yes, you can. You can take anything I hand you… then you can take some more."

I add a third finger and she's so fucking tight around me I hope I'm not hurting her. I go a little slower, just in case.

When her head starts falling backward, I have to remind her to get back on track. "Eyes to me, baby. Gotta act normal."

Her head snaps up, her eyes locking with mine. I swear I can see flames dancing in them, and a rose blush is staining her neck. "Finish me off, please."

"Anything for you," I say as I remove my fingers and change the tempo and pattern of my movements. She bucks against my hand with a whimper and leans her face forward. Her teeth sink into my shoulder, and if anyone is watching us right now, I think they'd know what we were up to. Another quick glance to the beach tells me no one is paying attention.

I slip my index finger back inside her and use my thumb to continue my strokes. Immediately, her body starts to tremble and she bites down on me hard. That's definitely going to leave a mark, but I could care less.

With only a few more touches between her legs, Rowan groans and her body convulses. She cries into my shoulder as the spasms fire through, and when they die off, she lifts her face to mine. I remove my hand and pull her bottoms back in place.

"That was some kinky shit," I tell her with a grin.

She smiles back and kisses me. "Yes, it was. Now I want you to take me back to the room and make love to me."

I kiss her back. "There's nothing I want more but you need to give me a few minutes. I can't get out of the water until my hard on disappears. Don't want to frighten everyone."

Rowan's eyes light up with a mixture of mischief and desire. "I have a better idea," she says.

"What's that?"

Moving one arm from around my shoulder, she drops it below the water. With just a few efficient moves, she's pulled the front of my swim trunks down and I spring free. I suck in a deep breath when her tiny hand curls around me. She places her lips near my ear and says, "How about I take care of you right now… then you don't have to worry about it?"

"Oh, God… please tell me you're not joking around?"

Her laugh is husky and rich as she strokes her hand against me. My toes curl down into the sand and I hope my knees don't give way, drowning us both. My head falls back it feels so fucking good, but she says, "Uh-uh, Mr. Caldwell. Eyes on me."

I raise my head and hold her eyes. Her hand moves along my shaft in the warm water, her thumb rubbing around the head every other stroke. She is like a siren rising from the sea, seducing me beyond my will, and I give surrender.

"You're amazing," I whisper to her.

She answers by increasing the pace and my body can't remain still. My hips start moving and I hope to God no one glances our way. But the truth of the matter is, I don't give a flying fuck. Right now, I'm a slave to Rowan's hand and the explosive orgasm that I can feel firing up.

I try to fight it off because I want to stay like this for eternity, but it's too overpowering. Stars burst inside my head as I shoot out into the warm Caribbean waters, and I have no choice but to kiss Rowan, otherwise I might scream from the intense pleasure.

CHAPTER 27
Rowan

THE SUN HANGS low over the water as we wait for Emily to arrive. The ceremony is taking place on a grassy, seaside cliff overlooking one of the blue lagoons. I'm amazed at the simplicity with which this wedding is taking place. As the daughter of a U.S. Congressman, I guess I sort of expected more.

More guests, more flowers, more everything.

Instead, the Caldwell and Burnham families stand in a semi-circle around Nix with the minister beside him. At Emily's insistence, everyone was to dress casually, preferably with a tropical print. Nix has on a pair of khaki pants and a white linen shirt. He's not wearing any shoes.

I chose to wear a yellow sundress with a white, palm-frond pattern along with a pair of gold sandals. Flynn stands beside me with his hand resting on my back. He's wearing a pair of white shorts, a navy and white tropical print shirt, and flip-flops. His skin is bronze from just one day in the sun and his hazel eyes are shining almost green in the sun's glow.

Emily walks toward us on the arm of her dad. I have to say seeing Congressman Burnham in shorts and an island shirt makes him seem less intimidating to me. There's no music to announce her entrance, unless you count the cries of the seagulls in the distance and the crashing waves against the rocks below us.

Emily's dress is simple and beautiful, with nothing but flowing, plain chiffon dropping down from a pleated empire waist. Tiny, pearled spaghetti straps grace her tanned shoulders. She confessed to me she bought it online because she didn't have the patience to go shopping. She didn't even bother picking out the calla lilies in her hand, or the wedding cake that would be served tonight. She told the wedding planner at the resort to pick something suitable, claiming she had better things to think of… namely, her wedding night. That cracked me up.

Emily is staring at Nix as she approaches, her eyes aglow with love for him. I turn to look at Nix and his eyes are intensely focused on his bride. The connection between them is almost palpable and I feel a lump forming in my throat.

Congressman Burnham… Alex… reaches his hand out for Nix to shake. After a few pumps, he takes Nix's hand and places it on Emily's. I expect her to step up gracefully beside him, but Nix apparently has other plans. He gives her a tug and she goes crashing into his body. His hands come up to frame her face and he gives her a passionate kiss, bending her backward. Her arms have no choice but to wrap around his neck, and then she's kissing him back as her flowers fall from her hand.

Everyone starts snickering and the minister has to make several coughing sounds before Nix finally pulls up, giving her a last delicate kiss on her nose. Oh, I'm going to give him so much shit about this on my next work day with him.

Flynn leans over and places his lips near my ear. "Do you think anyone would mind if I did that to you right now?"

I smile and turn my head slightly so I can whisper back. "I'm sure a few would mind. Now hush."

After the minister makes some surprisingly short remarks and reads a small passage from the Bible, Nix and Emily say their vows. They chose to write their own, so the minister takes a polite step back as they turn to face each other.

Emily goes first and she's nervous. She turns to Danny, who hands her a piece of paper, and she opens it with shaking hands. Smiling at Nix, she says, "I had to write mine down because I'm afraid I'll babble."

Nix says, "Your babbling would be beautiful, baby."

Giving a shy smile, she dips her head down and starts to read. "Nix… I may have ran you over with my car, but you're the one that completely knocked me for a loop. From the moment I laid eyes on you… I suspected you were special… in my mind. From the moment you first held my hand, I knew you were special… in my heart. When you opened yourself up to me, you proved to the universe that you were created by God so that I would have someone to look over me."

She folds the paper up and looks up to Nix. "You probably don't know this, but every night before I go to sleep, I pray. I pray for all the things people normally do… for the health and safety of my family, for me to get an A on a test, for world peace." Everyone laughs and she pauses a second until it's quiet again.

"But I end every prayer with a special thank you… I make sure God knows that I am forever in his debt for bringing you into my life, and I pray that you are never taken from it. I love you, Nix, and I always will."

I look at Nix and there's a sheen of tears in his eyes, and oh, crap… my waterworks start. Somehow Flynn knows, without even looking down at me. His arm comes around my shoulder and he pulls me into him while I surreptitiously try to wipe the wetness from my cheeks.

Nix lifts Emily's hand and gives it a kiss. He reaches into his pocket and also pulls out a piece of paper. This I'm not surprised by because Nix definitely doesn't seem like the type that would memorize his vows. He's so damn surly half the time I expect his will be short and gruff.

He opens the paper and scans it, his eyes flying back and forth over the words. Then he looks up, and glances around at all of us staring at him. He crumples the paper up and tosses it to the ground where it lands beside Emily's neglected flowers.

My heart lurches because I think for a silly moment that he's going to back out of the wedding, but then he starts talking. "I had written my vows too, but as I look over them… they're not really want I want to say."

He takes a deep breath and turns to look out over the ocean. A smile comes to his face and it's serene and full of peace.

He turns back to Emily. "All of this," he begins, gesturing with his arm out toward the water. "All of this would have looked like ashes to me before I met you. I saw the world and it had no color. It was dull and lifeless… like dirty dishwater. I lived in a dark place, somewhere between this Earth and Hell. But I don't live there anymore… not since I met you."

Nix's hands come back up and frame Emily's face. It makes me focus on her and I see tears streaming, which start mine streaming again. "All I see is color now."

He looks up to the sky. "I see the blue of the sky, and the white of the clouds."

He looks down to the grass. "I see green… a million

shades of green."

Nix looks back up at Emily. "And I see my favorite color of all… the amber in your eyes. I wish everyone could see the color I do. And it's all because of you."

Emily issues a low sob and then throws her arms around Nix's shoulders. He buries his face in her neck and they just stand like that forever.

I really don't remember much more of the ceremony. Instead, I focus on these new emotions that have been brought forth by watching such an amazing declaration of honor and commitment. I think about the type of parents they will make, and I wonder if that love will one day be enough for a child.

I'd like to think so but, based upon my experience, I'm just not sure.

♦

I FEEL LIKE I stepped into an enchanted fairytale world. The wedding dinner is being held in an old sugar mill ruin that sits down at the bottom of a hill, just outside the main restaurant for the resort. It's a crumbling building made of stone and mortar. The roof is long gone and our ceiling is the night sky, which is awash with twinkling stars. Windows dot the walls but the frames and glass are long gone. Instead, tall pillar candles have been set on the ledges and cast flickering light everywhere. The walls may be falling but a new wooden floor has been built and my understanding is this place is used to hold small, outdoor parties and dinners.

There is a huge dining table set in the center, laden with more candles and stargazer lilies that perfume the air. Another table sits to the side with a small, two-tiered wedding cake and bottles of iced champagne.

"You have sand all over your feet," Flynn says as he looks down at my sandals.

This I already know because it's slightly uncomfortable with the grains of sand rubbing between the leather straps and my skin. We went down to the beach after the ceremony while the photographer took photos of the happy couple, as well as the entire family. Cillian, Ever, and I tried to back away but it did no good. We were dragged into every family photo that was snapped and it made me feel strangely displaced… like I was committing a fraud. I didn't belong here with these people, and yet they were making sure we were immortalized forever in their family gathering.

Flynn bends down and undoes the buckle of one sandal. He lifts my foot out and I put a hand on his shoulder to balance. He carefully wipes all the sand away, and puts my shoe back on. He then does the same to the other foot.

I watch Flynn as he tends to my feet with a mixture of affection and morbid wonder. He is so caring toward me… always has been, and I wonder if this is because our relationship is new, or if this is the way it will always be. I wonder if I'm a novelty or I'm a potential permanent fixture by his side.

It's true… we've only been lovers for a few days, but we had each other's hearts long before then. Flynn speaks to me like no other person ever has. I want to wrap myself up inside of him, but there are moments where I just want to go back to the way we were. It was so safe and I had expectations that he never failed me on.

But now… this new relationship is odd and I'm having a hard time trusting the feelings that come with it. The intimacy we've shared… the sensual knowledge we have of each other… it overwhelms and confuses me. He's exposed me to feelings I never knew existed between two people. He makes my body want things that it's never even considered before.

He makes me want more, and yet, I'm afraid the more I taste, the hungrier I will get. I'm afraid I'll become dependent on him, like my body depends on water to survive. And the scariest thing of all—the thing I fret about all too much—is that if this doesn't work out, and I lose him, then I won't survive it.

Nix and Emily walk in, interrupting my thoughts, and everyone breaks out into applause. Several waiters move into action, popping open champagne and passing it around.

When everyone has a glass, Mr. Burnham steps to

the center of the floor and raises his glass to the couple. "Nix... I couldn't have picked a better man to entrust my little girl to. She's your problem now." Everyone laughs and Nix kisses Emily on the temple. "Emily... you do an old man proud. You've exceeded all of my expectations and you're going to make a wonderful wife and a loving mother. To Emily and Nix."

Everyone salutes with murmured affection and we all take a sip of the bubbly. Emily's mom ushers us all to the dining table and we take our seats to start the wedding feast.

♦

REGGAE MUSIC IS being piped in from somewhere and we're all on our way to getting drunk. Nix and Emily made their exit a while ago, and all the parents just left, including Danny and Ryan so they could get Amelia nursed and to bed. The only ones left are us single kids.

Flynn sits next to me, with his arm around my shoulder and his thumb rubbing my skin. Even with the monumental buzz I have going on, his touch manages to inflame me.

Cillian reaches over and pops another bottle of champagne. We're on our umpteenth one.

When he fills everyone's glasses, he sits back down and kisses Renner on her neck. "I hope we don't get so drunk I don't know what I'm doing tonight."

Renner pats his cheek. "You always know what you're doing, baby."

"TMI," Flynn whispers under his breath but I hear him and giggle.

Cillian stands up and wobbles slightly before he rights himself. "Another toast to Emily and Nix. That was a helluva wedding."

We all yell, *hear, hear*, and knock our drinks back, which really isn't couth to be doing with champagne. I let out a tiny hiccup and Flynn grins at me.

"I expected nothing less," Linc muses. "It was a helluva proposal."

"Oh, it sure was," Ever chimes in. "So romantic… I about died."

The look on Linc's face is adorable as he looks at Ever with undeniable fear over whether he can pull the same thing off tomorrow night. "Yeah, I don't know if I could ever be that eloquent," he grumbles as he stares at his flute.

"Well, if it helps," Ever says and then takes a small sip of champagne, "I'll say yes no matter what."

Linc's eyes snap up to Ever's. "You'd say yes?"

"Well, duh… why wouldn't I say yes? I love you, you big dummy."

"I just thought…" Linc says but then trails off, eyes still bewildered. I can see the wheels spinning in his head, wondering if he had just made a mountain out of a molehill.

Ever scoots her chair back. "Here… let's take the pressure off you." She hikes her skirt up, which luckily is long and loose, and still covers everything, and bends down on one knee in front of Linc. She takes his hand in hers.

Linc looks around at all of us, a near state of panic gripping him. I put the back of my hand to my mouth to hide my laugh and look over at Flynn. He grins back at me.

"Linc," Ever begins. "I lost you once, but then I got you back. I'm never letting you go again. There's no place you can hide from me, so don't even bother trying. I'm attached to your hip so you might as well get used to me. So in essence… what I'm saying is—let's get hitched. What do you think?"

With his mouth halfway open in amazement, Linc just stares at Ever. She watches him and when he doesn't say anything, she snaps her fingers in front of his eyes a few times. "Yo… Linc… want to get married?"

It is the most hilarious proposal I've ever heard of, made even funnier by the look on Linc's face.

Finally, a smile a mile long breaks out across his face. For someone with a gallon of champagne in him, he moves with amazing dexterity. He lunges out of the chair and picks Ever up around the waist, hoisting her high and spinning around. Her arms go around his neck to hang on.

She throws her head back and laughs. "Is that a yes?"

"Fucking yes," he yells out to the night sky.

We all get out of our chairs and hug the newly engaged couple. Linc gives me a resounding kiss on my mouth, for which Flynn pops him in the back of the head. We all have another glass of champagne and as we make small talk, Flynn leans over and rubs his nose along my ear. "All this romantic shit is making me horny as hell. You about ready to get out of here?"

I grip his jaw with my hand and push him back a few inches so I can kiss him. When I pull away, I say, "Oh yeah… I'm ready."

CHAPTER 28
Flynn

THE DAY AFTER the wedding has been fucking perfect and I don't want to go back tomorrow. I want to stay in this tropical paradise with Rowan forever. We spent the day lounging on the beach with frequent breaks back in the bedroom, where I made love to her over and over again. There wasn't a position we haven't tried yet but my brain is constantly working to figure out something new. I guess we'll have to just re-try all of those positions in new locations.

Rowan has taken the jump off the ledge and while I still see some uncertainty in her eyes, I'm going to continue to push her forward with me.

She's the one for me. I know it the way I know that fire is hot and ice is cold. While I wasn't necessarily a fan of her early proclamation that we should just be friends, it turns out that building the solid base of friendship was exactly what makes this so right.

"So where are we going?" Rowan asks me as I lead her down the lit path to the main resort building.

"Patience, o little one," I reply and squeeze her hand.

I lead Rowan off the path, through a small garden, and then we step out onto the beach. The moon is hanging low and throws a strip of white, sparkling reflection onto the water. The small dinner table is set to perfection with glowing candles, and just as Linc said, there's a bamboo tent erected over it draped in some white, frothy shit. I couldn't have dialed God up and asked for a more perfect setting.

Rowan stops and turns to look at me. "What's this?"

"Well, turns out Linc and Ever have decided to order in room service and 'discuss' their wedding plans. Plus, Linc wants to officially pop the question with the ring, but he figured a bed close by was a better setting. They offered this up to us and I hated to see it go to waste."

She releases my hand and walks forward to the tent. "It's beautiful."

Coming up behind her, I wrap my arms around her waist and lay my chin on her head. We just stare at the setup for a few moments, reveling in the magic of dinner on a secluded beach.

I release Rowan and pull a chair out for her. She sits down and I help her scoot the chair forward, which isn't easy in the thick, white sand. I take the seat opposite of her and pour us each a glass of white wine that has been uncorked and chilled for us.

Holding my glass up, I say, "To our last night in

paradise."

She clinks her glass against mine and we take a sip, smiling at each other.

Rowan glances out over the water and then back to me. "This is sort of surreal."

"I know. Linc is a true romantic."

She laughs… and it's a sound that I need to hear for the rest of my life. "I meant this setting… not Linc's romantic prowess for dreaming this up. I mean… look at the moon, and how still the water is. We have candlelight and chilled wine. Who lives like this?"

"We do. Tonight… we do."

A waiter appears and offers us a menu. We chat about the wedding, and last night's surprise proposal by Ever. We place our orders… grilled prawns and saffron risotto for Rowan and steamed, Mediterranean sea bass covered in olives, sun-dried tomatoes, and artichokes for me.

The food is wonderful and by my second glass of wine, I'm feeling more confident in the things I want to say to Rowan tonight.

After she takes her last bite of food, she wipes her mouth and looks at me. "Thank you, Flynn. For insisting I come. I don't have much in life, and really could never afford to do something like this. I'll treasure the memory of this trip the rest of my life."

"It was my pleasure. I'm glad you decided to take the

plunge."

My words have more than one meaning. I'm thankful that she loosened up her stubborn pride and didn't resist the offer of the trip. I'm grateful she decided to take our relationship to the next level, because let's face it… Rowan epitomizes my every waking fantasy. I'll never forget the tears she shed at the wedding, because that means her heart has the capacity to understand that apathy and rejection have no place in a loving relationship.

I hope she understands the strides she's made, and I hope she has more gas in the tank to push forward.

I'll certainly know after tonight.

We order one dessert and share it between us. The chocolate mousse is divine, and fuck if it's not sensual at the same time, as I watch the way Rowan licks at the spoon. It reminds me of how she went down on me this evening in the shower as we got ready for dinner. Of how she pulled me in close, with her hands gripping my ass hard, and took every bit of me down her throat.

After the last plate is cleared and we finish our wine, I say, "Let's take a walk."

I stand up from the table and help her from her chair. She looks stunning, more so than normal, and I'm not sure if it's the moonlight on her skin, the wine in my belly, or the fact that I've come to the realization that I love her like I've never loved before.

We stroll down to the water's edge, kicking our shoes off and dipping our toes in the water. I pull her in for a hug and she doesn't hesitate, laying her head on my chest. I know she can feel the way my heart is beating like mad, because I'm getting ready to lay my soul bare to her.

"Rowan," I say and she leans back slightly to look at me. I reach up and cup her face with my hands. Even though it's dark, the moonlight shines in her eyes and they look like the color of smoke when I lay water on a hot fire, and that seems apropos to me.

There are so many things I need to tell her. "Marney was the first and only girl I ever loved. And I know that when you're eighteen, you probably really don't even know what true love is… but I've spent the last eight years looking for something that would equal that. I've spent my entire career trying to fill that void… to make up for her loss."

Her eyes hold on to me but I can't read what she's thinking so I press on. "Then I met you, and my perspective changed. I realized all the things I thought were absolute truth, were nothing more than filters on the lenses through which I was looking. You became sort of a cloth that wiped away the grime of my past. I feel like I see clearly now, and once my eyes were fully opened… all I saw was you. All I want to see is you."

She doesn't say anything and her expression doesn't

change, but she doesn't break eye contact. "I guess what I'm trying to say… what I feel like you need to know before I can take one more breath… is that I love you. I love you more than anything I've ever loved in my life."

I finish with a deep breath and I let it out, glad to have that revelation out in the open, and hopeful that it will provide a springboard to strengthen this new relationship.

I wait… hopeful to hear those three words back. Almost expecting it.

But it doesn't come. Instead, her eyelids lower and she looks down, breaking the connection. I wait, because maybe… just maybe, she's trying to find the right way to tell me that she loves me.

When she looks back up, her eyes are now filled with sorrow and her lips are drawn down.

"Flynn," she says and there is apology dripping from my name. "I… I'm not sure what to say."

My heart drops but I try to take some measure of comfort in the fact that her first words weren't 'but I don't love you'. I hold out hope… that she'll give me hope.

"Tell me how you feel," I urge her.

She steps away from me and my arms fall to my side. Turning her back, she walks a few paces from the water's edge. When she turns around, the moonlight reveals genuine affection. "I care for you. You know I do."

She trails off, looking down to the sand.

"There's a 'but' in there… right?"

"But… I'm not sure I know what love is. Because… otherwise, my first thought would have been to immediately tell you that 'I love you, too'. Right? I mean, shouldn't that have been my first instinct?"

Yes, that's exactly what she would have said if it were true. I realize this with a small level of despair.

She walks back up to me and wraps her arms around my waist… putting her head back to my chest. My arms wrap around her and I hold her tight.

Her words are soft and sad. "My first instinct was… the first thing that came to mind… really, words that rang out loud in my head were, 'But what is love?'. I questioned my understanding of love, and I questioned yours. What does that say about me?"

I'm silent because I know what it says about her. She doesn't trust her feelings. And now I don't trust mine. What if I don't really understand it either? What if I'm so swept up in the amazing sex we've been having, that I've miscalculated what we really have going on?

But then I realize… no! There is something far more than sex going on here. Rowan has opened up to me the way she's never done before. I've brought the book she gave me for Christmas… her story… and I've read a little each night. She pulled no punches and she showed me the worst of what she's done. Which has made me appreciate all the more of what she's made of herself. The empathy she carries… the passion for her own survival.

Yes, I love her. That I do not doubt.

In fact, the only doubt that remains is hers, and I suppose the only two options I have are to back away or push forward.

Backing away would be contrary to what love is demanding I do, which is to guide her and hope she'll ultimately figure out that what we have is love.

I pull her face back again from my chest, stroking my thumbs on her cheeks. I lean forward and kiss her forehead.

"It's okay," I tell her. "Let's just go slowly so you can figure this out. No pressure."

She stares at me, with her eyes still sad and withdrawn. But she nods her assent. It's all she'll give me right now and I'll have to accept that.

♦

WHEN WE GET back to the room, I take her into my arms as soon as I shut the door. I seek her lips and to my relief, she kisses me back, wrapping her arms around me tight. My plan is to undress her slowly, and love her with all the tenderness that I have inside of me.

Our kiss deepens, her mouth moving hungrily over mine. Rowan reaches her hand down and cups me through my pants, and I grow hard from her touch. Her hands start to work at my belt, almost frantically.

"I want you, Flynn," she says in between kisses, and the desperate sound to her plea flays me open.

I know what she's doing. She's pouring every bit of displaced love into sex right now, because that's the only way at this point she's confident to show me how she feels. She's doing this to show me that she does feel something for me.

It's not what I'm seeking but I'll have to accept it for now.

I try to slow her down by removing her hands but she bats them away, unzipping my pants and taking me in her hand. Her touch is a little rough but it doesn't stop me from arching into her with a groan.

With one hand, Rowan pushes my pants and underwear down, and the other takes up a hard stroke to my dick. She only gives me about three pumps before she drops to her knees and takes me in her mouth, pushing me all the way to the back of her throat.

Fuck, but if she doesn't slow that shit down, I'm going to come in about five seconds.

I grab ahold of her head, trying to slow her efforts, and she growls at the restraint. It's not that I don't like some hard and fast fucking but God, I want this to last a little longer.

"Rowan… baby… slow down."

She pulls back and I slip out of her mouth with a soft

pop.

"How about I let you reciprocate then?" Her eyes are heated and challenging to me.

Reaching down, I put my hands under her armpits and lift her from the ground. Turning to the bed, I toss her there and she bounces lightly with a laugh.

"That's right," she says, her voice husky and rough. "Show me what you can do with that mouth."

I fall onto her, pushing her dress up around her hips. I don't even bother taking her panties off but just push them roughly to the side. Bringing my mouth down on her, I make love to her with my lips and tongue, causing her to cry out a strangled sound from her throat. It fuels my desire even further and I push my tongue into her roughly, causing her to cry out again.

"That's it," I praise her as I briefly remove my lips. "Let me hear you."

Her breath comes out in staccato bursts and her hands are gripping my hair tight. Plunging two fingers into her, I immediately feel her tighten around me and her thighs slam into the sides of my face as she starts to come undone.

"Flynn," she cries out as the orgasm tears through her.

I ride out the last of her spasms with my face between her legs. When she's finished, I stand up, swiping her underwear down her legs. She stares up at me, her eyes a little glazed, and I feel triumph rocket through me.

"I'm going to make love to you slowly now, sweet girl. Take that dress off for me."

I watch a fluttering breath come out of her lips and she sits up to disrobe. I shimmy out of my pants and whip my shirt over my head. Grabbing a condom, I tear the packet open and roll it over me. I'm so hard, I feel like I might burst the second I get inside of her, and maybe I'll just let myself go and do just that.

Crawling onto the bed, I settle on top of her to gather her close. I wrap my arms all the way under her, mashing her chest into mine. Resting my face in the crook of her neck, I swivel my hips so that the head of my cock finds its way home. I give a single push and slip right in, sucking air through my teeth over the rapturous feeling.

I move within her… slowly… lightly kissing her neck. I pull my face up once to look at her, and her eyes are closed, her lip stuck between her teeth, which is a look I adore. With a sudden move, I roll over and watch her eyes fly open when she finds herself on top of me.

"I know you can't say the words, Rowan… so show me how you feel."

She stares at me for a moment, her hands resting lightly on my stomach. I watch her… almost daring her to deny what we have between us.

She never says a word but she starts moving her hips,

pushing with her thighs to move up and down on my length. My hands come up to grab her hips and help her along, but she pushes them away. Because she wants to do this… for me. She wants to give me something, since she can't give me exactly what I want.

I accept it, because it's all I can do. I watch her the entire time, even as her eyes close as she gives into her urges. She builds even faster than I do and she cries out as she comes again. The look on her face is pained from the pleasure, and that's all it takes for me to follow her.

Because let's face it.

I'd follow her anywhere.

CHAPTER 29

Rowan

THE TRIP BACK to JFK seemed to take forever. I was lost in my own thoughts, staring blankly out the window. Flynn seemed to understand that maybe I needed a little time to come to an acceptance of his feelings, and maybe my own.

And while I do accept how Flynn feels about me… I mean, I truly understand that he loves me; I just have no fucking clue how to feel about him.

This is happening so fast now, and I have all these feelings of insecurity and a lack of self-worth assaulting me.

The memories of my parents plague me like they never have. I realize now that I have pushed them and the hurt deep inside of me, and now it's bubbling up like a fountain of lava. It's hot and it burns, threatening to engulf me in painful flames.

I know, in my heart, that I care for Flynn. Hell, as a friend, I love him. But that's because I know our friendship worked. It wasn't perfect, but it was as damn close as it could be. It was safe, and there were boundaries, and at the end of the day, I knew he'd be there for me.

But now… I don't know. There's something that is causing me to doubt everything. I don't need a shrink to tell me that my parents' lack of love and attention warped my perception of what a healthy, loving relationship could be. Add into that Flynn and I have upped the level of intimacy between us, and it exposes the nerve center of my heart. It has opened it wide and I'm vulnerable to rejection, loss, and pain.

In just a few short days, while our relationship progressed forward, it also became unstable in my mind, and now I have so much more to lose.

I'm terrified of being hurt again. I was able to claw myself out of my misery after I left Texas. I've done it once and it was the hardest thing I ever did in my life.

I don't know if I have it in me to do it again.

I don't know that I would survive Flynn hurting me.

We open the door to the apartment and Capone comes barreling out of my bedroom and down the hall to greet us. He almost knocks me flat on my ass when he launches himself at my chest. Fil had stayed over at our apartment while we were gone and cared for him, and while I was scared silly to leave my baby, he seems to be just fine.

After his mandatory licks to my face, he turns from

me and jumps on Flynn, who holds him in a big bear hug, and buries his face in his fur. My heart skips a beat as I realize just how much we've become ingrained in each other's lives.

Flynn raises his head and looks at me over Capone's shoulder, and the look is so filled with love, it makes me feel like there is a cinder block on my chest.

Standing up, I walk into the kitchen, immediately seeing a note from Fil.

Rowan/Flynn,

Capone was a good boy while you were gone. However, I didn't realize how big his crap would be. You owe me for having to pick that shit up.

Later.

F

Typical Fil. Straight and to the point. I need to make sure I hook up with her soon to give her the gift that we bought for her in St. Thomas before we left.

I feel Flynn's arms wrap around me as he looks over my shoulder at the note. "What's that?"

I hold it up for him to read and then step quickly out of his arms. He looks confused and it tears my heart up that I'm doing that to him. Turning away, I open the refrigerator and pull out a bottle of water.

"I think I'll get started on laundry since you have to go back to work tomorrow," I say in an effort to fill the silence.

Stepping up to me again, Flynn cups me around the back of the head. His eyes are warm and his voice filled with sensuality. "Or, we could fool around a little. A welcome home present to ourselves."

God, I hate myself but my body involuntarily pulls out of his touch and I turn my back on him. "I really should get this started. There's a lot of do."

Reaching out, Flynn grabs my wrist, his brow furrowed. "What's going on, Rowan?"

"Nothing," I say like he's crazy for thinking so. "I just want to get this stuff done so we can relax."

"Then why won't you look at me? Why won't you let me touch you?" His words are cautious… non-threatening. Like he's dealing with a wild, caged animal.

"I don't know what you mean," I insist.

Flynn isn't going to let it go. He pulls me to him and wraps his arms around me, leaning down for a kiss. He's daring me to pull away and yet, that's exactly what I do.

He cocks his eyebrow at me, as if to say, *See… I knew something was wrong.*

"What?" I ask, trying to sound oblivious to his meaning. "There's nothing wrong. Honestly… I just want to get—"

"Rowan!" he shouts and my eyes snap to his with attention. I've never heard Flynn yell before.

"What… is… wrong?" he grits out.

My eyes dart left and right, seeking a way to escape… this room, this man, this fucked-up mess. When I look back to him, his eyes are patient, even though he just shouted to get my attention three seconds ago.

Taking a deep breath, I sigh out my fear. "I don't know. I'm scared."

He starts to walk toward me, his face awash with sympathy. He stretches his arms out. "You don't have to be afraid. No pressure, right?"

I step back, not letting him try to comfort me. It will make this even more confusing because even though I'm scared shitless over what is happening, I find myself yearning to accept what he's offering. Shaking my head in denial, I say, "I don't think I can do this."

Flynn stops his forward progress, his arms falling to his sides. "Do what?" he asks cautiously.

"A relationship with you. It's moving too fast, and I'm afraid."

Raking his hand through his hair in frustration, he says, "I don't understand. I told you I wouldn't pressure you. I love you, but I'm not asking for it in return."

"But that's just it," I practically whine. "You do expect it. I see it in your eyes. I see I'm tearing you up every time I don't reciprocate. It's too much… your expectations."

"So what do you want me to do, Rowan?" His voice is angry and tired all at the same time. "Do you want me to just pretend I don't love you? Do you want me to just fuck you and keep all the feeling out of it?"

No, of course I don't want that, but he's making the point that I've known to be true deep down inside. There's no way for our sexual relationship to continue because it pulls me in too deep. That is what I'm afraid of. I'm afraid of losing myself completely to love… and taking my eyes off the danger that lurks below it all. I'm afraid I'll get careless and then when I'm least expecting it, I'll get slapped down by it all.

I'm panicking. I get it… but I can't stop being overwhelmed by this feeling.

"I think we need to go back to being friends."

Flynn doesn't even hesitate… doesn't even consider my request. "Not going to fucking happen."

"What? Just like that? It's 'not going to fucking happen'? You can't make me go forward," I say angrily, completely blown away by his dismissive attitude.

"And you can't make me go back," he says quietly and with authority.

I feel like I'm spinning out of control because none of this is going right. "It's not fair," I shout.

"What's not fair?"

"You knew," I point at him with accusation. "You knew I didn't want to ruin the friendship. You knew and you still pushed me into this."

Flynn's face mottles red and he takes a step toward

me, getting right in my face. "That's bullshit, Rowan, and you know it. I wasn't the one that forced your tongue down my throat or your hand on my cock. You went willingly into my bed and fucking enjoyed every orgasm I gave you. You can lie about your feelings all you want but don't say I forced you to do anything."

His chest is heaving in anger as he steps back, staring me down. I lower my eyes to the floor, unsure of what to do. "So, where do we go from here?"

I pray he has the answer because I'm all out of solutions.

"There's one thing you were right about, Rowan." His voice is so soft, I strain to hear it. "Once you take that step toward the intimacy we had… once that goes to shit… there is no going back. The friendship can't survive that type of hurt."

Oh, God, those words hurt. I don't know if they are true or if Flynn is reacting in anger. He turns his back on me, walks down the hall, and I hear his bedroom door shut softly.

I stand there for a moment, drowning in sorrow. Capone comes up to me and nudges my hand. Absently rubbing his head, I try to think of a way I can salvage things. I can't lose my friendship with Flynn. He's too important. He's absolutely essential. If we just slow down, take a step back… I can figure this out.

Needing to keep busy, I put our luggage in the kitchen and sort through the clothes. After I start a load, I open the refrigerator and ponder what to make for dinner. Maybe after we eat, we can talk some more. Surely, I can get Flynn to see that maybe we rushed into things. That maybe we need to focus on the friendship.

Even as I think those thoughts, I'm telling myself I'm being ludicrous. There's no way Flynn is going back. I'm not even sure I can go back, but I'm terrified to move forward.

I hear Flynn's door open and my heart starts racing. He walks into the kitchen and he has his duffel bag thrown over his shoulder.

"Where are you going?" I ask, fearful of what he'll say.

"I'm going to go stay the night with Tim. I need some space."

"But you go back to work tomorrow. I won't see you for three days." That seems like such a lame thing to say, because I've gone plenty of times without seeing Flynn for three days. Now, though… it seems like an eternity.

"Yeah… listen… I'm going to stay with Tim for a while. I just talked to him and he's cool with me crashing there."

Panic starts to seize me as I see Flynn fading before my eyes. "No," I plead. "You don't have to go. We can talk this through. You'll see… we can make this work."

"You mean we can just be friends and make it work,

right?"

"Well, yes… if you just give it a chance, I'm sure we can pick back up."

"Yeah… that's not going to work for me, Rowan. I'm an all or nothing sort of guy. I can't just fall in love and then fall back out. Your heart might be hard, but mine's not."

Oh shit that hurt, and the pain in his eyes is unbearable. The thought that I'm running him out of his home causes anguish to lance through me. "No, don't go. I can go. This is your home."

Flynn sighs. "It's your home, too, Rowan. Besides… I'm all packed."

I look at him, not knowing what to say. My friendship with Flynn is going up in flames and I'm powerless to stop it.

He turns away and walks to the front door. Capone stands there and he gives him a rub behind the ears.

"See you, buddy," he says softly and then he's gone.

I stare at the door, willing him to come back. Begging him to come back and push me past my own stupid boundaries. I don't have the strength to do it myself, and I plead to the angels above to make him come back to me.

But the door remains closed.

I walk back to my bedroom and lie on the bed, staring at the ceiling. Capone crawls up beside me and lays his head on my chest, looking at me with soulful eyes. He can feel my pain.

I hate you, Mom and Dad! See what you made me into!

Tears start coursing down my face, and I'm powerless to stop them. Just as I was powerless to stop this train wreck that is my life. I took the one good thing in my life, and I ruined it.

And while I would love to blame Flynn for putting me in this position, it's my own fear and insecurity that has done it. I'm the only one that has control of that, and apparently, I'm just not strong enough to overcome it.

Turning on my side, I wrap my arms around Capone. I know I need to figure out my next move. I have a few days and a little money saved up. I know I can start over again… somewhere new and fresh. Maybe a different state.

Yes, all of this seems plausible as I've started my life over before—why not again?

Except… the thought of leaving… of not having Flynn?

Well, that just fucking destroys me.

CHAPTER 30

Flynn

"FULL-HOUSE, BABY! READ 'em and weep."

I watch, disgusted, as Tim throws down his cards on the table and sweeps his winnings up.

Looking at my pathetic pair of sevens, I throw my cards facedown and say, "I'm done."

"Come on, man. Don't be a sore loser," Tim teases and the rest of the guys start laughing.

Well, I am a sore loser, fuck you very much.

I'm fucking sore as hell that I've lost Rowan and it's put me in a pisser of a mood. I let my anger ride me hard for the first few days back to work, so much so that I wasn't paying attention during an apartment fire and almost had a burning piece of sheet rock smack me down.

That earned me a good ass chewing from the Chief, which only goes to prove he cares, right?

Motherfucker!

To make matters worse, Rowan kept texting me. I'm not sure exactly what she wants, because she never comes out and says it, but she's begged me to come home when I get off shift. I've been non-committal and just asked that she give me space.

I haven't heard from her in over twenty-four hours, and for all I know, she's moved out of the apartment.

My anger has dissipated some but it's still there. I'm pissed at Rowan for not having the guts to be stronger, but I'm more pissed at her parents for making her this way. If her dad were standing in front of me, I'd throttle him. I've been thinking that over and over for the past three days.

Which gave me the most fucked-up idea I've ever concocted.

As if the stars were aligning, my phone rings and I see it's Buzz.

I connect and don't bother with pleasantries. "Did you find what I need?"

"Hello to you too, buddy. But yeah, I got the information."

"Let me have it."

"Okay, seems like the esteemed Judge Cleeden is medically retired. He apparently had a pretty bad stroke and is in a rest home. Word is he was a tough old goat… really hard on crime, but then I think most judges in Texas want to hang you for mugging little old ladies." He laughs over his joke but I don't have time for it.

"What else?"

"Well, it appears he and his wife, Susan Cleeden, divorced two years ago. She's actually remarried now to Peter Grantham, and he owns a construction company in Dallas."

"Addresses?" I say.

"Geez… you're in a mood."

"Yeah, I am, and you don't want to see it turn darker. Just give me the addresses."

After I take down the information from Buzz, I disconnect and head to the Chief's office. I have four days off starting tomorrow but I might need another day or two. It seems I'm making a trip to Texas.

♦

WELL, THE TRIP to visit John Cleedin was a bust. I got admittance to visit him easy enough but I left wholly unsatisfied. My dreams of punching him in the face evaporated after I saw the shriveled old man lying in the hospital bed. The nurses assured me his mind was still good, but he just couldn't communicate well. Once I realized I wouldn't be getting physical satisfaction, I did get a measure of joy by sitting in a chair by his bed and telling him about his daughter, knowing he couldn't stop me.

I told him all the ways that she proved him wrong, and how strong and wonderful she turned out, despite his best efforts to fuck her up. There was no way I'd ever let him know that he left her with unimaginable insecurity, because I'm still banking on the fact that she'll overcome that one day.

Before I left, I asked if there was anything else he wanted to know. He did nothing but glare at me, his body shaking, and he said "Fuck you" as a pool of saliva spilled out of his mouth.

I reached over, took the towel draped across his chest, and carefully wiped his face. I knew he'd hate being cared for that way, a reminder of how weak and powerless he was now, and I smiled at him the entire time.

I turned without a word and left.

Now I walk up to Susan and Peter Grantham's home. It's a modest ranch house outside of Dallas. There are two vehicles in the driveway, one a truck that has Grantham Construction on the side.

I ring the doorbell and hear a booming bark near the door. It opens and a man of about fifty is standing there. He's tall, well built, and tanned from hours out in the sun. He looks at me pleasantly while he holds a dog back by its collar that is straining to see who has come to visit.

I look at the dog and I'm almost knocked backward to see it's a Bernese Mountain Dog. I'm so stunned in fact, I can't think of anything to say.

"Can I help you?" the man asks.

I raise my eyes to his. "Yes… I'm looking for Susan

Grantham. Is she here?"

The look on his face remains pleasant but he's not about to let me in his home. "She is. Can I ask what this is about?"

"My name is Flynn Caldwell. I'm from New York. I came to talk to her about her daughter."

Alarm fills the man's face and he pushes the dog back, stepping out onto the porch. He shuts the door behind him and turns to me.

"Is she dead?" he asks, his voice filled with fear.

"God, no. She's alive and well, and well… I wanted to talk to your wife about her."

He stares at me for a moment, his eyes grave. He nods his head and says, "Come on in."

I follow him into the kitchen, with the Berner trotting on my heels. I can't believe they have the same type of dog that Rowan has. Unbelievable.

I get my first look at Rowan's mom. She's an older version of Rowan, except she wears her dark hair short in a pixie cut. She's dressed in a t-shirt and jeans, and she's pulling some muffins out of the oven.

"Honey," Peter Grantham says hesitantly. "We have a visitor."

Susan Grantham turns to me with a smile on her face. She sets the muffins on the counter and takes the oven mitts off, extending a hand to me. I shake it and say, "Mrs. Grantham… I'm Flynn Caldwell."

She gives me a warm smile. “Please… call me Susan.” She spares a glance at her husband as if asking, *Who is this strange man?*

I don’t hold back. “I’ve come to talk to you about your daughter.”

Susan’s face goes white and she reaches a hand out to brace herself against the counter. “Anne Marie? She’s alive?”

I nod. “She goes by Rowan now… Rowan Page.”

I’m not sure what reaction I expected, but it certainly wasn’t this. Tears start pouring down her face and she sags to the floor crying. Peter rushes over to her and kneels down at her side, holding her in his arms.

She looks up at me, disbelief in her eyes. “I thought she was dead. I searched for her for so long, but we couldn’t find anything.”

“You looked for her?” I ask, disbelieving her words. This is the lady that stood by while Rowan was practically kicked out of her home and told never to return.

“Yes,” says Peter as he helps his wife from the floor. “Up until about a year ago… when the fifth private investigator we hired couldn’t find anything.”

Following my meeting with Satan’s Spawn—aka John Cleeden—I really had some poor expectations for this meeting. I expected to find a socialite living in the lap of luxury with her new husband and new life, completely having forgotten about the daughter she had forsaken.

Yet, here I find a woman who has apparently been grieving over a supposedly dead daughter.

"You abandoned her though… all those years ago," I accuse.

"Now wait a minute," Peter says, stepping toward me.

"No, Peter," Susan says, laying a restraining hand on his arm. "He's right. I failed my daughter in many, many ways, and I'll answer for it. I hope I can answer to Anne Marie. I hope she'll let me beg her forgiveness."

"It's Rowan," I snap.

Susan nods her head at me in cautious agreement. "Of course… Rowan."

"Do you have any idea the damage you inflicted on her?"

Susan bows her head, sniffling. "I know I destroyed her."

"Wrong! You damaged her, but you could never destroy someone as strong as her."

She looks back up at me, taking a step forward to grab my hand.

"Please," she begs. "Tell me everything about her. Give me something."

I shouldn't. I should walk out that door and let this woman suffer under her guilt. But there is something in her eyes that stops me. She looks like she has truly suffered, and damn if that doesn't pull at my heart just a tiny bit.

The fact that she has Rowan's gray eyes makes me hesitate.

"She's wonderful," I tell her. "She's beautiful, smart, and kind. She's a survivor and I love her very much."

Susan's smile lights up her face and she walks over to the kitchen table, gesturing for me to take a seat. "Tell me more," she begs.

I sit down and I tell her everything.

♦

I UNLOCK MY apartment door and step inside, quietly shutting it. I immediately see Rowan on the couch and she pops up quickly, looking at me with relief. Capone bounds off the couch and charges me. I take a moment to lean over and give him a hug.

Looking back up, I see Rowan's eyes travel up and down my body, and well, shit… even as pissed at her as I still am, her look causes desire to sweep through me.

I push it back, because I have something else I need to do.

"You're back," she observes with relief.

I nod. I take a moment to look at her. She looks tired and pale, with dark circles under her eyes. She's clearly not been sleeping. I want to take her in my arms and hold her, but I don't know if she'd accept that.

I don't know anything at all.

"Where have you been? I called Tim and he said you were out of town."

Rubbing my hand along my neck, I nod. "Yeah… I took an impromptu trip."

She cocks her head at me with inquisition.

"I went to Texas," I tell her and watch her face blanch. "To see your parents."

Rowan's hand comes up to her throat and flutters there. She takes a step back and sits down on the couch heavily. "Are they… okay?"

"Your dad isn't. He had a stroke and is in a nursing home."

"You saw him?"

"Yeah. His mind is there… he understands everything. But he can't talk that well."

"Did he ask about me?" Her voice is small, and filled with a child's hope that perhaps she is actually loved by that fucker.

"I'm sorry," I say and understanding sweeps over her face.

She lets out a shaky breath. "I guess I shouldn't have expected anything. I guess… I guess maybe I thought he'd grown… matured. Maybe had some regret."

"I don't think your dad is capable, Rowan. I'm sorry. But I made sure he knew exactly how badly you proved him wrong. He'll go to his grave knowing he didn't break you."

She gives me a small smile, and then looks down at her hands clasped in her lap. "I guess that's something."

"I saw your mom, too."

Her face snaps up but there is fear. She's already been let down once by me, and I can see she's expecting it again.

"She left your dad a few years ago. She's remarried."

Rowan doesn't say anything and I can see she's holding her breath, her bottom lip trembling. Her pain is so visceral I can taste bile in my throat.

"She looked for you. Starting the night you left. The police wouldn't file a missing person's report for at least forty-eight hours, but she made your dad pull some strings. She hired several private investigators but they all kept coming up with dead ends. She even checked in all states to see if you changed your name. But, of course, you didn't do it legally so there was no paper trail."

"She looked for me?"

"Yeah… apparently your dad didn't want any part of it, and ultimately… that led to their split. She finally gave up about a year ago, when the last private investigator told her that you were probably dead."

Rowan lets out a short sob and I take a step toward her but she holds her hand up to stop me. She turns her back on me and looks out the window, her shoulders hunched. "I can't."

My heart falls, and I wonder if this has all been for naught. Maybe Rowan doesn't want to be any different than she is right now. Maybe she doesn't need love in her life.

Regardless, it doesn't change the fact that I've brought the past to her doorstep.

I turn and walk to the door. Opening it, I motion the couple inside. Susan and Peter Grantham step in, their hands so tightly locked together their knuckles are white.

"Anne Marie?" Susan says, her voice unsure.

Rowan spins fast and pins her mother with stormy, gray eyes. "It's Rowan."

Susan releases Peter's hand and takes a tentative step toward her daughter. "I can't believe you're alive. I had hoped for so long… but then they told us you were probably gone… dead."

Tears are streaming down Susan's face and Peter steps up to put a hand on her shoulder.

"Why did you look for me?"

Susan is startled by the venom in Rowan's voice. "Why wouldn't I look for you? You're my daughter."

"But you did nothing," Rowan says with deadly calm. "You stood by while my father told me to leave and never come back. You ignored me for years. So I ask again… why would you look for me? Surely you were better off without me."

"Never," Susan says vehemently. "You were the one good thing I made with my life. I was just too weak to see it. I was too weak to stand up to your father. And that is all on me. It's not on him, and it's not on you. It's my failing. I failed you because a mother should always protect her child."

My heart breaks for both women. Rowan stands there, so clearly wanting to believe she was actually loved by her mom. Susan is seeking absolution, a little something I know about personally.

"I'm so sorry, Rowan. For all the pain I caused you. I know I have no right to ask, but I need your forgiveness. Flynn told me how strong you are… despite what we did to you. I need your strength now. I need you to be strong enough to forgive me."

Rowan sneaks a glance at me, tears glistening in her eyes. I don't give her any indication of what I think she should do, because this is her decision alone. I hope to God she forgives her mother, because then maybe she can let go of the past.

But then she turns her back on all of us, crossing her arms across her chest. I see her shoulders are shaking and I die inside for her.

Susan puts her hand over her mouth to stifle a sob and Peter takes her arm. "Come on," he says softly. "Let's go."

They both turn to the door but when it opens, Rowan blurts out, "Don't go."

Susan turns around, hope filling her eyes.

"Please stay," Rowan says on the heels of a deep breath. "Let's come into the kitchen and talk. I'll make some coffee."

Rowan walks past me into the kitchen, giving me a look that's unreadable. Susan and Peter follow her in. I hear Susan say, "You know… we have a Bernese Mountain Dog, too."

I'm relieved that Rowan will give her a chance to talk. I hope that something good will come of all of this.

Turning away, I walk out of the apartment. I have to be on shift in a few hours.

CHAPTER 31

Rowan

I WAKE UP surprisingly refreshed after the emotional overload of last night. When Flynn had walked in that door, I had to restrain myself from jumping on him. He looked like my oasis in a hot desert and I was literally parched for him.

I had been doing a lot of thinking since he had been gone. I had done a lot of missing him as well, and maybe that's why he left. To show me what I'd be missing.

I missed lying in bed with him at night and having him wrap his arms around with me. I missed his soft kisses and the way his eyes would heat up when he looked at me. I loved the way he would swat my ass when I walked by and say, "Lookin' good, baby". I missed all those things so much and not one of those had a damn thing to do with friendship. They had to do with intimacy and I've apparently been an idiot to think those things were less important than the friendship aspect of our relationship.

I was prepared to tell Flynn all of those things and

more, but he threw me for a loop when he walked back into my life and started talking about my parents.

There was a moment—just a split second—when he said he went to Texas that I despised him. Anger surged through me, white hot that he would dare to dredge up those painful memories. But it left just as quickly when I came to the complete and absolute realization that Flynn did it out of love for me. He did it as a way to let me confront my past.

I would like to say I was devastated over my father's reaction, but I really couldn't even muster up enough energy to care about him. The fact he lays broken and withering in a nursing home really doesn't bother me at all. I wonder if that makes me a bad person, a numb person, or a realistic person.

When my mother walked through the door, I thought she was a ghost. I didn't spare a glance at her new husband, but stared at the woman who birthed me and then threw me away. Anger surged again, and I wanted to claw her eyes out. But then, that faded quickly and hurt and confusion took its place.

I couldn't believe the things she was saying. That she had failed me… that she was taking complete responsibility for everything that was done to me. She wouldn't even let my father take the fall, because as a mother… she said it was her absolute duty to protect me.

It was only when she was getting ready to walk out

that door that I let my heart make a split-second decision to let her back into my life. I certainly had no clue to what extent that would be, but I knew that for my own sanity and emotional well-being, I had to hear her out and I had to make peace with it.

She and Peter followed me into the kitchen and I waited for Flynn to come in. When he didn't, I walked back out into the living room and he was gone. This made me sad, because I really wanted him by my side, but with everything I had done to him… with the way I had let him down, I deserved no less than to have him walk away.

My mom, Peter, and I talked until the early morning hours. I learned that my mother had an early love-hate relationship with my father. She loved him for the security and companionship he brought, but she hated the control that came with it. I believe her when she said that she sort of drank the Kool-Aid he offered to her, and she let her maternal instincts wither away to keep him happy.

I also believed her when she told me that her wake-up call came within hours of me leaving. She begged my father to call the police and go after me but he refused. She got in her car and drove the roads for hours, searching for me. Ironically, she even went to the bus station but I wasn't there. I know I wasn't there because I sat across the street in a diner until my bus was ready to leave.

My mom stayed with my father but the relationship deteriorated badly. They fought constantly and, within just a month of my leaving, she was residing permanently in another bedroom. They separated not long after that, although she didn't make immediate moves for a divorce. She said it was almost too much work to have to fight him.

It was only after she met Peter that she had the strength to cut final ties and start her life over again.

Luckily for her, Peter was a godsend. He stood by her quest to find me, shelling out tons of his own money to hire private investigators. He held her at night while she cried herself to sleep, and he even arranged for a memorial service for me when the last investigator said I was probably dead. I look forward to getting to know this man better as he seems to be a genuine soul… like Flynn.

My mother and I have a long way to go to fully repair our relationship. The last five years of my exile are hard for me to accept, but knowing that she wanted me, and that she knew she made a terrible mistake, makes it easier to accept. Before they left, I told her the words she needed to hear.

I told her I forgave her.

My mom and Peter are going to stay in New York for a few days and we're going to get together for dinner tonight. I called Nix and asked him for tomorrow off so I could spend more time with them, and he didn't even bitch at me once. He must still be having post-honeymoon bliss or something.

Rolling out of bed, I slip on some clothes to take Capone for a walk. Then I need to get in the shower and over to the Station.

There's a firefighter I need to see about building a relationship with.

♦

WHEN I GET to the firehouse, I tentatively walk inside the large bay doors that are open. Thankfully, I see Tim standing there talking to another firefighter. He glances up and sees me, offering a warm smile.

He walks up and says, "Hey Ro-Ro."

I raise an eyebrow. "Ro-Ro? Since when am I Ro-Ro?"

He shrugs his shoulders. "I don't know. You just all of a sudden seemed like a Ro-Ro. Looking for Flynn?"

I nod. "If he's available."

Chuckling, he starts to walk toward the back of the bay. "I have a feeling he's always available to you."

I don't move and he glances over his shoulder. "Well, come on in… we don't bite."

Giving him a shy smile, I say, "I know… I'll just wait here though. I want to talk to him in private."

"Ah," he says in understanding. "A little dirty talk, huh?"

Snorting, I say, "Yeah… that's so not it."

"Okay, hold tight and I'll go get him."

I walk up to the fire engine closest to me, admiring the gleaming silver and shiny red paint. Several sets of turnout gear line up near the wall with the helmets hanging on pegs above.

Over the past few months, Flynn has taken a lot of time to satisfy my curiosity about his career. I'm always fascinated when he comes home from his shift, anxious to hear about all the exciting things he's done. Some of it scares me… the personal danger he is in, but I'm also extremely proud of what he does for a living.

And let's face it… firefighters are hot!

I start chuckling to myself over that thought and start imagining Flynn in his turnout pants and suspenders, with nothing else on underneath. My face flushes warm and I wonder… if I can put us back on track… could I talk him in to that.

Oh yeah, knowing Flynn… he's game.

"Hey," he says softly from behind me.

He's wearing his regular uniform of navy blue utility pants tucked into black boots. His navy FDNY t-shirt fits tightly across his chest and I can see the tattoos on his biceps peeking out. His hazel eyes watch me warily and his arms cross over his chest, maybe to protect his heart.

He doesn't look welcoming but I didn't expect much to be honest.

"How's work going?" I ask.

Lame-ass!

"Good. Thanks."

"Well… I wanted to stop by and thank you… for going to Texas… for bringing my mom back with you."

Smiling, he shrugs his shoulders. "It was nothing. You would have done the same, I'm sure."

"Yes," I tell him simply. "I would have."

Flynn glances down to his boots and when he looks back up, he takes a few steps forward. Casually leaning one arm on the truck, he asks, "So, how did it go last night?"

Taking a deep breath, I say, "It went good actually. We talked for hours. It was… healing to hear the things she had to say."

"I'm sorry your dad couldn't give that to you."

"I'm not. I know he never had it in himself to give."

Flynn nods in understanding. "I think you're right. But remember this—he's alone and has no one. That's what you get when you don't have love."

I wince internally because damn if that isn't a pointed jab at me, although I know Flynn probably didn't mean it that way.

"I'm going out to dinner with mom and Peter tonight."

"That's good. I'm happy for you that things are working. And Peter, nice guy, right?"

"Yeah, it's weird. I like, have a stepfather now. And can you believe they have a Berner? I mean, what are the chances of that?"

Laughing, Flynn says, "I know. I about died when I saw their dog. Crazy."

We both chuckle a little and then lapse into an awkward silence. This is killing me… this friendly banter. Which is completely ironic, since this is how we would normally interact when we were just friends.

But now it seems so empty and cold. It doesn't fulfill me in the way I thought it would. It makes me realize that what I could have had with Flynn would have been so much better.

Flynn just stares at me, waiting for me to say something.

"Are you going to come back home at the end of this shift?" I blurt out with an underlying tone of begging, which… okay… I'm swallowing my pride here.

Flynn glances away with guilt in his eyes, and then looks back to me. His eyes are sad. "I think I'm going to stay at Tim's for a little while longer. You know… give you some space. Figure things out."

"Oh," I say, my voice low and dejected. "Okay."

I wait and he doesn't say anything more. My heart is heavy but I put a smile on my face. "Well, I guess I'll let you get back to work. I just wanted to drop by and thank you for what you did with my parents. You're a good man, Flynn."

His smile is warm but it doesn't reach all the way to me. It's polite, with some satisfaction that he completed a job well done. "Sure thing. I'll catch you around."

He turns away from me and the minute he can't see my face, it falls, the smile disappearing into a world of hurt that's going on in my heart right now. I turn around, walking dejectedly from the station.

The man I love is slipping away, sliding through my grasp, and I tried my damnedest not to let it happen.

Except… I didn't lay *everything* out on the table.

Spinning around, I see Flynn just about to walk through a door in the back.

"Flynn!" I yell out to him.

He turns but doesn't make a move toward me. The door he was about to go through opens, and a few fireman come through, walking over to the truck we had been standing near. I watch for a moment as they open up a few compartments to place items inside.

He looks at me with question. He doesn't come any closer and he's not going to make this easy on me.

I take a deep breath and decide to jump in with both feet. "Do you still love me?"

The two firefighters standing there look up at me in surprise. They then glance over to Flynn and I follow their gaze. He starts walking toward me, and I'm mesmerized by a lazy smile that slides into place.

"You know I do," he says, having to talk loud so I can hear him.

The two firefighters now turn completely away from the truck, and lean back against it, absolutely content to forgo their duties and watch this drama play out.

Swallowing hard, and letting my nervousness go, I start walking to meet him halfway. When I stop just before him, he looks down at me with his beautiful eyes, and I say, "Good. Because it seems I may have been remiss in telling you the same thing."

Flynn's eyes flash hot and I see joy filter in. His dimple pops out before the smile even fully takes over his face.

"You love me?" he asks in wonder.

"I do. You're my hero, Flynn Caldwell. Not because you pulled me out of a fire, but because you pushed me into love. It's for that reason I love you."

His hand reaches out and tucks a stray lock behind my ear. He then cups the back of my head, just staring at me. "And when did you come to this realization?"

"Oh, only about two hours after you walked out of my life. The pain was unbearable. I'm sorry I hurt you. I'm sorry I let you down."

"You never let me down, Rowan. You just took a while to learn not to fear love."

"I don't fear it now," I tell him boldly.

He gazes at me… a long, deep look of devotion. "I love you, Rowan. Always."

"Kiss her," one of the firefighters yells out to us.

We both look over at him and start laughing. When we turn back to each other, the humor dies out and something hot replaces it. Flynn pulls me to him, framing my face with both hands. I love how he holds me this way and I close my eyes as his lips touch mine.

It's soft at first, a gentle touch to remind me of all the care in the world he has for me. But then he deepens it and my arms wrap around his neck, melding my body to his. I can hear his co-workers yelling catcalls, but then it all dissolves into silence so I only hear the beating of our hearts.

We kiss and kiss and kiss, not wanting to let each other go.

Even when the speakers jolt to life, emitting several loud tones and then a buzzer, we continue to kiss. We ignore the pager that goes off on his hip, and he kisses me deeper.

I'm vaguely aware of the back door opening and more firefighters running through. I can hear them talking, putting on their turnout gear, but I ignore it all. I only think about kissing the man I love with my entire being.

"Goddamn it, Caldwell. Get your ass in gear!"

I jump back from Flynn and look over to see an angry man with snowy white hair glaring at him.

"Sure thing, Chief," he says with a cocky grin but never taking his eyes off me.

Leaning down, Flynn gives me one more quick kiss and then starts trotting backward from me toward his turnout gear.

"Just wait 'til I get off shift. I'm going to rock your world, baby."

I blow a kiss to him. "You bet your sweet ass, you are."

Turning away, I practically skip out of the fire station and start walking toward our apartment. Not thirty seconds later, two fire trucks go whizzing by me, sirens blaring. The engine honks its horn as it goes by me and I give a friendly wave toward my man as he heads off to work.

EPILOGUE

Rowan

Four Years Later

"I'M AS BIG as fucking house," I complain.

"No, you're not," Flynn assures me.

"Well… I'm as big as Capone," I say, looking at the furry monster as he walks beside me.

"Not even."

"I look like a whale," I insist.

"You're way more beautiful than a whale," he tells me but I roll my eyes at him. "And you smell way better, too."

"Thanks!" I say, nudging him in his side and he shoots me a grin.

We stroll across the green grass toward the group of people sitting in the distance. We decided to meet in Central Park and have an impromptu picnic get together.

"Hurry up, preggers," Flynn urges. "I'm starving."

"I'm hurrying as fast as a fat woman can waddle."

Flynn turns to me and scoops me up in his arms. "You are not fat. You are decidedly pregnant with my child, and frankly… I like you like this. I think I might keep you pregnant from here on out."

"No fucking way," I assure him. "This is the only time I'm going through this."

I'm seven months pregnant and I can't believe I'm not ready to give birth yet. I feel like I'm ready to pop. My back hurts, my feet are swollen, and about the only good thing that has come out of this pregnancy is that Flynn seems to be hornier than normal so I get lots of sex.

He tells me that the fact I'm carrying his child in my belly makes him want to fuck me all the time. Which… now that thought makes *me* horny, and I have hormones coursing through me that tend to get out of control.

"Let's go home and make love instead," I say as he carries me across the grass.

Flynn's eyes turn hot and he actually looks back over his shoulder to gauge the amount of time it would take to get back to the car. Then he shakes his head. "Nope. Sorry… we have people waiting for us. We'll just need to make up for it later."

"But, baby," I whine. "I'm horny now."

"You're always horny," he commiserates.

"Well… so are you," I grumble but truth be told, I'm excited about this little outing.

It's summertime, the air is warm, and my clan is reuniting.

Yes, my clan.

Because when I married Flynn Caldwell three years ago, I gained a new family, and it's growing by leaps and bounds.

As we reach the group, Flynn sets me on my feet and I hurry—waddle—over to Danny, who struggles to her feet. She's seven months pregnant too and we bump our bellies together in a show of camaraderie. We told our husbands we want to share a room when we go into labor but I don't think they're buying it.

Hugging me, she says, "You look gorgeous."

"I look like a whale," I whine again, so someone will validate me.

"No, you don't," Flynn mutters on autopilot, because he's heard me bitch about my weight about twenty times a day. "Anyone up for throwing around the football? Please… anyone… to get me away from this crazy, hormonal woman."

The guys all laugh and stand up in unison. Most of them have been there and they feel sorry for Flynn.

I watch as the gorgeous group of men head off to play boy games. Ryan, Nix, Linc, Cillian, and Flynn. Now dayum… that is some prime meat right there.

Oh, God. I'm so hormonally horny!

Amelia runs after the men, shouting, "Daddy… I want to play, too."

Ryan turns around and scoops her up, tossing her

into the air. She is the spitting image of Danny and screams in delight once she's caught. He walks back and hands her to Danny. Kissing her on the head, he says, "Later, pumpkin. Right now the daddies are playing."

She pouts but then she sees Capone standing there and scrabbles out of Danny's arms to throw her arms around him. He flops on the ground and rolls on his back, groaning in delight when she starts scratching his belly.

"Can we get a dog, Mommy?"

"Ask your dad," Danny answers.

"Dad," Amelia yells, and Ryan turns around. "Can we get a dog?"

"Ask your mom," he yells back.

I burst out laughing when Amelia rolls her eyes at her parents and goes back to loving on Capone.

"Come sit down, you two," Renner calls out. She's sitting on a blanket nursing Ben, who just turned six months old. She has a blanket strategically placed over her breast and looks peaceful and serene. She and Cillian are staying with her parents for a few months this summer while his band is on break.

I walk—waddle—over to the blanket and ease myself down beside Emily, who's lying on her back with her hands tucked under her head. I find a comfortable position because I know I won't be getting back up until Flynn gives me a hand.

"How's the lima bean doing?" I ask her as I pat her tummy. Emily and Nix are almost seven weeks pregnant and they wasted no time in telling everyone. She made the calls while holding the stick she peed on she was so excited. Flynn and I waited until the three-month mark before we divulged our secret.

It was nice… sharing the most wonderful secret in the world with the man I love.

"He's doing great… or at least, the doctor says so when she showed us the ultrasound. He looks like a bean to me."

"Still convinced it's a boy?" I ask.

"Yup. Absolutely convinced but I think that's just because Nix wants a little boy so badly, he's about ready to pee his pants."

Laughing, I reach into the picnic basket and start rooting around for sustenance.

"Hey," Ever says. "We're not ready to eat yet."

I glare at her and growl, "Don't mess with the pregnant woman."

Ever laughs but I see the look of longing when she glances at my stomach. She and Linc have been trying to have a baby for the past two years, but aren't having any success. They've been trying IVF and she got pregnant on the first try, but lost the baby at six weeks. My heart broke for her then and sometimes, I feel guilty that it happened so easy for Flynn and me. I got pregnant within two months of going off the pill.

"How are things going with you?" I ask pointedly.

Ever puts on a brave smile and says, "It's going. We're going to try one more cycle and if it doesn't work, we're going to adopt."

Reaching over, I grab her hand and Danny lays a hand on her shoulder. "It will happen, Ever. Whether you get pregnant, or you adopt… it will happen."

Ever smiles and the light reaches her eyes. "I know it will. I'm just so anxious to be able to sit around with you girls and tell baby stories. I can talk hockey stats 'til I'm blue in the face, but I want to dish about baby poop."

Renner wrinkles her nose. "I'm so over baby poop. I'm ready for this kid to get potty-trained."

Danny laughs. "You have a ways to go, Ren. I hate to tell you that the poop is going to be around for a while."

"Well, I'm not looking forward to getting fat like Danny and Rowan," Emily pipes in. "You look miserable."

"Hey," I say in mock outrage. "I'm not fat… I'm pleasantly plump."

As if to prove my point, I find a piece of fried chicken in the basket and pull it out. Before I can even get the basket closed, Danny grabs it out of my hand. I look at her in surprise.

"Hey, like you said… don't mess with the pregnant woman," she says, and then takes a huge bite.

Shrugging my shoulders, I reach back in and grab another piece. Taking a bite myself, I moan in ecstasy. "Damn, this is good. Almost better than pregnant sex."

The girls all look at me with their mouths hanging open.

"What?" I ask with my mouth full. "Didn't you guys have sex like all the time when you were pregnant?"

"Nope," Danny says.

"No way," Renner chimes in.

"Hell yeah," Emily says.

I give Emily a dismissive glance and then look back at Renner and Danny. "Really? I thought it was a pregnant thing. Flynn and I are screwing like bunnies."

Danny chokes on her chicken and I give her a slap on her back. Gasping for air, she says, "Not Ryan, he's afraid he'll give the baby a concussion."

Ever starts laughing and bends over, holding her stomach. "You're kidding, right? He can't really believe that."

Danny chuckles. "I know. The doctors told him it's safe, but when we have sex, he goes at it with the speed of a turtle. He likes to be super gentle, and while I like it tender, there's something to be said about a good hard…" Danny stops and glances at Amelia, who thankfully isn't paying attention while she loves on Capone. She lowers to a whisper, "Well… you know."

"Well, when I was seven months pregnant, the only

thing I wanted from Cillian was for him to keep me supplied in ice cream and to massage my feet. He was a good sport though."

Ever, who is still snickering, says, "I'm not so sure I want to be pregnant anymore. If I had to give up sex with Linc, I'd die."

"Well, if you're anything like Flynn and me, you won't have to," I assure her.

"So, is your mom going to come in for the birth?" Ever asks.

"Yeah, she and Peter are going to come and spend a few weeks here. Thank God we moved into the larger apartment so we have room for the nursery and to put them up as well. It will be nice to have the help."

I am so looking forward to my mom coming in. Over the years, our relationship has healed and then grown very strong. Next to Flynn, she's become my best friend and we talk several times a week. At first, I know she was trying to make up for lost time, but I assured her we had all the time in the world to get to know each other again. My heart has never felt lighter because of it.

My dad… not much to tell there. He died about six months ago. My mom called to tell me and I had a moment of sadness that he died all alone. But then I put it out of my mind. He was a virtual stranger to me and there was no bond there to miss.

I did, however, gain a new dad with Peter. He's awesome and I've grown to love him very much. He walked me down the aisle when I hitched myself to Flynn.

Looking out at the guys playing football, I think about what type of father Flynn will be. It's probably the thing I'm looking forward to the most… watching him hold our child. We have no clue if it's a boy or a girl, both of us wanting to be surprised.

If it's a boy, we're going to name him Nathaniel Nixon and if it's a girl, she'll be Elizabeth Anne. I'm secretly hoping for a boy, but more than anything, I'm hoping for good pain medications.

Us girls lounge around and chit chat, dishing on babies and sex, but we find ourselves having to talk in code around Amelia. I eat another piece of chicken while Danny abstains and I wonder why I'm as big as a whale.

The men eventually tire themselves out, or get bored, since they're done playing in about fifteen minutes and head back to the group. Flynn sits behind me and pulls me back into his arms, so my back can take a rest. His arms come around my waist to rest on my belly. The baby gives a little kick in response and Flynn chuckles.

"I think it's a boy… that's a football kick if I ever felt one."

"Yeah, and I think it was to my bladder. I got to pee."

"Come on, hot mama. Let me help you up."

With Flynn's help, it's not so hard getting to my feet

and he walks with me to the bathroom.

"You don't have to walk with me to the bathroom," I tell him.

He grabs my hand and squeezes. "I'm never leaving your side."

"You can't go in with me," I tell him sternly.

"I'll wait outside. I've got your back… and hopefully your ass tonight."

"You have the most awesome pillow talk, baby."

We're silent as we walk, swinging our hands back and forth. I look down at my belly, taking note that I can just see the tips of my shoes briefly flashing with each stride. It's just one of the things I find I will treasure about pregnancy.

"Flynn?"

"What's up?"

"I feel bad for Ever not being able to get pregnant. I mean… as much as I bitch about it, knowing that she might not be able to experience this is kind of tearing me up."

"I know. Linc's having a rough time, too."

I'm careful with my next words, because this potentially could cause a fight. "What do you think about me offering to carry their baby for them? If she can't get pregnant?"

Flynn snaps his head toward me and looks at me in surprise. "You're kidding, right?"

"I don't think so. I actually think it's something I really want to do. I mean, they could say no, but I think I'd like to offer it."

"I thought you said you were never going through this again."

"Pfft," I scoff. "We're definitely having at least two kids… maybe three. Because it is oh so fun trying to get pregnant."

Flynn bursts out laughing. "That it is."

"I would never offer that to them though, unless you were on board. It's my sexy body you'd be giving up for a while."

Flynn stops walking and turns to me. Taking both of my hands in his, he looks at me with such adulation, that my heart skips a beat. "Rowan… you are the kindest, most wonderful woman on the face of the earth. I'm so proud to be your husband. If you want to do this for them, you have my full support."

Tears well up in my eyes—damn hormones—and I stand on my tiptoes to kiss him. "You've always given me devotion and support… from the day we first met. How many women can say that?"

"None," he says with a laugh. "They broke the mold with me."

"That they did," I agree.

Flynn gathers me in and kisses me… deeply. It sends a thrill straight through my body and I feel the baby's foot start a mad beating rhythm in response. I kiss him back, pouring all of my love and desire into it.

Pulling back, Flynn says, "Damn, woman. How about I go into the bathroom with you and we have monkey sex in a stall?"

I put my hands on his chest and playfully push him away. "Ewww. That's gross."

Turning to the bathroom, I throw over my shoulder. "I'm going to pee… alone."

"I'll be waiting for you… right here," he says, his eyes penetrating me.

"You're always there for me," I tell him.

"Always."

Looking for more Off Series? Go here to see all seven standalone titles in the Off Series.
sawyerbennett.com/bookstore/the-off-series

Go here to see other works by Sawyer Bennett:
https://sawyerbennett.com/bookshop

Don't miss another new release by Sawyer Bennett!!! Sign up for her newsletter and keep up to date on new releases, giveaways, book reviews and so much more.
https://sawyerbennett.com/signup

Connect with Sawyer online:

Website: sawyerbennett.com
Twitter: twitter.com/bennettbooks
Facebook: facebook.com/bennettbooks
Instagram: instagram.com/sawyerbennett123
Book+Main Bites:
bookandmainbites.com/sawyerbennett
Goodreads: goodreads.com/Sawyer_Bennett
Amazon: amazon.com/author/sawyerbennett
BookBub: bookbub.com/authors/sawyer-bennett

About the Author

Since the release of her debut contemporary romance novel, Off Sides, in January 2013, Sawyer Bennett has released multiple books, many of which have appeared on the New York Times, USA Today and Wall Street Journal bestseller lists.

A reformed trial lawyer from North Carolina, Sawyer uses real life experience to create relatable, sexy stories that appeal to a wide array of readers. From new adult to erotic contemporary romance, Sawyer writes something for just about everyone.

Sawyer likes her Bloody Marys strong, her martinis dirty, and her heroes a combination of the two. When not bringing fictional romance to life, Sawyer is a chauffeur, stylist, chef, maid, and personal assistant to a very active daughter, as well as full-time servant to her adorably naughty dogs. She believes in the good of others, and that a bad day can be cured with a great work-out, cake, or even better, both.

Sawyer also writes general and women's fiction under the pen name S. Bennett and sweet romance under the name Juliette Poe.

Printed in Great Britain
by Amazon

43505681R00243